THE BEARER'S BURDEN

Enjoy Joe's story!

~~DIANA ELIZABETH JONES~~

Diana Jones

FriesenPress

Suite 300 - 990 Fort St
Victoria, BC, V8V 3K2
Canada

www.friesenpress.com

First Edition — 2016

Author photo by Edward Ross Photography

ISBN
978-1-4602-8725-5 (Hardcover)
978-1-4602-8726-2 (Paperback)
978-1-4602-8727-9 (eBook)

1. FICTION, WAR & MILITARY

Distributed to the trade by The Ingram Book Company

TO BE FULLY ALIVE ONE MUST DARE TO GO INTO NO MAN'S LAND

You are braver than you believe,
stronger than you seem,
smarter than you think

—Christopher Robin

FOR

Richard and Linsey
Who fill me with life and love

And to the memory
Of Joseph Pullar

AUTHOR'S NOTE

When I decided to write a novel about a stretcher-bearer in WWI, I soon realized it would be necessary (and delightful) to live somewhere along what had been the Western Front in France. So for three months I took up residence in a village in Picardie, close to where the Somme battles ravaged from July 1 to the middle of November 1916.

I was fortunate to uncover, and in some cases, visit, the locations of the medical services in use during those battles. In *The Bearer's Burden* the places Joe lived and worked are all based on actual villages, towns and medical facilities. But, since *The Bearer's Burden* is a work of fiction, I had the luxury of inventing names, in some instances, for places and people as well as imagining events and characters with their dialogue and actions. While I deeply respect the accepted records of the Great War (and in particular the invention and introduction of new medical technologies), fictionalizing Joe's personal story won out over following strict historical accuracy in all its fine detail.

The long years between 1914–18 can be viewed through different lenses: as a series of military strategies, as a political situation, as the genesis of social revolutions, perhaps as the impetus for WW2. Ultimately, I believe, the only meaning lies in the stories, and each of the millions of lives lost had a unique narrative. *The Bearer's Burden* could have been one of them.

THE BEARER'S BURDEN

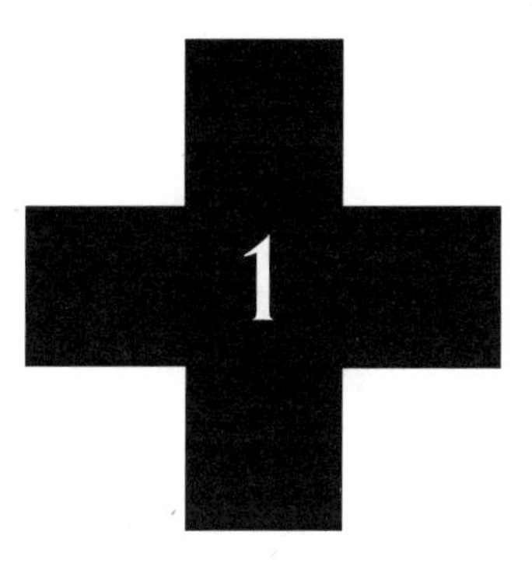

Monday, February 22, 1915 From his seat by the fire, Joe Mathieson leaned toward his ma's trembling hand, took the envelope she held out, and slit it open with his thumb. Couldn't she have let him have five minutes of peace after work before possibly unsettling them all?

"From Fred," she said. "I know his hand."

So this was why he had been summoned to her house, along with Kate and wee Ellen. He had to be the one to read it, to save her from making some excuse: Her glasses were nowhere to be found, her hands were wet... Her short four years of schooling made her nervous around squiggles on paper. He wished, almost, she'd had no word at all from his older brother. *No news is good news* circled his mind as his fingers traced the army stamp. His eyes wandered to the damp patches on the kitchen wallpaper, the rickety table, the chairs, sideboard, and bed crowded into the hub of her two-room house.

She turned her back and lowered a black iron fry pan onto the stove-top, put a match to the pilot light, coughed down the sulphurous odour from the coal gas, and wiped her thickening fingers on a faded floral apron. She turned to Joe. "He's okay then? No' one of them casualties? I couldn't bear it if he were killed and buried in France."

He thought she'd aged, the lines on her forehead deepened, since Fred left for the war. He left his chair and put his arm around his mother's back. "You said yourself it was Fred's hand, so of course he's fine. Alive and well." He felt he could read her mind. *What if he has a hand but no legs and is writing to tell us.* "Ma, if he wasn't, his wife would have told you. Lizzie wouldn't keep that to herself." He was proud his mother looked to him, seemed to have wordlessly appointed him head of the family since his father's death and Fred's departure. *One up for me, big brother.* He wasn't sure he liked that responsibility or was even up to the job. He gave her waist a slight squeeze. "And I'm sure the army's right pleased with him." But a niggle of worry tugged on the back of his neck, and he hesitated to draw the paper from the envelope.

"Are you going to read it then or keep us all in suspenders?" his wife said. She was at the sink by the only window in the room, with their toddler, Ellen, tucked under her arm. He cringed at his wife's full lips, narrowed to a hard slit, but stared down her over-the-shoulder smirk. He hated the way she looked for a fight in everything he did—or didn't—do. She tossed her head and bent over the frigid water, dripping from the brass cold-water tap, and tried to wipe the wee girl's hands. Ellen wriggled like a hooked fish, frightened by the rattling windowpanes. The wind that blew off the North Sea year-round was pounding a late winter gale at Methilane, the small mining town that jutted its chin from the face of the Fife coast, defying but never defeating the biting storms.

Joe dropped his arm from his mother's bony back, and squeezed past her and his wife. He poked at the extra flesh Kate'd put on her buttocks and belly since carrying Ellen. She slapped his hand away. He sat down at the hearth again, identical to the one in the house he'd moved to, down the road and round the corner, a year and a half back when he'd had to wed Kate because he'd put her up the spout. Hardly a move up in the world. Hard to imagine them ever getting out of there. Many a time he wished he'd walked away from Kate. Far away. Australia. New Zealand. But now he couldn't; wouldn't want to be without Ellen. He stretched out his long legs and crossed them at the ankles. The paltry heat from the coal fire barely thawed the soles of his stockinged feet.

"Where's that wee brother of mine?" he asked Ma as he shook out the lined and pencilled sheets of their older brother's letter. He'd had his differences with Fred over this war. Nothing new there. And of course, what he'd said to Ma about Fred being safe made sense. Nevertheless Joe crossed his fingers nothing unexpected and dreadful lay in Fred's words. "Where's Walter? I thought you said last week the lad was wanting to see us."

His mother scooped a tablespoon of fat from a scratched enamel bowl and chucked it into the frying pan. She turned to face Joe, ran a hand through her greying hair. "He doesn't come home for his tea as much."

Joe uncurled his hunched shoulders, squelched the irritation he felt at Walter's absence. "Och, I expect it's just his age, Ma. Me and Fred were the same at sixteen. Just wanting to be with our pals."

Ma looked away and swirled the sizzling fat. "Right. He could be at his pal Alan Barbour's. He sleeps over there sometimes. Even for days in a row.

"He should've let us know," Kate said, tensing her brow into furrows. "I'd give Ellen a skelp on her bum if she worried me like that."

"Since when are you the expert?" Joe shot back. He should say 'sorry', not pounce on her like that. It was Walter he was grieved at. Paying for his school, Joe felt he was owed some line toeing from his brother. "Who's this Alan Barbour he's chumming with these days, Ma?"

"His folks are the grocers in the High Street." Ma lowered a clutch of sausages into the spitting fat. "I expect he's there. Aye. That'll be where he is." She stabbed at the meat, freeing a peppery, greasy reek. She marshalled them around the pan. "Easier for the laddies to swot for tests, them having their own big house. They have the electric light in all their rooms. Easier for them to read at night."

"Then that's a good thing, Ma. We want him to do well, right?" Joe said. "And I know him well enough to know he wants to do right by us. He takes his studying seriously. He'll not be shirking." Joe looked at the envelope, wondering how long he could keep his mother's attention from it.

"I don't know where he is half the time. Haven't seen him since Saturday morning." She faced Joe, the cooking fork hanging limply in her hand. "If he's not come back when you leave, check The Brig, will you? I don't want him sneaking into a bar, spending his time drinking. Not at fifteen."

Joe laughed. "He'll be sixteen next week."

"Aye, well. There'll be time enough for pubs." She shuffled her cooking around the pan, making the fat spit and hiss, and leaned back to avoid the splatter.

Joe lost his chance to stay at school when his father got sick from the coal dust. At fourteen he was told to quit and go earning. Nine years ago now, the first six years on a road crew. No coal dust laying cobbles. Just poisonous hot tar fumes. He poked at the fire in the black-leaded grate and bit at a fingernail. Walter had better not be skiving away from *his* chance. He hoped Ma hadn't detected his irritation.

"Fred's letter, Joe," Ma said, pointing the wavering fork at his hand. Ellen tottered over to Joe's side and climbed onto his lap. He pulled in his legs and willed his face into a smile. Poker and letter in one hand, the other securing his daughter, he disturbed a few pieces of smoldering coal to arouse some heat. "Run over to your ma for a minute," Joe said into the soft white curls on his daughter's head, plopping her back on her feet. "Gran wants to hear about Uncle Fred." He fanned the sheets in her face making her giggle.

"Don't send her over here, Joe," Kate said, her green eyes blazing. "I'm helping your ma cook the tea. And mind she doesn't fall into the fire."

Joe pulled Ellen back to him, and stood her between his legs. Legs made strong from nearly ten years of physical labour. "Here." He tapped the letter and held it for her to touch. "Your Uncle Fred wrote words on this. So he can tell us what he's doing."

"Fed," Ellen attempted.

"Aye, your Uncle Fred. My brother. He's in France fighting a war for the English. Since six months back. What it has to do with him is beyond me. I'm not sure the Germans are any worse than the English."

Kate wiped her hands on a thin towel and dared him to be quiet with the glower he knew well.

He fixed his eyes on her. "Or us for that matter."

"Just shut your bloody mouth about all that, Joe."

"Please Kate, mind your language," Ma said, nodding towards Ellen.

Kate turned her back on her mother-in-law and fiddled with her thick auburn hair, twirling it into a loose bun at the nape of her neck. Joe caught the nippy in and out dart of her tongue, then a quick turn back to the cooking. Joe buried his face in the back of Ellen's neck.

"Well, your brother Fred's doing his bit," Kate said. "And earning better money than staying here. His wife's told me. If *you* went, Lizzie says you'd get even more than we have now because of me and the wee one." She folded her arms over her breasts. "And you could be helping your ma with the extra."

"Kate, I'm fine. It's not money I'm needing," Ma said, casting a smile at her son.

Joe pointed the poker at his wife. "Leave my mother out of this. I can well look after her here if I have to." He plunked himself deep into the fireside chair, feeling the cold fabric nip at his buttocks through the thin droopy cushion, and wrapped his arms around Ellen. This wasn't the first time he'd heard about the generous allowances the soldiers with families were getting. To be sure, the money would make a difference. He could help Ma with a few extras, maybe a night out now and then or a new fireside chair from the second-hand saleroom. And maybe he could move his own family to a house with an indoor lavvy. If Kate wouldn't keep harping on at him about it, he might share his thoughts with her.

"Fed," Ellen repeated and pushed the letter towards Joe's face. He took it and pointed the words out to his daughter. "The sun is shining today," Joe pretended to read. He stretched out the words for Ellen. "I am going paddling with my friends."

"What?" Ma said.

Joe winked at her and went on in his bedtime-story voice. "Tell Ellen she is my favourite wee girl and give her a kiss on her bonny red cheek." Joe kissed her and she snuggled into his chest. His ma nodded to him to read the letter.

"Dear Family," he read out loud, as he hoisted himself from the sagging chair, *"I am as well as you can imagine a man can be with scratchy trousers. Can't complain though as we've got all the clothes we need, including the warmest coat I've ever had. So that's a bonus. But like I said, it itches like mad. You'd get a laugh watching the lads trying to march."*

Joe hoisted Ellen onto his shoulders and marched her around the table that hogged the room. He held the letter out in front of him with one hand. *"Left, right, left, right,"* he read on. *"More like one, two, scratch, scratch. Our kit weighs a ton and some of the measlier boys—lads like Walter what shy away from real man's work—spend most of their time tripping over their own feet."*

"That's not a fair thing for Fred to say about his own brother," Ma said. "Walter works hard at his books. And he brings in an extra shilling with the part-time work."

"You're right, Ma. I'm on Walter's side. He sticks in. I've seen him at his homework. His fingers blue with ink."

His mother smiled. "And his shirt."

"I would hardly call him measly," Kate put in, laying plates and forks on the table. "He's a handsome strapping lad. And taller than Fred if it comes to that."

Joe's face hardened. "I'll not have him giving up opportunities as long as I have a say in it. My big brother has no imagination. Unlike Walter." He wiped a spot of spittle from the corner of his mouth. "Just because Fred was in a rush to sign up for the army doesn't mean there's something wrong with the rest of us. More likely he's the one with the twisted way of behaving. Running around some foreign land with a rifle in his hand trying not to get killed."

Joe froze when he saw a white stillness creep down his mother's cheeks and instantly regretted opening his mouth. "Here Ma, take Ellen." He lowered his daughter to the floor and handed her to his mother. "Let's see what else Fred has to say."

"We're kept well in rations. Bully beef, tea with the most sugar I've ever had. And the wages are not to be scoffed at. I still get half my wages from the mine. Five shillings. Mind you, I'm not sure the bosses will keep paying if this goes on for a while. (There's a lot more I'd like to say on the subject of 'the bosses' but we've been told to keep our mouths shut.) On top of that I get seven shillings in army pay, twelve as a ration allowance, as well as all these new clothes."

Joe quickly totalled the numbers. One pound four shillings. Close to three times what he was earning now, and Fred hadn't even mentioned the family allowance.

"I did well in the training. Mostly racing up to dummies with bayonets, acting fierce and getting a good clean stab at them. Haven't had a chance to do that to the Huns yet. 'Alleymen' the Frenchies call them. Not sure why. Maybe cos like us they're living in narrow trenches, like the alleys at the back of our houses. They say we'll be well ready when the time comes. Trick here is to shut up and do what we're told. You can imagine I'm not getting any medals for that. The officers swan around as if the whole thing was an afternoon in a gentleman's club. Strutting up and down, telling us lads to keep our peckers up! I wish! Sorry, Ma. Ignore that. Just joking. Hope you're all managing fine.

Your son,

Fred

P.S. Clean socks and decent smokes would be much appreciated."

Joe's stomach smoothed out. Thank God Fred really was fine. He carefully refolded the letter, lining up the creases and sharpening them with his forefinger. He placed the sheets back in the envelope and handed it to his mother. "He's his usual self."

She nodded and for a few moments all was silent save for the ticking of the clock on the mantel.

"Come and sit in," Kate said. She lifted Ellen onto a chair piled with cushions, tied a bib around her neck, and pushed her into the table.

"Let's wait a wee bit for Walter," Ma said. "Maybe he'll show up. If he does, he'll be needing some tea too. Maybe he's at his job, cleaning the lamps at the pithead." She continued looking at the clock. "Could've gone there right from school."

"The food's on the table and Ellen's hungry," Kate said. "I'm not waiting on him when he's likely chatting up some lassie somewhere and not giving a thought to us. C'mon, Joe."

Joe ruffled Ellen's hair as he went by her to take his spot at the table, next to his mother. He tucked into a forkful of meat and peas. "Fred really doesn't have that much to say."

"Mrs. Cluskey round the corner," Kate said, slicing her sausage, "says the soldiers aren't allowed to write about their work over there."

"How does she know?" Ma asked.

"Her sister's a maid in a house in London, and she heard the mistress talking on a telephone about a lad what got tied to a cartwheel."

"That's rubbish. What would they do that for?" Joe said.

"Wrote to the family of a friend, telling them the friend got shot and left to die." Kate spooned a mouthful of sausage into Ellen's searching mouth. "Right where he got shot, because there wasn't enough doctors. It's a fact."

"It's a fact, is it?" Joe said. "And this is what you want for me? The father of your bairn?"

"I was just saying Mrs. Cluskey got it right from her sister in London. She says the man what told got tied to a cartwheel and was like that for two weeks. Except for eating and sleeping. Like being cru ... crussi ... you know, like Easter," she said and shuddered.

Ma put her hand over her mouth. "My God."

"I didn't mean ... I didn't think ..." Kate, too, covered her mouth.

"Aye. Another of your problems."

Joe touched his mother's arm. "Ma, I'm sure they're not about to kill their own soldiers. That's rubbish," he said, throwing Kate a *shut-your-mouth* look. "Just women gossiping."

"I believe her," Kate said, her arms now crossed in their familiar huff position.

"Well, more's the reason for me not going." Joe stared at Kate. "Unless you have a mind to get rid of me." He watched tears collect in her eyes. "Well? Cat got your tongue now?"

Kate's hands shook as she put down her fork. She sheltered them under her armpits. "I was just saying that Fred can't write stuff—"

"And I'm just saying you haven't any clue what you're on about," Joe said. "And I'm also *just saying* I'm not getting involved, if that's what you're trying to get me to do," Joe said. "And neither's Walter. Got that? If the folks down in London have their knickers in a twist about whatever, let them fight it out. I'll leave it to the rich folk, if they want a war over their thirst for glory or honour, for whatever it's about and whatever they call it. I'm not into handing over my life for someone else's benefit." He pointed his fork at Kate, a plump piece of sausage dangling from one of the tines. "And I don't need any danger. I can get enough of that down the mine. Nor do I need to be around a gang of hotheads like Fred. I told him volunteering for the war could get him into trouble."

Ma gasped. Joe shoved the meat into his mouth and put his fork down. He patted his mother's arm again. "Ma, I'm just sounding off. It'll be fine. It was supposed to be over nearly a year ago, so it's gonna be done soon. Fred'll be back safe and sound afore we know it." He glared at Kate. "Let's eat our tea in peace."

Hard to fathom Fred had been gone nigh on half a year already. Back when he left, Joe didn't have the confidence in this war he was now urging his mother to feel. And still he was of the same mind. He sat in silence, thinking back to Fred badgering him in The Brig six months ago. Fred, Joe, and Joe's pal from the mine, John, were both putting away a pint at the ring-stained mahogany bar. "What is it you're wanting me to read?" Joe had said, as he picked up the beer-splashed *Courier* Fred had pushed towards him. He'd studied his brother's strong hairy arms before turning his eyes to the newspaper, dated Saturday August 22, 1914.

"Regiments are looking for volunteers. The Scots and the Argylls included. I'm thinking we should sign up," Fred said.

"What for?" Joe smoothed out the front page of the newspaper and squinted at the print. The grime-coated windows of The Brig foiled even the summer evening light trying to punch through. "A war?" He knocked back a slug of beer and skimmed the opening paragraph. "What's it about?" He looked at George the barman, drying a pint glass with a linen towel. George shrugged and moved towards the other end of the bar to fill a call for a rum.

Joe rested his right foot on the brass rail under the bar and tracked the beginning of the article with his finger. "Where's this Sar ... Sara ... whatsit? Never heard of it."

"Sarajevo. Aye, well you've had your face buried in a beer mug these last three month," Fred said. "*I've* been paying attention to what's going on in the world."

"All right then, give me the dirty. *If* I need to know about it." Joe elbowed their drinking buddy. "Me and John'll listen to your lecture, Mister Professor." His pal's presence encouraged him to try on a bravado he wouldn't normally dare around his older brother. He and John laughed, crossed their legs and posed, each with a finger on his chin. He was loving the blustering confidence he was dishing up to Fred.

His brother continued to scowl at them. "A couple of months back some idiot shot the Emperor of Austria's son, Franz Ferdinand, and his wife. In Bosnia-Herzegovina."

Joe and John both raised their hands and snapped their fingers as they used to in school to rudely get the teacher's attention.

"Please sir," Joe screeched. "Where's Austria?" He took a mouthful of beer and spluttered. "And the other place. Buzzin' something?"

"Quit being total fucking morons. Bosnia. They're both near Germany," Fred said. "A Serbian terrorist gang attacked them. The Black Hand."

"Ooh scary," John said and laughed. "The Black Hand. Bombs." He lobbed one of the little square beer mats over at Joe, who cooperated by falling off his stool onto the sawdust-covered floor.

"Grow up." Fred's face reddened. "This is serious stuff. Listen."

"You're making this up," Joe said. "Sounds more like a story from one of the penny dreadfuls Kate reads." He wanted to keep up this heckling, but he could feel his daring cheekiness slip away.

Fred slapped the paper. "It's right here," he shouted, the skin around his mouth and nose almost purple. "Read it for yourself if you don't believe me." He threw the newspaper at Joe's face. "You two are trying my patience. I'd walk out of here in a heartbeat and leave you two dolts to your fucking ignorance, if I wasn't trying to wake yous both up. Read."

Startled by Fred's little outburst, Joe clutched the paper, looked from his brother's blazing eyes to the cluster of round tables behind him. Would these old geezers sitting there, wet-nursing half-pints, take Fred's side? Many had seen the war in South Africa against the Boers. Would *they* put any weight in what Fred said the *Courier* was printing? What would they expect of his generation? Joe stared at them, trying to get a hint of an answer in their lined faces, but they sat the same as ever, pulling on their pipes and fags, shuffling and chapping dominoes and swapping stories. He was beginning to believe the war talk and didn't know what to do with this information. He certainly wasn't going to go off on some crazy crusade, but he was starting to fear his older brother would sign up.

Fred nudged him and pointed to the newspaper. "It's in there. A war coming. If men of all classes fight thegether, shoulder to shoulder against a common enemy, you'll see ... it'll change this world."

"And I've to take your word for all this brilliant future coming?" Joe said. "And I'm to join you? You're awfully sure of yourself. A big promise you're making."

Fred grabbed his wrist. "Don't you pay attention to *anything* but your sorry little life? Did you *ever* listen to our Da? Or his pals that sweated for years?"

Joe pushed off Fred's hand and stroked the sides of his pint glass. "Aye, aye, Fred. Enough of your speechifying."

Fred ignored him. "We're going to give the German Kaiser Bill and his cronies their comeuppance. And after this, nothing will be the same. There'll be big changes."

"Right, right, Fred," John said. "You tell him, that Bill man. Scare the shite out of him. But maybe it is time for a change." He turned to his friend. "How about you stand us a round, Joe? That would be a right change."

"You're an idiot," Joe said. "And *that'll* never change." He fumbled in his pocket for precious coins and threw down all he had. Enough of foreign devils and black-hooded assassins, or whatever they were. He nodded at the barman and turned towards the door. "Pour that joker and my brother a pint."

"I was just having a laugh on you," John Burns shouted to his back.

Joe spun around. "Aye, life's hilarious." He stuck the newspaper under his arm and shoved through the men at the bar. "I'm away for a walk."

Joe tried to shake off the talk of doom by heading to the shore, knowing he had time and light at hand. This far north, as the waters of the sea lapped against the pebbles, the summer sun merely dozed, never drawing the full blanket of night. He pored over the front page of the newspaper to check what Fred had been on about. It did read like an episode in a serial drama. He was skeptical about the truth of it all, yet still shaken. He tried to ignore Fred's warnings as simply ravings and obsessions about 'a people's war' but something about it all gave him the willies. He turned to the inside pages of the paper, where, as promised on the front, the 'full and awful implications' were revealed. This Austria Fred mentioned threatened an invasion as revenge for the loss of their duke. Short fuses from long-standing tiffs all over Europe had been ignited. Joe didn't know what these 'tiffs' were all about, and as far as he knew Scotland didn't have any enemies, but surely they wouldn't be printing stuff in the paper, frightening people about a war coming, if it wasn't true. All this argy-bargy was probably England's business. But if England was fighting, London might expect men all over Britain to sign up. He stuffed that thought away. He thrust the newspaper inside his jacket and rubbed his ankle. It was a couple of months since the runaway mine tram had run over his foot, but it still grew stiff when he sat too long. If Fred started badgering him again about signing up, he'd ignore him. He could exaggerate his gammy ankle, thank God, although he'd feel bad about playing that card forever. The army would love to get its hands on someone as big and strong as himself. He shook out his foot and wandered back to The Brig.

Fred laughed when Joe returned and settled again onto a barstool. "So I got you hooked? Convinced you, did I?" He nodded to the barman. "I'll stand my brother a pint."

"It says here," Joe said, waving the paper in the air, "the Canadians, South Africans, and Australians are joining up. Hundreds of Americans are going to Canada so they can join up. Is it really going to be that big?"

Fred pulled him to the quiet end of the bar. "All my talk all these years, Joe? About exploitation of us workers, the low wages, the dangerous conditions. You'll see. This is *our* war. This is our chance. To show our faces. Show them we can fight. They'll owe us. At the very least give all us men the vote, not just the ones with land. Our voices will be heard when this is over, if not before." Fred brought his stool closer to Joe and lowered his voice. "And it's not like it's away the other side of the world, like the South African war. Out of sight, out of mind. It's going to happen right close." He prodded the bar with his finger. "Right near here. In France and Belgium."

Joe traced some spilled drops of beer on the counter and stared ahead. He considered himself and his older brother in the mirror behind the bar, etched with an advertisement for Dewar's whisky. He watched them both as Fred's head came so close to his own he could feel a spectre of the spiky stubble on his cheek. His chest filled unexpectedly with envy for Fred's enthusiasm. And pride in his brother's fervour. And *caring*. He saw Fred's reflection stand and grip the edge of the bar.

Joe pulled his eyes from the mirror and stared into his beer. "But why's it up to the likes of you and me? If there's a fight, leave it to the army. The regulars. Like doctoring's best left to doctors."

"Not this time. Everyone's joining up." Fred drew on his drink and swiped the froth from his moustache. "So it'll be the likes of us that'll make up the fighting lines. We can dangle that over the government when the war's won. And they're saying that'll be soon. By Christmas." He swirled the beer around his glass, took a slug, and laid his hand on Joe's shoulder. "And that's why I'll be volunteering first thing in the morning."

Joe's stomach took a dive. He rooted his tongue around the inside of his mouth to waken up some spit. "The paper here says miners can be excused. We're too valuable apparently," he said, trying to ignore

Fred's pronouncement. "We can all stay home." He didn't feel valuable when he was lacerating underground walls with his pick. Necessary maybe. Worthless and dispensable more like.

"Or we could all go," Fred said. Even Walter when he turns eighteen, if it lasts that long. God help us if it does."

"I'll kill Walter myself if he signs up," Joe said. "That's not what this family's got planned for our brainy brother."

"You've got your own brains, brother. What about your life? How much value do they put on *your* life down in the pit?" Fred downed the last of his beer. "A couple of months back, you had a bloody tram mash up your foot. Kept you off work for six weeks. Lost your wages too." He flipped his flat cap onto his head. "And who would've looked after your wife and bairn if you'd been killed? Like I said, you'll know where I'll be in the morning." Fred pulled open the pub door. "Mind now. The recruiting office. Next to the library. I'd be happy to see you there."

An elbow jabbed at his ribs. "Have you heard one word I've said?" Kate asked.

Joe swivelled to face his wife, jolted away from the memory of Fred's last words and back to his mother's kitchen and Kate's voice vexing his ears. He stroked wee Ellen's cheek, reminded himself of the safe news in Fred's letter.

"The money's good," she went on, and worked her top teeth around her bottom lip. "If you went. . ."

"Enough with your havering nonsense. If our Da hadn't given his lungs to the mine, I'd have been the one like Walter getting a chance to get money from a decent job." He turned to Kate and pointed his finger so close to her nose she drew back. "Enough *what if.* Here's what *is*. We've got our own battles down the pit. They need us to get more coal out with less men working. That's a good hand to play for better conditions and more wages. Your dear brother-in-law Fred would've been better off staying here and fighting for that." Joe shovelled the last of his meal into his mouth, stood, kicked at his chair, and left the table.

"Stay, Joe," his mother said, her voice wobbling.

But he was already grabbing his cap from a hook screwed into the door. He put up a hand to fend off another appeal. "I'll see if I can find Walter."

He stuffed his hands into his jacket pockets as he made his way down the street to The Brig. Head down, cutting a swath through the biting winter wind, he thought on the gossip Kate reported. Most days he went down the pub, and like everyone, searched through the newspaper for news about the war. 'Spirits High', 'Victory At Hand', 'Kaiser in Retreat', 'Emperor On The Run', and similar headlines gave him no more sense of his brother's experience than the letter had. These captions hung over pictures of kilted soldiers relaxing against a haystack, bayonets used as backrests, cigarettes dangling from smiling mouths. Perfect moments of adventure and camaraderie.

But Joe, like his mother, did fret over Fred's safety. He *had* heard whispers. Of battles where every officer and higher up NCO in a platoon was killed, leaving the fight in the hands of a twenty-year-old corporal. Stories of bodies lying like a khaki blanket over the fighting area between the British and German trenches. An area they called 'No Man's Land.' Softly spoken murmurs about bodies lying unburied sometimes for weeks, and if buried, blown up again in the next onslaught. Many lads in the pub had heard stories from a sister's husband's second cousin in Liverpool, or from a letter someone's granny had received from a grandson who lived in Yorkshire.

Other friends told third-hand tales of villages in England where almost all the men had signed up together, calling themselves Pals regiments, and now, less than eighteen months later, a third of them were dead, another third home minus a limb or two. He couldn't decide whose version of this war to take on.

More unsettling was the talk that even with a couple million volunteers the government was saying they needed more. There was talk of conscription. Joe seethed at that decision being made for him. For while he wasn't sure what to believe, or how much to believe, he was sure in his belly that signing up would not change the world in the way Fred believed.

"You're buried deep there, my friend."

Joe looked up to see Bernie his workmate coming up behind him. "The wind. Got to keep your head down," he said, but suspected Bernie picked up the off-kilter sincerity of his response.

"I'm on my way to The Brig," Bernie said. "Looks like you could use one. C'mon. I'll stand you a half. It'll be warm inside."

"Aye, well ... okay," Joe said. "I can't stay long. I'm out looking for Walter. Ma hasn't seen him for three days."

"Aye, come to think on it, I didn't see him on the weekend at his job like I usually do," said Bernie, opening the door and waving two fingers at the barman. "Gone astray, has he?"

"Probably not, but my ma's worried." Flashes of anger punctured his concern about Walter. He was nigh on sixteen, already at that randy age. Maybe he *had* buggered off, decided he'd had enough of doing homework, and was diddling some lassie in one of Methilane's dark corners. Or God forbid, he'd actually come to some harm. There were always bands of pissed, bored lads roaming the streets looking for a target. Joe hoped he sounded more relaxed than his sombre thoughts were allowing. "I've been working nights mostly, so I never see him at the pit," he continued.

"Aye, a bit weird. Usually our shifts overlap." Bernie stroked his sweeping moustache. "But I didn't give it a thought. I just reckoned he wasn't well and had to stay in his bed."

"I know for sure he wasn't home ill. Can't believe Walter hasn't been in to his shift." Joe threw back his drink. "Thanks for the beer, Bernie. I need to go find him."

Out in the street, Joe lit a cigarette. With each exhaled puff of smoke, he struggled to blow off a growing worry. He pulled his jacket lapels up around his ears in a useless attempt to block out the North Sea chill and gloom. Head down, face into the wind again, he scurried the half-mile to the mine.

For three raw winters he'd walked six days a week to his job down the mine. Three years since his da died of the miner's dreaded black lung and he'd managed to wangle his father's place underground. For sure the pay was better down the pit than his previous job laying cobblestone roads, but swinging a pick at a coal seam didn't ask for any more brainpower than hammering a mallet against bits of stone. That road job had been severe in the winter, without a doubt, but the handful of warm days in July and August allowed him to strip to his undershirt, brought the intoxicating summer smell of melted tar, and toned down the boredom.

Joe remembered the chilly March day, three years since, of his da's funeral. A month after he'd turned twenty. After the burial, the male mourners rallied round Ma and joined her and the women folk, squeezed into the main room at the back of the house, in the same kitchen he'd just left in a snit. Nothing had changed since then. The walls were the same grungy cream paint, streaked white where Ma scrubbed a useless battle against grease and coal smoke. Even then the table crowding the middle of the room displayed a sad medley of scratches and gouges that weekly waxings and polishings couldn't defeat.

After the burial the women had helped Ma lay out the required whisky and sherry bottles. Fred, older than Joe by five years, helped himself to generous shots from the whisky bottles and tumbled into what Joe called 'his rantings.'

"I'm sick of watching our men coughing and spluttering their way to an early grave," Fred said, his voice grown huskier with each shot.

Ma's thin face fell and she started to weep, but Fred got in his next words before Joe rustled up the gumption to stop him.

"I'm sick of worrying about doctors' bills we shouldn't have to pay. And families left without a breadwinner."

Ma, across the table from her eldest son, took his hand and stroked the frayed cuff of his only white shirt. "I knew what could be ahead when I married your da. I knew the mine would get him sooner than later," she said. "It was the long drawn-out suffering that was the worst. Maybe the fifteen that were buried alive ten year ago in the disaster had it easier." She leaned back and covered her eyes with her handkerchief. "Been great for us if there was some other work, but the mine's all there is around here. He was my man and I stood by him."

"You were a good wife, Ma," Fred's wife, Lizzie, said and wound her plump arms around her mother-in-law's shoulders. "And think on those three strapping laddies he gave you." She handed the crying woman a dry handkerchief. "Here, dab your eyes." Lizzie reached for the Harvey's Bristol Cream. "Have a wee sherry."

Ma mopped up the tears from her cheeks with the white lace-edged cloth. When Fred thumped his hairy fist on the table, tinkling the cups on their saucers, she flinched and looked up.

"That's what I'm saying, Ma. None of us that go down the pits have it easy," Fred said. He stood and staggered away from the table over to Joe. "Dead or alive."

Joe had been trying to coax some heat from the pitiful pile of coals in the grate, stabbing at their undersides to throw off his annoyance at Fred. He'd never had the nerve to stand up to his older brother, or his stocky muscle, but he couldn't stand him badgering Ma. Not today, when she was worn down by the funeral. He clenched his fist around the poker, then forced himself to relax and let it drop. "I wonder you don't get sick of your own voice," Joe said, "gabbing on and on about things you can't do anything about."

Fred charged toward him and stuck out his chest, his fists clenched. "And what good are you doing this world, brother?"

Joe's insides felt like mush. "I'll tell you what I'm doing." He put his hands in his pockets to hide the quivering. "Neither you or me had a chance of doing any better than our da, but I'm going to make sure our wee brother sticks in at school. That'll do me and this family proud."

Fred was so close now Joe could feel the heat from his whisky breath. "What's that you're saying?"

"Nothing," Joe said, backing away. His voice trickled out thinner than he'd have liked.

"You'd be better making a real man of Walter," Fred said, pushing Joe against the fireside chair. "And where the hell is he? That wee brother of ours?" Lizzie flew at her husband, grabbed his forearm, and raised herself to every inch of her five feet. Joe slunk out of the couple's way. "He's in his bedroom," Lizzie said. "Reading. Leave him be and don't you go upsetting folk today. Have some respect for your ma. She doesn't need to hear the whisky talking the day we've put her man in the ground." She pushed him into the fireside chair, held onto his arm, and stared him quiet.

Joe smiled at the power she had over her belligerent husband, admired the way his sister-in-law's dark eyes grew big and unafraid, how her voice never shook, even as she tipped her head back to look up at Fred's solid jawline.

Lizzie's face smoothed out. She shook her head slowly and turned to the cluster of mourners. "A bad day for Fred. Not natural that. His da going afore fifty."

Fred shrugged himself free of his wife's hold, pushed her aside, got up, and assaulted the table again. "Just all of you remember that them what inherited these coal pits and got rich didn't inherit the right to exploit the muscle of the likes of us. If they want something of me, they can have my anger and my hungry bairns." He pulled at a splinter of wood that had caught the side of his hand. "It's about time you all woke up. We're twelve year into a new century. The twentieth century, for Chrissake. Mr. Lloyd George says it's the century of the ordinary man." He poked at a pock-faced cousin who, deafened by free whisky, had nodded off with arms folded across his chest. "That's you as well, Gordie." He waved his arms around the group. "All of you what go to the pit day after day, week after week. There's more than bodies trapped down there. You've all got your heads buried as well. Up your arses! You know what we are?" He banged one of Ma's best glasses on the table. It shattered, spilling the precious whisky. "We're sure-fire casualties." He wiped the spreading stain with his sleeve. "We just don't know the date of our own disaster."

"Right, Fred. That's enough." Lizzie resumed her grip on her husband's arm and dragged him towards the door. She offered a brief smile to the small crowd, who looked as weary and worn as their Sunday-best clothes. "Bobby, Jimmy," she said, shepherding two small, head-shorn boys to the door. "Get your coats and give your gran and Uncle Joe a wee kiss. And Uncle Walter too." She nodded toward the house's only other room across the hall. "Knock on the door first."

Ma was weeping aloud now, and pulled her black cardigan tight across her chest. She came over to Joe and clutched at his upper arms, her small hands unable to make a circle around them. He looked away from her. He feared her sobs would make him lose the composure he'd feigned all day and smash open the floodgates of his own sorrow. He kept quiet as his sister-in-law marshalled her family.

Fred looked over his shoulder at Joe. "And you're a moron, taking our father's place at the pit. How can you do this to Ma? She doesn't want more of us ending up like our father."

Ma let go her hold on Joe's arm and her hands flew to her face. Joe bit his lip and shuffled back to the hearth. Ma would be weeping non-stop, now that Fred had spilled the beans about him taking his father's job. He looked at his brother, uneasy at his aggression.

"So this is your life's purpose, then?" Fred went on. "Hacking away at someone else's black gold. Have you not your own ambition?"

Joe knew from the heat in his cheeks they were filling with colour. Embarrassed, he prodded the meagre fire. He had learned from an early age to keep his mouth shut and let his older brother have the parting shot.

Fred pointed his index finger at Joe. "You'd better come and talk to me afore going down that fucking pit Monday morning."

Now here Joe was at that same pithead. Funny, after all Ma's pleading back then. He hated being chained to that bloody mine, but here he was, crossing his fingers his wee brother was there. He rapped on the porter's booth. The window slid back. "Evening, Jim."

The lines on the face of Jim Laird, the old porter, cracked into a grin. "Joe, young fella. Thought this was your night off." He reached into a bundle of cardboard pieces and flicked through them. "Aye, that's right. I thought so. You're not due in until tomorrow." His face twisted as a coughing spasm gripped him. He picked up a newspaper lying on the table, opened at the horse racing, and whacked his chest with it. A splatter of greenish phlegm landed on the counter.

Joe stepped back. "You all right there?"

"Oh, aye. You know how it is. Forty-eight year down there." Jim nodded toward the shaft entrance.

Joe shuddered. The man's whole adult life had been spent in the dark corridors below them.

Jim waved the newspaper around the cubicle. "But it's right cozy in here," he said. "What can I do you for?" He succumbed to another coughing spasm.

"It's my wee brother. Walter. The family's not seen him and my ma … well mothers worry, right? Bernie Brown had the idea he might have signed off sick," Joe said. "Can you check the sign-in cards for me?"

Jim's hands, covered with woollen fingerless gloves, twitched over the cards. "Your brother's fine and well as far as I know. Maybe he'll write you a letter."

"A letter?" Joe said. "Why? Where is he?"

"Signed up."

"For what?"

"For France is what I heard."

Sunday May 16, 1915 Joe yanked the itchy grey blanket over his shoulders. Could barely take in he'd *volunteered* for the army, swearing to his mother his enlistment was only to find Walter. He hoped she'd bought his little white lie, his suggestion he could come home as soon as he found Walter. He hadn't expected to cool his heels and freeze his bollocks off in a field of bell tents barely seventy miles from home. Two months he'd been here. Other than scouring for Walter, he had no use for this training camp. He shifted to get more comfortable on the narrow canvas cot. Difficult when this apology for a bed was made for the average five-foot-seven Scotsman and his feet hung over the end. He drew his knees to his chest and tucked himself in as tight as he could.

The evenings, like now, were the most mind numbing. Now and then, if it was warm, the pipers stood in a circle and blew, enticing some lads to kick up their heels in a rowdy reel or the slower strathspey. The rest hooted, clapped out the rhythms, and stamped their feet. But tonight nothing was up except the tent flap, slowly and steadily slapping in the wind, and the rain splattering over his head. Joe was fed up and glum.

He pulled his shoulder blades together, fidgeting from the metal frame digging into his ribs. The only upside was the break from Kate. Her mindless talking of the clothes and furniture and dishes she wanted, and wheedling time away from him and wee Ellen to be with her girl pals, drove him mad, as did the bickering. If he was honest with himself, he gave back as good as he got from her tongue. Was *she* enjoying having him away? True, it wasn't just her fault she fell pregnant. But she was lucky he'd done the decent thing and married her. He'd never been short of attention from the lassies. He knew, when he looked in the mirror, it wasn't only Ma and Gran that thought him a handsome catch. His strong chin, full lips, and his mother's blue-grey eyes added up to a good-looking face.

But wedding her had its blessings. The warm ripple of joy when wee Ellen looked at him and gave him a gummy grin filled a part of his heart he hadn't known existed. One Saturday last summer, on a whim, he'd swept her up in his arms, raced her out the door away from Kate, for a dip in the sea. Taking her sandals off, he'd told her this was their day, was going to be *their* memory. At the edge of the lapping water, he'd sat down, gasped as the incoming tide iced his buttocks. When he raised Ellen over the water and dipped her toes in, she gurgled with delight and folded her little body over her legs trying to reach the source of her pleasure. He was jealous Kate now had that all to herself.

He scratched at a rough patch the blanket had made on his elbow. Ellen aside, maybe before he was a husband, before he was a father, he should've heeded Ma's bidding not to go down the mine. He settled on his back, arms pillowing his neck, and remembered her urging him to get away. The first time she brought it up it was the evening of his father's funeral, more than three years ago, after the mourners had left the house taking the warmth of their comfort with them.

"What are you doing?" Ma had said, allowing Joe to help her on with her coat.

"I'm taking you out so you can cheer up a wee bit afore going to bed." He handed her a muffler, the fur flattened and matted. "You'll need this."

On the ten-minute walk to the pub, Ma linked her arm with her son's. "Does this bother you?" she said.

"No," he laughed. "I'm not ashamed of being seen with my ma."

Hot air, smelling of seldom-bathed bodies, blasted them as Joe pushed at the etched-glass panel of the snug door. This was women-only territory, unless a sweetheart or an eligible son was being shown off. "You were very brave today, Ma," he told her, as he plopped down drinks on their table, a pint for himself and a sherry for her.

"Aye, well. What else can I be?" she said, clinking her glass to his. Fresh tears tiptoed down her cheeks.

In the three days since Da had lain waxen and silent on the bed, Joe too felt tears ready to spout at any minute from a deep well of grief. He swallowed hard, tugged at his lips to dam his own crying. "I'll look after you, Ma. Chip in and see you all right."

"It's not that, Joe."

"No? What then?"

"That was news to me when Fred said you're starting down the pit on Monday."

Joe shifted on the wooden bench. "Aye well. You'd only try and argue me out of it. It's not that easy to get hired on, but the foreman offered me Da's job, so I took it. It's steady work. And rent paying."

She twisted her handkerchief with shaking hands. "Joe, I want you to find something else. Anything. Get out while you're young and have no ties."

"If I live at home and work down the pit, we can keep the house. I can make the rent, and maybe make enough to keep Walter in school."

Ma put down her drink and faced him. "Listen to me, Joe." She grasped both his wrists and fixed her eyes on his. The same fierce tenderness on her face Joe remembered as a boy sick with the measles. When the fever chased away sleep, she would sit on the bed by him stroking his eyelids. He'd sunk into her cocoon of love and let it soothe his tight and twitchy skin. Now he shook his mother off, her touch embarrassing in such a public space.

She put her hands in her lap, but her gaze stayed fixed on him. "Every day your father went down those pits, he moved in a place I could never go. It drove him deep inside himself." She played with her sherry glass.

"Another?" Joe said, rising from his seat.

"Sit," she said. Her grey-blue eyes did not let up their stare. "You're a big lad now. Your own man." Her mouth softened. "But not so big you can't listen to your ma."

Joe wished he could run to the other side of the pub, join in the empty joviality of the men-only bar.

"Your da and me," she said, "that mine trapped us both. Peeled him away from me." A winsome beam smoothed the lines from her mouth. She held up and crossed her middle and index fingers. "We were like that in the beginning. Close. Always close."

Joe gulped his beer and cleared his throat. His cheeks boiled at the intimacy of her disclosure. He wondered if she had talked like this to his father. He certainly was never aware of devotedness between his ma and da.

"It'll be different for me," he said.

"Hear me out, son." She put her hand towards his arm. He put both hands in his pockets and fiddled with the few coins that rested there. She lifted her glass and took a sip. Joe felt the seconds ticking away like a clang inside his head, but he could hardly make an excuse and leave on this day, the worst in the life of the Mathieson family.

"Your future, if you stay," she said, her voice holding a steadiness that surprised him, "is as predictable as the tide going in and out on the North Sea. It'll be no different as it's been for all the Methilane men. Your dad, your granddad." She tugged on his sleeve. "What I'm saying, Joe ... you go down in that dark, it'll destroy you one way or the other. I wish you'd promise me you'd not go."

"I'm strong, Ma." Joe tapped his forehead. "Strong up here too."

"It'll get you, Joe. If it's not a cave-in, a flood, an explosion, or something falling on your head, it'll still get you." She played with the buttons on her black coat. "Before you know it, you'll be burrowing yourself like them all inside the pubs. When you're not down the pit, you'll be numbing yourself with whisky and pints so you can face another shift."

"It can't be that bad," said Joe.

"Be that as it may." Her voice became louder. "Never mind about the rent. I'll manage, Joe." She breathed out slowly and shifted in her seat. "Here's what you can do for me."

"What's that, Ma?"

"Get away. Anywhere. London, Canada. Australia." She forced a little laugh. "Even Glasgow. Take Walter with you if you have to."

This army camp wasn't exactly what she'd had in mind when she urged him to get away. What a joke. He *was* almost in another country. Another twenty miles and he'd be in England. He stared up at the point where the main tent pole pierced the canvas. Picked at his chin where the coarse blanket had snagged his stubble. The camp cot slumped under his weight and trembled when he shuddered from the cold drafts sneaking around the six beds in the tent. Remembering his mother's plea triggered the harsh understanding that came to him the day he had started down the pits: he'd likely never know anything different. He'd never know what lay beyond the row houses, the shops, the school, and the churches in Methilane, and the little he already knew of the Fife coast. A few times he'd visited the other mining towns: Leven, Wemyss, Cowdenbeath, Dysart, Burntisland. He'd been as far as Kirkcaldy, a dozen miles shy of Edinburgh, to cheer on its football team, Raith Rovers.

He should go outside, mingle with the others, hide from these dark ruminations, but the damp nipped at his nose and he buried his head under the blanket. Another month and this tedious training would be over. He heard the sergeant screaming and nagging at the lads taking their evening ease outside. How long before the ancient brute of an ex-soldier came in and hit him with his stick for the sheer pleasure of it? A heartless old geezer shunted out of retirement to make life miserable for him and the other newbies. Between chopping logs, charging towards scarecrows with lengths of wood in place of real rifles, digging holes to piss and shit in, and turning up nothing on Walter, he wasn't having a party here. At least at the mine he had his mates and the pints they shared at The Brig after a shift.

Joe got off the cot before the bastard could sweep into his moments of peace and wrench him to the ground. He swore the fucker would one day rip his arm from his body. How on earth had Walter got through all this? His wee brother who, at thirteen, had taken refuge in his books in the back bedroom the afternoon of his own father's funeral. Scared when Fred was making his ruckus and spouting his "we have to change the world" theories. But to Joe's surprise, a year back Walter joined the Boys' Brigade. He thought his brother more of a Boy Scout, a softer type. Likely the BB was mostly harmless marching and physical training. Keep Walter on the straight and narrow path the family had traced out for him. Maybe though, all that marching and the black and white uniform had put other ideas into Walter's head. Certainly no military ideas were in his head the day of the funeral, when Joe crossed the threshold to the wee back bedroom after Lizzie had dragged drunk, raging Fred home. "Was that him leaving?" Walter had closed his book and unwound his lanky frame from ma's old nursing chair when he saw Joe at the door.

"Aye," Joe said. "You're safe."

"Thanks," Walter said. "I can't stand Fred being stoked up so much. I thought he might simmer down, especially after the burial. I'm never doing the right thing according to him."

"It's not you," Joe said. He put his arm around his brother's shoulder as Walter stood, now only a couple inches below his own five-foot ten. "Everything's wrong in Fred's world. He'd turn it on its head if he could." Joe ruffled Walter's straight fine hair, so much like his own. "Go to the kitchen and be with Ma." He smiled. "Seeing you'll cheer her up."

Joe had felt sad watching his brother leave, heaving a sigh of relief. He had raised the window, polished to a sparkle by his mother that morning, and stared outside. The colourlessness depressed him: the grey stone houses, the grey slate on the roofs, still slick with rain from an early afternoon shower. Across the rooftops, the distant river Forth heaved its silver waters toward the North Sea. He knelt on the linoleum-covered floor, rested his arms on the windowsill, and remembered his da. How one summer his father had taken him and his two brothers up the coast to St Andrews. Even as a child Fred tested his younger brothers. On that occasion, Joe despised Fred's sneering dare that they jump into the brine. Walter ran off with Fred's jibes chasing after him, but Joe rose to the challenge. A crowd cheered when his father pulled him from the water and threw a thin towel around him. Da rubbed him so hard his skin hurt, but it brought breath back into his shocked lungs. Even on that July afternoon, the waters were frigid.

Steady raindrops spat at the tent walls. He was still mad at Walter for signing up. Angry and worried he wouldn't be able to comfort his mother now she had two sons in danger. No one at the recruiting office in the High Street had been willing to help him find Walter's whereabouts. One uniformed prick even laughed when Joe put to him his mother's request that they send her underage son home. Joe left the office with the soldier ragging at his back. "Tell your ma to look up the King's phone number in the book and give him a wee ring. I'm sure it's there. Under G for George. For sure he'll do her a favour if she asks nice and respectful." With that kind of help, he had no option but to do the job himself.

Ma couldn't turn off the water works when he'd told her he was going. "I can't have all my boys going to the war," she wailed. "What was Walter thinking?"

But in the next breath she was thanking him and shoving a picture of Walter at him. He held it in both hands. Walter. Squinting into the sun, black and white pillbox hat askew, at last year's BB camp at Aberfeldy. Lucky him, he got to play for a week.

"You always was the helpful one, Joe. The easy one. Thanks for not making a fuss."

Aye, that's me, he thought. His gran used to say, "Him what goes along, gets along." Going along. Where the Christ to, he had no idea. He put the picture into the inside pocket of his uniform.

"How long do you think?" Ma had said, holding both his wrists. "How long till this war is done?"

He didn't like her using that word. War. Wars were risky, scary goings on. The *Courier* was printing names and photos of the fallen. *The fallen?* As if the poor dead buggers could pick themselves up and soldier on. He laughed at his own wit, stroked his chin to massage back the seriousness of it all. His family was lucky. No Mathiesons had "fallen". So far. "You know I'm not for the war, Ma. I'm not Fred," he said, reassuring her. "I'm finding Walter and chasing him home. Bringing us both back. I promise." He turned on his biggest smile. "If you like, I'll try and persuade Fred to come home too. But I'm thinking that'll be a bigger order than dragging Walter home." But he had added to himself, *Just in case, look out for Ellen and Kate, will you? War.* Again the word hit him. Like a boot kick in the gut.

He tumbled from the cot onto the hard ground and rubbed his stomach to steady his breathing. *Geez*, he thought, *Ellen won't remember me*. And Kate? Would she weep for him like Ma did for his da? Was *he* much to lose?

He heard sergeant wheeze outside the tent, cough, and hurl a glob of spit.

"Button up your fly, you fucking disgusting wanker, I'm coming in."

Joe rolled under the cot.

"If I catch you whacking off, I'll have your balls for tomorrow's breakfast."

Joe watched the tent's entrance flap lift and the sergeant's puttees move towards the cot. *Away and bully some other poor sod*, Joe prayed. The sergeant snorted and left. Joe crawled out, lit a cigarette, and sucked hard on it. He waited through six puffs before he went outside, cupping the cigarette in his palm against the wind and rain.

A game of football was underway. Dark leaden clouds plodded through the pale sky. He had no mind to slip and slither in the mud like the lads running and shouting. Besides, they were bairns. Eighteen, nineteen years old. Twenty at the most. He took a step back, under the shelter of the tent canopy that slumped and bounced under the weight of the rainwater. Maybe it was his fault Walter left. Had he put too much on his young shoulders, insisting he stay at school? He'd thought his brother was fine with it, that he liked the book learning. But maybe he'd plunked his own ambition and hopes onto his brother. Like cleaning the cockerel's insides for Christmas dinner, going down the mine had taken the very guts from him.

Had Walter crumbled under the Mathieson family's hopes? Or revolted? He always cheered on Walter's relentless curiosity, was on at him to stand tall, tried to install confidence into his brother—a confidence he didn't feel for himself, squished in the family between feisty Fred and the future they all pinned on Walter. He'd always assumed Walter was the chosen one, was different in some special way. An old soul was what Gran, dead since Joe was fourteen, called her youngest grandson. Joe wasn't sure what she meant when she'd tug on Walter's cheeks and say that. He felt an ache in his chest thinking how his brother yelled, *"Ouch! Ouch!"* and squirmed away from her. But he, like his Gran, detected a special brightness about Walter. A light he brought with him when he entered a room, unlike the darker, denser weight that hung around his father and Fred. Maybe it was all too much for a sixteen-year old.

Joe threw his cigarette end into a puddle and watched until it stopped spluttering. Looked for the shit-faced sergeant. The bloody one-eyed idiot had been giving him an extra hard dishing-out since last Wednesday, when the medical officer discovered Joe was on the first-aid team at the mine and volunteered him for extra training to carry stretchers.

Joe couldn't breathe. He gasped and choked as cold water poured over his head. The fucking sergeant was bashing at the tent canopy's underside with a walking cane, releasing the final dregs from the lake lounging upon it. Must have sneaked up on him from behind the tent. He felt like tearing the skin from the bastard's face, screaming, and running all the way home. Fuck them all. Instead he shook the water from his head like a dog coming out of the sea.

"Gotta keep you on your toes." The sergeant pulled on his bristly moustache and glanced over his shoulder. "Over there, if a bullet's coming your way, just like this, you'll have no warning." He gave the canopy a last wallop and laughed. "You'll be dodging many a bullet, you being a fancy SB and all. Know what SB stands for?"

"Aye," said Joe. "Stretcher-bearer."

The fat man pushed him and he landed face-down in a mud puddle. "What was that you said?"

Joe wiped the sludge from his mouth. "Stretcher-bearer." He sat up and spat out some foul water. "Sergeant."

The sergeant swirled his boot in the muck and dug his foot into Joe's thigh. He bent over and hissed at Joe. "Silly bugger. *That's* what it stands for. Now get up and clean yourself up, you silly bugger." He wiped his boot on Joe's chest and marched off.

Joe was glad his mouth was out of commission, for he wanted to scream some things that would have landed him in big trouble. Now another wave of anger at Walter washed over him. Couldn't he at least have let Ma know where he was? Just to ease her mind a little? Couldn't he have replied to the letters Joe had written? All that education and not even a fucking note. And Fred? Joe went inside the tent and searched in his footlocker for a towel. He was still stinging that Fred, the one already in France, didn't seem interested in finding their brother. He had scoffed in reply to Joe's last begging letter.

It's not exactly a wee village over here, he'd written. *I can't just nip down to the pub and see if Walter's stopped by.*

Thursday June 24, 1915 Waverly Station was the biggest, grandest building he'd ever been in. Joe looked up and around, holding onto the back of his cap. Passengers bustled for trains; the giant metal clock with big black hands and numerals marched the crowds through the day. Fingers of light pointed down from the high-glassed roof; the power of the iron rafters made his breath catch. The pungent sooty smell painted the back of his throat, while the heat from the steam energized him. His anger towards Walter, his worry and fear for his safety, clashed with a grudging excitement as he found himself in Scotland's capital city: Edinburgh. He laughed to himself when he recalled his primary three teacher helping the class spell this important place. Edward Died In November Buried Under Robert George's House.

Did Walter leave from here? He would have been in seventh heaven. He'd talked to Joe about the novelists, poets, and patriots from Scotland's history whose bones rested here. On his way in, Joe had seen the castle, perched on its rock like a giant ornament on a Christmas pudding. One day, maybe on the way back with Walter, they'd go together and see the rooms where Mary Queen of Scots had slept, the jewels, the nooks and crannies where the plot to kill one of her husbands had been hatched.

He slurped at the tea in his mug, standing with a throng of men in the main forecourt. Only thirty miles from home, Joe already felt far away. Matrons barged among them handing out pies, sandwiches, buns, and hot drinks. He'd seen women like these at St. John of the Cross Church in Methilane, not that he went through its doors that often. These women were roughly the age of his mother, but big bosomed and well-fed, in frilly, high-necked blouses, and corseted under their linen summer skirts. They spoke in the clipped tones of the well off. A train wheezed and squealed behind him. He jumped and splashed hot tea down his trousers as he turned and watched the great engine slog to a halt and belch out a swoosh of steam. He pasted his free hand over one ear in a fruitless attempt to shut out the loud whistles and yelling.

"We've to line up." A lad Joe recognized from the training camp grabbed him by the arm and pointed. "Over there. Platform twelve."

"Ta very much," Joe said, and joined the other newly uniformed soldiers striding past the ticket office. He gasped when he came to the sign: London, King's X. This morning Edinburgh and now London.

Two officers, so young barely a whisker sprouted on their faces, inspected them as a corporal marched alongside, checking names on a paper clipped to a sheet of cardboard. A grey-haired man with three stripes on his uniform snarled at them to stand to attention. *Bugger me,* thought Joe. *Must be a sergeant's birthright to roar and sneer at recruits.* Pipers tuned and the sparse band whined out a halfway decent Scotland the Brave.

That *war* word sneaked up again. *You're off to war.* Was that why his thighs were shaking? Was that why his stomach weighed a ton? He rocked back slightly on his heels to steady himself. If only it were true what he'd hinted to Ma: that he could drag his brother back home. He still couldn't fathom how the wee bugger had managed to get away without the family having a clue. Joe wanted to clip him round the ear. How could Walter slink off without a word to their mother?

Ma was relentless with her postcards, three or four times a week. Have you heard anything? Is Fred looking for him? Have you found him? He saw her yesterday at the end of a four-day leave before setting off for France. She feigned many a smile, but often her face and eyes were puffy from crying. How could his brother lay this agony on their mother, already losing sleep from worrying about Fred and himself?

The kicker was his guilt. How come *he* hadn't suspected what Walter was thinking? Joe prided himself on having his younger brother's admiration and respect. It hurt to think he wasn't trusted enough to hold his younger brother's secrets. If he'd had the time and money he would've gone to France under his own steam. Never mind this signing-up nonsense.

Joe shouldered his kitbag and climbed aboard the southbound train, getting a bit of a push up from the lad behind.

"I'm right glad to be outta that hellhole training camp. Three months of my life wasted."

"Aye," Joe said, turning to the soldier behind him. They inched their way along the narrow corridor, kit bags banging against their knees.

"Personally," the lad said, "I've no use for learning to clean and fire a rifle or lunge a bayonet into a sandbag. As for marching up and down in lines for hours at a time, what is the point? And how come we can't be caught—not ever—with our hands in our pockets or with an unfastened button? Even when off duty?"

"What really sticks in my craw," Joe said, as he heaved his kit bag up onto the overhead rack, "is that we have to salute every officer in sight."

They sat down and Joe offered him a cigarette. "Joe Mathieson."

"Ta. Benny Smith." He pointed to the letters SB on Joe's sleeve. "I see you're a medic. Are you no' squeamish?"

"Why?"

"The blood. The guts. All that body stuff."

"It's interesting. Any roads, there's a chance I'll not have to put up with it for long. I'm on a rescue mission." He lowered his voice. "My wee brother ran off and joined up. He's only sixteen. Once I find him, I'll try and get back home."

The lad roared with laughter.

"Shh," Joe said. "I'm a miner. We're needed at home. I'll see if we can be excused. Maybe get us both out of it."

"Not once you're in. The brass have got bigger things to think about. When you're in, you're in. Till you're out. If you see what I mean. Here, have a nip from my bottle."

Joe's gut dragged and jangled again.

Once they were all seated on the train, eight to a compartment, out came more whisky and beer, cigarettes and laughs. Any spaces that might find the men lapsing into reflection were filled with jokes and singing. Joe had no great need for this false merriment, not if he could pull the miner ticket home. God knows he had to find a way to get Walter home. Besides, even though Fred had been proven wrong when he said it would be all over by last Christmas, it certainly couldn't last the year out. Surely to Christ, he'd be home with Walter in tow for Ellen's second birthday in November. He made himself see it: the family gathered at the table, the dark day already drawn in by four o'clock. Ma would boil up a cloutie dumpling. He'd let Walter light the two candles on the top. He'd watch his daughter's shining eyes caught in a small circle of light in the dim gas-lit room. He'd tell Ellen to make a secret wish. Joe smiled as he imagined her bonnie cheeks screwed up, making baby words inside her mouth like he would teach her. What would she wish for?

By one in the morning, halfway to London, the drink had worked its magic and the train puffed its way south with its cargo of sleeping Scots. More tea and fried egg sandwiches were doled out around seven when they arrived at Kings Cross. They scrambled, hung over and smelling of soot and sweat, onto buses that transported them across the city to yet another station to board the boat train for Dover.

Joe thought of each mile closer to France as checking off items on his "get Walter back safe" list. Boy, would he ever enjoy the tongue-lashing his brother would get from Ma. Now that they'd covered five of the six hundred miles to France, the job was close to done. As he stood at the stern of the boat, he could smell the English Channel, a dirty sweet odour so different from the clean North Sea tang. He clung to the railing with one hand and patted the head of a vomiting soldier with the other. Then something slipped. He could no longer find his place on the list. It was as if his soul hadn't been able to keep up with the speeding Dover-bound train and was lagging somewhere behind.

The boat bounced over the choppy waters between England and France, making it difficult for Joe to see where he was. One moment he could make out France ahead and the white cliffs of England behind. But the next moment all land was erased by a six-foot wall of water. Joe let go his sick pal and shielded his eyes to ward off the glare when the chalky Dover cliffs soared like a bird out of a wave. Fried egg and bacon rushed up his gullet and splashed between his feet. He leaned over the rail until the heaving stopped and wiped his mouth on his sleeve. Too soon he lifted his woozy head and stared at the coastline, smaller now than when he last looked. He squinted through watery eyes. The cliffs were no longer a smooth white mass, but riddled with black seams. He lifted his arm to hack at one, as he'd done the past three years down the mine. His knees buckled and he let himself fold into the gloom.

"You all right there?"

Joe tried to sit up, but two men held him down. Another wearing a corporal's double stripe on his arm stood over him, holding a water canteen. "Your war's not even started and you're having the heebie jeebies. What's your name?"

"Joe. I mean, Mathieson. Sir." A strong arm supported his back and he looked into a warm smile.

"Then you're one of *my* lucky buggers. Harry Gray. And I'm your corporal, not your sir. Here take a drink."

Tuesday, August 10, 1915 Joe plopped down on the grassy verge, wiped the sweat from his brow, and dropped his pack. "Right then, my lovelies, ten minutes and not a second more," Corporal Gray said. "Rifles piled. And that means the fucking lot of you." He lightly kicked Joe's shin. "You too, Mathieson. Maybe you got that SB armband, but don't be looking for any special concessions."

Gray's fourteen men went through the complicated routine, heaping their weapons into a tent-like structure, crisscrossed at the top like the poles on the wigwams Joe'd seen in his school geography book. Only after the corporal adjusted them to his satisfaction could Joe and the others relieve themselves of their kit. Sixty or more pounds—for many almost half their body weight—of waterproof sheets, clothes, grenades, a field-dressing set (in the unlikely case they suffered wounds so minor they could patch themselves up), close to two hundred rounds of ammunition, smoke helmets for gas attacks, a shovel and a pick, mess tin, water bottle, and rations. In combat, they'd been told, there'd be a further burden of coils of barbed wire and sandbags around their waists. One boy joked yesterday he felt like a tortoise, carrying the whole bloody house on his back. Joe would have a different burden on the battlefield. Not all this kit but a dead weight on a stretcher. He wished his thoughts hadn't turned to that expression.

Like a chorus line at a vaudeville show, the men dropped in unison to the soft ground. Most drew on their new ability to fall asleep immediately, propped up on their packs. They'd been following the same *one hour brisk walking/ten minutes rest* routine for the three days, since they'd left Étaples after a further month and a half's training. Already they were exhausted with the weight of their kit, their possessions a burden that strained and pained the muscles in their backs. At first, when they marched through a village, they'd sing and call out, "Bring out your daughters. We want the lassies." And sometimes, old women were there to wave them on, but quickly the men knew it was a joke that they'd come here to meet the "mamzelles". Any curiosity or sense of adventure they might have had as they disembarked in France soon hardened into fatigue and boredom. The exciting foreign land they first set foot on turned out to be a hard dusty slog as they marched, day after day, farther and farther away from home, not daring to think what might lie at their destination.

Joe didn't nap this break. He explored his breast pocket for a Woodbine, lit up, and took a deep drag. As he puffed on the cigarette, he glanced over at his armband, gave it a satisfied pat, and opened the great book they'd given him in Étaples for stretcher-bearer training. The book was half a foot thick, its grey linen cover embossed with gold letters: *Surgical Anatomy in the Field.* Joe licked his fingers and turned a page, thin as a moth's wing. He dragged a finger over a diagram of a human arm, mouthing the names of the muscles: *pronator radii teres, flexor carpi radialis, flexor carpi ulnaris.* He approached these strange long words with a relish and an enthusiasm that surprised him. Maybe if he'd come from a posh family—and with a father who hadn't withered away like Da—he could have been a doc, now that he knew he had a knack for learning this stuff. And all this reading was a first-class diversion for his brain besieged with worries about Walter. He scanned the pictures throughout his textbook, pictures that might turn many a stomach. Illustrations of bones sticking out through skin, holes in skulls, and detailed diagrams showing the correct lifting and carrying techniques for mangled bodies. But for him, the books and the days in his stretcher-bearing training awakened his brain. Sometimes he was so lost in the books he had to remind himself his real job was to find Walter.

"Those aren't a pretty sight. Think you're up for this?" The corporal sat down beside Joe, screwed up his mouth and pointed at a gruesome picture: a man missing most of his jaw. "No wonder we call you lot silly buggers."

"I'm a wee bit used to it from down in the mine. I got my first-aid certificate. Cleaned and bandaged legs and arms. Sometimes there was a rock fall." Joe laughed. "Or a pick-axe attack."

"What's that about? The attacks?" the corporal said.

"One time, one of the lads got found out he'd been having it away with the foreman's wife. Couple days later, foreman's pick-axe landed on the other one's shin. Accidentally on purpose, like. Right bloody mess that was." Joe drew on his cigarette and exhaled, squinting at Corporal Gray when the smoke stung his eyes. That story usually got a rise out of a listener, but the corporal was quiet.

"You study that book fast, Mathieson," he said. "Another two days we'll be at the front and you'll need what's in there." He took the book from Joe's hands. "But you'll not be much use if you're exhausted. We're ready to move on now, but I'm ordering you to get some shut-eye on the next break." Gray laid the book down by Joe's pack, rose, and went over to the mass of dozing bodies. "Up and at 'em, you lazy lot!" He prodded a few with his foot as he walked through the huddle.

The men helped each other put on their loads and set out again. The flat treeless landscape of northern France gave Joe's eyes no rest. The summer heat had dried out the roads. The ankle-twisting ruts threw dust over his thumping feet, squirrelling it up his nose and parching his mouth. Because it was punishable to sneak a swig from his water bottle outside of the break, Joe's thirsting throat silenced him and forced a retreat into his own thoughts.

He thrust his head forward and angled his sweat-soaked cap to the back of his head. Stared at the man ahead of him. *Fancy getting the chance to get away like Ma wanted for me and only getting to stare at the boil on Tom Harvey's neck.* The tendons in his own neck felt as if they would snap under the weight of his pack. Still, they'd stop soon for the night, and he let himself be satisfied with the delicious thought of lying packless on a pile of straw.

"Mathieson, get that cap on straight!"

"Aye, Corporal Gray. Right you are." Joe spent the walking time visualizing the diagrams in his medical book, amused at the memory tips someone had written in the margins. His favourite was *"Our old organ trembles terribly after fucking Anita's pale smooth hole."* He closed his eyes and tested himself on the twelve cranial nerves: olfactory, optic, ocular motor, trochlear, trigeminal, abducentes, facial, auditory, pharyngeal, spinal accessory, hypo-glossal. He wasn't sure he was saying them properly, but these unfamiliar words were so much easier to remember than the lessons in school. All that grammar nonsense wouldn't stay in his ears. But the words in this big book gave him an almost sensual pleasure as he rolled them around the inside of his mouth and imagined the nine cranial nerves lighting up his brain.

At day's end, as they closed in on the front, Joe got practise tending to feet oozing with blisters and hurting from calluses. He felt a new sense of importance when he urged the men to wait until their feet had cooled down so that their boots could be easily slipped off. He tried to scare them with stories of angry nodules caused by ill-fitting boots. He loved to describe in detail one he'd seen at the hospital at Étaples, an inch and half thick and a perfect impression of the patient's boot-lace.

Saturday, August 14, 1915 By the time the mid-morning break rolled around, they had less than five miles to go. Joe was picking up the last breadcrumbs from his lap when he heard the heavens rumble. Although the sky above was clear and the sun already throwing down shimmering heat, he searched his pack for his mackintosh to have it at the ready.

"Stop your dilly-dallying there, Mathieson." Gray stood over him. "No book reading today. Get as much kip as you can, for there'll not be much for you tonight." He was more tight-lipped than Joe had seen him the duration of the march.

"I'm not reading, Corporal. Just looking for my mac. Getting ready for the coming storm. It must be raining where we're going. I can hear the thunder."

Gray sat down beside him and patted Joe's arm. "Don't think so. My guess is sunshine all day. That's the guns at the front you're hearing. The music you'll be listening to until this nonsense is over."

4

Wednesday, August 18, 1915 Boom!

Joe dove for ground, grit spraying his gums.

Boom!

All week, and today was no exception, this was his wake-up call. 'The big guns', as the old hands called the artillery. Every five minutes, he jumped at the whizzing shells high above him. The whomping bursts forced him to keep low when moving along the endless troughs dug into the ground. He'd thought, when they reached the front, that at the very least they'd be living in tents as they did at the training camp. Miserable not having a proper roof over his head. But here they had no roof at all, and were living outdoors in these ditches. *Trenches* was the word they used.

Every explosion sent his heart racing and pumped out more sweat from his armpits. Each blast irritated him closer to thumping something—or someone. Bit by bit, he grasped he was in France, in *the war*, underground. He wasn't in the mine, nor anywhere near Methilane, but nevertheless living like a ferret or a mole. One of thousands and thousands of men squished together in these deep furrows. No longer was he in his homeland in the training camp or—to his surprise—lapping up the stretcher-bearer training at Étaples. There he had drunk in the strange words describing human anatomy, gave his full attention to the lectures on hygiene and disease prevention, hid his embarrassment when they paraded in men whose willies wept green pus. He paid heed to the demonstrations of how to put on French Letters—condoms they called them. Funny to think if he'd had one at hand when he started doing it with Kate, there'd be no wee Ellen.

He'd had no luck asking corporals and sergeants if they had heard of his brother and his whereabouts. All the activity here, the noise, and looking out for his safety was getting in the way of thinking about how he could locate Walter. At least he and the other stretcher-bearers didn't have to endure the stressful morning and evening '*stand-to*': in position in the trench closest to the enemy, on high alert either for an attack or an order to advance.

Clatter!

Another blast scythed the air above Joe. He dove with his hands over his head as another shell burst.

"Stand easy, there, Mathieson. They're just trying to scare us up a bit." Corporal Gray came towards him, the usual cigarette dangling from the left corner of his mouth. Joe and his section got to their feet and saluted. Joe turned his head from side to side. He still hadn't developed the knack of determining exactly where the noise was coming from. Was that from their side or from across the way?

"Too far off to do us any damage," Gray said. "I know, I know. When you first get here, you think it's going to take your hair off. You'll get better at reading them and which ones to duck for. Today the enemy's just showing off." He pulled a piece of paper from his breast pocket and waved it at Joe. "This says you get a few cushy days at the medical sections." He motioned away from the enemy lines with his head, squinting against the cigarette smoke curling up into his eyes. "Learning to tie bandages on, no doubt. Be ready here at eleven."

Thwack!

Another ear-splitting boom swiped at the air. "Down! Down!" Gray's shout was as sharp as a cuff round the ear. Joe dropped to his knees. "Christ, get down. This one's fallen short." Someone pushed hard into his back and flattened him against the wooden planks on the floor of the trench. His nose was driven into a space between the slats and pain seared through his head. A hand gripped him by the back of the collar and released his imprisoned face. He put his hands to his throat, trying to pry his shirt collar away from his Adam's apple. He huffed and spluttered as he rolled onto his back.

"Against the walls. Gangway. Gangway. Wounded coming through." Gray kicked him away from the centre of the trench and Joe, wheezing and puffing, watched him rush from side to side and push his men against the walls.

Joe pressed himself against the earth wall, hung onto the rung of one of the many fixed ladders the infantry used to climb out onto the battlefield. He hoisted himself to a sitting position. "Here," Gray said, flinging a rag at Joe. "Wipe your nose. You okay?"

Joe caught the cloth and put it to his nose. He felt his blood trickle over his fingers and warm his hand. "Aye," he said, cupping the rag over his nose. "Aye. I'm fine."

"Then hop to it Mr. Stretcher-bearer. To the dressing station. Run. Warn them. Wounded coming in."

Joe poured cold water from his canteen over the rag and held it to his nose. He could feel it swell and flame up. "Where?" he shouted back to Gray.

"Work your way back. To the rear. And get right back here when you're done. I'll need you for minor injuries."

Joe sprinted, struggling to get enough air through his swollen nose, willing his ears to sharpen and tune in to the direction of the enemy guns. The trench took a right turn, then a left, then another right. He mustn't get confused. His first assignment. He mustn't get it wrong, but this zigzagging and the pulsing in his nose rattled him. He stood for a moment. Quieted his breathing. He now clearly had a sense of the enemy guns behind him. He closed his eyes. He must do it right. He focused his attention on the skin on his face. Yes, he felt the breeze. The light wind cooled the left side of his nose. He ran on, navigating the turns, stopping every couple of minutes to check that the breeze was still hitting the left side of his face, until he came to a flatter area. Two gypsy caravans dabbed with red crosses and traces of painted flowers stood facing each other, as if puzzled by their new identities.

Joe ran up to a couple men in white coats playing cards. He heaved air in through his mouth as he turned and pointed behind him.

"Wounded coming. Back there."

"You one of them?" said the taller of the two.

"Bloody nose. That's all."

"Go inside and we'll get that fixed."

Joe's mind was set on his breathing, hard to do with his right nostril stuffed with gauze. He had just discovered a trick—in through his left nostril and out through his mouth—when he heard the wails, the moans, the screams, the whines, and the whimpers, all mashed into a chilling concerto. Next the smells. Rusty and sweet like the stink in his own nose as it bled. Dusty and dirty like soiled underwear. Warm and sweaty like meat left out in the sun. He couldn't quite take in the sight of it all. Two stretcher-bearers huddled over a soldier newly laid on the ground. One was pinning down his shoulders while the other cut away his trouser leg. The upper leg-bone ripped through the skin and stood almost to attention. Joe saw the marrow drip onto the stretcher. Two soldiers carried another whose split-open head lolled to the side, the eyes glazed and terrified. The column of carnage crept closer to Joe.

The medics, who only ten minutes ago had casually smoked, chatted, and played cards, who only five minutes ago had unhurriedly treated his nose, rushed out of a caravan. Now they were all business. Ordering, pointing, moving from stretcher to stretcher, marking foreheads. Joe was almost hypnotized. But the screams … he put his hands over his ears and scrambled to his feet. Should he help? He wasn't ready for this … this level of expertise. Gray had ordered him to *warn* the medics. He'd done that. Yes, he'd done that. He'd need to stick with the books if this was what they were expecting of him.

By nine all was quiet. Those who had been stretcher cases were patched up and had been told to rest. Joe sat in a dugout—this one a cubbyhole carved from the dirt of the trench wall—willing his breakfast porridge to settle in his stomach. Gray was pleased with him and that helped to dim the memories of the last couple of hours.

He'd lived and slept here the past four days, with the rest of the section, but didn't think it was so bad sleeping outside in the luxury of a summer heat unlike any he had ever known. Except for the flies and the waves of stink from the roiling bowels of the latrines. The explosion earlier brought back the jolting words slithering through his brain at the train station in Edinburgh. *Off to war. Off to war.* In a moment fourteen men's lives had evaporated or were changed forever. Had Walter any clue this was what he signed on for? Quite the little outdoorsman he was. Joe remembered Walter telling him how much he loved the summer camps of the Boys' Brigade. Ma often ordered Joe to help Walter carry his kit: a huge canvas tent, pots and pans, and a full duffel bag, to a rickety bus. A score of pimply boys piled in and set off to the Fife hills. Walter always came home freckled and full of stories. He'd spread out a frayed map on the kitchen table, place his compass set to north on the paper, and walk out their route with his fingers. Joe never paid much attention, but now he hoped Walter had learned some survival skills.

He reached into his breast pocket for a smoke and laughed at his own naivety. What was *he* doing? Trying to convince himself, because they were out in nature, that this was like camping? That his brother was protected from heavy artillery bombardment, enemy rifle-fire, and that horror he'd seen this morning, because he could read a map of the friendly Fife hills and woods? And had his own compass? And besides, this area was hardly nature. No more. Anytime Joe wandered through a trench lower than his own height and could see the surrounding terrain, there were no trees or much else left standing after the bombardments. Nature was blown to hell. The only thing he could call natural were the itchy lice that had taken up residence in the seams of his jacket and were driving him bonkers. Same as for Walter, no doubt, wherever the hell he was. Joe took in a deep drag on his cigarette, gulping down his fear. Two days ago, he contacted the military police but they were fucking useless and told him to bugger off when, politely, he *wondered if you'd mind putting on a search for my brother.*

His nose was still aching. He kicked at the wooden slatted floor—*duckboards* he now knew to call them—and looked up the length of the trench. How far did these things go? Gray said they stretched all the way to Switzerland and hundreds of thousands were stuffed into these two-foot wide, fifty-yard long connected ditches clawed out of the ground like long skinny burial plots. He wasn't sure if this was the corporal's way of comforting or scaring the shite out of them. Some of the men he'd talked to had been here on and off for over a year, and they weren't impressed with *their* outdoor experience. This trench was over six feet deep, capping even the tallest of the lads. Cut-down tree trunks laid horizontally two feet apart supported the walls. Some trenches he'd run through this morning, on his way to the dressing station, were less than three-feet high. He'd had to keep his head low so as not to be showered with shell fragments or catch a bullet.

On his way back from the treatment area, he'd made notes in his head of the little he'd seen of how the experienced medics dealt with the casualties. When he was safely back in the trench, he noticed an unpleasant tingling in his hands and shaking in his legs. He looked up these symptoms in the index of his fat medical book when he got back to the squad, but only came up with extreme conditions like brain cancer and Huntington's Chorea. He felt too well otherwise to believe something deadly was his problem. He wondered if he should ask some of the others if they felt this too, but when he discovered he could walk off the sensations, he kept his concern to himself.

By mid-morning the sun was already high. He took off his jacket, rolled up his shirtsleeves, and let the heat soothe his body. He settled with his notebook to study, a bit embarrassed to have the freedom from fatigues given the stretcher-bearers. He hoped none of the men down the lines of the trenches doing the necessary chores would give him a hard time.

He put his notebook in his jacket pocket when he saw Gray beckon him over. The corporal took the cigarette from his mouth and made an ear-splitting whistle with two fingers. A young lad, in full gear, appeared from down the trench. "Watch that rifle there in your hand, Carter. Shoulder it. You could kill somebody running with it like that." The soldier nodded seriously. Gray poked him. "Lighten up. You're supposed to laugh at my jokes. Okay, young Tommy boy, take this fella here with the fancy SB badge on his arm back through the lines to the dressing station. Hop to it then. Stand there long enough and the grass'll grow up and strangle your soggy wee piggy toes."

Joe followed Carter down the side trench, and took a right turn down another long trench, parallel to the front line. The mixture of long-dried sweat, unwashed feet, stale cigarette and cooking odours, laced with the smell of sewer and stagnant water, filled his mouth with bile. He quickly brought his free hand over his nose and spat onto the dirt floor. Men were seated along each side of its dirt walls. Some were sharpening bayonets. Others were examining some weird kind of gun.

Joe stopped. "What's that?"

"Machine gun. Amazing thing it is. Can fire hundreds of bullets at a time. Our secret weapon. We'll have one of these every hundred yards or so all down the front line. The enemy won't stand a chance."

Carter ducked up another side trench and Joe followed. Another right turn into the deepest trench so far, some three feet over Joe's head. Here some soldiers were stitching two blankets together. Joe nudged Carter. "What's the sewing for?"

"Burial bags."

Joe lifted a hand in greeting to those who met his eyes. He wanted to stop, examine the faces more closely to check for Walter, or ask if anyone knew him, but he had to maintain a half-run to keep up with the quick-footed Carter. The trench ran for about fifty yards before

Carter took a sharp left turn, pushed on for another fifty yards, and then turned again in the opposite direction. For about twenty minutes, they zigzagged, the trenches becoming deeper and deeper until the tops were more than five feet above Joe's head. He almost toppled Carter when the young lad stopped abruptly and knocked at one of a half dozen doors built into the wall.

"Geez," Joe said, "it's like walking along a street down here. Where's the shops so's I can buy some fags and beer?"

"Just wait till you get inside," Carter said. "There's plenty drink in there, although not for us, more's the pity."

The door opened and a tall captain ushered them in. Carter saluted and Joe followed suit, reciting his name, rank, and number.

"Thank you, soldier," the captain said to Carter. "You are free to go back to your post."

Joe took in the contents of the room as quickly as he could: a polished wooden desk with a telephone and typewriter on it, a large pile of buff-coloured folders, a bed—a real bed—in the corner, made up with white linen and a brown quilt. On another table, small and round, stood a framed photograph of a pretty dark-haired woman, in her mid-twenties, holding a boy about Ellen's age on her lap. A whisky bottle and two crystal glasses, one still wet with the golden liquid, filled up the space on the tabletop.

The captain tugged at the hem of his jacket and patted his holster. Its leather shone smooth at his side. "How's the nose?"

Joe put his hand to his face. "My nose?"

"This morning?"

"Bloody hell. It's you. Ta very much. Oh, beg your pardon. Sir." Joe pulled his heels together and saluted. The officer looked different, less doctorly, in his uniform. "Thank you. Sir. It's fine. Sir."

"Good, good. I'm the chief medical officer of the company. Captain Rogers. Royal Army Medical Corps. Stand at your ease while we wait for my lieutenant and some of the bearers we've recruited for this company. Where are you from, Private Mathieson?"

Joe caught him throwing a look over towards the drinks table.

"Fife, sir. Methilane. I was down the pits. And in charge of first aid on my shift." Joe drew his feet together and saluted.

"No need to keep doing that," Captain Rogers said, with a hint of a smile. "I'm from north of the Tay myself. Perthshire. Was getting accustomed to a nice quiet life as a GP when this all started. Not used to wounds. Just sniffles and sneezes, births and bunions. Not like this morning. But now here we are. Thrown together."

"It was horrible, sir. This morning." Joe couldn't believe he was confessing to an officer.

"I agree. It's dreadful. But from what Corporal Gray says, you're a quick study." He smiled at Joe. "I'm expecting good work from you then. Ah, there you are."

The door had opened and a short skinny man, younger than Joe, in an officer's uniform came in, followed by three privates.

"Ah, Atholl," Captain Rogers said. "Gellatley, Swan, Black, and Mathieson are yours." He smiled at Joe. "You four will report directly to Lieutenant Atholl as the leader of your platoon."

Joe could see barely a whisker on Atholl's face. *To you? Your face still as smooth as a bairn's bum?* "Now, my trusted lieutenant," Rogers said. "Let's get these men to the dressing station and get the ball rolling."

Joe stood to attention again. The other three privates followed suit, and they all saluted the officers' backs as they led the way deeper into the trench system.

He tapped the man in front of him on the shoulder and whispered, "What's all the zigzagging for? My head's fair spinning turning all these corners."

The man stopped and turned. He had the kind of dark, almost gypsy, looks Joe knew made lassies go weak at the knees. "Well your 'ead could be spinning right off your neck if it wasn't for your zigzagging."

Joe's face tightened at the English accent.

"Frank Gellatley," he said and shook Joe's hand. "Been 'ere five months and this is quiet, boring even, but when the enemy bombs start bursting, and the shrapnel really starts flying, there's less chance we'll get 'it 'cause of the way we've built it. And for a bomb that does land, less distance to destroy."

"Right. Takes brains to design a war. I'd never have thought on it."

"Keep up back there!" the lieutenant shouted, sorting his glasses, which had slid from the bridge of his nose. The group rounded another turn in the maze and came to a row of wooden doors built into both sides of the trench. The still growing grass above dipped over the top, like the fringes on poor haircuts. Lieutenant Atholl knocked on one of the doors and a medic with a haversack slung cross-ways over his chest opened it.

"What you got there, Corporal?" Atholl asked.

"A couple of cases of bad foot rot, sir."

"Perfect. Okay, everybody squeeze in and watch. Not very glamorous, but you'll be dealing with a lot of this. Carry on."

Joe and the others shuffled into the small room. The air rippled with a stink like the rubbish heap round the back of the butcher's shop in the High Street at home. The orderly waited until all four trainees gagged before handing them a cloth mask. *Thanks for nothing,* Joe thought. Horizontal wooden boards served as walls, with makeshift shelves built into them. Tidily arrayed were medicine bottles, enamel kidney dishes, and open canvas cases, like the ones his mother stored her knitting needles in, but with sewn-down slots for the surgical instruments. Bandages were stashed everywhere. Joe felt claustrophobic in this wooden hut.

At the top end of the room, two men minus their boots and socks lay on cots. The purplish-red skin of their feet reminded Joe of over-ripe plums about to split and burst. The orderly picked up a pair of forceps from a kidney dish lying on the breast of the first patient, and pointed at the man's left foot. "So what we have here is a nasty case of trench foot." Over the edges of the muslin mask, Joe stared at the mushy flesh.

"And over here," he said, pointing to the other man's feet, "we have two nasty cases of trench foot. Or should that be trench feet?"

"Very funny," the first said. "And pull my other one. The trenchless foot, that'll be. It's got bells on."

"We've brought these two chancers into the dressing station to dry their feet out and treat the blood blisters. I've got some good ointment here that'll reduce the spread of the fungus and the swelling. They may be left with a bit of nerve damage, but these two are lucky." He fixed his eyes on the first patient. "Or unlucky, if they've deliberately ignored orders about foot hygiene to get sent out of the trenches." He eyed both men, then turned to Joe and the others. "If that's the case, they'll be put on charge. So boys, other than not sleeping with your feet in a puddle, how can we prevent trench foot?"

Joe raised his hand. "Well-fitting boots, keeping feet dry and clean, keeping the toes moving, and greasing the feet aforehand if you think your feet are going to get wet."

"Good, good. Now sometimes we don't get them until the feet have turned black. What then?"

"Gangrene?" Joe said.

"That's right. And the cure for that?"

"Ask Mister Scotch that one too," Frank Gellatley said.

The corporal looked at Joe. "Amputation," Joe whispered. Captain Rogers stood off to the side, arms crossed, smiling at him.

"And right you are. Now each of you pick up a pair of forceps, take off as much skin as you can without bursting anything, do the ointment thing, and then get yourselves next door. There's a real black foot in there, gearing up for an amputation. Lieutenant Atholl will be doing it. He'll show you how to help."

The putrid reek of the rotted toes wriggled its way through Joe's mask and up his nostrils. He scrunched his nose, endured the ripple of pain from this morning's bashing, held his breath, and shut his eyes. But a shadow of the spongy strips of dangling flesh remained and would not disappear. He flinched and reached for the operating table. Hot breath tickled his ear.

"You can 'old my hand, if you like." Joe spun around. Frank Gellatley, the English stretcher-bearer, was grinning at him. Joe sneaked him a fingered V-sign. He wasn't about to give this cocky English bloke any chance make the usual Scottish jokes.

"Mathieson. Jolly well pay attention." Lieutenant Atholl's high voice pierced through the steady breathing of the patient on the table. "I'm deliberately doing this amputation slowly for your benefit. The least you can do is take advantage of the opportunity we're giving you."

Puny boys bossing to impress don't wash with me, Joe thought. He straightened himself. "Sir." "Get another blanket and elevate the leg more. Hold it in place."

Joe folded two grey blankets and placed them on top of the three already supporting the patient's leg, raising it as high as a can-can dancer's. *Higher,* he remembered from his books, *higher than the heart.*

"Tourniquet? Come on, soldier. This man can't wait all day."

Blah, blah, blah, Joe thought, as he tightened the rubber tubing already in place around the upper thigh.— the band that, tied tightly, would allow only minimal blood flow to the lower leg while the foot was being cut off.

"Tourniquet good, sir."

Atholl held up a gleaming blade. "Hold the foot, Gellatley."

Frank squeezed his way around Joe and cupped the heel in his hand. Joe tried holding his breath, rather than have the sickly sweet anaesthetic fumes touch his throat. Atholl sliced into the guideline he'd inked over the instep. Only a trickle of blood ran over the ankle and onto Frank's hand. The slit opened up like a gummy smile. Live healthy red flesh stared at Joe. He gulped and wished he hadn't, as the taste of blood and chloroform smeared his gullet. He gripped the leg tighter. The scalpel clinked into the metal dish. The bone saw hovered over the top of the foot. Joe was captivated now, as he watched the front of the foot fall away. Once it was separated, Atholl knocked the decayed tissue out of the way and it slid to the floor like a satisfied slug. Then he set to deftly creating a flap and stitched it down.

The rest of the day was spent going from one treatment room to another. Joe and the others watched wounds being irrigated and stitched. They learned to give morphine injections to soldiers coming out of the daze of anaesthesia. They accustomed their stomachs to the ripping tears of gunshot wounds and the slicing and dicing of shrapnel. The belly of a nineteen-year-old from Glasgow was a split-open hole the size of a dinner plate.

At four o'clock Captain Rogers poked his head in the door.

"That's it for now, boys. Tea will be brought to you outside. Twenty minutes, then I'll say some final words. There'll be one more exercise and you're done for the day. Any questions?"

Joe stayed behind as the other three pushed and shoved, stumbling to get into fresher air.

"Mathieson, you have a question?"

"Aye, sir. I was wondering if you'd seen my brother come through here. Walter Mathieson."

"Can't say I have. Name's not at all familiar. But then I usually don't have the pleasure of knowing any of the wounded personally."

"Thank you, sir."

Outside, Frank Gellatley was offering cigarettes around. "Joe I've met," he said, as he struck a match. "And I can tell where 'e's from. What about the rest of you?"

"Dan Swan," said one, leaning in his red-haired head to get a light from the match. "Newcastle."

"George Black," said the other, offering a firm handshake all round. "Haddington. Near Edinburgh."

"What about you? Where are you from?" Joe said.

Frank laughed. "Can't you tell, Jock? London. Centre of the universe."

Joe could feel a rise of annoyance. "A Sassenach. Well, likely you can't help being English."

Dan stepped forward and put his thickset frame between them. "C'mon Mathieson. We're on the same side here. That was pretty stomach-turning in there."

"Right," Frank said. "What were you asking the captain in there?"

Joe relaxed. "I signed up to find my wee brother. He ran off and enlisted, even though he's only sixteen. Any of you heard anything about a Walter Mathieson?"

"'E's probably not using 'is real name," Frank said. "That's what they do at the enlisting. Give a false name and stuff their boots with newspaper to look taller."

"Aye, well ... he's already tall, but I never thought of him lying about his name." Joe pulled out the photograph from his inside pocket. "Here's his picture and his real name is Mathieson. Of course. Same as me. Walter Mathieson."

Frank put his hand on Joe's shoulder. "We'll 'elp you out best we can."

"We'll keep a lookout," Dan Swan said. "Here comes the captain."

The men jumped to attention. A private following Rogers from one of the treatment rooms laid two stretchers on the ground and unrolled them. Joe took two quick final drags from his cigarette and threw the butt on the ground, grinding it with his boot.

"Right, men. Your first job is to pick up the wounded, so we'll practise that. A stretcher between two. One at the head and one at the foot. Good."

The private nodded to a mound of large stones and told them to pile twenty or so onto each stretcher.

"Pick the stretcher up, one at each end. Run about fifty yards and come back," the captain said.

Frank lifted the back end of one. Joe picked up the other. He tensed his thighs to take the weight. He breathed in, and on his out breath, hoisted the stretcher up to his shoulder. The short wooden handles were suddenly light as air in his hands and he crashed to the ground.

"Fucking bloody cockney." Joe was on the ground, rubbing the back of his neck. He picked up one of stones that had toppled to the ground and aimed it at Frank.

"Put that rock down, Mathieson," the captain said, standing between them.

"I was just having a joke on 'im, sir." Frank adjusted his lop-sided grin.

Rogers smiled. "I'll choose to believe you." He leaned over Joe. "Are you injured?"

Joe moved his neck from side to side. "Fine, sir."

Rogers helped him to his feet. "You've now learned rule number one. Both ends must be level with each other. You and your partner, or partners—sometimes four men are need to carry a loaded stretcher—must operate in unison. Tricky when one is much taller than the others. Practise to perfection. Uphill and downhill. For the next four weeks, all four of you will be based here. Twelve-hour shifts. Sorry, no days off as yet. Which one of you is Black?"

George stepped forward and saluted.

"You and Swan," he nodded at the ginger-haired Dan, "will be helping out here at the dressing station. Not just for the month but until further notice."

"Yes sir," they said, almost together.

"Mathieson and Gellatley, come the middle of September, I'll be sending you to the Casualty Clearing Station at Lillers to work the ambulance train to Boulogne."

Joe gulped down his annoyance. Wasn't there more chance of finding Walter among the thousands here? He didn't want to be confined to a train going back and forth. Nor did he relish the thought of coming across Walter on a hospital train. It gave him a jolt of anxiety thinking of seeing his brother's blood. The images he'd seen today, belly gashes, ankles dripping blood, and blanket burial bags flashed into his mind. And if they thought he'd be happy working with that swaggering Londoner they had another think coming. Joe couldn't stand all that south-of-the-border arrogance, especially from lads like him who couldn't get their tongues around *aitches* at the beginning of words.

"All of you report here at 0800 tomorrow." Atholl had taken over being in charge. "Pick up those stretchers and stones and find your own way back to your section. Try, just try, to use your imaginations.

Those stones are bleeding men with shattered bones. Certain death if you jar that bone and it cuts into muscle, or worse, an artery."

"Worse than certain death? What that might be?" Frank whispered to Joe. "Dead certain death?"

"I'd appreciate your attention, boy," Atholl said.

A slap across the chops, Joe thought. *That's what that twit needs.*

"Should take you about an hour," the lieutenant went on. "And you need to familiarize yourselves with the trenches. Get to know the markings that tell you just where you are. When things heat up, you could be ferrying the wounded from the battlefield all the way back to here. You'll need to know the way. Speed is always of the essence. The wounded must be transported back here within six hours, before infection sets in."

He tossed two cloth bundles, one to Dan and one to Frank. "Dirty laundry. Put it on the stretcher. Pretend it's your patient. And I'll be having someone count the stones and take the wounded soldier from you when you get back. So no taking the easy way. Go."

"Grab an end, 'ighlander," Frank said. "Are you 'urt? I didn't mean … I wasn't thinking the stones would roll. I really was just 'aving a joke on you. No 'ard feelings?"

Joe decided to put out his hand. "Pleased to partner you. No more Jock jokes then. And I'll quit the Sassenach teasing. One, two, three, lift. We'll beat those two lazy buggers back."

This way and that they ran, banging into the walls, hooting, and singing. Stones tumbled. Frank swore when one landed on his foot. When Dan and George caught up with them at one of the bends, Frank threw an armful of his stones onto the other stretcher and took off, only to stumble and roll the whole cargo into a puddle of mud. Dan and George came charging around the bend and crashed into the derailed front-runners.

"Shite," Joe said, sitting with legs outstretched in the mud hole. He shook the slime from his hands as Frank and the others started to laugh. "It's not funny," he said, splashing muddy water into George's face.

"No, it's not," George said. "It's hilarious."

"Aye, well," Joe said, picking George's bundle out of the mud. "You'll not be laughing when you get in trouble for drowning your patient in a mud hole."

"And look," George said. "A wee dog's just run off with yours."

"That's not a wee dog," Frank said. "It's a big rat."

"Jeez," George said. "How did it get that big?"

"Like the captain said, use your imagination. But 'ere's a wee 'int. It's got something to do with all the arms and legs lying about the place."

Wednesday, December 6, 1915 The metal monster hissed behind Joe. Another agonizingly slow train trip. Another expedition to the base hospital at Boulogne. He straddled an overturned crate on the platform at Lillers and savoured his last cigarette for a while. How many times now, in the past two and a half months, had he shuttled back and forth? On the plus side, when he worked with the injured men, he was too busy for much reflection or worry about Walter.

He no longer had the urge to flee from the appalling damage to the young men who travelled this route from the front to the safety of the coast hospital. How deft his fingers had become. How little he flinched, how clear his head, even as his days and nights reached a crescendo of chaos. The body's response to even the ugliest trauma grew less and less a mystery the more he peered inside ripped open abdomens, chests, and skulls. But there were gloomy times too, isolated in this secondment. Not even a snippet about his brother had come his way. Thank God Ma hadn't suffered the dreaded telegram. He hoped *No news is good news* held true. Yet he closed his eyes before looking at each new patient, silently praying it wasn't Walter. It became a ritual, a talisman, a way of magically keeping Walter unhurt. Wherever the bloody hell he was.

Joe shifted his buttocks on the hard wooden crate. These still moments before departure often sent waves of sadness through him. He ached for wee Ellen, longed to hold her soft squirmy body against his chest. A month had already passed since she turned two. Kate wrote about her toddling, the mischief she got into underfoot in the cluttered flat, her words ...

He wanted to *see* her, wanted to bask in the sound of her *"Dada."*

"Whatcha say?"

Joe toppled forward from Frank's back slap. "You'll make me swallow my fag one day. And then you'll be sorry."

Frank sat next to him and gave him another shove. "Before you make me depart this dear life, me old mate, give's a gasper."

Joe handed over his packet. Frank was medicine for his spirits. He talked up a storm with everyone, which was useful for getting the word out about Walter. Often Joe shook his head at Frank's schemes, the most recent buying a dozen pups from a farmer's wife and renting them out to the youngest officers, to kill the rats that roamed day and night in their living quarters. *Thank God for you, Frank*, he often told him, when the Londoner reeled off a long list of people he'd been in contact with: locals, girls in the brothels, officers, and men all agreeing to ask around for Joe's brother.

Frank lit a cigarette and pulled a package covered in brown paper from his haversack. "A treat," he said and winked.

Joe unwrapped it. Four brown eggs, each in newspaper. He was sure Frank had stolen them, like the dozens he'd already accepted, but he wasn't about to challenge him. He relished a fresh egg, scrambled, boiled, or fried. He nodded his thanks. "I'd better go. See you at the base hospital."

He crushed his cigarette end underfoot and walked the platform. The huge red crosses painted on the train's side fired up his brain. He was ready. He knew what to do. This new confidence, would it stay with him? If he found Walter today and somehow got home, would it vanish? If he were back working down the mine, would it just disappear in those black tunnels? Poof. Gone. He stepped aboard. Didn't matter, did it? He no longer had any hope they'd let him go home, Walter or no Walter.

He smirked as he watched a nurse fluttering down the platform, casting glances at a card in her hand. A snooty flapping female. He'd come across them before. Down from their upper-class perches to play a part in this game that didn't suit them. These girls thought the world, including the army and all the minions in it, would single them out as special. Aye, he'd seen them before. *They* got to go home. Yanked out by a *mama* who declared her daughter to be better employed serving tea and playing backgammon with convalescing officers in their converted ballroom. He could tell this one was rich by her uniform's cut and quality. No doubt Daddy had ordered it tailored to her whims.

Nevertheless he left the carriage to greet her. He straightened his jacket as she approached. “Help you ma’am?”

She put down her bag and looked at the card. “I’m assigned to carriage eight.”

Just his bloody luck they put her to work in his carriage. She startled as stretchers flurried past them and were loaded into the next carriage. He squeezed out a smile. “Follow me. We’ll set off any minute. We already have our … passengers.” He wondered if he should carry her bag but decided instead to give her a hand up into the carriage.

Inside, he secured a lantern to a roof strut. He purposely hummed as he concentrated on his task. He caught her staring at him and flashing glances at the stinking, bloody mass all about her. *Not what you expected, nursie lady*. She had a leather-gloved hand over her mouth. He saw her eyes dart from patient to patient.

“First time?” he said, looking over his shoulder and giving her a broad grin.

She gave a little cough. “Nurse Armitage,” she said.

“Well, Nurse Armitage, you take your time and get settled. I’m Mathieson,” he said. “I can hang up your coat for you and there’s a wee cupboard under the window where I can put your personal stuff. If you give me your gloves and the like. You’ll be needing your own light. I’ll get one.”

“Thanks,” she said. “Very gracious of you, but I can look after myself. Show me where the lights are kept.”

He pursed his lips, huffed at himself for his snap judgement of her, and nodded to a collection of lamps in the corner beyond the patients’ tiered bunks. “Don’t you lads be taking a loan of this bonny lassie,” he said to the wounded. “If you do, you’ll be feeling my fist. I’ll ram your teeth so fast down your throat, your stomach’ll think they’re rice pudding.” He chortled for them all. *Poor buggers,* he thought scanning the wagon, *most couldn’t lift a finger if their lives depended on it.*

He watched her pull at her collar and starched cuffs as she stepped to the spare lanterns. She was, as Ma would say, more handsome than pretty. Tall. Dark hair sneaking out from her nurse’s veil. Back long and straight. She fixed her light to the ceiling.

Wedding ring, he noticed. Where was the man?

“Have you classified them yet?” she asked. “What do we have for supplies?”

"I haven't had time to get them sorted." A snotty bitch or did she really know a bedpan, upside and downside? "These boys just got boarded afore you came on." She certainly wasn't a smiler. "As for stuff, we've got morphine, bandages, and not much more. Two cooks in a wagon ahead will keep us going with water. Cold and hot. They've a brazier. And they'll make tea and enough tattie soup to feed an army." He knelt down next to a moaning young man. "Joke," he said, turning to her. "The rice pudding thing. And the tattie soup. Just trying to cheer you up. You look a wee bit worried." At last a smile, showing white, dentist-paid-for teeth, unlike his own, yellowing with a space near the back upstairs where he'd already had a bad one pulled.

"Good joke," she said. "Funny." Another smile. "After all, the cook *is* feeding an army. Thank you. I do appreciate it. I'm not worried really. Not about the … this," she said, nodding around at the men. "I just want to do a good job and not let you down."

Joe swung around. "Me? Let *me* down?"

"They said you were good. You'd teach me a lot."

"Who's *they*?"

"Captain Rogers for one. My assignment was arranged through him." She blushed. "Friend of the family. He speaks very highly of you. Told me I'd be alongside Joe Mathieson, his prize pupil."

Joe's stomach flipped. He wanted to tug at her apron, and say, *"Really, really? What else did he say?"*

"I presume you're the Joe Mathieson Captain Rogers referred to."

"Aye, that's me all right." He wiped his right hand on his trousers and held it out to her.

"Adelaide," she said, her handshake firm and steady.

"Let's get the boys sorted out," he said. "Don't move them. A mark on the bare shoulder." He nodded at his haversack on the floor. "In there. Pencils."

She undid the buckles and dug out two pencils, the kind used for marking china.

"We do three grades," Joe said. "Three marks for the most urgent we think we can help now and will be off-loaded first at Boulogne. Can you make your own decisions about that? Two for the next most serious. One mark means they can wait until later and ... and some we'll not mark at all."

Adelaide nodded. Her lips moved as if mouthing the instructions to herself.

They cut away cloth, washed and dabbed, removed blood and pus-soaked bandages, and redid the dressings. They built a mound of violated clothing, injected generous morphine doses to float the men away from the worst of their agony. An hour or so passed. Quietly. Occasionally he heard her whisper, *I'm going to lift your shoulder … I'll be as gentle as I can … This might hurt a little … You'll feel a slight sting … I'll be quick.*

"Joe, I need you! Joe. Help!"

He stumbled up from sitting on the floor, re-bandaging a head wound.

"Up here! Can't see for the blood."

He scrambled over to her at the other end of the carriage until he was against her legs, braced and set astride, as she held onto a soldier hanging from the edge of an upper bunk. A scarlet fountain surged from his mouth.

"Joe, he's falling. I can't see."

Blood poured over her head and down her arms. Globs splashed on his face. Together they rolled the man back on the bunk and Joe pinned his shoulders down. He ripped the veil from her head and dabbed her eyes.

"Get up there. Roll him onto his side. Facing us. I've got him."

She stepped onto the lower bunk and heaved herself up, her skirts brushing against Joe's face, and she knelt behind the man. He pulled the patient's left arm towards him.

"Get your knees under his back and hold his head up"

"Got it," she said.

The soldier coughed and choked. More blood flooded from his mouth and saturated Joe's shirtfront. He tried to say something with panicked watery blue eyes fixed on Joe.

"Easy there, Jimmy. Easy there," Joe said. "There's a lovely lady at your back. Try and breathe. Real light. Gentle. Slow." Joe felt the warm liquid soak through his shirt to his chest.

Adelaide wiped the soldier's face with her bloodied veil until it became a sodden useless ball. She ripped off her apron and wiped away the deluge now coming from the man's nose. It was as if inside him a raging river had become undammed. The dry metallic smell spat at Joe's face.

A warmer more fetid stench whiffed from the bunk. "I'm going to be sick," Adelaide said. "He's fouled …" She scrambled to the bottom of the bunk, meeting a wet puddle of feces. Joe heard her vomit splatter over the floor. Quickly she was back, holding the young man's gurgling head.

"I'll manage," said Joe.

"I'm fine now." She leaned over the soldier's hair and looked into his face. "Good. The bleeding's stopped."

"Aye, you're right. It's stopped. For good."

Her hand flew to her head and tears moistened her eyes.

Joe rolled the boy onto his back. "Sit on the edge. Careful now."

She inched her bum beyond the man's head and sat with her legs dangling over the side.

"Be still," Joe said. "Let me." He put his hands on her waist and lifted her down. "Have you clean clothes?"

She nodded.

"Go change. I'll clean this up and see to him."

"I'll help first," she said. "Then I'll change."

The train stopped. Adelaide stretched her back and went to the window. "What's happening, Joe? Why have we stopped?"

"No problem. Happens all the time, so them that are able can take a … you know, relieve themselves. You rest a wee. I'll get us each a tea. Can't guarantee the best from Ceylon, but it'll be warm and wet."

He opened the door. Fresh, crisp night air rushed over him. He jumped down, breathed in the glow from the moon, stole some of its energy. "I'll get us some soup too!" he called back to her. "And a treat." He eased his way through a few wounded men from other carriages, who were able to leave the train unassisted. Joe nodded at them as they shook themselves out, turned their backs to the train to urinate, and smoke cigarettes.

It only took him fifteen minutes to return to carriage eight, carefully balancing a black pot filled with soup and two mugs of stewed dark tea. And the special treat. Frank's four eggs, fried and flipped to perfection. Adelaide was kneeling by an unmarked patient in a lower bunk. He nearly blurted out his arrival but was stopped by a spell of calmness she appeared to have woven around the soldier. The right half of his torso was like a shadow, a soft mush of blackened flesh. Resting on his chest was a cardboard identification tag attached with a necklace of string. Joe peered over her shoulder at the name. Robert Houston, Private S/21643, 1st/7th Battalion, Argyll and Sutherland Highlanders Regiment.

The heat of the tea and the soup burned through Joe's fingers. Holding his breath, he lowered the food and drinks to the floor and knelt behind Adelaide, mesmerized by her voice. Softly, she touched the soldier's hand and stroked his face. He moaned gently and gazed at her. The pleading in the dying man's eyes did not seem to frighten her. She leaned towards his ear and Joe heard her whisper. "Robert, I'm looking after you now. You'll be home for Christmas."

The soldier's eyes became fixed and he exhaled. Joe waited for the next in-breath. None followed. Adelaide drew the soldier's hand to her mouth and kissed it. She closed the dead man's eyes and stroked his face again. The train tooted and the engine sputtered into action. She stood and held onto the bunks.

"I've something for you," Joe said.

She jumped and put her hands by her sides. "Sorry."

"Don't be. If he could, he'd tell you he was grateful not to be alone."

The train lurched again and Joe put out a hand to steady her. "Sit." He handed her a mug of tea, a fork, and a plate with another covering it. He bent over her and whipped of the top plate like a magician producing a rabbit from a hat. "Oofs."

She stared at the two glistening fried eggs. "Oofs?"

"Frog talk," he said.

"Ah, oui Monsieur. Des Oeufs. Merci. Where…?"

"Ask no questions and you'll get no fibs," he said, scooping up his own eggs with a piece of bread.

After, Joe ladled soup into mess cans lined up on the straw-covered floor, picked one up, and offered it to a soldier. He propped him up against the flimsy sidewall, cradled the youngster's head, and steered it toward some nourishment. He insisted she finish her tea and have some soup before she resumed her work. Then while the train resumed its journey, they toiled in silence, side by side. Joe barely noticed time passing. He and Adelaide rarely needed to exchange words. They moved about the wounded and each other like well-practised partners. Sometime deep into the night, they agreed they were finished. The train stopped again and once more Joe opened the door and jumped down. This time he offered Adelaide his hand. She held onto him and plopped down onto the tracks. He led her to a harshly pruned chestnut tree some twenty yards away, where he sat on the hard ground and beckoned her to join him. She shook her head and stayed standing.

"Would you mind taking a little walk?" she said, wrapping her nurse's cloak around her.

"Aye. I'll walk with you," Joe said, getting up.

"No." She smiled. "Just you. I need to ... I need to go behind the tree."

"Behind the tree. What for?"

"It's not so easy for us women."

Joe slapped his hand over his mouth. "I'm so sorry. I didn't ..." He started running toward the train. "I'm gone. Shout me when it's safe."

Her face was impassive as she brushed a blood-stiffened curl from her cheek. "I counted forty-one men," she began. He had packed away his embarrassment and rejoined her under the huge tree. Its spiky winter branches cast quivery fingers in the moonlight. "Fourteen have died since we left Lillers," she continued. "We should see if there's an empty wagon and move them out of the others' sight. Eleven need urgent attention as soon as we reach Boulogne. Don't you think we should have them closest to the door, so they can be the first to be loaded onto the ambulances? I'm assuming there will be ambulances waiting at the station when we arrive."

"You can rest your legs while you're telling me. Sit down." He patted the ground and she lowered herself, wrapping her legs in her long skirts. "There'll be ambulances for us to hand them off to." He pulled a matchbox and a packet of cigarettes from his top pocket, tapped out two and lit them both. Offered her one.

She put her hands over her chest and leaned back against the mottled trunk. "Oh, no, I don't. I have never ..." She looked straight at Joe's tired eyes.

"You've earned a break," he said, still holding out the cigarette. "Relax a wee."

"Why not?" She smiled, took the cigarette, and gingerly placed it against her lips.

"Have you heard the latest?" she said, pulling a strand of tobacco from her mouth.

"The latest? What's happened now?" Joe said.

"I am just wondering how the war is going. Are we winning? What news are they telling you?"

Joe laughed. "They don't tell us anything. I haven't the foggiest idea who *they* even are. I just do what I'm told. That's my job."

"I'm sorry. I wasn't trying to make you uncomfortable. I hope you aren't insulted."

Joe shook his head.

"And thank you, Joe. You are splendid. Just like Captain Rogers said. You were so calm, so confident. You kept me going, you know."

And you're okay yourself, he wanted to say, but she wasn't a Methilane lassie, the kind he'd have no problem speaking his mind to. Good or bad.

The train squeezed out a warning blare. They both leaped up and dashed toward the open door. Soon Joe was far ahead. He turned and shouted back to her. "You did good!"

"What?" he heard her call. He was glad he'd said it but relieved she hadn't heard him. At the open door, he jumped up and waited to help her into the carriage.

Once inside, they squatted side by side, staring at the dead. Fourteen men laid out, silenced and still.

"Penny for them," Joe said.

"Pardon?"

"You look deep in thought."

"I'm angry to tell you the truth. From all my father's stories—he's a brigadier—I thought I knew about army service. I've built up a picture of his fighting endeavours as adventures conducted in a civilized, even polite, fashion. Now as I look at these poor men I feel duped. Surely, if the country knew these lined-up corpses were the truer picture, it would be stilled with sorrow."

Joe sat cross-legged on the floor and took a deep breath. "I'm with you, but what you're seeing is all I've ever seen since I joined up. I'd like to say you'll get used to it." He stood and stretched. "But that would be a lie."

"My father *must* have seen horror like this," she went on. She turned to Joe and smiled. "An army man. Runs in the family. I wonder if my mother knew how it was ... if he talked to her."

"I wouldn't think so," Joe said. "Are you okay? We need to carry on."

"Yes. Very good." Adelaide took a notebook and a pencil from her bag. "I'll record the name, rank, number, and regiment from every tag of the fourteen."

"Write down a wound description and the date of death, too," Joe said. The train trundled on, dirty smoke gusting by the carriage window, unaware of the suffering in its belly. Another two hours. Wheels clattered and screeched against the iron rails before its laboured puffing became a soothing hiss. Joe leaned a shoulder against the door and unlatched it. A dreary, pale light hovered over Boulogne and the waters that separated France from Britain.

"Where will they take the ones who died?" Adelaide asked.

"They have a mortuary at the hospital, and they'll be…taken care of. Don't worry."

"Then I'm going with them to the hospital," Adelaide said.

"I can do that. I've to report in anyways."

"Thanks Joe, but I'd like to see them safely delivered."

"Is that your orders?"

"Not exactly. I'm supposed to get some sleep and return on the train tomorrow. But I want to talk with the base surgeon."

"Well, I'll be off then." He hoisted his haversack higher on his shoulder and hesitated before adding, "You can be proud. Of yourself. You have a talent." He nodded his head as he walked off. "Yes, the lady shows promise."

He left her standing wide-eyed, smiling, on the platform, and searched among the other stretcher-bearers for Frank, knowing he'd have some antic up his sleeve to wash away the journey.

Joe sat slumped over a table in the hospital canteen, his head thumping. Nowhere in the hospital had he been able to get hold of a headache powder. A hand whacked him on the back, driving his nose farther into the stained wooden table.

"Morning me old mate."

"Get lost," Joe said. "This is all your fault, Frank Gellatley."

"I brought you a cuppa."

Joe raised his head and squinted against the light. "Thanks for nothing." He tossed back the tea in one go. "Remind me never to go gallivanting with you again. Or drink that wine blank. Gut rot it is." He held out his cup. "I'll have another. Toot sweet and the tooter the sweeter."

"Yes, master," Frank said and took off.

Joe leaned back in his seat. He would've loved to put his feet up on the table, but instead crossed his legs out in front.

"Hello, Joe. Did you sleep well?"

He drew his legs in and jumped to attention.

Adelaide laughed. "I thought for a moment you were about to salute me."

"I never know what to do with you nurses. Some act high and mighty—not you, mind—and treat the likes of me like dirt."

"I hope *I* didn't treat you badly. After working with you, I'd say you're one who demands respect. You're fearless when dealing with those wounded men, aren't you?"

Joe was pleased she'd noticed. His rising confidence was becoming a secret pride in him. "Wouldn't help the men if I showed them how I really felt about their predicaments. I'd say you were pretty calm for your first time."

"Thank you. I must admit I was very uneasy at first." She shook her head and smiled. "I'm glad my parents weren't here to see me yesterday when I . . . got flustered. They were so against me doing any real work. My husband is different. He believes we women have something to contribute. First I was relieved I could come over. Father pulled some strings to get me here after I got the letter about Robert. My husband."

Joe wanted to sit down again, rest his brain from the words flooding from her.

"Then I was terrified. I am trained, you know. Almost a year at Amersham. That's our local hospital. On the wards. And three months at Guys."

"Guys?"

"Big hospital. London. Of course I couldn't refuse after all the fuss I'd made with Mother and Father."

Joe pulled out a chair and steered her toward it. "Take a breath. Sit."

She arranged herself on the wooden cafeteria chair and smoothed her veil. "Sorry. Rambling a bit. All so new to me."

Joe nodded and sat opposite her.

"Other women, like my mother, are satisfied rolling bandages. Smug even. I want to do more. I told my mother I want to bind wounds not bandages. Really help. I insisted on getting nursing training. Didn't go over well with either parent. Especially when I sort of volunteered for France."

Joe never referred to Ma and Da as his *parents.* "I volunteered too," he said, "Came to look for my young brother who ran off and joined up."

"So he's missing too? Like my husband."

"I hope not." He swallowed hard. Knew what was hidden behind the message when the army informed a family their soldier was *missing*. "Aye, I suppose he is. For sure, I can't find him."

Frank came between them and set two teas on the table. "This is Frank," Joe said. "Another SB on the train. And he's trouble." He nodded at Adelaide. "Nurse Armitage."

She swivelled in her chair and offered Frank her hand. "Delighted. It's Adelaide." She stood. "Sorry. I'm intruding."

"No. Stay," Frank said, and pushed his own teacup toward her.

"Joe was telling me about his brother," Adelaide said to Frank. She pulled a brown envelope from her dress pocket. "I'm in the same situation, but it's my husband who's missing. The base surgeon here is an acquaintance of my father. He may be able to help me, although I haven't located him yet. Look," she said, pulling a sheet of paper from the envelope. She handed it to Joe and pointed at the print. "That's my husband."

Joe had heard of the dreaded telegrams and letters and was curious to see one first hand. He studied it, with Frank reading over his shoulder.

No. 3547 Army Form 104–83
(Please quote this number on all correspondence)

SIR OR MADAM

I regret to have to inform you that a report has been received from the War Office to the effect that (Rank) Captain
(Name) Robert James Armitage
(Regiment) **OXFORD AND BUCKS**
was posted as "missing" on the 26–10–15

The report that he is missing does not necessarily mean that he has been killed.

"How could Robert go missing?" Adelaide said. "He's been a soldier since he left Oxford and even then he was in the OTC. He's an officer, for goodness sake. In charge of men's lives. Experienced. Responsible."

Frank said, "Everyone knows missing likely means—"

Joe kicked him under the table and held up his hand. He glared at Frank. "Let's finish the letter." He put the document on the table and smoothed it out. All three bent their heads over the letter.

He may be a prisoner of war or have been temporarily separated from his regiment. Official reports that men are prisoners of war take some time to reach this country and, if he has been captured by the enemy, it is possible that unofficial news may reach you first. In this case I am to ask you to forward any letter received at once to this Office, and it will be returned to you as soon as possible.

Should any further information be available it will at once be communicated to you.

I am,

SIR OR MADAM,

Your obedient servant

J. J. R. St. Claire

Officer in charge of records.

Important – Any change of address should be notified to this Office immediately.

(4-7 -21) W 8000-8543- 674 Form B104-83/2

Joe folded the letter and handed it back to her, giving Frank a *keep-your-mouth-shut l*ook.

"That's why I want to speak to the base surgeon," Adelaide said. "You know what they say." She smiled. "Always check for missing persons at the hospital. Just in case. But I'm sure he's not hurt. Someone would know." She stood and looked at Joe and Frank. "They would, wouldn't they?"

"Aye. Of course," Joe said. "Like the letter says, sometimes it takes a while to get it all sorted out. Or he's a prisoner. And if he is, he's protected by rules. Rules that keep them fed and helped if they're injured. We learned that at training camp. In case we found any enemy wounded. We *have* to treat them well. Isn't that right, Frank?"

"Absolutely. Absolutely. That's the truth," Frank said. "Once you're at the nursing a bit longer, you'll get a better idea what a big job it is keeping track."

"You'll certainly be the first to know," Joe said. He didn't add that *missing* men rarely turned up with body parts intact and limbs attached. "You're best to rest like you were told." He put on his cap and tipped it to her. "All the best. Me and Frank have a train to catch."

Wednesday, May 24, 1916 A fresh day. Barely past five in the morning. Joe slurped away at his porridge, watching a rosy pink dawn creep over the fields. He had time to stay a while and soak up the already warm sunshine. He clambered down a verge, lay on his back on the bank of the River Ancre, and stretched his limbs as far they would go, annoying a pair of nesting larks. His gaze followed them as they soared singing into the clear sky. He splashed his face in the river, watching new light tap-dance on the water. He checked his watch. He had an hour. Bliss. He'd soothe his feet in the lapping river before the start of the slow day's march to the southwest. As usual, no one had told them where they were going or why.

But this May day was a longed for improvement, a heavenly change from months and months cramped inside the ambulance trains with their fug and inescapable cloying stench. He'd never voiced any dissatisfaction, knowing he was blessed compared to thousands upon thousands of men in the trenches day and night, squished against each other, threatened and miserable and too often scared or bored out of their minds. At times he too was bored, and frustrated to have to write the same letter over and over to his mother: *I'm fine. No sign of Walter. Have you heard from Fred? Does he have any word?* He was thankful, though, for the learning on the trains. He felt more sure of himself, liked having the skills and know-how to be doing something really useful. Helpful. Valuable. And he could lighten up, not having the likes of the four-eyed prat Atholl interfering over his shoulder, faulting him for this or that.

He wondered what had happened to the Adelaide woman. The nurse. He took one foot from the water and shook it. No way her poor bastard of a husband was ever going to turn up. It made him think that maybe he'd hear some news about his brother now he was back amongst the troops.

Yesterday the whole battalion, some twelve hundred men, had set off from the south side of Albert following the horse transport. After a ten-hour march, they'd spent an exhausted night in tents on the outskirts of Buire-sur-l'Ancre, a hamlet of thirty or so brick and stone cottages. Huddled together with their constant companion, the steepled church. At the outset, the day's march had the appearance of an outing. Sunshine filtered through the new green leaves and lifted their spirits. Potato and beet plants birthed their way through the soil in the fields. The earth smelled rich with the promise of good summer eating. The soldiers' blood danced through their veins. In the Picardie villages they crossed, the inhabitants too seemed intoxicated by summer's onset, acting merry and relaxed. They came from their houses, their shops, their workshops, often waving a towel or a handkerchief and trying to join in as the men sang *"It's a long way to Tipperary, farewell to Leicester Square. We didn't know how to tickle Mary, but we learned how over there!"*

Joe's troop had marched an hour or more away from Buire when they realized they had a new recruit: a French boy, around twelve years old, who refused to talk, not even to give his name. They tried shooing him away like a stray dog, but he wouldn't budge, and in the end they adopted him. During the ten-minute breaks, they rustled up some khaki clothing for him: long underpants with a button front, a mud-splattered jacket, and even a knitted cap. An officer gave credit to the adoption by making him a pay book and entering a day's wages into it, and naming him Buire—soon degenerated to Booey—after his village.

At Bretonvelincourt around noon yesterday, his company—over two hundred—were ordered to stand down. The officers allowed them to pile into the old *estaminet,* where the villagers had been recruited to help the owners pour beer, slice hams and cheeses—some yellow and hard, some with their white creaminess oozing—all slapped onto plates with freshly baked bread. After lunch they stood in parade formation, while the moustached mayor handed each man a medal inscribed Avec Notre Etèrnelle Gratitude Et Notre Indefectible Amitié Pour La Nation Britannique.

Frank turned to Joe and muttered, "Didn't know we'd done anything 'eroic already."

"Well not us personally, but I'm sure plenty buggers already have. Certainly the ones I saw on the hospital trains." Joe fingered his award. "I've no doubt we'll be getting our chance sooner than later."

"Will you take a look at this! I think we're the chosen few." Frank gave Joe such a nudge he was jolted out of his review of the previous day and nearly toppled from the weight of the pack on his back.

"Bloody hell," Joe said. "It's like a castle." He pushed his helmet back and wiped away the sweat of today's march. Eight hours and twelve villages. The length and heat of it made it hard work, but he'd lapped up the invigorating fresh air and the memory of his quiet moments of solitude down by the river that morning. Now here they were, at five in the afternoon, at the edge of some parkland within sight of yet another village. Lively green grass and trees stretched ahead for some two hundred yards to a very large house. He shielded his eyes from the lowering sun.

Frank elbowed him again. "It's one of them cha-toes."

"How do you know that?"

"Look at ze sign, idiot."

"And since when did you learn to read like a Frenchie?"

Frank rubbed the side on his nose with one finger. "I have ze scoop from our boy Booey. You know 'ow I can charm the locals."

"Well," Joe said, pulling Frank's nose, "I've been chatting up our wee French friend myself. I'm sure Booey wouldn't call it cha-toe, or any kind of toe. It's sha-toe. 'Sh' as in sh-shut up, and quit sh-showing off."

"Well, whatever it is, it's bloody magnificent," Frank said. "I can see myself as lord of the manor for the duration. Lay in a ton of food and drink, invite the mamzelles and carouse the war away. I bet there's even a swimming pool round the back."

They were called to assemble on the lawn, close to the big house, for a headcount. The horses were unhitched. The men could then line up at the cook wagons for water, chat amongst themselves, and laugh to shake off the dust and effort of the day. Joe sat cross-legged on the soft grass, took a long slug of water, and lifted his cheeks to the sun.

What a day! Most summers he'd spent only a couple of heavenly restful days down at the seashore, although never going more than the few miles to Burntisland and its fine-sand beach. Rarely had he felt any real heat soak into his bones. Not once as an adult had he put on a swimming costume. The North Sea air, even at the height of summer, was too hostile for that. While he'd been off work, injured from the pit accident in the summer of 1914, he'd regularly gone to the water at Methilane with Ellen. It was the closest he'd come to having a summer holiday. He often wondered what it would be like to have money and be able to go to the continent, as the rich folk called it, to laze on a foreign beach with his skin exposed, feeling the sun's rays bore into his core and be really, really warm. The French weather he'd experienced up until now, since signing up, wasn't much different from home. The winter had been all too familiar: constant damp, musty-smelling clothes, and chills that worried his stomach and made him feel sick. Now here he was, on the continent indeed, the sun so warm it heated the ground even as dinnertime grew near.

Nothing was asked of them, so Joe walked off, following the sun as it arced down toward the horizon. He found himself on a pathway of tiny stone chips that cut through a flourish of purple and pink irises in full bloom. Beyond them a wisteria-laden covered bridge arched over a pond. Dragonflies darted and flicked. He'd never seen such a wealth of flowers. His granddad, when he was alive, had grown a few daisies and dahlias in his allotment but nothing like the spectacle before him. He walked to the middle of the bridge and gulped water from his canteen. For a few moments he felt completely happy. Then he corrected it to: *If I knew Walter was safe, and if I was helping Ellen sniff these flowers, I'd want for nothing more.* He thought of Kate and their frequent quarrels and felt a tightening in his chest. Even on his two-week leave a month ago, they'd quickly fallen back into their bickering dance. He wondered what it would have been like if they'd been of a different class, freed from dismal, small living spaces and meagre means. What if they'd had been able to take a grand honeymoon, staying in a fine country house such as the one here, the Château de Gaudechat? Would it have been easier to get along with her if they'd had such luck? He turned and gazed at the tall windows. He imagined Kate in one of the rooms, dressing in a fine white muslin dress for dinner on the terrace, her nose sun-kissed and her freckles smiling from her cheeks. He'd write tonight and tell her all about this place. Or would it just make her mad at him for enjoying himself?

He rested his elbows on the bridge and reminded himself he was not here to worry about troubles with his wife but to look for Walter. The invisible grip on his lungs tightened. He took a deep breath and filled his brain with the dazzling colours around him.

He lit a cigarette and made his way back down the path and through the trees. In an unploughed field close to the big house, a football game was in full throttle. The men had stripped off their helmets, jackets, puttees, boots, and socks, rolled up their trousers and shirtsleeves, and were chasing one another like wee boys set free from school. Abandoned clothes marked out the goal posts. A whistle blew. The footballers grabbed their clothes and scampered towards the front steps of the house. Joe ran after them and could see the kindly Captain Rogers, who'd first trained him, walking out the French doors onto the terrace with his puny stuck-up sidekick, Lieutenant Atholl. Another captain, a couple of younger officers, a middle-aged man, and a woman in beautiful clothes followed. The whistle was still giving out sharp spurts. As Joe got closer, he recognized the sergeant who had barked orders on the two-day trek from Albert. He had the whistle stuck between his teeth, all the while continuing with tinny blasts as he waved his arms around, getting the men to gather on the lawn in front of the house. Once they were all lined up, he ran back inside the house and then reappeared with two chairs. He placed them on the terrace at the top of a flight of stone steps. First the woman, shading her head with a white parasol, sat down and then the man, adjusting his trousers.

"All right, you lousy lazy lot. Listen." The sergeant blew another blast on his whistle. The woman on the terrace shielded one ear with a white-gloved hand. "Listen up all of you." The officer who had been chatting to Rogers all the while stepped forward.

"Good evening, men. Or may I say ..." He turned briefly and nodded to the seated couple. "*Bon soir.* I am Captain Comstock and I have gathered you all here on this fine evening to outline your duties for the next while. You may all sit down. Rest your legs after the long day's march." He gave a little bow to the woman. "The Princesse d'Auchon-Gaudechat and her husband, Monsieur Mailly, are most generously lending us their magnificent summer home for an unspecified period of time. We will be using this fabulous residence as a hospital." He gave a little cough and pulled his jacket down at the back. "Yes, indeed. We will be converting the lower floor to a hospital. All personnel, including ambulance drivers and stretcher-bearers, will play a key role in the preparations. Report here to your sergeants at seven tomorrow morning. And now for some very happy news. The upper two floors will be your billets."

A cheer went up from the men. Comstock put up his hand for silence and the sergeant blew his whistle again.

"Quiet. Quiet. It will be a crush, but you can all rest easy being a safe fifteen miles from the front. This is an opportunity, thanks to the princess's graciousness, for quieter nights and better rest. Take advantage of it. As I speak, the transport is being moved behind the château. The kitchens, mess tents, and workshops are being set up. Your evening's task is to enjoy your meal back there, and avail yourselves of the baths being prepared in the largest of the dining tents. All clothing, including underwear, must be removed and sent for fumigation. You will be issued clean garments once you have bathed."

Another cheer.

The major waited a moment then resumed his speech. "A few rules. And they must be rigidly adhered to. First, you may go into the village. But only when you have a full day off. On duty days there is to be no sneaking off in the evening. I am imposing a curfew of eleven in the evening, but it goes without saying that drunkenness will not be tolerated. Any violation of these expectations will be treated with the utmost severity and punishment will be forthcoming. The full name of the village, by the way, is Gaudechat-en-Bruy and it's that direction." He pointed over the heads of the men, and a couple of hundred heads turned in unison. "I've heard you boys calling it *good chat.* I don't care what you call it among yourselves, but go-de-sha is what you ask for if you get lost. Learn how to say it.

"And now a final word. You will treat the locals with the utmost respect and consideration. Men, women, and children. And especially the young women. We are here to alleviate their suffering, not add to it. Now I bid you a pleasant evening." With that he walked back to the French doors, opened them, and gave a little bow as the princess and her husband walked through.

Frank came and sat beside Joe on the grass, took two cigarettes out of his packet, and gave one to his friend. He took a deep drag.

"Something's up. I'm sure they're not treating us this well out of the goodness of their 'earts."

"Suspicious lump, aren't you? But you're probably right." Joe could see Frank wanted to get into some kind of discussion, questioning their superiors' motives and plans, but he was loathe to come out of the good mood he'd been in all day. "I'm sure they're not about to tell us anymore than they already have."

"I think they're gearing up," Frank persisted. "There's only one reason I can think why they'd need an 'ospital made ready."

Joe stood and fixed a smile on his face. "C'mon you. Cheer up. Let's go. Bathe or dine first, your lordship?"

Joe itched to get more of what he now came to think of as his summer holiday, to get out and explore, to lie in the sun with nothing expected of him. But the first week at the Château de Gaudechat, his platoon worked from sun-up to sundown converting the main floor. Joe and his company took down paintings, wrapped them carefully with muslin, and placed them in crates with wood shavings for protection. They knocked down walls, re-plastered and painted the scarred seams. They rolled up carpets and carried gilded furniture up to the attics. They laid out mattresses and folded blankets on top of them.

They conscripted the waif Booey as their apprentice and had fun flinging English words and phrases at him, many of which miraculously stuck. The men removed stag heads and boar busts from panelled walls. One time Joe touched the spot, just behind the left antler, on an astonished-looking stuffed stag's head, where the rifle bullet had entered its skull.

"Hey, wee Booey," he said, dragging the young French boy over and pointing to the hole hidden under the hair.

Booey, his clothes as dishevelled as a runaway urchin's, raised an imaginary rifle to his armpit. "*Fusil,*" he said. "*Pffft, tu mourros.*"

"Tomorrow?" Joe shook his head.

"*Oui.*" Booey raised the gun to Joe's head and pretended to pull the trigger. "*Tu mourros.*"

"Ah," Joe said, suddenly understanding, "you're telling me I'm dead." He staggered and fell in a heap on the floor. He lay motionless for a few moments then leapt to his feet, grabbed the imaginary rifle, chased Booey over the parquet floors, and screeched, "Tomorrow! Tomorrow!"

Immediately after the mid-day meal, the bearers were given special physical training. They lifted heavy bales of straw while squatting to develop their thighs. Lifted them above their heads to develop their chest muscles and shoulders. Joe, already fit from his work down the mine, thought he was in heaven building up his body in the fresh air and sunshine. Every afternoon, Captain Rogers and Lieutenant Atholl took turns giving the medics a lecture on anatomy for two hours, and for another hour, practical first-aid instruction: applying tourniquets and dressings and attaching a trellis-like contraption to hold a fractured limb rigid while the patient was jostled on a moving stretcher. A *splint* Captain Rogers called it, said the new-fangled device increased the soldier's chance of survival from seventeen to eight-three percent. Joe wondered how they came up with those figures but was nonetheless impressed that there'd be less wandering bone fragments to puncture a major artery, especially in the leg.

On one of these afternoons, a youngster who had been chopping firewood in the woods for the kitchen cut a finger badly and was brought into the classroom. Joe watched fascinated while Atholl used catgut and a short, fine needle to stitch up the wound. After the instruction, they were given an hour to read up on the topic of that day, in preparation for a test the next day. Most, including Frank, would use the hour as an opportunity to hide in the woods for a snooze or simply laze together, smoke, and tell jokes. But for Joe, the world of his textbook was never dull. The section on sanitation was less than riveting, but the information about germs—the book called them microbes—and how they could get into the human body through what a person ate, drank, or touched was intriguing. And he liked the feel of words longer than he'd ever known. *Haemorrhage, tourniquet, innoculation.* He would get a biscuit and a cup of tea from the kitchen wagon and find a shady spot under a briar in one of the side gardens. Under this parasol of tiny pink roses, he'd devour every word he was assigned. It all made sense to him: the meanderings of arteries and veins, the way muscle was connected to bone ...

Friday, June 2, 1916 A sunbeam hit Joe squarely between the eyes. He pulled his pocket watch from under his pillow. Twenty past nine.

"Jesus Christ," he said. Then remembered it was Friday, his first day off. He lay back with his arms behind his head. It had finally come: the real beginning of his summer holiday. He pulled on his trousers and shirt, shoved his feet into his boots, and put his jacket under his arm. He set out for some breakfast and a think about how to spend this day.

"Morning mate," Frank said through slurps on his tea, as Joe pushed back the flap and ducked into the dining tent. "Another bloody day in 'eaven. I picked up a letter for you." He slid the envelope along the table then leaned back in his chair, and stretched out his arms. "So what's your pleasure this fine morning? Spot of 'unting, fishing? Or," he mimicked Comstock's private school English accent, "I say, what about a spot of frolicking with the ladies? How about that, dear chap?" Joe gave him a quick swipe across the back of the head.

Frank squealed as he fell off his chair. "Ouch. That 'urt, you bugger."

"Got to keep you honest," Joe said, helping him up, sitting him back down, and ruffling his hair. "But let's get out of here for the day. I'll just get myself some bacon and tea, read my letter, and then we're for the off." He cupped his hands around his mouth and shouted down the length of the tent. "Who's up for a tour?"

May 12, 1916

Dear Joe,

A while now since you finished up yer leeve here and I hope your still getting along fine back where you are. Ellens been greetin a lot since you left. She canna understand that you had to go again. Poor wee soul. Apart from that weer all fine here exsept Ellen had the runs for four days what a mess but she is all better now. Your ma had a letter from Fred the other day have you run into him. He seems fine no wunds or anything. Hes still rantin on aboot the officers and how he cood do a better job. You no him and what hes like. Nothin changes. I have big news! No Im not expecting cross my fingers. Im going to Gretna Green to work in the munitions there. Its exsiting coz I'll be almost in England. Canna believe Im getting a chance to travel and the money is amazin and your ma says she will look after Ellen for us. Hope thats ok with you. Theres five of us goin from here. My pal Jean and her two sisters is going and so is your mothers pal Flora and we can all go on the bus thegether. I can rite when I get there. Im goin a week Thursday Me and Ellen hope your gettin on ok.

Luv (I meen it) your wife
Kate

Why hadn't she mentioned any of this when he was home? In the three years he'd been married to her, he had yet to understand whether a move like this on her part was as much as a surprise to her or whether she was a sneaky planner. Like the way she'd wheedled him into marriage. They'd been at the pictures one Saturday afternoon and he was walking her home. Thoughts of getting away to Australia had taken firmer root in his head after tedious months down the mine.

"What a grand picture," she said. "Did you like it?" She eased out a sigh. "*From the Manger to the Cross.*" She slipped her hand into his pocket, rooted around his groin and snuggled into him. He shuddered without meaning to. Since she'd offered herself to him that first night—November 1912 it would have been, the same year Da died—they'd been doing it most times they got together, usually at her old Gran's house while the ancient woman's snores drowned out their moans of pleasure and grunts of gratification. But he was careful not to succumb to all his cravings for a female body.

"So romantic," she said. "Them having a wee baby, and so sad when they hung him on the cross. I was so sorry for his mother. What a heartbreak. Why'd they call cradles mangers back in them days?"

"It wasn't a cradle. It was a manger."

"Is it not the same thing then?"

"No."

"Aye, well you're the clever one." She continued stroking his cock through the fabric of his trousers.

His body's needs were at odds now with his resolve to take her straight home.

"What about tonight?" she said.

He pulled her hand away. "Can't."

"How not?"

He saw her lower lip tremble. "I told Walter I'd go and watch him."

"Do what?"

"His Boys' Brigade's putting on a parade. I tried to persuade Fred to go too. Wanted to show him that our wee brother is not just a bookworm, but Fred—Mr. Man of Action—refuses to believe it. I promised Walter I'd go. And…"

"What?" She took her hand from his stiff willie and covered her mouth.

He stopped and turned her toward him. "You know I like you, Kate, and I enjoy going out with you but not all the time. I think maybe we could take a wee break. You're young and good-looking. You should be seeing other lads. And I want to sort out a few things and that."

"Like what?" She gnawed on her pinkie.

"Ma wants me to leave the mine ... get away, maybe even New Zealand or Australia. I need to think on it."

She clutched his arm with both her hands and fixed her eyes on his. "We could come with you."

"Who's we?" Joe said.

Kate pulled away from him and leaned against a shop wall they had come to.

"What are you on about?" Joe said and went to her. She turned her back on him and he realized she was crying. He took her by the shoulders and turned her around. "What is it?"

She covered her face with her hands.

"Shush," he said and kissed the top of her head. He held her out at arm's length. "Whatever it is, it's not the end of the world."

She hurled herself against his chest and her groaning sobs beat against him. "For me it is if you go away. I was going to tell you tonight. I'm in the family way."

Joe felt his stomach take a dive, almost down to his knees.

He married her three months later, in the June of '13.

It was close to eleven before six of them finally set off for their day's outing from the château, not knowing where they were going. They kept the sun at their backs, warming their shoulders, now so light and pain-free without the weight of their usual packs. The pitted dirt road cut a straight swath through fields where potato and sugar beet plants were already a foot high. Several times they waved to men and women working in the fields, their backs bent as they hoed. In less than an hour, they came to a village, Tourbièrecourt, but as they were all feeling so alive in this sunshine that had gone on for nearly two weeks, it was easy to keep going. They stopped once at the entrance to a field, passed round cigarettes, sat cross-legged, and dealt a round of Gin Rummy and a few more of Nap, then they were off again. Sometimes one would break into a run and the others would chase him for a bit.

Around two, when the sun was just tipping past its highest salute, they arrived in Bercordie, more of a small town than the tiny villages they were used to. The imposing double columns of the abbey got only a glance when they spied a red sign across the street: Café, Bar, Tabac, Presse.

"My dream's come true," Frank said, and went through the already open door. Sprinkled throughout the bar were half a dozen men with ruddy country faces reading newspapers or chatting, sipping coffee or nursing a glass of wine.

"Bon jooer," Frank said, and led the line of men up to the bar. The barman, a small squat fellow with a large nose, wiped his hands on a white apron tied around his waist. None of them understood his words, but they knew what to do. Frank indicated the row of wine bottles behind the bar and held up six fingers. Joe pushed his way up to Frank and pulled his hand down.

"Don't be ridiculous, Frank. It's not even the middle of the afternoon."

Frank smiled, stood back, and put his hands on his hips. "Who put you in charge? Next you'll be wanting me to call you 'sir'?"

Joe laughed. "Just looking out for your health, my friend. Away and sit at a table at the back and take the others with you. I'll get this. We can square up later." He held up two fingers for the barman who uncorked a couple of bottles of white wine from the shelf. Joe took a swig. The liquid soured his tongue. He spat it out onto his sleeve and walked over to the table where the men were now seated, expectantly, their cigarettes already lit.

"I saw that," Frank said. "But anything cold and wet's fine by me. More for them what likes it. Give over the bottle."

"Suit yourself," Joe said. "I'm not in the mood for staying inside the day. I'll see you all back at the château."

Frank swilled back the wine bottle and coughed. "Draw my bath for me. There's a good man. 'Ot and ready for when I get back." The boys around the table hooted.

Joe turned to the group. "Look after this idiot friend of mine. He'll not even be drawing his own breath if he keeps knocking back that French piss. I'll see you all later."

Joe turned to his left from the bar and came to the town square, where the market was in full swing. Tethered pigs, cows, and pens of chickens lifted the noise level. He walked past stalls selling fish, most of which he didn't recognize except for the salmon and the whiting, and platters of whelks which made him gag. He loved the sampling of a three-inch long shrimp he was offered. Walking straight for about ten minutes, he came to a grassy spot where two rivers met. He strolled upstream of one for about fifty yards, sat down, took off his boots and socks, and dangled his feet in the clear water. A woman, about fifty, was riding a bike in his direction. He waved her over. She stopped, putting one sandalled foot onto the dirt path.

Joe pointed at the river. "Ancre?" he asked her, remembering the moment more than a week ago when he had lain so contented on the riverbank at Buire.

She looked almost horrified. *"Ancre? Mais, non. C'est plus formidable que l'Ancre. C'est la Somme."* And with a self-satisfied look, she rode off.

"Somme," Joe said quietly to himself, disturbed by the way the sound vibrated against his lips.

Joe headed back towards Gaudechat for something to drink and a meal. He'd treat himself to a proper French meal, an exotic change from the army diet. He passed the bar again, almost went in, but instead kept going, back over the bridge and the railway line, where two train wagons were stopped with their doors slid back. He heard voices and crept towards them. There, some hundred yards or so from the train tracks, scores of men dressed like him on his working days—trousers with no puttees and a light shirt—went in and out of a three-storied run-down building. Ladders leaned against the walls. Workmen patched holes in the walls with trowels and mortar, while others glazed the broken and missing windows. Six large tents, fatter and taller than the huge dining tents back at the château, had been erected on the grounds around the building. He got on his hands and knees and sneaked closer, snooping at men by the open wagons who were unloading iron beds, armfuls of blankets, and crates onto the shoulders of others who ferried them into the brick building.

Jesus Christ, they're getting another fucking hospital ready. A cold wave trickled over him, washing away last week's warmth. He rose and ran along the road, keeping Tourbièrecourt in his sight. He was sure he heard the rumble of guns to the northwest. Just his luck that his summer holiday was turning out to be no more than a dream. But his darkest thought was whether Walter would end up in one of these hospitals. Or worse.

He sank to the roadside, lit a cigarette, pulled the smoke hard into his lungs, and willed his hands to stop shaking. Maybe he should have stayed with Frank and the others, drinking himself into an ignorant illusion of happy summer days.

The tobacco calmed him enough to set off again, half-walking, half-running on the straight road, all the way to Tourbièrecourt without stopping, where he stumbled into a café, bought a beer, and signalled to the woman behind the bar he wanted something to eat. He took a seat by the window and put his head in his hands, trying to steady himself with deep breaths.

He felt a hand on his shoulder. A pleasant fragrance floated around him.

"Monsieur?"

He looked up into eyes the colour of cornflowers. He wiped his hands on his trouser legs.

"La carte?" the waitress said, handing him a menu.

"Oh, aye. Thanks." Joe opened it quickly, not wanting the bright blue eyes to wander away from his face. He pointed at the first thing. "This."

"C'est tous?" She pointed at something else then waited.

Joe pointed at the first item again.

She shrugged and walked away. Joe watched her slim straight back disappear behind the counter. She said something to an older thin woman who was pouring wine into a glass. Joe caught them both looking at him and gave them a little wave. He took a swig of his beer and felt the liquid soothe his insides. He kept his gaze on the waitress as she went from table to table. A bit younger than himself, maybe twenty or twenty-one. Joe watched the other customers cheer to her smile, become animated, and grin when she talked. She lifted a plate slapped on the bar counter, and with a flourish, set it down in front of him.

Joe caught her scent again and it made him dizzy.

"Okay, Monsieur?"

A plate of chips! *What an idiot,* he thought. *I finally get the chance to have some French cooking and I go and order a plate of chips.* She remained standing by the table. He wished he could take in her wonderful smell forever. He couldn't recall Kate smelling in a way that made him want to get close to her skin, and now some foreign waitress was casting a spell on him because of her sweet perfume. He was suddenly embarrassed. She raised her finger, leaned over, and whispered something in his ear. Joe had no clue what she was saying, except she was now pointing to where the kitchen must be, through a door behind the bar.

He decided his best smile was the right response. She disappeared through the hinged door and came back a couple of minutes later with a metal skewer pierced through lined-up pieces of beef. With the skewer, she shuffled his chips to the edge of his plate and laid down her gift. "*Brochette,*" she said pointing to the meat. "*Bon appétit.*"

The café's lunchtime hours were over. Customers left, waving goodbye, some kissing the woman behind the bar on both cheeks. The cook appeared from the kitchen, took off his white hat, and left. The barwoman wiped the counter, spoke a rapid succession of words to the waitress, handed her a broom, and left. A bell jangled as the door slammed shut. The waitress locked the door. Joe stood up and made to leave, but she came over and gently touched his shoulder, lowering him into his seat.

"*Mangez,*" she said, pointing at his plate, her smile showing small white teeth. He stared at her mouth and had a sudden desire to kiss it. He grabbed his fork and chased the last bit of meat into his mouth.

She brought him another beer, then set about clearing the tables, wiping them down, and sweeping the floor. Joe couldn't take his eyes from her. He watched the muscles in her slim back rise and fall under her thin dress as she hefted the broom. He noticed how her trim calves gave shape to her legs, as she leaned over to pick up some crusts that had fallen on the floor. He saw how the sash of her apron marked the slight swell of her slender hips. She caught him staring once but simply gave him a smile and indicated he should eat. He turned his face away, sure it was burning red. When he peeked again, she had gone and he felt a loss. He jumped up, grabbed the broom that leaned against the bar, and in between darting back and forth to his plate to shove a handful of chips into his mouth, he finished off the sweeping for her.

He could hear water sloshing around in the kitchen, went to the door, and cracked it open. Her arms were in soapy water up to the elbows; her face was flushed from the steam rising from the sink. She blew a stray strand of hair out of her face with her bottom lip stuck out. Joe thought he had never seen anything so beautiful. He watched her pile all the dishes onto the draining board, then dashed back to his table and carried his plate and glass into the kitchen.

"*Merci, Monsieur,*" she said, and blew at her hair again.

He lifted the damp curl and arranged it behind her ear. She stared straight at him with those blue, blue eyes. He turned her around, pressed the back of her waist against the sink, and kissed her. She brought her hands up against his shoulders, hesitated for a moment, and then pushed him away.

"I'm sorry," Joe said. His head buzzed with excitement and the shame of having acted on impulse. He put both hands over his heart. "I am so sorry."

She rinsed off the dishes, wiped the sink, then took off her apron. He couldn't see her face. Couldn't see whether she was upset ... maybe even crying. Christ, he'd nigh on attacked her. She squeezed past him and he followed. "I really am sorry," he breathed, as they reached the outside door. He went after her and stepped out into the street. She locked the door and offered her arm. He took it and they headed to Gaudechat together.

He pointed to himself. "Joe." She did the same with a soft smile. "Marguerite."

She chatted away at him and he nodded as if he understood. When she raised her voice in a question and looked up at him, he took a turn talking. He told her how much he was enjoying the relaxed atmosphere at the château, the warm days, the clean clothes, the baths, and the lectures.

She watched his face, and every so often said, "*Oui*," smiled or squeezed his arm.

"Where do you live?" he said, and drew the shape of a house in the air.

"*Gaudechat.*" She laughed as if to say, "Where else?" "*J'habite à la ferme.*" She made an oinking noise, rounding her shoulders and sticking out her nose.

A flush came over Joe, warming him as much as the golden sunshine. He stopped and took her hands in his. "You live on a farm. *Ferme?*"

She nodded and lightly patted him on the back.

"In Gaudechat?" Joe said. "Where in Gaudechat?" He drew a question mark on his arm.

"*Au château.*"

"Show me," he said, pointing ahead. He took her hand and dragged her along in a run. At the church on the outskirts of Gaudechat, they slowed down to a stroll. She led him off to the right, past the duck pond and through the large archway of the three-storey building that opened onto the Princess's parkland. This building, like the tenements at home, housed a slew of families but was prettier, with boxes of geraniums at the windows. She pointed up at one of the topmost windows, then at herself. She took his hand and, led him back through the arch, and pointed at the church.

"*Demain,*" she said. She feigned sleeping, then popped her eyes open. "*Demain.*" She held up eight fingers.

"Aye, aye. Tomorrow. At the church. Eight o'clock. I'll be there. Tomorrow."

She stepped away from him, a look on her face that made Joe think she was afraid. He tried to calm her and imitated her word. "*Demung*. Tomorrow."

She put her hand over her mouth and giggled. "Tomorrow," she mimicked.

He loved the way she said it, squeezing the *t* past her pursed lips.

She ran off back through the arch, turning once to give him a smile.

Lying on his bunk back at the château, Joe could not still the racing in his chest. Frank and the others had not yet come back. He had time and peace to reflect on the hours he'd spent with Marguerite since yesterday. He counted. One in the café and one to walk home. Two this evening. Four perfect hours. They'd walked arm-in-arm along the edges of fields with cuckoos calling, through an avenue of plane trees, and along a path where mice and rabbits rustled the hedges. He held her hand and smoked his cigarette while they sat hidden by a row of raspberry canes, the light slitting through bushes. Everything since yesterday was light. The curtain of murk that blighted his days in Methilane had lifted. Gone was the dourness, the monotony as if he was asleep. Of course it was likely his fault as much as Kate's he'd never had much fun. He wasn't ever in a light mood with his wife. Or in the mood *for* her. Even that first night, when he had her against a wall in the shadowy street behind The Brig, he wasn't *with* her. There was him, there was Kate, and he was doing something to her. Something that had nothing to do with love. That night he'd let himself fall down a tunnel of craving, rushing through the mess of her clothes to get his cock inside her. He remembered, at the end—likely no more than twenty seconds later—how he hadn't expected it to be over so quickly and wondered if she thought he'd done a good job of it. He'd been left with a release, not this delicious ghostly trace of Marguerite he was feeling now.

He stroked his arm. It felt the same, muscled and smooth, the hairs downy rather than rough. But inside his head something had sloughed off. He'd grown a new, more brilliant skin. At the edges of his mind though was the knowledge that hospitals were being prepared. The anxiety over Walter's safety loomed bigger than ever. He lit a cigarette and blew those dark shadows away.

It was still light at curfew. Joe was in a contented semi-sleep when Frank clattered into the bunk beside him and crashed his boots onto the floor. Soon his friend was snoring and snorting as loud as a train thundering through a tunnel. But not so loud as to drown out the sound of Marguerite's voice in Joe's head, until he finally dropped off to sleep with the lilt of her words rippling through him.

Sunday, June 4, 1916 "Someone shut those bloody things off." Frank sat on the edge of his bed, his head in his hands. The booming chimes of the church bells filled the large barracks room on the first floor of the château.

"I like them fine," Joe said, and hummed in time with the bells.

"I swear to God they're going to bash my brains in," Frank said.

"Serves you right going drinking, getting stocious two days in a row." Joe started to sing, matching the one, two, three pattern of the chiming bells.

Summertime, summertime, summertime.
The sun shines, the day is warm.
Our breakfast of greasy bacon waits
What more could young men want?

He stamped his feet and marched up and down the tiny space between their beds, shrilling his anthem into Frank's ear. He fired up his singing into a howl.

Summertime, summertime, summertime.

Frank threw a boot. Joe ducked as it went flying. "Shut the fuck up," Frank said. "'Ave some respect for the wounded, will you? What's got your dicker up and dancing around so early?"

Joe stopped belting out his song and turned his back on Frank.

"You dirty wee bugger, Joe Mathieson. Who is she?" Frank jumped over toward Joe and turned him around. "Okay, boy. Spill. Ah, now I get the song and dance about us drinking too much, you not wanting any part of it, and 'ere was me thinking you was a God-fearing man thinking only of 'ome. Well, are you and 'er ... you know?" Frank thrust his hips back and forth. "Just be sure you use a johnnie. Unless you want to leave a little froglet behind."

"No. We did not and you're the dirty bugger for thinking of that." But Joe was smiling. "Put your clothes on. Let's go eat and I'll tell you, but you have to promise to keep this to yourself."

Over breakfast Joe told Frank about walking Marguerite home, and taking her walking the previous evening. "I might need you to cover for me. I'm meeting her again tonight. If I'm not back afore the curfew at eleven, stuff something in my bed in case they come around."

"Christ, you're off your 'ead. You're a married man. Couldn't you just get a prossie?"

"Don't want to shag her." He laughed. "Well I do, but it's her I want to spend time with. Just talking like."

"Jesus, Joe. 'Ow can you talk with a French lass? You can't understand a word she says. Give it up. The regimental band's playing out back tonight. Near the woods. The locals are invited so there'll be dancing. Come instead. Don't be stirring up trouble for yourself."

Joe patted Frank on the shoulder. "Thanks for your loving concern, but I'll be fine."

Frank pushed away his hand. "We might only be 'ere a few weeks. Just keep it in your trousers. You'll not be any good to your brother if you get caught and they shoot you at dawn. Like a rabbit in a field."

"I haven't heard anyone getting shot for taking a girl for a walk. And you'll be covering for me." He punched Frank's bicep. "Right my friend?"

It was almost one in the morning when Joe dropped Marguerite back at her house. He could still feel where she had placed a little kiss on each of his cheeks. He could still hear her voice. *Tomorrow?* It would take him ten minutes to run up the long driveway through the farmed areas of the château grounds. Ten minutes and he'd have thought of a way to see her again tomorrow.

"Tomorrow," he said aloud. "It's already tomorrow." The tall, thin trees flanking the pathway were still and shadowed in the quarter moon. The stars were sharp and bright. Joe could feel their power sizzle into him.

"Halt! Put your hands up!"

Joe heard the bolt on a rifle being pulled back. "Don't shoot me," he wheezed at the prod in his chest. A light blazed in his face and he dropped one hand to shield his eyes. "I live here. I mean I'm billeted here."

"Keep your hands up. Name?"

"Mathieson, Joseph. I've been sent with the field ambulance to get this place ready. Lieutenant Atholl'll vouch for me. Or better still, Captain Rogers."

"Well, sonny, we'll not be disturbing those fine gentlemen from their beds to speak for the likes of you. Walk. And keep your hands up."

The figure came round behind Joe and poked the rifle butt into his lower back as he walked and stumbled into a room at the rear of the château being used as a guardhouse. A couple more military police were lounging with their feet up on a table. They both stood and rubbed their hands when Joe was ushered in. His heart thumped in his chest. He'd heard how brutal these men could be. One pulled his pay book from his pocket. The one he'd had the misfortune to meet on his walk home kept the rifle pressed into his left kidney. Maybe they'd scare him up a bit, play the bully. Best he go along with their game until they had enough of the sport and shooed him on his way.

"He's in possession of this Mathieson's pay book, but how do we know he's him?"

"Well, who else would I be?" Joe said. The rifle drove farther in, arching his back. A fist slammed into his belly from the front. He doubled over, but the rifle-toter jerked him upright by the scalp, and held his head still while the other punched him three times in the nose. Joe spluttered from his own blood trickling down his throat.

Then he felt the wooden rifle butt clobber him on the cheek and he was shoved into a dark space. He fell to the ground, banging his head on a tin bucket as he went down. The door slammed and he heard the soldiers outside laughing.

The light hurt Joe's eyes. Someone had hauled him to his feet, grabbed him by the collar, and frog marched him out of the guardroom. Only then did he realize it was morning and the grip belonged to Captain Rogers. "Walk with me, Mathieson. Talk. Where were you? What were you up to? You were warned there was a curfew. You're the last person I expected this from."

"I was just out walking. Lost track of the time."

"That's your story?"

"Yes, sir."

"And you're sticking to it?"

Joe was relieved to see a smile start at the corner of Captain Rogers' mouth.

"Yes, sir. I haven't done anyone any harm. Honest."

"No, I don't expect you have, Mathieson. But look ... here's the thing."

Joe stopped and looked at him.

Rogers gave him a prod. "Keep walking, man. I don't want those goons back there to think I'm not doing my job. Let me tell you. The worst is we could have you up for desertion and that is a capital offence. Get that? You could be shot. But I need you, Mathieson. You're one of the best. I like the way you learn and I need you to keep learning PDQ."

"That I will, sir."

"But I can't let this go unpunished. They'd have me up for that. So here's what we'll do. There will be no days off until the end of the month."

"But, sir—"

"But nothing, Mathieson. Most men in the village are away in the army and they are desperate for manpower on the farms. On what would have been your days off you will go to the farm and put in a ten-hour day there. Any task they ask of you, be it haying or swilling out the pigs, I expect you to cooperate. Do you understand me?"

"I do, sir." Joe couldn't believe his luck. They were sentencing him to spend time with Marguerite.

"Any questions?"

"Yes, sir. One. I was wondering if you had a French book I could learn from. You know, in case I run across some Frenchies, I mean French soldiers, in the hospital when it's ready. And maybe I'll need to talk to folk at the farm. To ask for my orders. And with no days off, sounds like I'm going have time on my hands."

"Wonderful idea, Mathieson. Not sure how much it will help, as the folks around here speak a very strong dialect. A bit like the English trying to understand Rabbie Burns. But your request is further proof of why you impress me. I'll make sure you get a book at my next lecture. Now, get yourself cleaned up and fed. I'm taking you over to your partner to dress that wound."

Frank was polishing his boots when Rogers led Joe into the dormitory. He jumped up and saluted, staring at Joe's face.

"Look after your friend here," Rogers said to Frank. "Get him cleaned up and I'm holding you responsible for his behaviour." He threw up his hands and left.

"What the fuck 'appened to you?" Frank said. "I told you, didn't I, that you were courting trouble? I knew you'd get that smile wiped off your face."

As they walked down the hall to the dispensary, Joe told Frank of his night.

"And Rogers bailed you out?" Frank said, pushing open the door, steering Joe through, and sitting him upon a table.

"Aye," Joe said. "Must have caught him on one of his 'no drinking' days. Och, I shouldn't run the man down."

Joe winced as Frank patted the dried blood from his face.

"You're serious?" Frank asked. "No trace of whisky on 'im? Lucky for you. But I feel sorry for 'im even if 'e is an officer. I 'ates to see good men go to drink."

"He's been more than decent to me."

"Likely easier for 'im 'ere too. Who wouldn't be in a good mood? You'll be seeing 'ow good it is 'ere now that you'll be staying out of trouble. Like an 'oliday camp 'ere. Good grub and sleep. I've almost forgotten there's a war on. Enjoy while we can. I think the real fun's gonna start soon."

"Are all your family such sunshines?" Joe said.

Frank reached into his satchel for a bottle. "If you're middle of nine nippers, you learn to keep everyone 'appy."

"Ouch," Joe said when Frank dabbed iodine from a pad onto the cuts on his cheek. "So you've not got over thinking something's brewing?"

"For sure something's coming. Gossip is there's 'ospitals all over the place. I just 'ope it's not too big. Mind you, I've 'eard the words *big push*. Rumours about 'undreds of thousands, a million even, being got together to shove the enemy back where they came from."

"Seems a bit far-fetched," Joe said. "They'd never send hundreds of thousands out at once. That's gotta be a story. There can't be that many in the armies of the whole fucking world."

Frank daubed more iodine on Joe's face. The pungent spiciness pricking his nostrils, reminded him they were preparing a *hospital*, laying out beds and equipping operating rooms. His knees trembled and he gasped at the sting of the iodine.

"Easy there. Easy. You should be like me, mate. Don't think or worry about what or what might not come," Frank said. "I'm enjoying myself 'ere. Each day's like a present. Sun, food, football, baths." He smoothed the sticking plaster over Joe's cheek. "There. You're done."

Joe told him about the assignment to the farm.

"I'm warning you again," Frank said. "I don't 'ave a good feeling about this. I can't see 'ow any good can come of it."

As each day grew warmer. Joe made a real effort to follow Frank's advice. Now almost halfway through June, the sunshine lifted the men's spirits higher and higher. They worked bare-chested. Their skin became golden. They grew fitter and filled out with the ample rations, most of which were sent up from the village farms: large round cheeses, hams, fresh bread, roasted chickens, large brown eggs with bright yellow yolks, fresh tomatoes, and vegetables like radishes and lettuce that Joe had never seen before. Everything, everything—except for Ellen not being around—was better than home. The weather, the food, the music in the evenings as he lolled on the grass, Frank's friendship, and the camaraderie with the other medics. The men were invited into homes, they flirted with the village girls. He was thankful for the chance to stretch his mind under the instruction of Captain Rogers, who was true to his word and showed up with a battered French textbook. Joe was proud of himself. One more thing would make it damn near perfect. Marguerite. Every day.

Monday, June 19, 1916 Joe was down at the farm by six. Guilt itched in him that he was looking forward to the day, a day he would not be among the troops and asking for Walter. He stuffed his responsibility into a tiny corner of his mind and whistled his way to the milking shed. By eight he had carried more than twenty buckets of milk to the barn, fed the pigs, and collected dozens of eggs. Told to take a break, he went outside and sat on a patch of grass, the sun already hot enough to evaporate the dew. He saw her. Coming toward him with a small white bowl in her hand. She knelt down beside him and handed it to him. The aroma of milky coffee flavoured the hot air. "I am sorry," he said. He pointed up towards the château. "They've taken away all my days off." He pulled the dictionary out of his pocket, licked his middle finger, and turned the pages. "Work, work ... *travail. Je suis desolé.*"

She clapped her hands. *"Bon. Très bon."*

How different her reaction from Kate's if he'd disappeared without explanation.

"Mon Dieu," she said, drawing back when she saw the scabs and yellowing bruises on his face. She flung her arms around his neck and kissed his forehead.

"It's okay. Doesn't hurt. But you can still kiss it better." He put his coffee bowl down and pulled her toward him.

"Marguerite!" A chunky woman waved at her.

"Shit," Joe said, letting her go.

"Sheet," she mimicked.

"Yes, *beaucoup* shit."

She got up and brushed grass from her blue skirt. "Tomorrow?"

"Oui. Tomorrow."

She ran off, looking behind her, and he blew her a kiss.

That evening after supper back in the field behind the château, Joe painstakingly wrote Marguerite a note, carefully forming as many French words as he could find in the language book the captain had lent him. He could write to her of his run-in with the MPs, and about his confinement. He told her that after every seven days he would be at the farm and drew a calendar for her, putting xxx for the days he would be there and see her. He told her he wanted to see her. He said nothing about his wife and child.

She seemed delighted the next day when, instead of supper at the château, he ran to the farm and gave her the letter. Although she often screwed up her face as she read it, hesitating and running the words around her mouth, she smiled when she recognized what he was trying to say. He loved watching her. It gave him the same kind of thrill as when he watched his daughter. Like Ellen, Marguerite would laugh or smile when she caught him looking at her. Not Kate's harsh *Whit you looking at?* He knew Marguerite was making all sorts of excuses to her folks so she could come and see him.

The days he worked at the farm, she brought him coffee—and a lingering kiss—first thing in the morning, and bread, cheese, and tomatoes at ten. She came to get him for the main meal at two and always contrived to sit next to him before she left for her job in that lucky café in Tourbièrecourt. Then he had another agonizing seven days of confinement to the château, restricted to the company of men. But he had his textbooks and his French book. He was making progress with both.

Monday, June 26, 1916 He was up with the sun. On the half-mile to the milking sheds, he stopped at one of the rose-laden bushes leading to the vegetable gardens. He got out his knife and hacked at the thorny branches, collecting a bouquet of pink roses for Marguerite. He wrapped them in his shirt. Sucking at the bloody scratches on his fingers, he ran the rest of the way and worked furiously to make the time pass quickly until she came with his coffee and kiss.

She came right at eight, running with a hand over the coffee bowl to catch the splashes. She had barely set it down when Joe was lifting her up and swinging her in the air, kissing her face. He gave her the flowers and she unwrapped a cloth bundle. Strawberries, red and ripe, tumbled onto the grass. *"Pour toi,"* she said, her cheeks flushing as she put her fingers into his mouth and deposited a fruit. They talked a while, but mostly they just sat close while Joe slurped his coffee. He flicked to the dictionary at the back of his French book and pointed to *swim.* She didn't look at the page, but smiled at him. He breast-stroked his arms. "Swim. Swim."

"Oui, oui," she said, nodding her head and pointing at the woods. *"Allons nager. Après le déjeuner."* She mimed eating and held up three fingers.

"After our meal. At three." Joe held up three fingers as well.

"Oui," she said. She picked up the bowl and left, blowing him a kiss.

Each second of the next five hours passed as slowly as a minute, but eventually his day's work was done, and he, the only male of shave-able age, was sitting beside Marguerite at the long wooden table in the farmhouse kitchen. He wanted to wolf down the meal, grab her, and run off. But he patiently paced himself through the soup, the salad, and the main course of simmered pork and carrots. He touched her ankle under the table with his foot. Then the torture of the cheeses, the dessert of chocolate cake and cream. Marguerite got up as the dishes were being cleared away and whispered something to her mother, who looked over in Joe's direction. He saw Marguerite put her hands together as if in prayer, begging her mother for something. The woman looked over at Joe again, then nodded to Marguerite. She gave a little jump and kissed her mother, then came over to Joe and led him out of the room.

She ran with him about halfway up the drive to the château, then veered to the left and pushed her way through the trees for another four hundred yards or so, until they came to a clearing with a large pool where a stream had been dammed. They flung themselves down on the bank, side by side, their arms and legs outstretched, soaking up the sun. Joe rolled over and planted a brief kiss on her nose, then jumped up and started pulling off his boots and his socks. He pulled his arms out of his braces, unbuttoned his trousers, took them off, and flung them behind him. He pulled his shirt over his head and jumped into the pool in his underwear. He sank about six feet to the bottom and felt the cool water ripple over his skin. He came up and spat out a mouthful of weeds. Marguerite was sitting on the bank, hugging her knees and laughing. He waved at her to get in beside him, but she shook her head. He scrambled up the bank and tried to hold her to his dripping body, but she pulled away, still laughing, and ran up the bank. He ran after her, carried her back over his shoulder, and sat her down where his clothes were lying in a heap. He put a finger on her lips. "Ssh."

"Ssh," she said, and started to giggle again.

He took her head in his hands and kissed her. He tried out his new words, *"Je t'aime, tu es belle,"* but wished he could speak properly to her, to tell her how he felt every part of him rising to his mouth to offer himself in one kiss. He wanted to tell her that he would make this kiss go on forever if he could.

With her mouth still fixed to his lips, she pulled her arms from around his neck and began unbuttoning her blouse. He took his lips from hers, gently pushed her hands away, and one by one, pried the little white buttons from their holes. He slipped her blouse off, lifted her to her feet, undid the hooks on her skirt, and let it fall onto the ground. He stepped out of his long underpants, unashamed of his hardness. He lifted her shift over her head and removed her knickers. He placed a soft kiss on her mouth, took her hand, and led her into the water. She gave a little gasp as the water hit between her legs and rose onto her tiptoes. But then they were in up to their necks and treading water. He felt her relax.

"Here," he said. "Come close."

He lifted her legs and wrapped them around his waist, put her arms around his neck, and rolled onto his back. With her lithe body floating on him, he spread his hands over her buttocks. He felt her soft belly press into his erection. He kicked his legs and swam back and forth across the pool with her fitted on top of him. When he tired, he let go of her, rolled her onto her back, and side-by-side they floated like starfish. He stared into the sun, all his thoughts on the lovely girl holding his hands, on this force that had flooded his being with life.

"Joe," said Marguerite. He loved her soft pronunciation of his name. *"Tu rèves?"* She flicked water onto his face, her eyes smiling at him all the while.

"I am. I *am* dreaming. Of you. And I hope I never wake up."

"Pardon?"

He pulled her on top of him again, working his legs to keep them both afloat.

"This is what I dream of."

He whispered in her ear. "*Je t'aime.* I love you my darling smiling Marguerite." With her still in his arms, he swam to the bank, led her up the slight incline, spread out his clothes as a blanket, and laid her down. He saw her blush and cover her breasts with one hand and the hair between her legs with the other. He took her hands away and lay on top of her, taking his weight on his elbows. A noise in the trees startled her and she bolted upright and clung to him. Joe grabbed his shirt and covered her back. They held onto one another, still and quiet. He could feel the thumping of her heart. He put his fingers to his lips and turned her head toward the thicket of trees behind them. A young deer, still sporting his baby spots, watched them, ears cocked and head to one side. Marguerite fell back laughing.

A swell of happiness filled Joe's body. He lay on his side and gazed at her loveliness. He wished he could suck it up and spray it over the dark memories he'd stored in his body since he'd left home. Smooth some of it onto Walter to keep him safe.

Her laughter changed to a shy smile and she laid an arm over her breasts. Joe kissed her lightly and removed her hand. He touched the warm skin around her nipple and felt her shudder. He paraded kisses around her breasts and in a line between them down to her navel.

She squirmed as he drew his tongue across her belly. "*Ça me fait rire,*" she giggled. She pushed him onto his back and tickled him with her nails down the sides of his ribs. He drew up his legs and wriggled away from her. She crawled after him, pressed herself into his back, and stroked the front of his thigh. Her hand brushed against his erection. He held her hand there and felt her warm breath on his ear as she whispered, "Joe, *je t'aime. Oui, je t'aime.*"

His brains flashed. Frank shaking his head. *No good.* Ma shoving Walter's photo at him. *Bring him back. Promise now.* Kate posting an envelope from Gretna. *A pound from my wages for Ellen's keep.* Ma wiping his daughter's face. *Bonny wee lassie. Your Daddy loves you.*

But he couldn't hold onto the messages. He turned and faced Marguerite, and settled his cock between her legs. She rolled onto her back and pulled him into her.

The sky was still bright when Joe crossed the front lawn of the château. A blackbird starting the overture to his evening song was the only sign that this day would end. Joe scrolled through the events of the last fifteen hours, a good day's work, the golden fields, the blue sky, the juicy green grass on the bank of the stream, the silver glints on the surface of the pool, the stomach-filling feast in the afternoon. The smell of Marguerite's skin, her wet hair, the faint coffee whiff on her breath. The way her soothing voice said *tomorrow* as they parted back at her house. And now, her love.

He walked round the back, hoping the kitchen wagons hadn't closed up for the day. He could do with a bite after all that swimming. He laughed out loud, but stopped suddenly when he saw the men streaming from the back of the château and assembling out front on the grass. He pushed his way through until he found Frank.

"What's happening? What are you all doing outside?"

"Don't know," Frank said. "Just doing what we're told, but I'm thinking the party's over."

"What?"

"You, me, everybody 'as to muster 'ere at nine-thirty." He pulled out his watch. "Five minutes."

"What for?"

"I told you I don't know," Frank hissed at Joe. "If you weren't off getting your end away or whatever you do at that farm, maybe you'd be able to tell me."

Joe turned his back on Frank and strode off.

"Wait up," Frank said, and grabbed Joe's shirt. "We need to stick together if there's a problem."

"Aye, you're right. Let's see what the fuss is all about."

Captain Comstock walked quickly up to the assembled men with the whistle-blowing sergeant who called them to attention.

"First thing tomorrow—the exact time yet to be determined—we will be moving out. Make yourselves ready for a march. It goes without saying of course that all days off and leave are cancelled. Ensure nothing personal is left behind and that whatever you were working on here is left in an orderly fashion."

The men turned to each other to ask the questions they wanted to ask Comstock. Where were they going? Why? What was happening? Were they coming back? Joe had to stop himself from rushing up and punching Comstock in the face.

The sergeant was blowing furiously on his whistle, but Comstock shushed him with a wave of his hand and gave the men a couple of minutes to settle.

"Make sure you all get a good night's rest."

"Sounds fucking scary to me," said Frank. "Told you something was up. I've a nose for it. All of us where I come from can sniff out the bad what's coming."

Joe's bowels gurgled and he worried they might empty right there and then. First Walter gone and still nowhere to be found. Now he was being wrenched away from Marguerite. Christ, was there no lasting luck at all?

Joe lay smoking on his bed, listening to the rum-fuelled snores of the others as his mind darted from images of Marguerite's small slim body and her fair curls to traces of her scent on his skin. He was instantly aroused. He was a little embarrassed but went ahead touching and stroking himself until he could get his mind back on the problems he now faced. Should he write now and tell Kate he didn't want to be with her anymore? Or should he wait until he had some more home leave and talk to her face to face? Would she quit her munitions job and take Ellen away from him after he told her? Could he get himself untangled from his marriage?

He slipped into a fantasy, into a wonderful life he could see as clear as the sparkling water of the pond where he'd been only twelve hours ago. He and Marguerite in a tucked away cottage on the Princess's estate at Gaudechat, shielded on one side by trees rippled through with sunlight. He works on the farm, a good strong help to her family. It's around two in the afternoon, and sleepy from their midday meal, he and Marguerite lie down. They talk kindly to each other. Make love. Now it is evening. The children are asleep; Ellen, two boys, and another girl. He and Marguerite, his beloved wife, in their big fluffy bed make love again and fall asleep, their bodies wound around each other. He helps the doctor in the village clinic clean and stitch minor wounds from farm accidents. Ellen, grown tall, wears the skinniness of a young girl. She's doing well here with fresh air and farm-grown food. Her French is fluent. She and Marguerite adore each other. Ma is here too, learning a bit of French and living out a long and care-free life.

The images faded and he rolled onto his side, put his hands to his head to shut out the hammering thoughts of reality. At home when Kate found out, what havoc would she wreak on this life he wanted? Then the thought struck him. If the troops were moving out, it was time. Just like Frank had said. A big battle. The hospitals were in place. The fighting could begin. Now he was fretting about his own fate. He might not even get home from this war. At least the trains were mostly safe from shells, shrapnel, bullets, fire, poison gas, and all the other paraphernalia that rained on this poor country. He kneaded his temple and tried to loosen the tension gripping his forehead. He shook his head. He couldn't take in that yesterday the world had showered a dazzling happiness on him and now … what darkness lurked, ready to pounce with an ugly blast?

By five in the morning everyone was up and dressed. The usual chitchat and happy morning humming was stilled, allowing the cockerel's crow to punctuate the hush in the dormitory. Even Frank was wordless as he pulled on his clothes. Joe folded his two blankets and laid them on the bare mattress ticking. He wondered how long it would be before he saw a bed again. At breakfast, the cooks collected plates, ignoring cries of *Hey, I'm not finished yet,* anxious to pack up their business. The horses were brought from the stables. Whinnying and lifting their front legs high, they revolted against being tethered to the wagons after nearly a month of grazing and sleeping in the sun.

Joe sat cross-legged on the grass by the kitchen wagons, still stunned by last night's marching orders. After the captain's announcement, rum rations had been handed out and the men talked at and above each other, venting their disapproval. Fired by fear and feeding on their own rumours, they ranted and raved about the rotten turn in their luck.

Joe mopped up the runny yolks of two fried eggs with a slice of bread and plotted how to escape notice for a few minutes, enough time to get out the dictionary and write a note to Marguerite, telling her he was not abandoning her. He needed her to know they were being moved out, to where he did not know, but he'd come back for her. But when he climbed the stairs to the dormitory to collect his kit, he had to fight his way up through the others on their way down to the muster.

"Morning, slacker."

Joe looked up at Frank coming down the stairs, his own kit bag and Joe's slung over his shoulders. He flung Joe's bag over the advancing soldiers' heads, hitting one when he overshot Joe's reaching hands. The soldier crumpled and the moving mass became a melee, arms and legs flailing in all directions. Frank, feet astride, cupped his hands to his mouth and offered up his best officer's voice.

"Sorry. So sorry, boys. Now get up and proceed in an orderly manner to the assembly point."

The soldiers, without thinking or looking for the voice, obeyed. Joe picked up his kit bag and walked down with Frank. He couldn't help laughing at his friend's mimicking talent. "You could've started a fight and got me into more trouble with the MPs. And believe me, that's no picnic. Fucking brutes."

"Indeed I could 'ave, Private Mathieson. But I didn't, eh? Now smarten up and fall in, there's a good boy."

Joe gave Frank a shove and they made their way to the forecourt, where the men were already mustered and the horses were straining against their harnesses. By eight they were passing through the château grounds with an honour guard of farm women waving handkerchiefs. Joe almost broke rank when he saw Marguerite standing alone, her hands crossed over her pale blue apron. He gripped the shoulder straps of his knapsack, digging his nails into his palms when their eyes met. As he passed her, he turned his head and mouthed, *"Je t'aime. I'll be back. I promise."*

Once they left the grounds of the château of the Princesse d'Auchon-Gaudechat, the men, four abreast, filled the width of the road that headed to Tourbièrecourt. This was not the leisurely cheerful march of a month ago. Today, the mood was sombre, the air silent save for boots crunching over gravel. Some twenty minutes into their march, they came upon a mass of soldiers waiting where the road intersected with a wide path. Joe's company, the men from Gaudechat, were halted and told they could sit. There was a brief conversation among the senior officers of the two groups before the other troops were marched off in front of Joe's company. As morning stretched into afternoon, this troop build-up was repeated and repeated until a moving column of khaki-coloured insects streaked and slashed the green countryside.

Shortly before two in the afternoon, the order was given to fall out for a lunch break. The men wearily dumped their heavy kit bags, assorted tools, and other equipment on the ground, groaning as they laid their tired and aching bodies on the roadside. Most had opted to clear aside the beet leaves and lay themselves on soft ground. A sweaty reek conquered the sweet smell of growing plants. Joe was settling himself when Rogers called him over.

"Mathieson, I'm going to give an order for all the men to remove their boots and socks and give their feet the air while they are eating and resting. I want you to organize a walk around with as many stretcher-bearers as you can rustle up. Check and treat any blisters. I don't want the headache we had with foot problems last winter."

"Yes, sir. But if it's okay to say, can it wait for ten minutes? It's better to let the feet cool afore taking the boots off. They might not get them back on again. And for those what have blisters, we should wash and dry the feet and put on a plaster bandage."

Rogers frowned at Joe and lifted one eyebrow.

"It was in a book you made me read back at the château."

"Of course. Glad you did your homework. I'll be giving the sergeant a list of orders for the men. I'll make sure your suggestion is part of that." He smiled and Joe saluted, making a note in his mind to keep his eyes peeled for his little brother Walter's familiar feet.

By six in the evening, so many troops had accumulated the landscape of rolling downs, fields, woods, and streams was no longer visible. It had become a moving mud-brown sea, pierced here and there with a spiking turnip plant, a tree in full leaf, or a high mound sprouting a beard of grass. All the men now knew they were walking a long and terrible road to something. To actually battle with the enemy was a prospect full of terror and inside each man was the awful anticipation of pain or death. Few words passed between Joe and Frank the last couple of hours, as they marched side by side, Joe barely enduring the added agony that each step took him from Marguerite, from the best happiness he'd ever known. Suddenly, the ground felt unsteady under him, he lost his footing and toppled over. His knee crushed a pale blue bird's egg. He grabbed Frank's arm and shook the gooey innards from his uniform.

"You okay?" Frank said.

"Fine," Joe snapped. "Sorry. I'm okay, mate. Just exhausted."

He pushed Frank's arm away and stepped up into the rhythm of the march. "And you? Are you worrying about what's up for us?"

"I think it's obvious what's going on 'ere. What's up for us."

"I suppose. When I came over from home, I didn't have much thoughts of battles and stuff like that. Just wanting to find my brother and get the hell home. Even among all these men we've seen today and the months I've been here, I haven't been able to get a glimpse of him or any news no matter who I ask. Not a peep." He pointed to the rolling sea of soldiers. "Fucking nightmare, this is."

"I'm thinking you've 'ad a couple of good days."

"I didn't reckon on meeting Marguerite."

"And getting your leg over. I've 'ad to put up with you mooning around like a fifteen year old getting 'is first taste of it. You should know better, being a married man and all."

Joe grabbed Frank's arm again, this time digging in his fingers. "I swear if you keep talking like that, I'll end up hitting you. I love her and I want you to respect that."

"Okay, okay. Keep your 'air on," Frank said, throwing off Joe's arm.

"I mean it, Frank. And I don't want to fall out with you over this." He lowered his head. "I've never been in love. Never had this with Kate. Never felt like this about any lassie. I know I've got myself into a right pickle, but I'll find a way to be with her. I just have to. She loves me too. She said so."

"Are you serious?"

"I am that. I've got a pile on my mind and now God knows what's going to happen to us in the next while. So when we get to wherever, leave me be. I'll be off to write to my ma."

"And," Frank said, "to your lady love, no doubt." He put his arm around Joe. "You 'ave my permission, my friend."

Joe read over the letter he'd written so far. He wanted to tell Ma about his work, give her something to be proud of, but had he taken out enough bits about blood and mangled bodies?

Thursday, June 29, 1916

Dear Ma,

I'm just thinking I'm glad no one's invented some amazing thing so's you could hear the racket that's going on over here, for it's earsplitting. Ever since I got here the artillery's been bombarding Jerry across the field, scaring them up. I was behind the lines last night visiting the gunners cos a couple of the lads there had their eardrums burst from being so near the noise and they was needing first aid. They're working round the clock, stripped to the waist, sweat running down their faces and chests. Word is we're having a real big battle, starting on Saturday. No weekends off for us! Was supposed to start yesterday, but it's been raining heavy. Ellen would be excited to hear the big thunder and see the black clouds of rain rolling across the fields. The rain's stopped now but the trenches are still full of water. I had to help a man yesterday who went through a sodden duckboard—remember I told you the trenches have wooden boards as a floor—and broke his leg. The Captain was right pleased with my work fitting him right to the stretcher so's his bone wouldn't jangle as we moved him back to the treatment post. I got to give him the ether to take away the pain. He'll be good as new in a month or two.

He didn't say that with his patched up leg and limp, the poor bugger would be shoved out again onto the battlefield.

I'm sitting up in the front line trench writing this. Came up to do a reccie and shoot the breeze with the Edinburgh platoons. The shells are flying over my head. They bang away for eighty minutes at a time. We've been clocking it. We bet cigarettes and try and guess where they'll land. So you see we're not worried and are having some fun with it all. I'm not very good at the game and am running out of fags! Send more if you can. And toffee. It's hard to think, just like with Guy Fawkes fireworks, but I'm trying to take a quiet moment for myself to write to you.

"For Chrissakes, get down!"

Joe crouched low, expecting a shell to have fallen short of its mark, but when he looked up a sergeant was pounding a young soldier he had pinned down. The soldier was spluttering brown mud from his mouth. "For Chrissakes!" yelled the sergeant. "If I have to sit on you to make you get down, I will, and more. What the bloody hell was you doing that for?"

The soldier coughed and wiped his nose on his sleeve. "I was just trying to see what a war looks like."

"Don't mind that. It'll all be coming to you soon enough and sooner than is good for you if you don't keep your head down."

"But I can't see anything from down here." The sergeant wrenched the man to his feet and pushed him up against the trench wall. "Those foreign boys over there can see you and snipe at you from seven hundred yards." He wiped mud from the lad's jacket and dragged him away. He turned to Joe and shook his head. "Youngsters. Need some sense knocked into them."

"Aye, they do that," Joe said. He watched them disappear round the zigzag bend and let his mind wander to his own wee one. He picked up the letter and started writing again.

I can't believe I was home on leave a few months back and we were taking Ellen up to the park. It was raining then, too. Remember? I had a good rest this past month but like they say all good things come to an end. Too bad it's not the same for bad things. I wish they'd sent me back to work on the ambulance train rather than here. But here at the front I'll be more able to search the trenches for Walter. So far no sign of him. Anyway I'll keep looking. Here's the good news. Word is from my medical pals nobody's seen him hurt. It's getting dark now so I'll sign off as I have to get back to our own trench, way back from here, far from any firing line so you can be sure I'll be safe this night.

Tell Ellen to be a good girl for you until I get more leave and see you all again.

Your loving son

Joe

He was nearly an hour getting back to his own trench, an hour he'd spent scanning what felt like a thousand young faces for Walter. Faces like the peeping soldier, faces of boys not old enough to feel the pull of mortality. Joe chuckled, supposing that at twenty-four he too was considered one of the youngsters. It had been a while since he'd felt young and green. When he'd gone home on leave back in April, Kate had whined that he had become as dour as an old man, was cold, and no fun. She'd huffed and withheld her attentions. His mother had fussed over him like she had when he was a child, but she too commented he looked older.

Certainly he knew more, lots more, and the suffering he'd seen on the ambulance trains he'd worked for nearly eight months had thrust him into some very grown-up responsibility. It shocked him then when he'd got a good look at himself, undressed, in the mirror down at the public baths. He liked that he was leaner and tighter and his shoulder muscles had ballooned. But he was disturbed at how pinched his face looked. He had peered closely in the mirror trying to see behind his eyes. Was it just tiredness that made him look so drawn? Thank God for the month at the château that had returned a youthful lift and smile to his face.

Evening stand-to was in full swing, the unlucky buggers in the front-line on high alert watching for signs of an attack. Joe had the luxury of sitting down in a support trench some three hundred yards back. He gobbled up his evening rations from his canteen: the fatty lumpy bully beef, a chunk of dry bread, and a dollop of raspberry jam. Sitting against the wall, he couldn't stretch out his legs since men were running back and forth carrying food, weapons, and ammunition to the front-line trenches. All the while the big guns boomed from behind and occasionally a cheer would go up if screams from across No Man's Land proclaimed a successful shell explosion.

After his meal, Joe licked the end of his pencil.

Dear Kate,

We've been sent up to the front. This is only our second full day and the mail service is not organized yet so I have no idea when I'll get a chance to post this letter, but I need to tell you something important.

His mouth dried up as if he were already being asked to speak the terrible announcement he'd one day have for his wife. His hand started shaking. His thumb seized up and stuck out a right angle from his clenched fist. He banged it against the ground until the spasm passed. He erased the greeting and his wife's name.

My darling Marguerite

We've been sent up to the front. This is only our second full day and the mail service is not organized yet so I have no idea when I'll get a chance to post this letter but I need to tell you something important. I love you and have not deserted you. I never would. I'm told we're near a village called Teepval (I don't know how to write it in French). Maybe that's a secret. If it is, no doubt the censor has already crossed this out.

I will be back. I don't know when, but I'm coming back for you. Keep smiling for me and I will keep myself safe for you.

Your loving (forever and ever)

Joe

P.S. I hope you can get someone to read this for you in French cos what I've said is very important.

Wake-up call the next morning was at five. The rain had stopped and already warmth massaged Joe's shoulders. Steam rose as the sun's heat sucked the moisture from the sodden earth. The breakfast wagon did its rounds, and as Joe was slurping up the last of his bland porridge, the bombardment started again. Eighty minutes of deafening noise, fifteen of anxious silence. Joe went into the dressing station and cut two small pieces from a rolled bandage and stuffed them in his ears. On and on the shells shrieked as they roared through the air. Atholl and the other lieutenants barked at the men constantly. Check the bandage supply. Check the morphine syringes. Arrange the forceps, the scissors, the lances. Scrub the cots. Count the tourniquets. Wash the pans. Run to the first three lines. Remind the lance corporals that the men's haversacks should be filled with their personal first aid supplies: iodine, two bandages, and one field dressing. Joe ran miles, up and down the trenches, round and round the bends, crashing into troops moving up to the front line from the reserve trenches farther back, the support trenches behind them, and from even farther back, the villages where thousands more had been billeted. He pushed his way through swarms of men who were trying on the newly issued tin helmets, cleaning rifles, and sharpening bayonets. For the umpteenth time that day, Joe tapped the letters in his breast pocket. The post boy still had not come.

The early evening was a beauty. Soft warmth hung in the air and Joe thought he could hear a blackbird singing in the lull of the bombardment. Around seven, when he was sitting outside on a dry patch of grass at Dressing Station Row—as he called the strip of treatment rooms—he was summoned to treat two gunshot wounds: a shaking nineteen year-old with a mangled, mushy knee and an older man, maybe forty, whose left thumb was hanging by a sliver of tendon. Both were howling. Joe and Frank patched up both as best they could, while two military policemen screamed at them. *Sissies. Slugs. Yellow-bellied fuckers.* As soon as Joe had pinned the last bandage and written up a wound tag for Atholl, who would be responsible for further treatment, the two bawling men were marched off with rifles pressed into their backs.

"What's that about? Where's the pity?" Joe said.

Frank shrugged as he collected sodden dressings. "Did it to themselves."

Joe's stared at the backs of the two being pushed out the door by the MPs. "What'll happen to them?"

"After they're fixed up, they'll be taken back beyond the trenches, given a quick trial, and maybe shot."

"Then why the bloody hell did they bring them to us?'

"You're asking me to make sense of any of this?" Frank said. "Give your rags over 'ere and I'll take the lot to the incinerator."

"Get your kits together, you two." Atholl had come into the room and was waving his baton like a fairy wand over Joe and Frank. "Find those other two bearers I trained with you."

"Swan and Black, sir," Joe said.

"Well, get them and yourselves up front. The night raids have been stepped up and you four are to carry a stretcher for retrieval. Get a move on."

Joe's stomach twisted in fear. He still hadn't been on an actual battlefield and wasn't in a hurry to go there. He'd enjoyed the training, gobbled up the information in the books, and was fascinated watching the surgery. He wasn't part of the raiding parties who went out at night, in the dark, putting themselves at great risk, crawling on their bellies, throwing petrol bombs towards the German line, and cutting the barbed wire so the infantry could get through when the battle started. Sometimes the raiding parties were ordered to get right into the German trenches and bring back prisoners to extract intelligence. He shuddered at their bravery, but now he was being asked to go close to the creature called *the enemy*. This was a whole other ball of string. And not one he was dying to unwind. He'd heard stories that the Germans were huge, were living in luxury in their trenches, that they had proper beds and even electric lights and radios.

"Are you hearing me, Mathieson? Get up to the front, have your supper up there, grab some sleep, and be ready to go out when told. You're to scour No Man's Land, right up to and through the German wire, and rush any wounded back to the dressing station. Now skedaddle."

The trip to the front was unhampered by the bustle and busyness of the day that had come to an end as night fell. Joe and the other three made their way forward. He carried the stretcher over his shoulder. His mask, which would save him from the evil tinned-pineapple-smelling gas, nested in a bag against his chest. Two haversacks with medical supplies, one cross-wise over his shoulder and the other strapped to his back, signalled his role. He and the other bearers stepped over hordes of infantrymen settled into a huddled khaki mass, trying to sleep in spaces too small even for a child. There was a huge throng up at the front line. There the men stood, shoulder-to-shoulder, jostling for every bit of space.

"Clear a passageway! Clear a passageway!" a sergeant was shouting, pushing men aside as he walked up the middle. Joe's first thought was this clearing was meant for them, that they were being afforded special treatment. He winked at Frank, tickled that stretchers-bearers were given favoured status. But when the sergeant shoved him and his three comrades more roughly than he had the men, Joe was quickly deflated and laughed at himself.

"Something funny, soldier?" the sergeant said, spraying spit into Joe's face.

"No sergeant," Joe said.

"Then stand aside and make way for the Brigadier-General."

Joe looked back down the trench and saw a party of officers advancing. In the lead was indeed a Brigadier-General. Fiftyish, slightly built, and at the most five foot five. Much shorter than Joe had imagined a very senior officer would stand. His uniform dazzled with gold stripes; his riding boots were polished like mirrors. The excitement Joe had felt during the day suddenly left and fear passed through him again. It was true then, really true. There was going to be a big battle. This visit was meant to reassure and encourage the men, but looking around at the attentive faces, he could tell dread had infected them all.

"At ease, men." The brigadier's voice was rich and imposing. "I stand before you atop the promise of a battle that will go down in history as one of glorious success. Tomorrow you will face the enemy. There are sixty thousand of you stretched along eighteen miles." He paused. "And that's just our front line." He stuck his chin out and looked around at the men for a response but none came. "We are strong in numbers," he continued, "and mighty of heart. When you go over tomorrow, you are assured of victory. We expect casualties to be less than ten percent, so any dead men you meet will be the enemy's loss. Not even a rat will survive our valiant onslaught. By suppertime tomorrow, you will be back here, victorious, lighting your pipes and cigarettes, and we'll have a grand celebration. God be with us!" He turned, saluted his party, and moved on. The guns started again.

Just after one in the morning, Frank nudged Joe awake. "We've 'ad the word. Let's go. I'll get the others. You and me stick together." They made their way to one of the ladders built into the wall and silently left the womb-like safety of the trench. Joe's heart thudded in his chest, but when he came up into the half-mile stretch between the front lines, it was quiet, and eerily peaceful. A sliver of moonlight cast a glow on the ghostly outline of burned trees. The smell of spent shellfire tickled the hairs in his nose, and he felt a sneeze rising. He put his hand over his face to stifle the noise.

All plant life had vanished, the once level fields now rutted and pitted with shell holes. Half-crouched, the four bearers ran through the colourless night in short bursts, dodging the holes, before lying flat for a few seconds, then rising up and running a few more yards. In ten minutes, they reached a tangled snaking of barbed wire, over three feet high. They lay flat and looked around but saw only other groups of bearers. Nobody immobile or in need of attention. Joe jerked and squealed when he felt a pulling at this shoulder. A stinking mud-encrusted hand was clamped over his mouth.

"Shh, I'm one of you."

"Jesus," Joe said rolling on to his back and picking dried mud from his lips. "What's up?"

"Actually not much. This is the quietest night we've had. Only one wounded. Over there at two o'clock. Get him and then you can all go back. We're going back in too. Easy night."

George Black stood. A crack shattered the quiet air. He quivered, like a rampant eel. A dark stain spread out from the centre of his chest. He folded in half and dropped to the ground.

"Christ, no!" screamed Dan. "It can't be." He was running around flinging his arms out to the sides. "Jesus Christ! George!"

"Stay down! All of you," Frank yelled.

Joe lay flat on his belly, arms protecting his head, legs shaking.

"C'mon," Frank said, "let's get 'im."

Joe kept close to the ground and pulled the stretcher towards him. He grabbed George's body by the legs, dragged it, and rolled it onto the stretcher.

"Mind him," he said to Dan, whose breath was coming in gasps through his sobs. He beckoned to a squad of bearers. "Can you carry the wounded guy? We'll take our friend back."

"Is he?" Dan said.

"He's dead," Joe said.

"Just like that, he's gone?"

"Aye."

Joe, Frank, and Dan scurried as fast as their load would allow, back to the dressing station where they delivered the bodies. Joe removed one of George's two identification disks, the red one to send to the orderly room, along with his pay book where Joe had written the date and *killed in action*. Frank checked that the other disk, the green one that identified the body, was secure around George's neck. Dan suggested they empty their pockets of cash, and along with the few shillings in George's boot, send the money on to his widow. The word seemed strange to Joe as he blew it out through his lips. Widow. It made him think of his mother, grandmother, and the other husbandless women he knew. All of them old, past their mid-forties. Strange, not right, to use it for George's young wife.

"Get some sleep. All of you," Atholl said from behind them. "No knowing when you'll next get a chance." He tapped his watch face. "I shall want the three of you awake in a couple of hours to be at the front line trench by six-thirty. And, Swan, report to the SB post for a new partner."

The three men gave a cursory salute as Atholl moved off down the support trench, followed by Frank and Dan.

It was still dark. Joe was alone again. Despite Atholl ordering them to get some sleep, he could no more fill that command than an order to shoot himself. On the other hand, maybe it wouldn't be that hard to shoot himself like the two malingerers he'd tended to earlier. He wondered if this close acquaintance with death was why stretcher-bearers weren't issued rifles.

Like earlier in the day—yesterday he corrected himself— he was again seated against a trench wall. But this time he had no wish to stretch out and savour the moist meat that had filled his canteen. He wanted to bury himself in the dirt, close himself off from the sight of George's last trembling moments, and disappear in the forever darkness of the clumped earth. He wanted Marguerite's arms around him. He wanted sex with her. Sex. Yes sex. A fuck. He needed it now. He drew in his legs and put his arms around himself. His shoulders relaxed and sank down. This was what he really wanted. A hug. Release. Comfort. He stood up and shook out his arms and legs. He lifted his hands to his face. As he was lowering them, he saw the blood. George's blood. On his hands. He held them out in front of him and watched them. They vibrated as if they were in tune with the ground trembling from the continual waves of the bombardment. *Stop. Stop shaking.* He smacked them against his thighs. He got out his pencil and dug in his haversack for some paper. He looked up to the lightening sky.

Saturday, July 1, 1916

My dear wee Ellen,

Did you say, Rabbits, Rabbits, Rabbits, this morning? Remember I taught you to say that the first of every month? For luck. It's four in the morning here, already tomorrow and I've just said it, so it's sure to be a lucky day for me.

Joe imagined lifting Ellen from her bed and whispering the words in her ear, making her laugh. Kate wasn't into that kind of frivolous play. He scolded himself for being so hard on his wife. Hadn't she sweated and laboured to bring this darling child of his into the world? He thought of the comfort Ellen gave him when he held her. The whole of her wee body fitted against his chest, slotted into his heart. And to think he'd been horrified when Kate said she was up the spout. It made him laugh now to think he hadn't wanted Ellen to exist. Aye, that was a day of fear too. November 2, 1913. The day she made her entrance. Joe suddenly felt as if he were right back in the early afternoon on the day of her birth.

He had propped his back against the rain-slicked wall outside the flat he and Kate rented, had drawn up one knee to steady himself, and sucked deeply on his cigarette. Another shriek from Kate made him grit his teeth. *Shite. How long is this bloody ordeal going to go on?* He checked the time on the gold pocket watch that once belonged to his da. Twenty-five after one. Kate had been at it over nineteen hours, since tea time yesterday, labouring to give birth to the bairn. His child.

His stomach rumbled. He needed a bowl of the soup from the big pot Ma had brought over, and he should dare himself to check on Kate again. When he last went in to see her, she hadn't wanted much to do with him, especially when a pain gripped her. She'd reached out to her own mother and to Ma. He wished it was a workday and not a Sunday, and he wouldn't have to know any of what was going on in the over-heated all-purpose back room of the two-roomed flat. As he started his climb up the outside stairs to his house, he heard her scream again. His heart thumped wildly and he rushed in over to the bed in the recess. Although settling for marriage and fatherhood was not how he'd wanted his life to be at this age, he would be gutted if anything happened to Kate.

The midwife leaned over the bed, listening to his wife's exposed belly through a thing like a trumpet. Kate thrashed about, her hair tangled and soaked with sweat. Her short, tubby mother was trying to still her so she could wipe her brow and let the midwife do her job. Kate pushed her away, hoisted herself, and vomited into an enamel basin her mother held out for her. When the spasms were over, she began to whimper. Joe went over to her and tried to hold her hand, but she pushed him away and dropped her head back onto the pillow.

His own mother led him over to a bare corner of the small rickety table and set down a steaming bowl of broth. Newspapers, scissors, clamps and other metal tools he didn't recognize, enamel dishes shaped like large kidneys, and piles of cotton swabs covered the rest of the surface. He gasped and slurped his soup, relieved to have a reason not to go to Kate again. For one thing, he thought he'd seen blood on the sheet and that threw him into a panic. "The first is always the hardest," his mother said. She sat at the table, encouraging him to concentrate on his soup. "We've had to send for the doctor."

"What?'" he said, seeing the serious look on her face. He covered his ears as Kate let out another howl that bounced off the walls and pierced his chest. He jumped up, rocking the table and sending a wave of soup onto it. The doctor? How was he going to pay for him? He covered his face, humiliated he'd had such a thought when poor Kate was in such agony. And that was his fault. "Is she going to die?"

"Don't be daft." Ma lowered him back to his chair. "He'll give her a whiff of chloroform, take the edge off the pains. It'll be fine. You'll see. Now eat up, and away and see your friends, or Fred and Lizzie."

It was coming up for midnight when Fred's wife shook him awake. He was relieved to see Lizzie was smiling. "A wee lassie. Eight pounds, four ounces. You two make them big and healthy."

He ran the length of Fred's street letting his scarf flap in the wind. He turned the corner and belted down the hundred yards or so to his own flat, took the stairs two at a time, and flung open the door. Kate was sitting up in the bed, sipping a cup of tea.

"Where is she? Where's my wee girl?" Joe said, putting his hand to his chest, trying to steady out his panting.

"I'm feeling fine. Thanks very much for asking," Kate said, and clamped her teeth on a toasted crumpet.

He'd gone over to her and sat on the bed. Lifted her long hair and combed it with his fingers. She closed her eyes and the cup tilted toward the edge of the saucer. Joe took them from her. "Was it awful?"

"It's over, that's all that matters. I just want to sleep."

Kate's mother—her sleeves still rolled up, her eyes ringed with dark circles from missing a night's sleep—laid the precious parcel in Joe's arms. He pulled back the edges of the shawl from the baby's chin and fixed his eyes on the wrinkled, pink face. Fear spread through his chest. "Is she all right? She's not moving."

"Touch her. She'll not break. And I'm away to my bed. I'm done in. Put her on her side in the cradle when you're finished holding her." He remembered his mother-in-law adding, "Your daughter needs her rest too. It wasn't easy for her coming into this world."

Nigh on three years later, two countries and hundreds of miles away, Joe's pencil hovered over the letter to his child. He brought to mind how, with his newborn daughter in his arms, he'd gone over to Kate, but she was slumped against the pillow, snoring gently. He tucked the baby in the crook of his elbow and covered Kate up. He'd placed a kiss on her lips and got a faint whiff of the chloroform. "Thank you," he said. "I swear I'll do my best for the both of you."

A few drips from his eyes at that memory. He wiped his cheek and continued writing.

You're probably fast asleep still. I hope your dreams are sweet, full of happy bunnies running in the fields. I can see clear across the fields here to a lovely wood. The birds are chirping away in their wee houses in the trees. Last night I went for a walk and guess what? I found a blue eggshell. I'll bring it home for you. A wee bird came out of it and now he's snuggled in his nest with his ma. Lots of colours here. Little yellow flowers, red poppies, and a brilliant blue sky. Almost all the colours of the rainbow. I saw a rainbow yesterday. It rained a lot, then the sun came out and made a rainbow. I wished on it that I could see you again soon. It's spitting rain again, so maybe I'll see another rainbow today.

Your Daddy sends his love

He folded the letter and placed it in his jacket pocket, nestled beside the others: the one for Ma and the other for Marguerite. He lit up a cigarette, pulled his pay book from his breast pocket, and opened it to the back page. Again he wetted the end of his stubby pencil, and on the space for soldier's last will and testament, he wrote:

There are three letters in my pocket. Please see they get posted. All of them. Whatever I own, and it's not much, I want it to go to my wee daughter, Ellen Margaret Mathieson. I'd like to leave her a better world, but I'll have to see what tomorrow brings.

Joseph Mathieson, Private

Saturday, July 1, 1916 4:15 a.m. Joe climbed onto a foot deep alcove dug into the trench wall, sat side on and drew his knees towards his chest. Light rain started to fall. Maybe it would cause a further delay. Maybe the battle wouldn't start until tomorrow. Maybe the rain wouldn't stop. Maybe they'd call the whole stupid thing off, so he could stay here curled up. Maybe Walter would come strolling by. They'd hop an ambulance train for the coast and then a hospital ship that would take them both somewhere quiet and safe for a good night's sleep. He dozed, on and off, until nearly six.

The rain stopped. The sun had already risen. This waiting, this nerve-wracking space before it started, was killing him. To distract himself, he fished for the letter he'd been handed before he left Gaudechat. Found it deep in his trouser pocket. When he first had it in his hand, his heart sank with disappointment—Kate's laboured pencil printing.

Gretna Gren
Dear Joe,

Dinna even know what day it is. I think Thursday. We work twelve hour shifts so I'm tired a the time and ma head is buzzin wi a the noise so I dinna know if I'm comin or going. Also I'm swelterin a the time But what we are doing is important keeping yu a in shells and bullits so I canna whine about it. My job is fillin the brass shell cases with cordite. How are you getting on? No word that yuve been hurt or anything so that's good. All the lassies here in the munishun factory are like me there man is away fighting or theyr no married and was in service so they are happy to be away from that and earnin better money we get three pounds, two and four a week the men get more than us of cours four pounds I think but still its good money for me. I send yur ma a pound for her and Ellen so I'm no being chintzy with my money. You wid get a good laff if you seen me at work. We hav to ware clogs on oor feet with wood soles so as no to coz a spark, a funny hat and wait til yu hear this. Troosers can yu see me what a laff. Aye, we have to ware overalls and weer no allowed metl, no evn pins in wir hare. anuther funny thing is yur skin turns yellow and yur hare kind o gingr, kind o gren. For that we hav to drink a lot o milk so that's good coz they say we can get unwell. But dinna wurry. Ellens fine too. Ma says shes tokking lots and asks fer yu.

Yur wife
Kate

Hardly a love letter, he thought, but then she hadn't exactly had any from him. He read the letter through again, folded it then scrunched it into a ball. The rustling of the paper smudged the silence.

By twenty past six, he'd scrounged some tepid water for a quick wash, then made his way forward. Away from the quiet of his improvised bed, the trenches had come alive. Soldiers flowed through these underground channels like an unstoppable flood. The closer he got to the front line the denser the deluge. He stuck his rolled-up stretcher out in front of him, held onto the sides, and pushed his way through soldiers crowded up against each other. As always, he scanned for Walter but the swollen river of men moved as one. As soon as he fixed his eyes on a face, it became another and another. Never his brother's. And it was hard to concentrate with the renewed thunder from the artillery behind him. He bumped into a cook dragging a canteen cart. The grey smell of boiled oats reminded him he'd had no breakfast.

"What's on the menu this grand day?" Joe had to shout into the cook's ear. The short unshaven man rolled up his sleeves.

"We've porridge without milk, porridge without cream, porridge without bacon, porridge without eggs. What's your fancy? An' I have fresh brewed tea." The cook lowered his voice. "Tell you the truth. I've not had many orders this morning." He rubbed his stomach slowly. "Lots of nervous tummies."

Joe painted on a smile and pantomimed indecision. "I'll have a porridge without bacon, another without eggs. And I'll try that swill you have the nerve to call decent tea." He put the stretcher against the wall and pressed himself against it, his back to the enemy lines. He slurped down the runny breakfast. Next to him a priest stood amongst a huddle leading them in reciting the Hail Mary. Some finished up canteens of porridge; one polished his shoes on the back of his puttees, as if he were about to be paraded before the king. Some slumped against the wall caressing the faces on photos they'd taken from their pockets.

"Hey, Joe! Over here."

Corporal Gray was waving him over. Joe handed off his unfinished canteen and mug to a sobbing pale-faced youth crouched by him and squeezed his way to Gray. The corporal ladled rum tots to the men who would be first to go forward. Pushing and shoving lads blocked his way as they tried to work out their tension on each other. "Oy, oy, that's enough," he said to the lads. "Get in an orderly line." He held out a metal mug half full of rum to Joe.

Joe waved the drink away. "I need to keep my head clear. But thanks."

"Right, of course. That's good," Gray shouted at him over the din. "You're looking well. Must be getting special treatment back there." He put down the rum bucket, pulled out a pocket watch and checked it. "Hang about for a wee. I need to get these men organized." He waved to the soldiers to close in around him. "Okay, listen!" he barked.

Joe put his hands over his ears. Gray's shouting and the noise of the guns scaling to a crescendo scratched at his eardrums. Gray looked back up the trench where the soldiers had tried their best to clear a path for their platoon lieutenant and a barrel-chested sergeant. He turned around to face the officer and saluted. "Ready for your orders, sir."

The lieutenant turned to the sergeant. "Time?" he asked, his voice squeaking. He put his hand over his mouth, coughed, and ran a finger inside his khaki shirt collar. The sergeant grimaced and looked down at the watch in his hand.

"Time, sergeant?"

"O six fifty-nine, sir."

The lieutenant nodded. "Repeat the orders to the men, sergeant."

The sergeant saluted and turned to the men.

"In fifteen minutes you will go over the top and crawl on your bellies into No Man's Land. You will keep in tight formation with the lieutenant here, Corporal Gray, and myself. Keep us in sight at all times. If you get hit, crawl into a hole for protection. Fix yourself up as best you can and wait for the stretcher-bearers to pick you up."

"When will that be, Sarge?" asked one.

"When they've had their bacon and eggs and they're good and ready to come for you."

Joe couldn't stop a smile.

"You will not make a sound. Watch. Listen for orders. Absolute silence. No mucking about. This is critical. Understand? Corporal, instruct your men to load their kit."

Without a word from Gray, the men heaved their loads over their shoulders, onto their backs, and around their middles: two hundred rounds of ammunition, a waist-full of grenades, empty sandbags and a shovel, wire cutters, and wiring stakes. In their haversacks, slung crosswise over a shoulder, lazed two days' water rations, tins of corned beef, malt extract, biscuits, jam, and chocolate. In addition to his drag-down load, one man carried two homing pigeons inside a cage that would be released to send back written signals. "All ready?" the lieutenant said. "You there, stretcher-bearer." He pushed Joe back by the chest. "Get out of the way. Go back to your post. Doesn't do the men any good to have you standing around showing off your stretcher and armband."

Joe nodded and moved back a few yards, embarrassed at his ignorance, but grateful he wouldn't be snaking over the ground with a sixty-pound kit strapped to his back. Some had already turned their backs to him as if the sight of his armband and stretcher was a black omen. A young lad, a row of yellow-tipped pimples on his chin, bumped his hip against Joe. "I want you. If I get hit. You'll look for me, right?" He bumped Joe again as if he were a touchstone. "Let my mum know." Joe looked up and nodded.

It would be another hour or so before he was needed to attend to any wounded. 'Ten percent,' the brigadier had predicted last night. So one, maybe two members of Gray's section might need help. Multiply that by twelve for the number in the company. Roughly twenty casualties that he, Frank, Dan, and George's replacement, Hamish Cameron, would attend to. He quickly calculated that the whole brigade could lose a couple hundred men, more than he'd ever met in his life. He gathered up his stretcher. How many might a whole army lose? Maybe a couple thousand. More than he could imagine in one place at a time. He tied the handles of his stretcher together so he could easily drag it behind him to the SB assembly post. Likely ten trips from the field back to the dressing station at roughly an hour for each delivery. Plus, he calculated, maybe three hours giving first aid. He was glad now he'd eaten the lousy porridge to tide him over. It could be a long busy day.

Gray stood to attention and faced his lieutenant.

"Ready, sir."

"Fix bayonets!"

Joe squinted at the flashing metal as Gray checked on every one of his men, adjusting bayonets as he went down the line. Then he came over just as Joe was moving off, laid a hand on his shoulder, and whispered. "You're a good lad, Mathieson. Make yourself a worthwhile life after all this. Been good knowing you."

"Don't say it like that," Joe said. "I'll see you the morrow, same time, same place." But he too laid an arm on the other man's shoulder.

The barrage ceased. The enemy guns too were suddenly still. The men looked at the lieutenant for an explanation, a reassurance. Instead he nodded to his sergeant. The men knew then it was their time. They froze. One slumped to the ground, shrieking and shaking. Gray picked him up under the armpits, and with one hand over the man's mouth and the other grabbing his chest, slammed him against the trench wall. Joe heard Gray whisper in the trembling soldier's ear, "Bloody well look normal or they'll have you minced. Got it?"

Joe looked away from the young soldier's soaking crotch and scanned the twitching faces of Gray's men. Someone snickered.

The corporal turned his head toward the men. "Enough," he said. He went close to one. So close they almost touched noses. "You want something to laugh about, soldier?"

"No,"

"Sure?"

"Yes, corporal."

The lieutenant put up his hand for silence, inched his way up the fire-step ladder, and slowly climbed up and over the top of the trench. From below, Joe studied the lieutenant's pressed trousers and long polished boots until they were hidden by the swarm of men following him with weighted-down backs.

As the men crowded at the fire-steps, Joe looked to the sky. The sun had risen and burned off the mist from the early morning showers. He closed his eyes and let the quiet and warmth relax his muscles, soaking in the pleasure of the perfect temperature. By mid-afternoon it would be a scorcher. The flapping of bird wings cracked through the silence of the resting guns. He fixed his eyes on the cloudless blue above him. A pair of partridges swooped low over the trench, and for the first time in a week, a freshness filled in the spaces as the cordite stink from the guns wafted away. The white chalky dust disturbed by the guns had floated back to the earth and spotted the duckboards. Joe sucked in some clean air.

The silence, at odds with the scene a few minutes ago in the trench, confused him. He looked up and down to remind himself where he was. Men as far as he could see down the line were still using the ladders to depart the trenches. He followed a group up the nearest ladder, moved off to the side when he was over the top, lay on his belly, and shut his eyes. He prayed that when he opened them, men would be lazing on green grass, smoking, chatting, and laughing. But when he dared to squeeze them open, he covered his mouth to smother a shriek. The colours covering the French countryside, which had brought him such delight in June, had been blasted into a murky grey monotone. Men advanced, most on their bellies like slugs, some on tiptoe with their knees slightly bent, inching forward, bayoneted rifles raised to chest height. He scrambled back down into the trench and crouched. The sunlight up top had bitten into his eyes. Tiny red flashes danced behind his eyeballs. He shut his eyes again, imagined that if he looked over the top again he'd see a stand of trees in their full summer brilliance. Or beet fields with their silvery green tops pushing up through the yellow flowered weeds. Maybe men hoeing the rows in wide brimmed hats to keep the flashing sun from their eyes, women going up and down the rows handing out bread and metal mugs of cool water, girls picking poppies, or boys running and shrieking, flying kites.

He rubbed his eyes and opened them. The pair of partridges flew over again and broke into his thoughts. The trench was now full up again, packed from side to side with more soldiers in full kit, bayonets fixed and rifles at the ready. But still all was silent and he watched the activity as he might have watched a film with Kate during their short courtship: a crowd scene where the actors moved wordlessly like an ant colony. He moved down the line a little, pushed his way through the new faces, and stepped up on the ladder again. A dark ocean of churned up dirt rolled and rippled soundlessly as far as he could see, for the guns had done great damage. Waves of men pressed on like small bobbing boats. Thousands more crawled on their bellies, their haunches flicking from side to side.

Suddenly, just beyond where Joe reckoned the enemy lines began, the land rose up in a huge black cloud. As tall as a Highland mountain in the picture calendar on his kitchen wall at home, it spewed out chunks of dirt and rocks. Embers fell in perfect arcs like the sparks from a giant's Roman candle. A second later the awful boom of the explosion reached him. His eardrums beat against his brain. An arm pulled him down from the ladder and flung him to the ground. The owner, a captain, stepped over him and onto the first rung of the fire-step. The officer put a whistle between his lips, and raised a hand holding a pocket watch high into the air. On his back, Joe watched him fix his eyes on the watch. Then came a blast from his whistle. Another blast. And another. All up and down the line, whistles shrilled in quick succession like falling dominoes. The artillery started again, a hundred thunders shaking the very bowels of the earth. Men clambered over the top, and flattened Joe against the trench wall.

A sound new to his ears battled the booming guns. A lightning-quick chain of bullets. He peeked over the top. Wave after wave of men fell as if a scythe was swooshing through long stalks of legs and bodies. Stones, dirt, and sod were flung into the sky. Splashes of red painted the smoky grey air. Screams and howls competed with the guns for distinction. Joe closed his eyes and shook his head. Was he really seeing this carnage? What if he replayed this scene? Would it all have righted itself? If only he could look again, see it for what it should be, what he wanted it to be. He eased his eyes open, willing the men to be walking upright, side-by-side, friend-by-friend. But the picture was worse: the air darker, the falling men screaming louder. Joe clenched his fists as he stared at the next trenchful of men ordered onto the battlefield. They too were shot down, tumbling like skittles. He hurled himself to the duckboard and curled into a ball. How could they order him into that madness? He tried to drive out the terror that stiffened his whole body. He shielded himself with his stretcher and reached into his pocket for his watch, the one that had been his father's, needing to fill his brain with a thought he could understand, and wipe out the pictures from over the top. He tried to summon some spit into his mouth as his shaking hand held the watch. Seven-thirty. Ma would be boiling an egg for Ellen's breakfast. Marguerite would be making coffee in the sunny farm kitchen.

7:56 a.m. Joe quit counting how often the front-line trench refilled. Flood after flood of full-kitted young men. Handsome in their tidy uniforms. Shining in their youth. Time after time the trench vomited a horde of infantrymen up onto the battlefield. Above him another freshly shaved captain stood, legs apart, on the trench lip. Again and again he expelled the air from his lungs into his whistle. Urged his boys towards their enemy. Joe wished the rules here were like a football match: the whistle blew, play stopped, the fracas was sorted out, and then opposing teams resumed respect. But instead the continuous roar of artillery fire, a full orchestra of destruction: bass, treble, and tremolo.

He yelped and staggered under a jab in the small of his back. He turned around. Two military policemen poked rifles at him.

"Over the top, you slacker," the fatter one screamed. A spray of his saliva scummed Joe's chin. His heart thumped in his chest. Tapped the Red Cross on his armband. Stuttered. "W-w-waiting for my order to see to the wounded."

"There's wounded aplenty out there," the other MP said. "Bloody massacre it is. Fucking butchers over the other side. Got your work cut out for you. Go on then. See to our boys." And they moved off butting their angry rifles into the kidneys of men who, having seen what was ahead, opted to stay behind.

With adrenalin prickling his muscles, Joe raced the quarter mile back towards the Regimental First Aid Post. His stretcher scraped along the duckboards beneath his feet and banged against the sidewalls as he took the corners at full speed. About halfway there he ran into Frank and the thirty or so other stretcher-bearers from his company.

"Where the bloody 'ell have you been? We're on our way out. Now!" Frank shouted above the din into Joe's face. "We've to get into the front line. Atholl's screaming for your blood. You were supposed to be 'ere."

"I've just come from…" He looked over his shoulder to the front line. "There."

"'Ow is it?"

Joe gaped at Frank, his face blank. He had no words to give shape to what he'd seen.

"We've not to go beyond our own wire." Frank yelled above the din and dragged him away. "For our own safety."

"What about them that get hurt farther out?"

Frank shrugged. For a moment they stared at each other, then ran as best they could through the crowds and didn't stop until they reached the front trench where Atholl waited. They melded with men huddled together. Joe wondered if, by touching each other's bodies to form one connected mass, they felt less vulnerable. Atholl threw him a look. Joe bet he wasn't beyond giving him a bawling out even at a time like this. Instead Atholl shoved his way to the fire-step, raised himself on two rungs, cupped his mouth, and yelled.

"Bearers up!"

The words sliced through Joe. He had to go up. Get out there. Now. He closed his eyes, threw the stretcher over, and climbed out. Frank was already ahead and picked it up. The smoke from the shelling and shooting made it difficult to see. Bullets whizzed about them. One pinged Frank's helmet. Joe leapt on him and brought him to the ground. "Frank! No! No!"

"Get off me you idiot."

"I thought you'd copped one," Joe said.

Frank sat up, dusted off his uniform, and laughed.

"I'll cop you one for dirtying my coat."

They pushed on. Joe waved, as if swimming one-armed, through the haze. Rabbits and moles, disturbed from their burrows, tickled at his ankles. He did little dance steps on his tiptoes to avoid trampling them and tripped over a soldier who grabbed at him. Joe knelt and dared himself to look at the man. Blood seeped through the soldier's trousers at mid-thigh. Joe remembered the grisly shrapnel wounds he'd seen during his training and on the trains. Had never wanted to see those old images again. He took a deep breath, got the scissors from his haversack, and cut away the clothing around the wound as he'd been taught. He breathed out with a puff when he saw a small clean cut.

"It's your lucky day. A wee nick. Get your dressing kit out, tear the cardboard off the iodine bottle. Pour it on a dressing pad and hold it there. Watch you don't pour the iodine directly on the cut. It'll hurt like hell. Then get yourself to the first aid post, 'bout half a mile back. You'll be fine. Crawl or keep low until you get back to the trench." He turned to Frank, who was kneeling over a man and holding a dressing with both hands over the man's throat. "What you got there?"

Frank's hands and lower arms were soaked in blood. The injured man lay very still and made not a sound. His blue eyes stared straight at Frank. Then Frank let go and sat back on his haunches. "It's stopped," he said. "The pouring blood. It just fucking stopped."

Joe leaned over and closed the man's eyes. He removed the red tag, almost hot from the fast rising heat of the morning, and the pay book from the man's breast pocket. "Rest in peace, Graham Davidson from West Calder." He put the man's final belongings in his own haversack for safekeeping.

"And we're not even allowed to bury 'im," Frank said. "Poor bastard."

They both looked around. The smoke had cleared a little, allowing them to see about fifty yards in all directions, a fifty-yard circle of moving screaming earth. "More work than I figured," Joe said, then turned back and leaned over the body. "Sorry, Mr. Davidson. Sorry you'll not have a proper funeral."

All around them the guns drummed on; black smoke came in waves. Each time it briefly cleared, the ground changed from a hint of green, where stubborn leaves of turnips and beets dared to survive, to the natural pale russet of the bare earth or a uniform hue-less grey. Joe's knees ached and his thighs burned as he crouched among the dead, searching for a twitch, a groan, a scream, a sob, or any sign that a soldier was still alive and could be saved. He added up the numbers as he and Frank walked on their knees. Lost count of the dead at fifty something. And that was just in the small radius allowed by the smoke. Talk was useless over the bedlam of exploding shells, raining shrapnel like summer hail. A new instrument joined the cacophony on the moaning field: a fierce bra-ta-tat, bra-ta-tat, brata, brata, bra-ta-tat. *So it's true,* Joe thought. Here it was. A machine that fired bullets non-stop.

A cough came from Joe's right. A man lay on his back, hands folded over his stomach. A dazed serenity veiled his face. Joe crawled over, removed the man's hands from his injury, and saw where shrapnel had ripped him open. He stared into the crevasse that had once contained the man's organs, now a glistening bowl of pink and red slime and mud. He put two large dressings over the wound and held the man's head up so he could swallow the two morphine tablets Joe had taken from the man's kit.

The man waved away the pills. "It doesn't hurt," he said.

Joe was surprised to see a strange smile curl the edges of his mouth. "Take them. Just in case," he said, and laid the man's head flat again. The sun was hot now. An unpleasant meaty smell snaked up his nostrils. Joe thought of the ugly wound in the soldier's belly. The words *frying* and *grilling* and pictures of dogs scrapping for offal at the butcher's back door plugged his head. He thought he might vomit. He sat back on his haunches and took a couple deep breaths. He signalled to Frank to help him lift the man onto the stretcher. His first passenger. A shell exploded about twenty feet in front. Joe dropped to the ground and looked up between his outstretched arms. A body, a person, rose fifteen feet into the air, haloed by soil. At first his fall was graceful, like the downward arc of a trapeze. Keeping his head covered, Joe crept over to where the man should have come to earth. He found only a small pile of bony grit.

"What are you doing? Get back 'ere." Frank tugged at Joe's boot. "Your belly wound died. I've put a different one on the stretcher. We need to get 'im back. Dan and 'amish's got their own. There's so many we're lifting in pairs, not four men to a stretcher."

Slowly Joe got to his knees, clawed at the ground, and sifted the debris through his fingers. "What's 'appening?" Frank asked. "C'mon."

"Nothing," Joe said. "Nothing. I'm on my way."

"I'll take the front," Frank said. "The feet. You watch 'is face. We'll drop 'im if 'e dies and get another."

Together they heaved the weight up onto their shoulders. They made slow progress, their knees often buckling when they stumbled over churned up ground. Joe was reminded of how his Uncle Tam, Fred, Walter, and himself had carried his father's coffin into the church and then to the burial plot that chilly March day over four years ago. Maybe his father was lucky to die when he did and be spared this bloodletting.

With every step, the polished wood of the stretcher handle rubbed against the space between Joe's thumb and his palm. With every step, he could feel the skin thinning and knew it was soon going to be a raw and painful blister. *Fancy with all this slaughter around me,* he thought, *all the wound tags I've filled in—gunshot/chest, shell/thigh, bayonet/neck—I'm moaning about my hand.* Still the thing bloody hurt. And the heat. More intense than any he'd known. Sweat trickled down the inside of his thighs.

At the first aid post, they were told the man's injuries were more than Lieutenant Atholl and the orderlies there were equipped to deal with. They hoisted the stretcher again and plodded to the dressing station farther back. Joe thought his shoulder tendons were strained to their limit and might snap. It was another half an hour or so before the pair staggered into Dressing station Row.

In the first cubicle, Captain Rogers bent over a screaming soldier lying on a trestle table. He looked up when he saw Joe and Frank. "Drop your load off next door and come here and give me a hand." Joe did as he was told and went over to the table. Captain Rogers had taken off his jacket and shirt and was sweating through his undershirt, his braces dangling around his hips.

"Come to the side of me," Rogers said, nodding to his left. "Hold down the shoulders."

The patient was quiet now, silenced by a pad dripped with chloroform. The sweet smell grasped at Joe's throat. He touched heads with Captain Rogers, who had taken up a saw and was starting to cut just below the man's elbow.

"Down, I said. Hold them down. Flat on the table."

Joe caught another whiff. Whisky on the officer's breath. He turned his head away as the saw crunched through the bone. The removed limb was thrown off to the side onto some rubber sheeting, which had already caught a dozen assorted limb parts. Joe half expected the abandoned legs to get up and run away from this reeking place. He continued holding the patient down while the captain packed the wound with lime chloride powder and gauze. When he'd finished, Rogers walked to the door opening and yelled. "Next!"

He turned to Joe. "Now get out of here and let me get on. Get back to your duty."

Joe scurried away and met up with Frank, whose cheeks were bulging. "Managed to scrounge up a couple sugar buns," he muttered, spraying crumbs and tossing one to him.

"Thanks," he said. "You're a right pal." And both ran forward towards the battlefield, unable to speak with their mouths full of dry bread and dust.

Seven runs later, Joe had lost count of the number he had assessed, given first aid to, and transported to the first aid post or farther back to Dressing Station Row. Then there were those who were not badly hurt, newly named *the walking wounded*. Joe's orders were to patch them up and send them back to their troop where after a brief rest, a smoke, and — if they were lucky— something to eat, they'd go back out to fight again.

One was a boy with a grazed forehead. "An inch lower and you'd be blind. You're a lucky lad," Joe said, dabbing at the scratch with a cotton pad dipped in iodine. He forced out a joke like they'd been advised in training. That was more Frank's department, but Joe had certainly handed out enough tired expressions today. "You'll live to see another day," was one. He said it now and laughed at his own banality.

"Is that supposed to be a consolation? 'Cause it's not," the lad said, and burst into tears.

Recognizing an accent similar to his own, Joe put a hand on the lad's shoulder. "There, there, son. Where are you from? What's your name?"

"Tom Patterson. From Kirkcaldy. It's in Fife."

"I know well where it is. I'm from Methilane. Been to Kirkcaldy many a time to the football matches. Cheered on the Rovers."

"Methilane," Tom said. "Do you know Willie Melville? He's from Methilane."

"Never heard of him." *Weird. It's a wee place and I thought I knew all the men from home that came over.* "What's he look like?"

"Fairish hair. A bit sandy. Pretty tall, maybe five ten." He eyed Joe. "Aye. About your height."

Joe's gut tightened. "How old?"

"Says he's nineteen," Tom said, "but that's a lie."

"How's that?"

"First, he doesn't look that old. Then I was asking him about his family and he said he had two brothers and the next up from him is twenty-four."

"Same as me," Joe said. He felt the blood was emptying from his head. He held onto the lad's shoulders.

"He said the brother was seven years older, so that would make him more like seventeen. Sixteen when he signed up."

Same age as Walter. Joe had to sit on the ground. He fuddled around in his breast pocket for a cigarette. "When did you last see him?"

"This morning. We went over together close to half eight. Haven't seen him since. Dead or alive."

Joe dragged on the cigarette. "What battalion are you with?"

"I'm signed up with the Glasgow Boys' Brigade Battalion, 'cause I was in the Boys' Battalion at home. Been in the BB since I was thirteen." The lad started to cry again, bubbles of snot leaking from his nostrils. He touched the dressing on his forehead. "Don't send me back there. I can't do it again."

Joe took out a bandage, pressed it into a narrow strip. "I'm doing you a wee favour," he said. He looked around, knelt down, dipped his fingers into a puddle of blood in a shallow shell hole, and daubed a red cross on the bandage. "In turn I want you to keep your eyes peeled for this Willie Melville." He tied the bandage around Tom's left upper arm. "Now you're a real silly bugger—a bearer. You stick by me though." *You're my big hope for getting to Walter.* "When we get back to the first aid post, grab a stretcher, and if you can't find one, get a sheet of corrugated tin. There's tons lying around. Watch you don't cut yourself on it. And round up a partner. I'm sure there's thousands of walking wounded like yourself along the way. If anyone says anything, tell them Corporal Gray ordered it."

The lad saluted. "Aye, corporal. Aye!" Joe's spirits were alive again. The numbness that had curtained off his brain all morning thinned. Maybe this was a false trail to finding Walter, but it was the closest he'd come. And just maybe…

1:55 p.m “Your boy’s a good worker,” Frank said, nodding over to where Tom and his partner, a lad with a bandage around his head, were loading two soldiers onto their tin stretcher. “Not easy in this ’eat. That tin is scalding to the touch.” He gave Joe a friendly shove. “But not as ’ot as the water you’ll find yourself in if Atholl finds out you’ve put yourself in charge of recruitment.”

“Talk of the devil,” Joe said, pointing at the lieutenant coming at them from the direction of the enemy line.

“Who are these two?” Atholl asked.

Joe gave Tom and his partner a quick look.

“Reinforcements, sir.”

“Good. Good,” Atholl said. “I expect the regiment organized that. The enemy has called for a short truce. To clear away the wounded. Get some nourishment as well. If there’s any to be found.”

“For ’ow long, sir?” Frank asked. “This break.”

Atholl peered over his steel-rimmed glasses. “And that is your business because?”

“It’s not. Sir. Wondering is all.”

“Leave the questions to the officers.” Atholl looked at his watch. “Almost two now. You’ll know it’s over when the firing starts again. Were you instructed in the triage system?”

“The what?” Joe said.

“Triage. We assess the wounded in three groups. First, those that can take care of their own first aid. Your job here is to do a quick assessment and remind them to use their own dressing kits and tell them to walk back to the first aid post.

"Aye," Joe said. "We've been doing that." He wanted to say, *We have got brains in our skulls. Did that stuff for months on the trains, you little ponce. Didn't need a fancy word for it.*

"The second lot are more seriously wounded," Atholl went on. "They will require your assistance and transportation. You make that decision. The troops are instructed to plant a rifle into the ground as a signal if they are wounded. Should make your job a bit easier. I think you've seen enough this morning to be able to assess who might survive."

"So the third group is the dead?" Frank asked.

"No. Those we will leave to the burial parties. If you can help with that, good, but your first priority is to get the wounded to us doctors.

Us doctors. Like us bearers don't matter. "What's the third then?" Joe asked. He knew perfectly well those were the men on the brink of death, but he wanted to see if Atholl would squirm.

"Those you assess as being beyond help in any way." He pushed his glasses to the bridge of his nose. "Clear?"

"Not quite," Joe said. "What do we do with them, sir?"

"Leave them."

"Sorry sir," Joe said. "Didn't quite catch what you said."

Joe saw Frank smirk and turn away.

"Move to the next patient." Atholl fiddled with his jacket buttons. "Carry on then," Atholl said. "Don't get any closer to the enemy wire than this point. There's enough wounded between here and our own trenches to occupy us for days. And ..."

"Something else, sir?" Frank asked.

"No," Atholl said. "Just that ..." He fixed his eyes on Joe. "Well, I'm glad you are unharmed."

"You too, sir," Joe said, embarrassed at his own meanness. Frank and the other two nodded.

2:05 p.m. Joe worked his shoulders free from his neck. Good to have some quiet and feel his body uncoil from the morning's tension. His mouth was parched. No one had appeared with food. He walked over to where Frank had joined Tom and his partner, John, trying to impress the hell out of them with some story or other. "Off your arses."

"Fag break first," Frank said. He waved his cigarette at Joe. "'Ave one on me."

Joe took in Frank's dark-circled eyes, then nodded at Tom and John. They rooted around in Frank's squished packet, tamped down the tobacco on the backs of their hands, and lit their cigarettes with their own matches. "I'll get started," Joe said.

Tom jumped up.

"Okay, okay. Sit, for a wee while," Joe said. "Puff away. I'll give you five minutes, but only five and then you catch up with me."

All the guns were silent now. The only noise was a low droning from those who carpeted the ground waiting for medical help. The softness of the sound reminded Joe of the bees buzzing, working over the heather on his summer walking trips in the Ochil hills. The sound here, though less shrill than earlier, still set his nerves on edge. The sky blazed bluer, more cloudless, and the air hotter than any he'd experienced in Scotland. As he stepped over bodies, doing the quick assessments, the sun's burning yellow eye stung his face. A number of bodies, chubby as well as skinny, muscular as well as flabby, had their clothes blasted completely away. The naked exposed genitals made Joe feel he had intruded, uninvited, into an intimate moment. Often he looked into the distance, all the way to the enemy wire, and saw the scope of the slaughter. He could not get into his brain that men, ordinary men, men he might enjoy a beer with, inflicted this bloodbath. He lay down and squirmed on his belly right up to the wire. Imagined the trenches beyond filled with huge blond German men who might jump out and chase him as elderly women had when, as a boy, he and his friends went chapping at strangers' doors with false bravado. And like those neighbours, the big German boys would turn out to be friends and they'd all have a laugh. But the sight around him wasn't funny. It was disgusting. Cluttered. Torn and bloodied bandages messed the fields. Burst haversacks spewed their contents over the ground. The insides of thousands of pockets created a litter of papers, letters and postcards, photos. God, he didn't even have a picture, other than the one in his head, of Ellen. Strips of fabric from all sorts of clothing, boots, and caps trashed the fields. It was like a snapshot he'd seen in the Sunday Post of the infamous riot between Rangers and Celtic in the 1909 Cup final, the pitch a mess of abandoned scarves, jackets, hats, and team pennants. The game had been called off. No winners that day.

A faint squawk caught his attention. He lifted his head and closed down the thoughts of his younger days. Two tiny beady eyes looked straight at him. A partridge, with one wing flapping, had a claw tangled in the wire. Joe put down his haversack and took out his wire cutters. He cradled the bird in one hand and cut a small piece from the barbed line. He put the cutters back into his pocket, stroked the top of the bird's head, and with both hands set him loose up into the sky.

An unexploded mortar bomb, sent over to blast its way through the enemy wire, clunked against his boot. They were everywhere. Scattered like apples from a swollen tree. Delinquent in their role of wire destroyers. Joe willed his heart to be still, as if the slightest noise might set off the duds. *Calm, calm,* he told himself. *Settle, settle. If they were live and dangerous they would have gone off on impact.* He wanted to kick one, taunt it, chastise it for its uselessness. Instead he glared at the uncut barbed wire. Followed its stubborn intactness as it rose ten feet or more. He scanned the length of it and gasped at the upshot of the impotent shells: hundreds of men impaled on the barely damaged wire. Uniforms ripped apart by a welcoming party of bullets. He crawled up closer and touched one on his naked chest, a handsome dark-haired corporal who lay with his arms outstretched, and flaccid, like a shirt pinned to a clothesline on a windless day. He wanted to scream, to cover the arms, the thighs, the floppy willies, and shrivelled balls. *Is it not enough to murder them? To take their lives? You have to steal their dignity? Humiliate them for all eternity?* He fell to the ground, clawing at bits of cloth, and tried to dress one's legs with the rags of a tattered uniform.

"Are you out of your fucking mind? Are you trying to get us killed?" Frank was behind him, grabbing his ankles and trying to yank him backwards.

Joe turned his head and stared at his friend.

"What the bloody fuck are you doing over 'ere?" Frank said.

Joe continued to gawk at Frank.

"We've got to go!" Frank screamed. "The shooting could start again any minute. If Jerry doesn't get you, Atholl will 'ave you and me and these two kiddies"—he pointed at Tom and John —" shot. We've disobeyed orders."

Joe finally found his voice. "Dead. All dead. Everyone."

Frank lifted Joe up. "That's right, mate. We'll leave them for the burial party. Okay? Let's make our way back."

"Sorry. Just had a … a wee moment. I'm fine now. C'mon. Get going." He stood. Tom came toward him. Joe put an arm around the lad and turned him away from the image that had burned itself inside his own head.

By four o'clock, working at top speed, they had already made three more runs back to the Dressing Station. It was faster now that the smoke had cleared, and easier to run without crouching to avoid bullets. Wounded men had indeed driven their rifles into the ground, to signal their need for help. The harmless-looking bits of metal and wood swayed slightly, like birches in a breeze, but sprouted a new hazard: the risk of a nasty whack on the shins. Guns and wounded. Guns and wounded. The words whizzed through Joe's head as he dodged this two-feet-high shrubbery of erect polished wood and metal. He wanted to be whisked away from it all. Back to the safety of home. He sneered at the problems he had back there: Kate, his da's illness and death, and his own envy of Walter's chance at school. Now only wounded and more wounded. Pain, shrieking, and death.

On their fourth run, the shells and guns screamed again. Insistent and demanding all Joe's brain space. He felt his energy escape. He wanted the din to stop. Now. He wanted the quiet of the short truce to return. He wanted to eat. He wanted a drink, preferably a strong one, but some tepid water would do. He wanted to forget about Walter, close his eyes, and open them back home. He wished it was a usual day coming off shift at the mine, soaking the day's toil away in the bath at the pithead, scrubbing himself clean so he could rub a smooth cheek up Ellen's pudgy arm all the way to the top of her head.

"Private!"

Joe followed the yelling upper-class voice. An officer was splayed out on the ground. An important one by the amount of gold thread on the wrist of his uniform.

"Stop a minute," Joe said to Frank. They laid the stretcher down and went over to the officer. Joe knelt down to do his assessment. An easy task, as the officer's right leg and the bottom half of one arm were nowhere to be seen. Blood and his worm-like intestines slithered from a foot-long, two-inch-wide gash in his lower belly. The officer let out a scream so shrill Joe wanted to scream back at him to shut the fuck up.

"I'd call 'im a three on Atholl's tree thing," Frank whispered in Joe's ear. "But tell 'im we'll come back later. That 'e's next up."

"You," the officer said, nodding his head at Frank. He wailed again and writhed in an agony Joe could not imagine. "My pistol. Take it."

"You'll be fine, sir," Frank said. "We'll be back for you. Twenty minutes tops."

The officer drew in a rattling breath and exhaled it like the shriek of a stuck pig.

Joe came over and laid a hand on the man's chest. The officer pushed it away. "No. No. My pistol. Shoot me."

"I'll give 'im two morphine tablets," Frank whispered to Joe. He got them from the officer's kit, found a water canteen fixed to his belt, and put the pills and the water to his lips. The officer spat them out at Frank.

"Do it, man. That's an order. Shoot me." He puckered his lips. "Please."

Joe knelt down beside him and took his hand. "Take the tablets. The surgeons can help you. They've been saving lives all day." He turned to Frank. "Give me all the pills he's got." He lifted the man's head, pried open his mouth, threw in the blue pills, and trickled some water on top. He clamped his hand over the man's mouth. "Like my partner said, we'll be ten minutes. Twenty at the most. I promise."

Joe nodded to Frank and they walked off to retrieve their stretcher. "Just a minute," Joe said. He walked a few yards, his hands clasped round the back of his head. Certainly, as Atholl would say, the officer was on the brink of death. Joe paced back and forth. But how long might the poor soul hover on that edge before he slipped over? Seconds? Five minutes? Hours? Joe blew out his breath in a chain of puffs. He turned and came back to Frank and pointed at the now limp patient. "Sit him up," he said.

"Why?"

"Just sit him up, then go to his side. Not in front." Joe took the pistol from the man's holster, and went round behind him.

Frank ignored the wounded officer's groans, pushed him to a sitting position from behind, then sat at his left side.

Joe knelt down, pointed the pistol, and fired it into the back of the man's head. Slick globs of brain matter and blood spewed out in all directions. Joe fell backwards, his legs shooting into the air.

"Jesus Christ!" Frank said, as he scrambled away from the body, picking chunks of tissue from his uniform.

Joe crawled over to the dead man, put the pistol back in the officer's holster, and slumped to the ground next to Frank. He could barely share his thoughts with his friend, but he had to get the words out. "Atholl would have done it if he was here. Officers are ordered to."

Frank put the water bottle to Joe's lips. "Then you did a brave and merciful thing." He wrapped his fingers around Joe's, cupping his friend's jerking hands. "Drink," he said.

It was well past nine in the evening before the sun started to dip. Joe saw Atholl walking toward him, silhouetted in the setting sun.

"Mathieson, round up all the stretcher-bearers you can. Get them to the support trenches. Search out some food and catch some kip."

Joe noticed the tremor in one of Atholl's skinny legs. Saw the lieutenant place his hands on his thighs. "During the hours of darkness I'm sending out every man I can spare on retrieval. This time your order is to cover as much ground as possible right up to the enemy wire. Report to the first aid post at midnight."

"Yes, sir. You can leave it in my hands." Joe gave Atholl a quick salute. "You come with me," he said to Tom. "We're not going back overland this time. We're going back through every trench I can find. I want you to look for this Willie Melville you was telling me about."

"Why? Who's he to you?"

"Shut up."

"Just wondering what's so special about him?"

Joe clenched his fists at his sides to stop himself from hitting Tom in the mouth. He forced his shoulders to relax. "Let's just say, I think I know this man. Now do as I ask."

"Sorry. Right you are," Tom said.

After they'd travelled the breadth of No Man's Land, they lowered themselves onto the edge of the front trench and prepared to drop the seven or so feet to the duckboards.

"Oh, my God!" Tom screamed. He stuffed his fist into his mouth. Joe looked down. The trench was solid with dead bodies. He wanted to spear them out a couple at a time, like he might pilchards or sardines from a tin can. These were the young men who had queued up innocently that day waiting to do their bit, to follow their pals out there to do something they thought heroic. Joe patted Tom's arm. "Poor buggers. Sorry, young Tom," he said, shaking out a roll of bandage and handing it to him. "Tie this around your mouth and nose. We have to go in there."

Tom and Joe jumped down and flopped onto a giving mound of flesh. Joe got to his feet, and as best he could, stood erect, straddled over the backs of the dead. He lifted one by the scruff of the neck, examined his face and let him flop back onto the pile. He threw off his haversack and clawed at more bodies. He rolled them over two at a time and threw them back down.

"Help me," Joe snarled at Tom.

"Do what?" Tom asked.

"Find that Willie Melville. Check the faces."

The more faces Joe turned over, the faster he worked. The more he floundered over the bodies, like a Saturday night drunk, the harder he breathed. What if he found Walter in that heap? Was it not better to suffer the worry and anxiety of not knowing?

A shot flew over his head. Joe fell onto a body and was as close to it as when he and the toddler Walter cozied up in the same bed. Tears pushed at the back of his eyes. An MP yanked him to his feet. Another pointed a rifle at him. His heart raced and thudded in his chest. Not these brutes again.

"Up! State your business!"

Joe tottered to his feet, straddled two dead backs to keep his balance, and put his hands up. He glanced over at Tom and watched his young friend do the same. "I'm following orders. I'm—" He stopped and pointed to Tom's armband—. "We're to be at the first aid post. For a break. Food. Orders to be out again in a couple of hours."

"Come with us then. We've got some stew at our post."

Joe shoved Tom in front of him and the four men picked their way down the trench in single file.

Sunday, July 2, 1916 12:30 a.m. "Help needed over here!"

Joe followed the voice ripping the midnight darkness. A shadow leaned over a soldier on the field.

"Tourniquet? Have you a tourniquet?"

Joe squinted at a priest outlined against a writhing soldier.

Joe wriggled his haversack off his shoulders and delved into it. He brought out his little carbide lamp, clipped it to his jacket, and did a quick check over the man's body. No blood or gouges other than the upper leg, where the man in the shadow was tying something white and stiff around the man's leg.

"I was ministering to a fellow over there," the priest said. He swung his head around and indicated a body behind him. "I thought this one was dead. Hard to tell the wounded and the dead apart in the dark. I heard him moan, saw him twitching, and came over. He's bleeding badly. I'm afraid my tourniquet won't quite do the trick, but it's all I had."

Joe looked at the leg and smiled at what he saw. He got it now, the ministering and the tourniquet.

"I'll see to it, Father. Thanks." Joe tied on a proper tourniquet and removed the priest's dog collar from the man's leg. "You just saved another soul."

They worked the brief hours of summer darkness in a shadowy pantomime. The burial parties—an army itself of spade carriers with rolled up sleeves—dug holes and heaved bodies into them. Clerks trailed behind them, collected tags, and recorded information in notebooks. The stretcher teams scurried back and forth. Often they tripped and hissed curses at a hole that twisted an ankle. There was some sniping at the wounded but mostly the night obeyed the moon's shushing dimness and slow silence.

Even the wounded sensed the need for quiet. Many Joe helped had slipped into sleep before he came upon them. He hated waking them from perhaps a delicious colourful dream back into the reality of a torn body and an anguished mind. Others had waited so long—some twelve hours or more—for attention, they had given up and passed on. Their infected wounds were rotting already, with a stink that lodged in Joe's throat. A smell so cloying and stubborn he thought he'd never be able to scrub it out. And all around them, despite the gently warm night, fear skulked, its limbs waiting to grab him. He was good at keeping going, Had always been praised at school for effort and stick-to-it-ness. Hadn't he ploughed his way through those thick medical books when others had yawned and settled for skimming? But the spectre of fear exhausted him now. He looked over some twelve yards to the enemy wire. He stood up straight, stared at it, and tried to chase the ghost of it back underground.

The voice was faint. Joe tiptoed forward towards the wire and dared himself to go right up to it. He slashed away his fear that the voice luring him might have one of those fancy new machine guns that had torn up so many bodies. A German boy, his uniform blown off, staggered on his knees with his arms outstretched. Just a boy, a naked boy, sixteen at the most. Two black holes where his eyes had been dripped yellow pus. The left side of his head was a mush of splintered bone. Joe edged towards him and sat on his haunches.

The boy said something again, and collapsed.

Joe crawled over to him and cradled him in his arms.

The boy's pale fingers traced Joe's face. "Bist du Mutter?"

Joe had no idea what he was saying, but he knew it was a question. He offered the boy one of the two German words he had learned.

"Ja."

Sunday, July 2, 1916 5:40 a.m. Joe stopped about a hundred yards forward of the first aid post. He had to get himself together before he could face the other medical personnel. He slid down the trench wall, showering himself with dirt. Sat, hugged his knees, and wished he could worm into the earth. An endless stream of walking wounded bunged up the trench on their way to the medical post. He kept himself curled tightly in his little sanctuary, fending off the fear of being swamped by the barely moving stench of pus-soaked bandages and blood. He tried to hold a lit match still enough to connect with the cigarette in his mouth, but his hand shook so badly the flame travelled too quickly down its shaft and flicked at his thumb. Three times he tried before stuffing the unlit cigarette back in the packet and putting the Vesta matches back into his pocket. He rubbed his aching thighs in an attempt to coax some life back into them. He tried to shrug out the fatigue in his back and shoulders. A headache was brewing behind his right eye, his relentless fatigue a winner in his battle to stay alert. His eyes closed against the rising sun and he let his body surrender.

"Sorry, I needed you to let go."

Joe's cheek stung and he toppled sideways then forwards, bouncing his head on the duckboard lining the trench floor.

"I didn't want to hit you."

He struggled to sit up, to avoid the plodding caravan of wounded men. He touched his face and felt blood paint his fingers. Tom Patterson knelt beside him and hauled him away from the forest of feet.

"Are you okay? Sir?" he said, and stuffed a handkerchief into Joe's hand. "You had a go at me, but I didn't mean to hurt you. It was just—"

"Just what?" Joe asked, patting a corner of the handkerchief on his left cheekbone.

"Nothing."

"What's this then?" Joe said, pointing to the blood on the cloth. "I could report you to the corporal for this. Explain yourself."

"I saw you sleeping, Thought it was a great idea. I dossed down beside you. My haversack clunked on the duckboard and your hands flew at me like bats out of hell. You had your fingers crushing my throat. Tried to strangle me you did."

"I did not," Joe said, and again examined the red splotches on his handkerchief.

Tom rubbed at his Adam's apple.

"I'm sorry," Joe said. "It was a dream."

"More like a fucking nightmare," Tom said.

"Aye, aye. A nightmare. You keep this quiet. Right?"

"You needn't worry."

"Thanks."

"And ... sir?" Tom said.

"What?"

"How could you report me to the corporal? I thought you was the corporal." Tom smiled. "Or maybe your stripes fell off. Makes no difference to me." He took Joe by the shoulders and gently pressed him back into the trench wall nook. "Go on. Catch some kip. I'll lie here beside you and do the same."

Joe nodded off for about an hour until his body twitched him awake. He rubbed his eyes, trying to erase a particularly gruesome image. A shell had ripped through the belly of one young lad he'd attended a few hours ago. Now all he could see was that gaping hole ... the man's liver sucked in on itself by the blast. In fascination, despite the horror, Joe had stared as the smooth organ bulged and pulsated and finally exploded, showering him with blood. Now he wanted to cry, but if he did he might never stop. He closed his eyes and tried to conjure up happy pictures. Ellen playing with his mother. Swimming with Marguerite's naked body next to him in the pond at Gaudechat. But even those thoughts could not quench his fear. He banged on his head to stop the gruesome images spewing as rapidly as bullets from the new-fangled machine guns. Bra-ta-ta-tat. Ma looking tired and haggard. All three sons away had taken their toll. Bra-ta-ta-ta-tat. The rent man at the door. Bra-ta-ta-ta-ta-tat. Ellen howling for her absent mother and father, her wee cheeks inflamed and puffy. Bra-ta-ta-ta-ta-tat. Kate, finished her shift at the munitions factory, sipping a sherry in a pub, too close to an Englishman with his arm in a sling. Bra-ta-ta-tat. *Cheri, cheri.* Marguerite's sweet words in his ear. Bra-ta-ta-tat. Bra-ta-ta-ta-ta-tat.

"You all right there, my friend?"

Joe raised his eyes. Frank stood over him, looking awful: his jawline shadowed by two day's whiskers, his black hair stringy and oily, his eyes bleary.

"Aye. Fine. Just tired and I can't sleep." He pointed to the sky. "Too bright. Doesn't seem to bother young Tom here. Sleeping like a baby. Light me a fag, will you?"

"What did your last servant die of?" Frank said. "Overwork?"

Joe lunged at his friend and yanked at his breast pocket. Frank grabbed him by the shoulders and squeezed until he crumpled to the ground.

"Easy, easy," Frank said, still holding Joe's shoulders. "It's okay. We're all fit to drop. I'm whacked too." He let go, took two cigarettes from his pocket, and lit them both. "Take a big drag. I'll get some porridge for us, then we're off out again. Atholl's got you as lead bearer."

"Me? Atholl? He hates my guts."

"Fucking scared like the rest of us. That's all. Someone's got to be 'is punching bag." Frank laid a light fist on Joe's upper arm.

"You up for being our fearless leader?"

"Aye, of course."

"Good," Frank said. "Sit there till I get back. Enjoy the fag."

Joe's hand shook as he stabbed the cigarette into his mouth. Frank turned his head away.

Yesterday morning, up at the front line trench, there'd been some backslapping camaraderie. Men had thrown out jokes, bolstered by being crowded together, intoxicated with both rum and adrenalin, itching in perverse excitement at finally getting at the enemy. But this morning it was glassy quiet. Soldiers sat alone or in twos or threes, talked quietly, and supped their breakfast porridge from canteens. The parapet, that sturdy edge separating the men from possible safety below ground and likely injury up and over there, held such fascination twenty-four hours ago. Now it was an ogre, a giant curtain of sandbags that, when drawn back, would usher many to their deaths. Joe and the other stretcher-bearers lined up to follow the troops when they were given the order to attack again. He lingered at the back, his body no longer primed to get over the top as it was yesterday. An intermittent tic in his left eye tested his patience. He tried rubbing it. He tried holding his eyelid taut. He tried covering his eye when no one was looking. But the eye danced to its own convulsing beat. Joe pulled his helmet forward on his head to shield the pesky eye from the sun that had now woken up the whole sky.

The platoon sergeants strutted through the porridge slurpers and announced extra tea would be available today. And bacon. A cheer went up. Joe could already smell the grease. It hit his throat and triggered his gag reflex. He rushed away from the boys and chucked up his porridge. His helmet fell off and landed in the puddle of his vomit. The tears that had queued up behind his eyes now found their way forward and soaked his cheeks. The release felt good. Thank Christ no one was looking in his direction. He pulled out a handkerchief, the same one Tom had given him to stem the blood flow from his face, wiped his mouth, then his helmet, and threw the stinking cloth away.

Back with the platoon boys, the breakfast was cleared away. The command filled the air. "Firing line, fix bayonets!" Another workday awaited them.

It clouded over quickly around one in the afternoon and the darkened sky released a violent rain that smashed the last day and a half's heat. Joe and Frank were about hundred yards from the enemy wire, about halfway across No Man's Land, when the raindrops tap-danced on their helmets. Soon the load they carried became impossible to ferry through the soaked ground, now a quagmire of mud and debris. Their patient was a young captain who'd had both feet blown off. Joe applied tourniquets around the man's upper calves. With a speedy transport to the dressing station he could be saved, which was something—one thing—to feel good about, to get him through this Sunday afternoon. Halfway up to their knees in the goo, Joe and Frank lowered the stretcher onto ground that wobbled like jelly as the weight displaced the mud.

"Always a problem to solve," Frank said. "But this one's a right pickle. Any bright ideas?"

"Nope," Joe said. He leaned over the wounded officer and made sure the tourniquets were doing their job. He suspected Frank was checking out his hands and was relieved they felt steady and competent. "We need to get him out of here quick or we'll all drown in this muck. Let me have a think."

The rain had stopped now. Joe watched the sun burn through the shrinking clouds. He lowered his helmet to shield his eyes and glimpsed a half-dozen or so enemy soldiers crawl through a hole in their wire, about fifty yards away. They stood. One waved a white flag on a pole, the others showed off white cloths with red crosses on them. Two British officers walked towards them with their pistols raised at the ready. Joe prodded Frank. "One problem solved," he said.

"What the bloody 'ell?" Frank said.

"I'm thinking it's another lull to clean up this mess. Like they did yesterday. Well, at least we needn't worry about keeping our heads on till we sort out how to get Sir here seen to."

The patient tried to sit up. "What's going on over there?"

"Short truce, sir," Joe said. "Must have heard you was hurt and needed some peace to get to the station."

"Then let's get a move on. Can you hurry?" He tugged at Joe's sleeve and whispered. "Will I live?"

"Sure as rain. Just lie back and take it easy. I'm assembling the bearers for your special carriage, sir." He nodded over to Frank and then glimpsed Tom and three others tending wounded.

"Over here," Joe yelled at Tom. "And bring your stretcher."

Tom and the others slogged over, puffing and sweating, lifting their knees through the mud, dragging their makeshift metal board through the sodden ground. Joe and Frank rolled the patient on his stretcher onto the rigid tin and lashed him and it all tightly together. Joe made six large webbing loops, pooled from their kit, and wound them lengthwise around the whole invention.

"Here," he said, and gave each man a loop. "Stand inside this so it's around your waist and we'll pull him back through this muck."

"Sea of mud, that pitch," Joe remembered his father saying after a Saturday football match when the rain lashed down. Ma too had used the expression as she scolded her boys "See you two," she'd said, cuffing his seven year-old ear as well as his eleven year-old brother Fred's head. "Trampling a sea of mud into my house." Now with Frank, Tom and John at the feet end, himself and the two others at the head of the stretcher, he grimaced as they all struggled up to their thighs in the sludge. He could feel the mud resist his thighs, and watched the liquid earth ripple as they forced their way through. The land rose and fell. Joe felt dizzy and a little nauseous. His patient whimpered as his boat rocked and rolled on the sea of mud.

Joe gave the order to lower the stretcher to hip level. He shoved his gas mask in its bag from his front to his left hip and lowered his hold on the stretcher to his right. Focus. Focus on this. Stem the wooziness.

"Good work, boys. Don't lift your legs. Wee steps. Wee pushes against the mud. Slow and steady."

By the time they delivered the patient to the dressing station the truce was over. The same old *whomp* and *skoosh* of the guns soaked the air, the same *ping ting* of bullets on helmets, the same screams as men were hit. The same cold breath of fear.

Darkness was closing in as Joe and Frank made yet another two-hour slog back to the dressing station. This time they passed a couple hundred men commandeered as burial parties for their friends who had not survived the past two days. These temporary undertakers had donned the mouth and nose-pieces from their gas masks to numb the stench as the corpses rotted, like sewage in an open ditch, in the still rising heat. Joe gagged many times at the stink of spilled shit and held his breath against the foul gases wafting from abdominal wounds. And since the word was already out that the soil could infect the bearers as well as the injured in minutes, some gravediggers had emptied sandbags and tied them on as mittens.

Joe sat outside the stretcher-bearer's post under a stringy overhang that had once been a dense hedgerow. Hunger chewed his stomach. Thirst scraped his throat. He was fed up now. The pain, the blood shooting like geysers from limbs and necks, the desperate agonies of the dying, and the ghoulish sight of the butchered. He was bored too, hearing his own voice echoing lies to hide impossible recoveries. You'll be right as rain. Shut your wheesht now, you won't die; don't be daft. It's just a scrape. Lucky you, you've copped one that'll send you back to Blighty. He'd even run out of chat with Frank. His friend knew the real conversation. Wh*at's the point of wasting a bandage? There's no* *way it can hold your head together. What a stench. You're going to be in the worst blarsted pain. Pain you can't even imagine. Will your girl still want you with no arms, no legs, no dick? You'd be better off dead.*

All Joe could think of was just getting through it. He knew it had to be the same for Frank. He didn't envy the surgeons—even Atholl, the puny little toad—the job of rooting inside these stinking, mangled bodies.

It was impossible to get time to sleep. Any opportunity he did have, he couldn't relax enough to get any rest, was scared now to even close his eyes and expose himself to the magic lantern show replaying all he'd seen during his waking hours. Those episodes when he'd gone for Tom and rushed at Frank worried him. It worried him even more that Tom might say something to his pals. Throughout the day he'd felt Frank watching him. Watching for signs. He didn't shake when he was at work, so that was good. The busyness and the constant vigilance for Walter were steadying.

He took the cork stopper from his water bottle and threw back a slug, tried to empty his mind. A thought filled the tiny space he managed to clear. What was the war about? What was so big that men were sent to die? *I'm beginning to sound like Fred,* he thought, as he took another swallow of water. *Maybe I should have listened to him.* His older brother seemed to be in the know and convinced enough of the importance of it all to go and volunteer. What *were* they fighting over? What great changes would come to him back in Methilane? To the men down the pits? To their wives who struggled to support house and home and keep their bairns fed and healthy? What could be better for those dead boys' mothers and fathers? They were doomed now to a life of grieving. Their sons had sacrificed themselves to spoil their folks' lives? Madness. And what was in it for all those newly minted young widows? All those bright-eyed lassies? Never to produce their husbands' children. Never to enjoy unborn generations of grandchildren.

"Where's Gellatley?" Atholl's bellow hurt Joe's ears. Despite what Frank had said about Atholl being affected like them, Joe was getting sick of the way this young snob ordered him around.

"Frank?"

"If that's Gellatley, then yes. Where has he skived off to?"

"At the latrine. Sir."

"Can you boys drive a motor? I need two bearers to load up an ambulance and drive over to the casualty clearing station at Bercordie."

"Learned in my job back home."

"Excellent. You and Gellatley collect the wounded for transport from the dressing station. Get some sleep while you're at the ccs. Be back no later than noon tomorrow."

Joe couldn't believe this turn in his luck. It would take them less than an hour each way. His tiredness fled like a greyhound out of the starting gate.

"Noon?"

"Yes. You know, twelve o'clock? You have a problem with that?" Atholl asked and moved off.

"No, no. It's great is what I mean. Thank you, sir," Joe called after him.

Atholl turned around. "I do have a heart, Mathieson."

Joe ran over to the latrines and banged on the wooden wall.

"What the 'ell?" Frank said as he came out, buttoning up his trousers.

Joe grabbed Frank and pushed him ahead toward the dressing station. He told him about their assignment and his hope of getting to Gaudechat. He tugged at Frank's sleeve. "Are you with me? We'll get to bed early, get a good night's sleep, up by six, over to the château in the ambulance, and still be back here by noon."

Frank stopped and turned to face his partner. "Listen, my friend. You've already 'ad one run-in with the MPs. Don't push your luck. You're no good to your fancy lady bruised and beaten. Or dead."

"Frank, I can't be that close to her and not try."

"Tell you what. Me and you go to the ccs, chat up a few nurses, get some sleep, and take it from there. Maybe ... and just maybe, you wanker, we could get over there in the morning. Now get your chauffeur's cap on and drive me out for a jaunt in the country."

"You're a joker. I can't drive. You'll have to. I reckoned it was worth a wee fib to Atholl."

"Sometimes I think you've got an 'orseshoe up your arse."

Marguerite. Marguerite. Her name danced through Joe's head. It was too tantalizing not to think of her. He'd be crushed if he didn't get to

Gaudechat. He wanted to share stories about her, but his friend at the wheel was too tired to listen. Frank ground the gears and steered the unfamiliar motor forward. In the silence, Joe moved his mind again to Fred's rantings. What was it he was always on about? Freedom for the working classes, a new social order? How was that supposed to come from all this slaughter? What did it mean anyways? A new social order? Anger rose up in him like vomit rushing into his mouth. Why hadn't the powers-that-be bothered to tell him what they were all here for? He looked over at Frank, who pursed his lips as he concentrated on manoeuvring the ambulance. Did Frank feel like him? That this was all a fucking frightening mystery? Did Frank or the others feel any more a part of this fracas than he did? He just couldn't see any good in this pile of shite.

There was his training. He'd learned a lot for sure, all the medical stuff. He was good at it, a quick learner. He knew how to clean and fire a rifle, though as a stretcher-bearer he never carried one and would never fire one. He'd learned to march, to obey orders, to look up to his officers, and hadn't he been a good leader to the younger boys like Tom? He'd even learned some French. Who would have thought that would ever happen? His thoughts dashed back to Marguerite. There he was again. Thinking of her and the wonderful feelings she aroused in him. How could that not be good?

Sunday, July 2, 1916 11:05 p.m. Joe hesitated at the entrance to the only building at the casualty clearing station. If Walter fought yesterday in this area and was wounded, he could well have ended up here at Bercordie. A current of fright skipped through him. He couldn't register this was the same ccs where only a month ago he'd come upon its renovation—a sight that had unhinged him then—and warned of the casualties he'd dealt with the past forty hours. He fiddled with the collar of his jacket before putting his hand against the door. He urged spit to wet his mouth. He stepped over the threshold, walked down a short corridor, hesitated again when he came to one of the wards. He was glad to be alone. Easier for him to drum up courage in his hunt for Walter among these gravely wounded men. Frank had taken off in search of friendly off-duty nurses as soon as they delivered the patients half-an hour ago. But Joe needed to be by himself to calm the nerves pricking at his stomach. Neither his mind nor body would shut down after the chaos and frenzy of the last two days, although he was sorely in need of some kip.

He pushed open the ward door, almost whacking an orderly on his way out. The sharp smell of carbolic fought a losing battle against the stench of unwashed wounds and stung the inside of his nose. Red-stained bandages dazzled against the white of the nurses' aprons and the sheets. Joe soft-footed down the ward's length to get a good look at the dirty and bloodied faces. He nodded to nurses as they went about their work, dodged wheeled trolleys heaped with basins, clean dressings, rubber tubes, and urine bottles. He went up close to men who were lying flat on their backs, many with a leg or an arm held up with metal contraptions. Offered apologies and smiles. No Walter. He examined the features of men sipping from cups with spouts, like little teapots. No Walter. Relief washed through him but his ribs remained tight. Still three wards to check.

No freckle-faced young brother suffering in ward two either. Or three. Dread pounded in his chest as he walked slowly into the fourth. He scanned the room from the doorway. No one he recognized but the battle's damage and the bandaging made it tricky even for a mother to pick out her own boy. He slip-stepped up the first of the three rows of beds. Shook his head. Halfway down the second row, perfectly lined up down the middle of the ward, a lad hurled his last meal. Two beds farther down he recognized a youngster he'd delivered to the dressing station and handed over to Captain Rogers and his whisky breath. Now the last row. He forced his feet to approach each bed. His eyes took in details: hair, fair and dark, sticking out from dressings. Bodies, tall and short, fat and thin, lay scrunched or stretched on tidy cots. Like a cat searching for prey, Joe kept his eyes on high alert. No familiar face. No Walter. Just sixty or so unlucky buggers riding different levels of pain. He blinked against the sweat that dripped into his eyes, and wiped his face with his sleeve. Next came the old sting of anxiety *not knowing* where Walter was. And still the eight or nine massive tents in the field behind the building…

He peeked into the sluice room near the exit. The posh nurse with the straight black hair he'd worked with on one of his train runs, leaned against the sink. Her hand hovered over the tap. "Hiya, Nurse…" He couldn't quite recall her name. Adelaide something. She hunched over the sink, not moving. The tap ran at full blast. A large older woman pushed in front him. He quickly moved back, didn't want to come in contact with her formidable breasts.

"What's taking you so long, Nurse Armitage?" she said. "And that water is precious. Who are you?" she barked at Joe as she turned off the tap.

He stood up straight. "Mathi…"

But the sister had already marched out of the room.

Adelaide jerked upright and turned to him. "Hmm?" She rubbed her eyes. "Yes?" She rubbed her temples and stared at him. "Good God. Joe, isn't it? Sorry. I didn't recognize you at first. My brain needs a minute to switch back on." She gripped the edge of the sluice sink again. "I think I nodded off." She turned back to the sink and worked at a clutter of bedpans and urine bottles.

"Who's the old bat? Didn't even give me a chance to answer," Joe said.

Adelaide laughed. "Sister's okay. Likes to keep us on our toes. Sorry about the haze. Lack of sleep. But I suppose you know all about that. Right now my mind is a kaleidoscope shuttling pieces to form something I can recognize. It's lovely to see you again." She clutched the edge of the sink more tightly. "What day is it? Sunday? Yes, Sunday evening. I can't remember when I last slept in a bed. We worked through the night, sorted through what seems like an uncountable number of wounded men." She stood taller and tugged at her veil. "Sorry. I'm rambling. And all about me. I am rude. How are you? It is so much worse for the men. I feel embarrassed now about complaining. Can I get you something?"

"No, no. I'm fine. It's okay," Joe said. "Take a breath." He took her arm and steered her to a chair pushed under a small table. "Sit for a minute."

"No," she said. "I have to get this job done. You sit. Hard to take in, isn't it? All this."

Joe pulled the chair away from the table, glad to sit and still the wobble in his legs. "I came to see if my wee brother I told you about had ended up here."

She spun around. "Gosh. Is he?"

"No sign of him," he said. He'd spent enough energy on Walter for now. The stroll down that ward had been gut-twisting. "What time did the first ambulances get here?"

"Around one this morning. I saw such agony on those hospital trains and frightful wounds. Remember? But until last night, I'd never seen such…" She put her hands over her eyes. "Such … such … destruction of human flesh. And the numbers." She pursed her lips. "I can't get over how amazing these men are, how little they complain."

"They're too tired and shocked," Joe said. "Or maybe ashamed they feel relief away from the firing line."

She turned away from the sink, her hands red from the hot water. "Barely a moan as we worked." She flexed her fingers. "Spooky. One or another would ask quietly for a cigarette. Politely. Always the first request: 'Can I have a smoke?'"

Sister came into the sluice room again with a sheet of paper in her hand. She glowered at Joe. "Why are you still here and just who are you?"

"With respect, Sister," Adelaide said, smiling at Joe. "He is an assistant chief stretcher-bearer from the front and has come all this way to check on some seriously injured men he carried from the battlefield."

"Ah, Nurse Armitage. I trust you do not jest." She rested her folded arms on her bosom and looked at Joe over the steel rims of her spectacles. "Well far be it from me to chastise one of our heroes. Nurse, I have devised a new roster for tonight. I am putting you on the moribund ward from ..." She ran her finger down the clipboard. "From two a.m. until eight. Report to Nurse Jeffreys. She's in charge."

"But I was down for sleep tonight."

"Are you complaining?"

Adelaide lowered her head. "No Sister. I am not."

"We volunteered for this. To do our duty to these poor wretches and to our country. I'm sure your friend here would not question an order." Sister lifted Adelaide's chin. Her steely grey eyes softened for a moment. "I know. I know, my dear. We're all worn out."

"Thank you, Sister. Of course I will do whatever is asked of me. Which tent is Nurse Jeffreys' ward, please?"

"The one farthest back from the railway line. Stands a bit off from the others."

"I'll just finish up here and be on my way, Sister." Adelaide turned the tap on again and resumed cleaning the bedpans.

Joe raised his voice over the din and moved closer to her. He coughed against the smell of the disinfectant. "What's this place you're off to?"

Adelaide shrugged. "Not sure. Come with me if you like."

The wee hours of the morning closed in, but the dirt and sparse grass beneath Joe's bare feet were still warm from the heat of the past few days. Adelaide, too, took off her shoes —stout black lace-ups—and sat on the hillock next to him. She rubbed her feet and wiggled her toes, took in a huge breath of the warm night air. "I am so thankful to be free from ether and chloroform. And suppuration. Makes me gag." She stretched out on her back and closed her eyes.

"If I did that, I'd fall asleep," Joe said. "In an instant."

"I'm trying to remember what it's like to be in a bed with cool white linens. I can no longer summon up my old world, where a whole night's sleep is a given, not a tantalizing luxury. On summer nights at home I loved to be in bed and listen to the owls hoot in the trees."

"Sounds nice," Joe said, "this place you come from. Nicer than what we have here. We must be a good six or seven miles from the front and still the guns rip at my ears." He lay on his back beside her and thought of the larks he'd heard the other day.

Adelaide sat up, checked her watch and shoved her feet into her shoes. "Quarter after one," she said and stood. "I should go. Are you coming with me or will you lie here for a while?" She bent and tied up her shoelaces. "Joe?"

"Hmm?" Joe sat up. "See I told you I would fall asleep. Drifted off. Just like that."

"I was saying I should go."

"Wait," he said and stood beside her. "Your husband? Any news?" Surely she no longer harboured any hope he'd be found alive.

"No. Nothing. And I've not had time to think about it."

"Maybe it would help?"

"Help what?" she snapped.

He put out his hand towards her, but she turned her back to him and moved off. "I just meant, you know, see him in your mind. Sorry. I'm being nosey," Joe said when he caught up to her.

She hung her head. "I'm the one to apologize. For my rudeness." She lifted her eyes to him and hugged herself. "I promise myself every morning," she said, "that one day, when I get decent time off, I'll go for a long walk. Be alone, away from all this. And I'll think only of him."

Joe touched her elbow. She pulled away. "I'm afraid I've reneged many times on that promise." She strode away with Joe hurrying to keep up with her. He took the hint that no more talk on the subject of her husband would be welcome and kept quiet the rest of the walk to the moribund tent. He wanted to ask her what *moribund* meant, but was embarrassed at his ignorance. Whatever the meaning, it was one of the tents he still had to search. The silence and darkness put him on edge. He glanced at the sky from time to time and enjoyed the stars, the dancing pulses keeping him awake. A distraction, too, from the gruesome thought he might find Walter in that tent, or one of the others ahead.

Adelaide pushed back the tent flap and Joe followed her into a vestibule where a desk sat empty, save for a large ledger, a hand bell, and a lit candle under a glass cover. She rang the bell. Joe opened the book and flipped through the first few pages as Adelaide looked over his shoulder. Names in one column, ages in another, and regiments in a third.

"Hello there." A blonde-haired nurse, wiping her hands on a linen towel, came from inside the tent. "You must be the heaven-sent Nurse Armitage. Ah, my book," she said and took the ledger from Joe and stuck it under her arm. "Couldn't remember where I'd put it. Lose my head if it weren't screwed on." She extended her hand. "Phillipa Jeffreys. And who's the handsome man with you? My, my, such blue eyes."

"Private Joe Mathieson, ma'am. Stretcher-bearer."

"Ah, another of the famed silly buggers. Must be my lucky night. You're the second good-looking man to come visiting." Her huge brown eyes shone as she giggled. She put her fingers up to her mouth and whistled into the tent.

Joe laughed as Frank came into the vestibule, mussed up and ruffled. Joe smacked him on the shoulder. "You little toe rag." He envied Frank, moving from moment to moment apparently not overly affected by whatever had already passed. Only a few hours since they'd shared the same terrible workday and now his pal was chasing some skirt.

"Actually we should be quiet," Nurse Jeffreys said, and put her index finger to her lips. She now spoke in a whisper to Adelaide. "This dark good-looking one is Frank. I was entertaining him to tea. Frank served under my brother before the war with the Buckinghams." Frank's eyes were firmly set on Nurse Jeffreys as Adelaide offered her hand to him.

"Pleased to meet you. Again." Adelaide said. "We met on the trains. Last year. I remember it so well. My first posting and your friend here," she nodded at Joe, "was so patient with me. It's a pleasure to see you again."

"I remember you too," Frank said. "You impressed my mate 'ere." He kept hold of her hand. "What's this you've got 'ere?" he said, and pointed to the underside of her middle finger.

"Probably nothing. Just a scratch."

"It's too red and swollen for my liking. You want to keep an eye on that. You might 'ave picked up an infection from one of the lads."

Joe and Nurse Jeffreys laughed and Adelaide blushed. "What he means is…" said Joe, and paused, searching for the words.

"Go on Joe," Frank said and stood back, his short muscled legs astride. He crossed his arms. "Tell us what I mean." Then he whispered something in Nurse Jeffrey's ear. She nodded. "All right boys. That's the fun over for a while. Off with you!" She turned to Adelaide. "We're hatching a little plot," she said, and tapped the side of her nose. "I'm sure these men need a bed for the night."

"That's right," Frank said, and rested one hand on Phillipa's hip. The other stifled a faked yawn. "I'm exhausted."

She gripped each man at the shoulder and propelled them into the tent. "Let's get the lady a bandage. What's your first name? I'm Phillipa. Did I say that already?"

"Adelaide. Adelaide Armitage."

"Any relation to Robert Armitage from the Ox and Bucks? Met a fellow by that name. At a dance before the war. Through my brother."

Adelaide brought her hand to her mouth, then gripped the edge of the table. Her shoulders quivered. A soft keening flowed from her. Phillipa gave Joe a questioning look. He put his index finger to his lips, then silently drew it across his throat.

Phillipa lowered Adelaide into a chair and put her arms around her shoulders. "Brother?"

"My husband."

"I am sorry. So sorry. When?"

"Last October." Adelaide reached for the handkerchief in her pocket. "No. I am sorry. He's reported missing, you see. I didn't mean to let go like that."

Joe felt an urge to comfort her, to hold her. Grey lines of fatigue and worry had scored her skin. He'd seen hundreds, maybe thousands, of dead soldiers, but in Adelaide he saw for the first time the anguished face of a mourning wife. He clenched his hands into fists. Adelaide's husband is missing. He could turn up ... and cows might fly.

"I'm just done. From the workload. Same as us all." She dabbed at her eyes and blew her nose. "I'm fine. Show me the ropes."

"First we see to your finger. Don't want you coming in contact with the men's wounds if you have an open cut." Phillipa steered Adelaide through the curtain into the ward.

"I'm going to have a turn around the beds," said Joe.

"No, no. Where are your manners?" she spouted in her clipped upper-class accent. "We'll see to Adelaide first. Follow me." She laughed and strode off with the confidence of the privileged set.

Joe bristled at her superior air, and her poise, so unlike the women he was used to.

Adelaide sat at the nurse's table and held up her hand. "You boys may be right." She'd pulled herself together and smiled at Joe and Frank. "I've probably picked up an infection from a septic wound."

"First some iodine," Phillipa said. "Stinging?" She then wound a narrow bandage over Adelaide's finger. "Keep it covered." She fastened the ends. "That should do it. Seems clean enough but you jolly well keep an eye on it."

Joe looked over to Frank, and behind Phillipa's back, flicked at the underside of his nose and snickered. Frank pushed him ahead to follow Phillipa to a cupboard at the left of the entrance flap. She lifted a ring of keys from her waist, unlocked a small door at shoulder height, removed four small cardboard boxes, and handed them to Adelaide. The morphine ampoules inside nattered as Adelaide set them on the table.

"I hate that noise," Phillipa said. "Reminds me of last breaths. But they should see our men through the night. All of you grab some needles from the third shelf and we can start our rounds."

"Whatever you say, ma'am," Joe said. He let Phillipa's slit-eyed look slide off him.

"We'll do the first *together*," Phillipa continued. "That's you too, Mr. Mathieson. I'll teach you the drill then we'll take turns. That way we'll each get a little shuteye. No one's going to come in and check up on us. We're hardly dealing with acute injuries."

Frank elbowed Joe. "Do what you're told."

Joe drew his lips into a tight line. He was itching to check for Walter, didn't need to be lectured, nor be giving injections.

"Keep your 'air on," Frank said, under his breath.

Four rows of ten beds filled the tent, with only a handful empty. Whispery breathing wrinkled the air. No snoring, no calling out for a bedpan, a cigarette, or relief from pain. Only the almost soothing rise and fall of air drawn in and let out. No tubes, no cages to ease the weight of bed-covers off shattered legs, no slings to support broken bones, no rustles of stiff, starched nurses' aprons as they moved through the ward. Joe sniffed. It smelled the same as the main wards. The rancid throat-catching odour of flesh gone bad. He shivered and looked at Phillipa.

"Are you afraid?" Phillipa said.

"Afraid?" he said. "Of what?"

"These men. Triaged a three from the main wards."

"They're ... done?"

"Well, yes. Why do you think it's called the moribund ward? They're as good as dead."

Joe wanted to slap away her sneer.

"We don't want them to take up space and effort in the main areas," she went on. Her voice chafed at his tired brain. "If the doc says there is no chance of survival, we send them here. Keep them clean, comfortable, and sedated. None of them stay long."

His annoyance faded as panic surged through him. He fought off the desire to race among the beds, to search for Walter. 'Done,' he'd said to the nurse. Done. *Please God. Don't let Walter be done.*

Phillipa's high-pitched posh voice wrenched Joe out of his thoughts. She spoke directly to Adelaide. "Sedation. We spare no morphine here. And a little extra never hurts, does it? Give the injections, chart the time. No need to write in the amount. If one dies, record the time." She tapped the ledger that Joe had skimmed in the vestibule. "In here. We're required to keep track. Some nurses sit with them if they're not busy, but if you find that too uncomfortable, no one will hold it against you. For myself, I'd rather get my beauty sleep. Questions?" She turned away from them.

"I do," Joe called to her back. "I have a question. Have you a lad here by the name of Walter? Walter Mathieson. Or Willie Melville? William Melville, I suppose."

She swivelled to face him. "Please lower your voice. But the answer is no. To both names."

She walked away and led the march down the ward. Frank snickered when Joe stuck out his tongue behind her back.

They worked their way up and down the rows. They took pulses, dripped water into mouths, swabbed lips with glycerin, gave injections, and charted their work. Joe relaxed each time he saw an unfamiliar face resting on a pillow. He counted the beds: thirty-six occupied, three empty, and a portable screen pulled around one other. They didn't go behind the screen and he didn't ask why. He didn't want to have any conversation if he could help it with that Phillipa nurse and her grating voice. He would have a peep when he did his solo round.

Phillipa checked the fob watch on her apron. "That took just over forty minutes. Let's have some tea and biscuits. Mummy sends them in her parcels. Makes sure I always have a supply."

A few minutes later, when they were all seated around her table, she raised her mug. "Cheers." She reached for a ginger snap. "I always feel a bit guilty eating here, but at the same time relieved we have so little to do. No meals to serve and clear away or wounds to dress. Quite a cushy assignment really if you can ignore why we're here." She opened a drawer in the table and took out some knitting. "Socks, socks, and more socks," she said. She wound the wool around her pinkie and forefinger.

The knitting pins clacked over Joe's brain like nails dragged over slate. He could no longer contain his scorn. He jumped up and stared at her. "I'm going for a smoke."

Frank wheeled his head from Phillipa to Joe. He spotted the irritation around his friend's mouth. "Me too," he said and followed Joe outside.

"That bloody woman's driving me insane," Joe said, and took his squished pack from his breast pocket. He put two cigarettes in his mouth, lit them both with a single inhalation, and handed one to Frank. "Tea and Mummy's biscuits and bloody socks. Who gives a shit?" He drew hungrily on his cigarette. "I just want to double check Walter's not anywhere here at Bercordie, then put my head down for a few hours. I should do that first and take an early turn around this ward, but I'll fall over if I don't have at least a few winks." He slapped Frank's back. "Then we're off to see Marguerite."

"Take it easy, mate," Frank said. "You don't need to take a turn first off. I'll tell 'er you'll do the 4:00 a.m. Just get yourself to an empty bed and sleep." He put his cigarette in the corner of his mouth. "I'm going back in." He walked back to the tent flap and turned. "I'll tell 'er to wake you." He pointed his finger at Joe. "And you be nice to 'er when she does."

Cigarette finished, Joe crept two-thirds down the right outside row of beds until he came to an empty one, stiffly made but inviting nevertheless. He shuddered, realizing he was about to sleep among the almost dead. His chest tingled. He thought he could feel the air shimmer with a curious energy, felt he could reach out and play with the dancing vibrations as he stepped through the candlelit space. Yesterday these men, young men, were alive. Like him, they had a life. Any moment, tonight or tomorrow, they'd be no more. He slipped off his jacket and boots and lay down. The mattress curved around his weary body. Almost as good as Marguerite's arms.

A soft moan came from the bed on his left. Joe swung his legs to the floor and knelt by the soldier's bed. Sour bile rose into his throat. The right side of the sandy-haired youth's face was gone; a sweeping arc of blackened skin outlined what had been his eye, his ear, and his cheek. A superbly cleaned-up wound so Joe could see right into the boy's pulsating brain. The skin on his arms, outstretched on the counterpane, was so smooth he could have been twelve years old. He lay so quietly Joe thought he might have passed away. He placed two fingers across the downy stubble on the boy's intact upper lip and felt a weak puff of air from his nostrils. He stroked an arm. The patient stirred, his one eye flickered, and he grabbed Joe's hand. Joe pulled away, but he remembered Captain Rogers' words during his training at Gaudechat. *Do not pull away or flinch; look straight into their faces and smile. Things are bad enough for them without you showing horror and fear.* Joe took the boy's hand, held it in his, and stroked the smooth knuckles. The young soldier let out a raspy breath and was gone. Joe wondered whether he should tell Phillipa but found the opportunity to lie down for more than an hour too enticing. He closed the dead man's eye and put his arms inside the sheet.

He walked up and down the rows of beds. Long, long rows that stretched off into a hazy distance. He stopped at one and drew the white sheet back from the covered face. A congealed mess oozed over the bottom sheet and he recoiled at the sight of his brother's face. He staggered to the next bed and did the same, and the next, and the next. Each time he drew back the white top sheet, his brother's face became a sludge pool, seeping and sliming over the bed. Then he came to a bed with blue sheets that glowed and shimmered like a mirage. He pulled back its cover and there was Walter. Reaching out his arms to embrace him.

Joe bolted upright, waving his arms to fight off the dream. He grabbed the pillow. Bit into it to stifle the sobs that pulled at his throat. He wiped his face dry with the sheet, stumbled out of bed, picked up his jacket from the floor, and checked the time. Twenty to four. Thank goodness he had woken before anyone could catch him in this pathetic state again. He stepped into his boots and laced them up.

A light snore crinkled through the still atmosphere. He put on his jacket while tiptoeing up the ward toward the sound. He traced it to a bed that had been empty when Phillipa did her orientation. Adelaide was fast asleep on her back, with her arms over her head like an infant. He gave her a gentle nudge. She stopped snoring but did not waken, only rolled onto her side and folded her hands under her cheek as if in prayer. But someone else snored in this quiet place. Again he tiptoed to the source: the screened bed. He looked through the space where the screen was hinged. He gulped down a deep breath. What if that dream was preparing him for this?

He pulled back the fabric to get a clearer view of the snorer. Phillipa. Curled up fast asleep with Frank spooned into her back. His arm circled her slim waist. Joe stood like a statue, dumbfounded. Frank and ... *her?* He watched Frank twitch, saw him slide his fingers up the nurse's ribs and cup her breast. His hands tingled as they remembered Marguerite's firm breasts, and how her nipples hardened to his kisses on the grassy bank by the pond. Phillipa's snores softened. She sighed and reached for Frank's hand. His own cock stiffened. He looked about, embarrassed at his envy, his excitement. Angry, too, that while Frank wantonly felt up a stranger, he had to wait until this night was over for the slight chance he could lie with Marguerite.

He'd start a 4:00 a.m. round, distract himself, calm the craving in his body, and the ache in his balls. Then he remembered Phillipa would be waking him. If he stayed here, Phillipa might guess she'd been seen. Joe bent over and took off his boots again and tiptoed down the ward to the bed where he'd slept. His socks slipped just as he got there and he banged his ankle on one of the bed's iron legs. He stuck his fist into his mouth to stifle the scream that wanted to come. With the other hand, he tried to grasp his leg, but it threw him off balance and he ended up on the floor. That same bloody ankle he'd injured down the mine. Joe rubbed at the throbbing bone. He would not let the pain be the gateway for more tears. He sat there with his eyes closed for about ten minutes, rubbing his ankle and cursing under his breath. He cooled his head against the cold of the iron bed, and took deep lungfuls of air.

"I see you're up already. Or rather I should say down."

Joe looked up at Phillipa's shoes and black stockinged ankles. "Tripped in the dark."

"Did you get some sleep?"

"Aye. I'll get my boots on and be ready to go. Do you want the bed? I can smooth it out for you. I didn't go under the sheet."

"Relax, Joe," Phillipa flashed back. "No one's in a rush here. None of these poor sods are going anywhere." She straightened her belt buckle. "I've got a bed going, the one behind the screen. Can't wait to hit the hay again. Any chance you could work right through? I've been on my own for three days. Only been able to snatch a couple of hours here and there. I'm bagged."

He fixed his eyes on hers, wanting her to know he knew. "Of course. I'll handle it. I had a good sound couple of hours. You get some proper rest."

"Good then. I'll see you at around seven-thirty for your report. Breakfast's around eight. Need some help with those boots?"

"Thanks but I think I can manage." Joe stood and forced his swelling ankle into the shoe. She hurried back up the ward, back to her little secret.

"Oh, ma'am," Joe called softly after her. "A boy died." But Phillipa had already disappeared. He returned to the dead soldier and lifted the sheet over his still face. He did his round, moving silently from bed to bed. Thoughts of Walter slipped into the slits of his fatigue. He kept them at bay by focusing on the patients drifting over to death.

He checked his watch. Half an hour before the 6:00 a.m. round. A cup of tea would keep him alert, ready to check the remaining tents for Walter before setting off with Frank for Gaudechat. If Walter was here, but not in the moribund ward, someone had already decided he wasn't going to die. He settled at the table and opened the drawer to look for a spoon. The ledger Phillipa had rescued from him and Adelaide in the vestibule lay underneath a nest of yarn. He lifted the book and ran his fingers down the lists on the first few pages, hoping to see someone had survived this ward. But beside each and every one was a pencilled cross. He should mark a cross against the name of the boy who died. He gathered up the ledger and a pencil and walked down the ward to the boy's bed. Picking up his chart, Joe wished the lad's mother could know that when the end came, her son had passed away peacefully. He wrote the soldier's name, Stephen Miller, and put a little cross beside it. He added *July 3, 1916. 6.a.m.*

"Someone died?"

He jerked around to the voice behind him.

"Sorry. I didn't mean to give you a fright," Adelaide said.

"I thought you were sleeping. I saw you earlier." He put his fingers to his lips. "And that's not all I saw."

"What do you mean?" she said.

He nodded towards the screened bed. "Frank." He lowered his voice. "Sharing a bunk with Nurse Phillipa."

She shook her head at him. "I don't want to make that my business."

Joe shrugged and held up the book. "I did make a new entry," he said. He handed the ledger to her and they walked up the ward. "If you make me a fresh cup of tea," he said, "I'll tell you all about you know what."

Her frenzied and exhausted look of a few hours ago was now the kind intelligent face he remembered from their time of the trains. "I'm sure it's very romantic, but I have to do my round," she said, pushing past him.

"Hardly a love story, I'd say. But better than the story we're in." He looked down the ward. "Uncanny this place. But right, you're busy." Joe smiled and shooed her away. "I'll make my own tea."

He'd give Frank another hour, and then shake him out of that bed, cuddly nurse or not. Still time for the side trip to Gaudechat and to get back before reporting at noon to Atholl at the dressing station. His anxiety over his fit of temper earlier that day had faded, the worry over his outbursts against Tom and Frank gone. Exhaustion and no sleep had caused it. Nothing more serious. He leaned back in the chair, put his feet up on the table, and sipped his tea. Amazing what even a few hours of kip in a real bed could do. He picked up the ledger and turned the pages, licked his forefinger and dragged it down the columns. *Please, please. No Walter Mathieson.*

"Any tea left in the pot?" Adelaide's soft voice cut short his reading. "Were you looking for a specific name?"

Joe's felt his heartbeat speed up. "I was. I … Can I talk to you?" His hands sweated. "My brother." His shoulders tensed.

"Of course. Come. Sit next to me. I've got some time before I have to wake Nurse Jeffreys." She smiled. "And your friend. I can listen."

He poured two cups of tea, and in low whispers, told her about his search for his young brother, his frustration, and how he'd been unable to find any trace of him until recently, and then only that he *might* be with the 16th Battalion, under the name Willie Melville.

She listened, saying barely a word except to dig out a physical description: tall for a sixteen-year-old at five foot ten, sandy hair, and blue eyes. "A younger version of you," she said. Occasionally she nodded, touched his arm, or asked a question.

"Hobbies?"

"How would that help find him?" Joe said.

"Might have volunteered for or managed to steer himself to something he enjoyed."

"Like?"

"Oh, I don't know, Joe. If he likes horses—"

"Books. He read a lot of books."

"Not sure we have a library division. So somewhat introverted, would you say? Has a … a quieter face?"

"He's not a fairy, if that's what you're saying. He likes lassies. A lot."

Adelaide patted the back of his hand and smiled at him. "So we're to look out for a tall, handsome, somewhat serious young man." Her smile faded and her eyes glistened. "Not unlike my Robert." Her face relaxed again. "Like every mother's darling boy." She stood and picked up the ledger. "I know it's hard, but I think you should finish checking."

Joe felt his toes curl and dig into the soles of his boots. "I'd better go." He reddened at his croaking voice. "Should see to the motor ambulance afore I get Frank up. Thanks for your ear."

She touched his elbow. "Would you like me to look through the book? Before you go? I'm sorry I have forgotten your family's last name."

"He was using the name Melville. Our name's Mathieson," he said, sat down again, and squeezed his hands between his knees.

"Right. Yes. I remember now. I'll check them both."

They sat with their heads together as she turned the last few pages and ran a finger slowly down the lines. "Oh," she said. Her hand stilled over a line. "Oh, Joe. I am so sorry."

"What? What is it?" He jumped from his seat. "It can't be. I was checking afore you had your tea. And there's no one in the beds. It can't be." He dropped back onto the chair. "You've found Walter?"

Adelaide found the entry then gasped. "Oh, my God. I am mistaken. I wish I hadn't alarmed you."

Joe looked at where she marked the place. *July 1, 1916. Mathieson, Frederick John Pte. S/20130 Royal Scots.* He clutched the back of the chair. How could he not have worried about Fred? Fred. His strong and feisty older brother. The one who always won a fight. Shame coursed through Joe, burning the inside of his head with regret. What a bloody selfish man he was. He'd never given much, if any, thought to Fred's safety. Ever. Not even these past two years since Fred stomped off to volunteer. His big brother was a tough man. Indestructible. Adelaide put an arm around his back.

"You two look cozy." Frank emerged from behind the screened-off bed, buttoning up his trousers.

Adelaide put up her hand to silence him and he looked over to Joe.

"What's up?" Frank said, putting his arms in his jacket and hoisting it over his shoulders.

Joe stood. Kicked the table leg. He heard Adelaide say something to his friend, as he pushed aside the flap and raced from the tent. "Oh, my God, no!" Frank cried. "Joe! Wait up!" He yanked Joe's arm just as he jumped into a motor ambulance. Frank hauled him out the driver's side door, dragged him around to the passenger side, and shoved him into the seat.

"Okay, fine! You drive this fucking thing!" Joe screamed. "I've gotta get to Gaudechat. You've had your night off, your good night's rest. Go!"

"Shh. Shh," Frank said, and put his hand on Joe's shoulder. "I am so sorry. 'Orrible it is."

Joe shook him away. "I have to get to Marguerite. Now."

Frank started the engine. "I'm taking you back to the stretcher-bearers' post."

"Oh no, you don't. This is my big chance to see her." Joe pressed the heels of his hands against his eyes and let out a moan.

"Not a good plan," Frank said, as the motor inched them forward.

Joe punched his elbow against the door. "I'll tell you a good plan. Forget the post! Forget Gaudechat. Drive this fucking thing back to the English Channel and into the bloody sea!" He kept smashing his elbow against the side of the vehicle.

"Sounds like a not bad idea but we're going back to our post. 'Ow did it happen? To Walter?"

"Walter?"

"The nurse said he's killed."

"It's not Walter." Joe thumped his fist against the door.

"Oh, thank God. But she said—"

"It's Fred. My other brother." Joe wept now.

Frank stopped the ambulance and leaned over to Joe.

"No, keep going. I'm fine," Joe said and wiped his nose on his sleeve. "Keep driving."

"I will, but we're not 'eading for Goodchat or 'owever it's said. I'm taking you, both of us, back to post."

"I need Marguerite. I'll desert if that's what it takes."

Frank faced Joe and took him by the shoulders. "Listen good, my friend, she'll still be there when this is all over. Right now you are going back and will write a letter to your mother."

"I can't tell her."

"The telegram'll give her information, but she'll get comfort with a letter from you," Frank said. "Do it straight away, mate."

"It's gonna kill her." Joe fisted at his temples. "Poor Lizzie. The bairns. Bobby. Wee Jimmy." He looked out the window, drew in a loud breath and finally nodded. "It's gonna rain. Let's go afore this road's a sloppy mess. Like me."

"Go ahead and bawl. I'm not going to tell anyone." Frank geared the motor forward.

July 3, 1916

Dear Ma

You'll have heard the terrible news. Must have been awful for you and Lizzie. Was someone with her when the telegram came? I hope so. Aye, our Fred is gone. Killed. I can't believe it. One of the thousands and thousands in the last three days. I know that's not a comfort to our family. Just means all them families are heartbroken like us. And not even a funeral. I'm hoping it's a consolation for you that the hospital grounds where they'll bury him is a nice place, lots of trees and a river. The nurses are very kind, so they will have done their best for him at the end.

I think a lot more these days about Fred saying he wouldn't have minded dying for the better world he was always going on about. I don't see it happening yet, but we can hope maybe it will turn out good in the end. Talking of hope. Here's cheery news for you. I ran into a lad the other day from Kirkcaldy who seen Walter alive and well. Smashing, eh? I still haven't traced him exactly but looks like it will be soon. I wish I was at home right now to ease your grieving. I miss you. And Ellen. I'm worried too about Kate going off and working in the factory and getting sick from the munitions. Maybe you can talk her into coming home to look after Ellen again. Take the load off you.

He read the letter over, crossing his fingers that the wee lie about Walter read true. He grasped that with Fred's death, he was now the oldest son and he felt the weight of that responsibility press into his shoulders. Seemed at odds with his desire to bury his head against his mother's chest and let loose his own anguish over Fred. And Marguerite. He wanted to tell his mother about her. How much she liked him, how much he cared for her. He wanted to be able to describe her laughter, which brought such light into his small, darkening world. He wanted to scream out how much he wanted Marguerite. He needed to touch the life in her. He thought maybe Ma might understand. Might even whisper to him it was okay.

Give my best to Fred's Lizzie and the two bairns. It'll be a real struggle for them but maybe the government will see the widows all right. I'll try and send some money to help them out. Ask Kate to send some too. She seems to have plenty for herself these days.

You are all in my thoughts and prayers.

Your loving son

Joe

"Mathieson! You've had enough of a holiday. Put that away." Lieutenant Atholl stood over him, ankle deep in the mud. The rain that started earlier had not eased up, turning the chalky Picardie earth to a mush like potato soup. "Captain Rogers wants you in his dugout. On the double."

"Aye, sir. I'm on my way." Joe wished he had the nerve to thumb his nose at the lieutenant. Instead he gave Atholl a weak salute.

Joe folded the letter and put it in the top pocket of his tunic. The rain came down harder than ever. His boots squelched into the mud. When he managed to pull a foot out, the glutinous earth stuck to his soles and wrapped itself around his boots and his puttees. With each step, he collected more muck on him, making the going slower and slower. He moved off the duckboard to the side, where the water had collected into puddles, and tried to rinse off his boots but the mud had stuck like glue. He aimed all his rage onto the innocent dirt. He took off one boot and hurled it against the upright crisscrossed twigs that shaped the trench. It landed in a pool of water and slowly sank.

Grey-faced infantry, marching to the rear trenches for rest, made their way toward him, two abreast, and trampled his boot deeper into the earth. Joe grabbed at one soldier who walked right over it and landed him a punch in the jaw. Four or five jumped on him and buried Joe in thrashing flying arms and kicking legs. He fell against the side of the trench. One arm stuck in a wooden support. He managed to pull it free and cover his head with his hands. An arm yanked him to his feet. "Joe Mathieson. What the bloody hell's got into you?"

Joe uncovered his head and put his hand on his thigh, throbbing from the attack.

"I'm talking to you, Mathieson."

"Corporal Gray. Hiya," Joe said. The delight at seeing his old superior thinned the fight inside him.

The line of soldiers stopped to nosey. Quickly the trench gridlocked. Gray shouted, "Keep moving you lot. Keep moving. The show's over." He went over to a soldier rubbing his jaw. "Do you need a medic?"

The young lad shook his head. "I kinda lost my rag," Joe said, and slumped to the ground again.

"Got a good reason for that? Other than the usual that everyone's got a gripe about?"

"Found out this morning my brother got napoohed."

Gray squatted down beside Joe and handed him his boot.

"I'm sorry, Joe," he said. He shook his head. "Too many, too many. Really, I'm sorry."

"Thanks." Joe could feel the blubbering rising again. "Aye. Thanks." He balled a fist against his mouth and nose. "Good to see you. You've survived then?"

The trench bottlenecked again. "Keep moving," Gray shouted ahead. "Not a scratch. One of the lucky ones. I have to go. You take care, my friend." Gray soon receded into the throng but shouted back. "And don't worry about the fisty-cuffs. I'll see you all right."

Joe shook the water from his boot. As he pushed his foot into it, some mud squirted out and landed with a plop in a puddle.

He easily found his way to Captain Rogers' office. Already he knew the lines, the curves, each corner of these trenches as well as he knew his way around the streets in Methilane. How many times in the last three days had he zigzagged through these trenches from No Man's Land? The first aid post just behind the front lines—a dugout in a hedged bank where a road had once been—became a second home to him. From there he had navigated his way over and over again, ferried the more badly wounded farther back to the dressing station where Rogers and the other doctors had performed emergency surgery on those they could. He knocked on the post at the entrance to the captain's dugout.

"Come," Rogers called.

Joe ducked through the low lintel and saluted. A whisky bottle on the side table stood almost empty. Joe ran his tongue around the inside of his dry mouth. Had news of what he'd done to the soldier in the trench already reached here? Why would Rogers even care? Surely a tongue lashing or worse needed only come from a corporal or at most a sergeant?

"Good God, man. You look awful. Tell me what happened."

Here it comes, Joe thought. *I can't be locked up. I promised Ma I'd get on with finding Walter.* And he still had to somehow get to Marguerite. This fuck-awful fighting got in the way of everything.

"Been for a roll in the mud?"

Joe thought he might embarrass himself by tearing up in front of the officer. He licked his lips again. He really didn't want it to show that the loss of his brother was affecting him. All right to do that with Frank or even Corporal Gray but not here. He looked down at his clothes.

"Tripped, sir. Tripped and fell. Must have been in the wrong trench. Got tangled up with men marching back from the front lines."

"Well, just a word. I won't keep you, as I'm sure you want to get cleaned up. The rain has come as a blessing in disguise. The advance will be halted. At least for a few hours. Gives us a bit of a breather to do some reorganization. I have reassigned you. As an orderly. I'd forgotten until the other day that you'd worked the trains. With that, and your recent experience, you obviously know your way around a body. And it didn't escape my notice that you were very conscientious about your studies at Gaudechat."

A bead of sweat dripped from the edge of Rogers' moustache. *It's got to you too,* Joe thought.

"I'm taking you with Atholl and myself as a surgical orderly to the advanced dressing station at Lauretteville. The sergeant will give you all the necessary information. Your experience is wasted carrying stretchers when we're so desperate in the operating areas."

Joe's mouth opened in surprise.

"This is a promotion for you, Mathieson. Only a slight one in rank, I'm afraid, but you show such a knack for learning. It pleases me that you have taken my instruction seriously. And if your work proves to be as good as I expect from you, I can possibly get you posted to a casualty clearing station. The work is horrible and demanding, but your personal safety is more guaranteed. How's the reading by the way?"

Before Joe had a chance to say that the last thing on his mind these past few days was cracking open a book, Rogers carried on. "Get yourself cleaned up and be in the dressing station at four this afternoon. We've quite the backlog and we're working round the clock." He handed Joe something soft wrapped in brown paper.

"What's this, sir?"

"Now you're with us, the medical corps, you'll need them." He nodded at the parcel. "Your official red cross armbands. Off with you now. Acting Lance Corporal Mathieson."

"Thank you, sir. I'll not let you down." Joe saluted and left. He needed to go back and ask where exactly he was going, or more to the point, how much farther away from Gaudechat and Marguerite. But as he turned back toward the entrance to Rogers' dugout, out of the corner of his eye he saw the doctor walk over to the whisky bottle. He'd ask Frank where Lauretteville was when he went to say cheerio.

He went deeper back into the trenches and chose a spot to light the little stove he kept strapped to his belt. When the water he'd poured from a puddle into his canteen bubbled good and hot, he stripped to the waist, washed round his neck and under his armpits. He unrolled his housewife—the canvas wrap that protected his sewing kit, cutlery, and razor. He had a quick shave. Shaking as much mud and grime as he could from his clothes, he redressed and combed his hair. He read over the letter he'd written, added the information about his promotion and that he was now an orderly. With the Royal Army Medical Corps. Ma would be fair pleased about that. First, he would go back to the first aid post, hand in his letter for mailing, and bid his farewells to Frank. He'd miss him, but he could keep in touch. He saw those words in the ledger again. *Mathieson, Frederick John.* He imagined Fred's Lizzie reading the telegram to Ma. 'Died of wounds' it would say. He'd see plenty more of those at this new post. He willed away thoughts of Fred for now, and patted down his hair. Acting-Lance Corporal. At an advanced dressing station. A flutter of excitement passed through him.

Thursday, August 24, 1916 Joe shielded his eyes from the sun streaming in the open barn door and shoved the blanket off his sweat-soaked chest. "What time is it?" He hoisted himself onto one elbow.

"Nearly six. Rise and shine if you want hot water to shave with," Alec Young, one of Joe's new bunkmates, said loudly. He smiled as a young French girl who lived at their billet, eight or nine years old, handed him a pitcher of water. "Thanks, love." He kicked the hay bale Joe was lying on. "Look at this. Room service included. I keep telling you, it's a swank hotel."

"Shh," said Joe."Too early to be shouting."

Alec poured some water into a large white porcelain bowl enamelled with pink roses. "Sorry, lance corporal." He tapped the left side of his head. "Hard of hearing." He saluted Joe.

Joe laughed. "Stop that nonsense." He heaved himself upright and looked around the barn. He'd been here over a month and it was still a luxury being a couple of kilometres away from the front. Ten of them shared this outbuilding but each had enough room to make up a straw bed, with space in between to stash their belongings. Always enough hot water to wash and shave—heated in the farmhouse and delivered like this morning—cool water to drink, fresh eggs, and bread. The fifteen-minute walk in the sunshine from the barn to the Lauretteville advanced dressing station was a precious time for Joe. He'd come to feel less alien in this foreign land, more accepting that he was *here* and not only putting in time until he found Walter. This fifteen minute walk was his Marguerite time, where he replayed and replayed their time together: her laughter, her blue eyes that spread a smile through his whole body. He admitted to himself, not without some shame, that the summer hadn't been all bad. Frustrating, though, that this posting left him farther from Gaudechat and the café in Tourbièrecourt where Marguerite worked.

This morning the songs of larks and often cuckoos filled the late summer air. His head was clear and he felt well rested after a day off yesterday. A whole day! He'd thought of setting out for Gaudechat but a thirty kilometre walk there and back wasn't realistic. He'd also thought of going forward up the line to see Frank and his other stretcher-bearer pals, but after eight fourteen-hour days since his last break at the ADS, the temptation to sleep had won out.

Alec was cheery and a friendly companion, but he missed Frank. Poor wee Alec, all twenty years and five-foot-three of him, had been wounded at the start of the year. Now bald and scarred on the left side of his head and missing an ear, he considered himself luckier than lots of his mates. The jovial Englishman had been helpful when Joe started here at Lauretteville six weeks ago. Alec had time for all his questions, and always had a joke at hand—his favourite, *lend me an ear, you lucky bugger.* Joe made sure he laughed every time, and in turn had been allowed to make fun of his workmate the first time Alec slammed his feet together, saluted him, and shouted, "Young. Alec." And from that first introduction, Joe called him "Youngalec".

Invigorated from the morning's walk, Joe arrived at the ADS, two large marquee tents and the remains of a house, shortly before eight. Wounded men, picked up from the battlefield during the night, were laid out or sat on a lawn that had once been a village family's back garden. Joe moved among the wounded, doing a quick triage. Three wooden lawn chairs and a table had stubbornly survived, alongside rows of peas, leeks, carrots, and beans. Shells had almost flattened the house, but the intact cellars made for perfect treatment rooms.

"Hey, Doc!" Someone waved a slinged arm at Joe. "Over here."

Joe dodged his way through stretcher-bearers accompanying horse-driven carts laden with wounded. "Right you are," he said, and bent down to the injured man lying against a pile of boards cut for reinforcing the trenches. "What can I do you for? Are you next?" Sometimes, he thought, looking around at the waiting wounded, he felt like the doctor's wife at home, who acted as the receptionist at the surgery where he once took Ellen when she had a bad rash on her bum. The woman—he tried to remember her name but it wouldn't come—would forever roll her eyes around the waiting room, making sure no one skipped the queue.

"It's this lad right here." The soldier pointed to a bundle almost buried under the pile of planks. "I dragged him into a shell hole yesterday morning, but we didn't get picked up till dark. We've been out here all night, waiting our turn. I don't think he's too good. He's frigging cold. I covered him with my jacket for the night. Now I can't get him to wake up. He's my pal."

"What about you? What's your name?" Joe said, and cradled the man's arm. The soldier flinched.

"Dave Tattersall. Lancashires. I'm fine."

"I think your arm's broke. We'll get it splinted and it'll mend."

"Later. It's him I'm worried about."

Joe got to his knees. He tried to draw back Dave's jacket from the man's chest, but his blood had dried hard and stiff and glued the fabric to his skin. He lay two fingers against the lad's neck. "Your friend here has passed. I'm sorry," he said. *One less ripped apart body to try and patch up.* "I'll let someone know. Let's get your arm seen to and plastered. C'mon. One of your lads from the Lancashires works in here. I'll see you get special treatment."

"What about my friend?"

"It'll all be taken care of. Dave? Right? Don't worry." He didn't add that they had their own cemetery a couple of hundred yards away and the lad would be in the ground before lunch, sharing a space with many others. "Here, take my arm."

Joe led Dave across the garden up close to the abandoned house. He led him down a few stone steps, the entrance to the cellar dressing station.

Dave unhooked his arm from Joe's. "I'm not going in there." He pressed himself against the sandbags piled round the entrance like a jute bower. "No sirree. Not me. Me and him were in that hole all night. Thought we could be smothered in dirt any minute. I'm not going back into another one."

"It's okay," Joe said. He tugged at Dave, who held up his injured arm between them. "Look, watch me go in." He pushed open the wooden door. The dank smell of never dry earth and years of old stored vegetables squirmed out. Joe ducked, went in and closed the door behind him, counted to ten and came out again. "See. No problem, I can go in," Joe went in again, this time leaving the door open, "and I can come out. This is where the doctors work. We've converted two cellars. Like a hospital it is. Look."

He pointed farther down the back of the house at the entrance to the second cellar. Two orderlies stood outside, having a smoke and chatting. They stood aside and pressed themselves against the sandbags as a couple of bearers carried a fellow in on a stretcher. The wounded soldier half-sat up and gave the orderlies a wave as he was carried down the steps. "See," Joe said. "Safe as houses."

He stepped toward Dave again and saw him shaking. "You'll be fine in here." He lowered his voice. "C'mon, let's see if we can find Youngalec. He's the lad from the Lancashires I told you about."

Dave nodded and went in front of Joe down the steps. *Poor sod,* thought Joe, although he was better off than most of the twelve hundred or so injured men that came through the ADS each day. Many of them were led, like Dave, into this crypt-like area. The two cellars each covered about a hundred feet square, barely enough space for a couple of chairs for the patients and the two tables where the doctors operated. Mostly it was minor surgery, setting bones and sewing up wounds that would heal without further intervention, although scraping away infected flesh and amputations were not unknown. The dirt floor chilled right through their boots, despite the air outside holding the lingering warmth of late summer. When the thunderstorms came, and there were many, the rain flooded down the cellar stairs and the men felt they were back in a trench or out on the battlefield.

Every half an hour or so, he or one of the other orderlies swept out the accumulation of sodden bandages with a bristly broom. After nearly two months, the earth had been scoured so thin the damp rose faster than the heat of the crowd of bodies could warm it. But no amount of sweeping banished the cold metallic stink of the blood that soaked into the dirt.

In the bustle and competition for the small space, Joe had lost count of the number of times he'd banged his head on a hanging lamp or on the shelves nailed into the timbers of the walls to hold bandages, surgical instruments, and bottles of fluids to clean and treat wounds. But always he reminded himself things could be a lot worse for him. He was sure his little 'turns', as he thought of them, when he'd had a go first at Frank and then at Tom was in the past. His hands were steady too. Rogers would not have taught him how to assist at some of the minor surgeries if he had any worries about his state of mind. The captain had even shown him how to stitch skin together, and the other day, he'd let Joe have a try. He had allowed himself a moment of fantasy. Dressed in a white coat, a stethoscope bobbing around his neck, one of a crowd of white-coated young men who followed Dr. Rogers from bed to bed in the infirmary in Edinburgh. He nodded in understanding as Rogers poked, palpated, and questioned each patient. *Fat chance for someone like me. Once this war's over, it'll be back to the way things always have been, everyone back in the same old place on the social ladder.* He didn't have the same faith as his brother Fred in the notion that the walls separating the classes could be torn down. Captain Rogers treated him with respect, but he didn't run the show. *The likes of me'll no' be of use when the last bandage is burned,* he thought.

He had the last two days of August off. The weather was still warm, not even a hint of chill in the mornings like there would be back home in Methilane. He lay back on his straw bed, taking pleasure as he anticipated the next forty-eight hours. Two whole days of a slower pace and the warm dry hay smell in the barn instead of the dank cellar. Enough time to get to Gaudechat. First he'd take his paper and pencils, sit in the farmyard, and reply to the letter he'd had from Ma last week. He thought he should also write to Kate, but what did he have to say to her? Besides, he'd had no word from her since the middle of July and even then all her words were about how much she made at the munitions and what her and her pals got up to on their days off. She'd signed off with *I havna heard no bad news of you so that'll mean your ok.* It seemed like an afterthought. He'd write to Fred's wife instead. It might comfort Lizzie to know they'd laid her man, his *brother,* to rest in the cemetery behind the casualty clearing station at Bercordie. He'd tell her he would get there one day and would pay his respects at the grave.

He'd make a grand outing of the rest of the day. Find some food, put together a picnic, get over to Gaudechat, and surprise Marguerite. Maybe he'd get lucky and get a lift in a cart or be able to borrow a bicycle. Still not one letter, or even a note, from her. Even in the days of the heaviest fighting, the mail service rarely faltered. He wrote to her most days. She *had* to think of him unless … only one reason could explain her silence: She didn't love him. Or maybe the mail only went back home, he consoled himself. Not to addresses in France.

Alec was bent over one of the enamel washbowls set up on trestles in the yard when Joe made his way to the latrines out the back. "You coming to the feast tonight, Joe?" He lathered his face with a shaving brush.

"Don't know anything about that, Youngalec. I'm off for a wee holiday. Got some friends with a château I have to visit." He gave Alec a thump on the back.

Alec jerked the razor away from his face. "Sorry to be the one to tell you this, but Atholl came round and we've all to help."

"With what?"

"Harvest."

"You're joking me," Joe said.

"Nope. You'd better telephone your important friends and tell them you're unavailable." He checked his shaving job in the little mirror nailed to a tree. "It's that time of year. All hands on deck. If we muck in, we get to join the party."

"Shit," Joe said.

"Cheer up. A day in the sun'll do us both good."

Joe lifted Youngalec's basin and emptied it on the ground.

"It's not my fault," Youngalec called after Joe, who had stomped off, raising dust and stones as he kicked the ground.

Joe and Youngalec walked together away from the ADS down a narrow road, its hedgerows still intact and busy with birds and insects. Alec sang off tune, Joe spluttered and cursed at Atholl's orders as they veered to a narrow path that took them down the side of a field. Already a score or more of workers were spread out over the land, backs bent as they lifted the crops.

And it was good, as Alec had insisted. The physical effort of hefting huge baskets of potatoes and beets for the cattle onto carts liberated the frustration in his muscles. As the day wore on, he took over the job of driving the horse and cart. He tipped cartloads of vegetables, building ten-feet high piles at the edge of the field. The mindless tasks relaxed him. The good-natured teamwork of the men and the women gave him hope of a chance of cooperation among folk. The pain and misery of the wounded seemed a thousand miles away. But Gaudechat, and hopes of ever seeing Marguerite, began to crash. A blistering charge of disappointment threatened to dash away the good of the day. He lit a cigarette, and after a few deep drags, promised himself he'd not let Marguerite slip away that easily.

Every two hours, girls brought round jugs of cider and the harvesters took a break, sat, and rested their backs against the growing mounds. It was during one of these breaks, as Joe watched the bees gather nectar on a bush thick with flowers, he dared think back to June and his so-called punishment at the farm. His heart saddened as he recalled the pull of Marguerite's flowery scent. *Lavandre*, she called it. He swore the sweet oily perfume would haunt him for the rest of his life.

Around seven in the evening he walked back from the fields. Two women ran up from behind him and linked their arms in his, with a jig in their steps despite the long hot day. Joe guessed they might be younger than their leathery faces, wrinkled and brown with heavy-lidded eyes, led him to think. He nodded and laughed whenever they paused in their chatter, as they led him round the back of his barn. Close to a hundred people sat or stood chatting and laughing around long trestle tables. The smell of real meat roasting on spits over open fires made him dizzy with hunger. The women showed him to a space at a table and pushed him down on a wooden bench. The young girl who brought the hot water in the mornings leaned over his shoulder and poured cider for him.

"Good day, right?" Youngalec said. He stepped over the bench and sat on Joe's left so he could tilt his good ear to any conversation. Another young farm girl pushed between them and set down two piled plates. Youngalec leaned over and gave the food a satisfied sniff. "Okay, let's dig in."

Joe explored the food with his knife: huge chunks of pork, steaming potatoes slathered with butter, and some vegetable like a pale grey turnip. He shoved a forkful into his mouth. "Might as well."

"Ah, c'mon Joe. It's good to help them out and I'm sure they're grateful. Most of their men are at the front. Even with them what've come from the farms around here to muck in, they still don't have enough manpower."

Youngalec was right. Men made up only a quarter of the crowd. None seemed under forty. The impact of the war, the price men paid, charged at him again. "I don't know what they'll to do when the dancing starts," Youngalec said and laughed. He spluttered out a spray of mixed vegetables. "Looks good for *us* though."

"What?" Joe said.

"Well just look at all those *boootiful* mamzelles." Alec waved his fork down the length of the table. "Even I stand a chance."

Joe looked up the table. *Aye, mostly women.* His heart froze in his chest. At the far end, perhaps ten people down the row, a familiar stray curl peeped from the edge of a white bonnet. He jumped up, knocking over his drink. Youngalec quickly lifted his own plate and spread his legs, letting the cider run over the table. "Watch it! You clumsy clot," he said. "I'm getting soaked."

Joe kept his eyes fixed on Marguerite as he moved away from the table. She put her finger to her lips and shook her head at him. Her mother, next to her, talked to her neighbour and wigwagged her fork about in the air as she spoke. On her other side sat a dour man, his droopy moustache pointing to an ugly red scar smothering his chin. "While you're on your feet, get a cloth from the farmhouse and clean this up," Youngalec shouted after Joe as he shook drips from his fingers.

"Aye, aye," Joe said. He made his way up the table, passing behind Marguerite. All the while he kept his eyes on her even as he crossed the yard. At the farmhouse door he hesitated. She put her hand to her head, said something to the man, and left the table.

She came into the farmhouse kitchen, looking over her shoulder at the outside. Joe nodded to her that he'd go out the back. At last he had her in his arms. He lifted her up, twirled her around, and covered her face with kisses. He stood before her and walked his hands all over her, from her shoulders down over her breasts, and squeezed her waist. He felt her shudder. He pulled her into his own body and slowly traced her lips with his tongue. He worked her lips open and kissed her deeply. She panted and he inhaled the heady scent of her breath and her skin. He pulled away to look at her, but she grabbed him behind the ears and pulled him to her, locked his lips onto hers. Finally she ran out of breath and laid her head on his chest. He ran his fingers through her hair and let his racing heartbeat slow to the rhythm of her quiet sobs.

"I can't believe it," he said, holding her head between his hands. He kissed her again, but she pulled away, said something he couldn't decipher as she looked back towards the house. He took her hand and ran, pulling her towards his barn. Inside, he closed the door behind them and stacked three straw bales against it. She held up her hand to stop him dragging her over to his sleeping spot.

"Non, non. Je suis désolée. Mon père." She pointed to the door. *"Je dois partir."*

So that's the father, he thought. The miserable looking bugger who sat next to her. Joe knew the mother liked him well enough. Thought she even encouraged him when he'd sat around the table with them at the château farm back in June. The father he'd never met and no one mentioned one. He assumed the father was away with the army or already dead.

He whispered in her ear. *"Je t'aime. Je t'aime."*

She flushed, and for a moment Joe thought she would run away, but she took his hand and kissed it. *"Moi, aussi. Je t'aime."* She turned to leave. *"Mais, je dois partir."*

"Okay, okay. But come back." He pointed to the ground. "Here. Come here." He lifted her up and kicked away the bales. He opened the door. Marguerite was yanked from his arms. Joe heard the sharp slap on her cheek. Her father's sweat stank and made him recoil. He wanted to strike out at the small swarthy man but the rancid puffs coming from his almost toothless mouth made Joe think of an angry bull. The father shoved his daughter away and Marguerite ran off without looking back. Joe took a step back as the unshaven man moved closer. He didn't have time to grab the arm that came toward him before he plummeted to the floor, stunned by a jolt of pain. Joe covered his mouth and tried to halt the gush of blood. He watched the father leave, turning around every few paces to scream a torrent of French at him. Not a word did Joe recognize, but he got the drift all right. He looked past the father and screamed after Marguerite.

"Here. Tomorrow!"

The father turned and loped back to Joe. He waved his fist so close to Joe's face he could feel the air flapping. Her father's words splattered his face.

"Bé, ti aussi tu mourros!

Into his mind flashed the urchin boy Booey at Gaudechat, with the pretend rifle fitted under his armpit. *"Fusil. Pfft, tu mourros"* he'd laughed. "Pfft, pfft. You're dead."

He had the worst night. Sleep would not release him from the evening's agony. He tossed, he turned. The straw itched. He gave up on rest. His instinct was to go after Marguerite, even follow the family all the way back to Gaudechat, but as he paced around the farm throughout the night, his head became clearer. In the end, he figured it would cause more trouble for her if he went. And for him. Besides, if he went absent without leave, there'd be no way he could continue his search for Walter.

Occasionally he threw his hands up and howled. How had he got himself all these problems? Life back home was a drudge but none of this serious shite. If only he could get out, go back home. He thought of the tiny house back in Methilane, of Kate whining at him, of wee Ellen without either her ma or pa. He'd signed on willingly for "three years or the duration, should the war last longer." *And here was me thinking I'd be gone a few months. What a joke,* he thought. Then his thoughts turned to Marguerite's words. *Je t'aime.* I love you. So his worst fear was not true. She *did* love him. The father must have found his letters, forbidden her to have anything to do with him. Even threatened her. Joe patted his split lip, stirring up the throbbing. Thank God, her bastard father wouldn't understand his letters. Words that lingered on their love-making. He leaned against a pile of fodder beets, the hard round vegetables digging into his back, and gave in to the tears that came so easily these days.

"What on earth happened to your face, Mathieson?" Atholl said.

"Had a bit too much cider at the feast, sir. Not used to that stuff. I banged into a beam in my billet. It's fine. I'm ready for work."

"Don't you still have some time off? I didn't expect to see you today. Maybe I'm confused. One day seems like the next."

"No, you're right, Lieutenant," Joe said, removing his jacket and following Atholl into the cellar. "I was bored. Needed something to do with myself."

Joe's mind drifted back to Marguerite in the barn. That had been far from boring. Questions battered his brain. Was she safe from that brute who slugged him? Where was she now? Would her father send her away? How would he ever see her again? Comfort her? Touch her?

"So of course we are having her here. I am relying ... Mathieson, are you paying *any* attention to me?"

"Sir?"

"You're miles away. And your face is all screwed up. Are you in pain?" Atholl asked.

"You could say that, sir."

"Get yourself a couple of aspirin." Atholl scowled at Joe. "I'll have to start all over again. Pay attention." He looked past Joe's shoulder. "Ah, there you are. You poor soul. Let's get you sat down."

Joe turned around. An orderly helped Adelaide Armitage to a seat outside a treatment room. Joe waved to her, smiled, remembered how kind she'd been to him at the casualty clearing station when he found out about Fred.

Atholl put his hand on her forehead. "Hmm. Bit of a fever. We'll have you fixed up as quick as you can say Jack Robinson." He turned to Joe. "Get this lady some aspirin and tell Captain Rogers that Nurse Armitage is here."

"Hello, Joe," Adelaide said. "You just vanished ... that day."

"You two know each other?" Atholl said.

"We've worked together," Adelaide said, and gave Joe a thin smile. "He's one of the best." She touched him softly on the shoulder. "How are you, Joe? I've thought a lot about you, and again, I am sorry for your loss."

Joe wanted to fling himself against her and bury his pain in her kindness.

"Get going, man," Atholl said. "I'll see to this lady, look after her until the captain can see her." He turned to Adelaide. "I'm sorry, it could be long enough. It's a madhouse here today." He waved Joe away and turned back to Adelaide with a big smile.

It took Joe only a couple of minutes to return with water and a handful of aspirins and pass them to Adelaide. He touched her bandaged hand. "What's happened? You look awful weak," he said.

"Is that your medical diagnosis, Mathieson?" Atholl said. "Weak?"

"Lieutenant," Adelaide said, "I am sure you have more pressing cases to attend to than a cut finger. As you said, it is a madhouse. I'd hate to deny a wounded soldier the benefit of your skill. Joe can stay with me until Captain Rogers is free."

Joe felt the burn of Atholl's glare as he nodded and left.

"You're a brave one," Joe said. "Put him in his place, bloody—"

Adelaide touched Joe's arm. "He's young. And probably scared."

"And you're too kind. Let's have a look at that finger." She looked up and smiled at him. "Remember the infection you said I picked up from one of the wounded men?"

Joe blushed. "Right. I do. And you haven't looked after yourself like I told you."

"It was getting better. Truly. And I did keep it clean."

Joe unwound the pus-stained dressing.

"I didn't want anyone to know. They might send me home, and I can't do that. I have to keep busy." Her eyes rolled. The glass of water fell from her hand as she slumped into a faint.

"Sir! You need to see to Adelaide, Nurse Armitage, now!" Joe shouted to the back of the room, where an orderly lifted a soldier off the table. Captain Rogers leaned against the enamel basin the surgeons used for washing their hands. He was dressed in a pair of khaki shorts and a short-sleeved shirt as if he were in the tropics.

"Get her onto the table then, Mathieshon," Rogers said.

Joe eased Adelaide out of her faint and helped her onto the table.

"Where's Atholl?" Rogers barked.

Joe turned his head away from the waft of whisky from Rogers' breath. "Next table, sir. Working on someone else. I can help if you like."

"Well, you'll have to do, I eshpect." Rogers slurred.

"I've already given her some aspirin for the fever."

"Give her some more and shcrub your hands."

Once washed and with a clean white apron over his shirt, Joe gave Adelaide a whiff of chloroform. Rogers set to work, cleaning out the top of her finger. "Shee that," he said to Joe, shoving the tip of the forceps deep into the wound. "I've taught you about it."

"Gangrene," Joe said.

"What do we do?"

"Nothing to be done except amputation."

"She's lucky, though. It's only on the tip," Rogers said. His shaky hand continued to probe the open wound. "We can cut it above the first knuckle. Hand me the bone saw and give her another drip of the whachamacallit."

"Chloroform?"

"Right. That stuff."

Rogers swayed a little, then held onto the table to steady himself before he removed the tip of Adelaide's middle finger, with a deftness that surprised Joe. The captain secured the blood vessels and prepared a flap of skin to cover the naked end. "Get Atholl to sew this up. I'm off to lunch."

Joe looked over to the other table. Atholl's head was almost buried in a man's abdomen.

"He's busy right now."

"Goddamn the man. I need my lunch."

"I think *I* could do it," Joe said.

"Well, can you or can't you?"

Joe took a deep breath, decided not to take offence at Rogers' sharpness. "You showed me yourself. Aye, I can do it."

Wednesday, September 6, 1916 At three in the afternoon, warmth still streamed from the sun. Joe sat at the edge of the cemetery, a few hundred yards from the advanced dressing station. He balanced his canteen between his legs, opened a bully beef tin, and spooned out the meaty mash. A bare arm grabbed him from behind and pressed a stinking cloth over his eyes. He dropped the spoon and tried to wrestle the fabric away. Then as suddenly as he was blinded, the fabric was whisked away and Joe swung around. "You idiot," he said. "What if I'd had a knife in my hand? You wouldn't be standing there now."

Frank grinned. "Thought you'd be pleased to see me." He scooped up a handful of Joe's meat and stuck it in his mouth. "I see you get the same fine dining as us." He wiped his hands on the handkerchief he'd wrapped around Joe's head. "I've been over 'ere a few times looking for you, to see 'ow you're doing, wondering if you've found your other brother. But your Atholl friend shoos me out of the way. Gets on my tits, 'e does." He sat down and looked over at the mounds of earth. "This isn't a very 'appy place."

"I like it okay. It's quiet after all the screaming, the blood, and guts. It's good to think they're,." He pointed over to the rows of little wooden crosses. "It's good to think they're not hurting no more. At least Walter's not in there. Any road, what's up with you?"

"Same old, same old. Shelling and sniping at night, lads sent over during the day. Sometimes I think we might as well send the 'ole bloody lot over at once, mop up the bits and bodies and be done with it. We move the wire out a bit. Then next week it's back again where we started or even farther fucking back. Can't see the point." He helped himself to more of Joe's meal. "We still go out there every night, in the dark, picking up and running to the dressing station." He coughed and sprayed mushed meat into the air. "Try to get as much kip as I can in the day." He smoothed down his shirt and puffed out his chest. "I've become a sporting gentleman."

"What game are you up to now?" Joe smiled and nodded to Frank to sit.

"It's true. Listen, 'ere's what. I borrow, or more like take, a rifle from one of the lads what's sleeping and go off and get myself some rabbits. Made a nice little profit selling them in the support trenches for sixpence a go. I can get you some. On the 'ouse. Just say the word. And as you can see, I'm still 'ere. Touch wood." He tapped the top of his head. "But look 'ere, mate. When are you next off?"

"In two days. Saturday," Joe said. "How come?"

"Do you remember Bercordie?"

Joe's mind flashed to the day he met Marguerite. If he hadn't left his pals to the drink in the bar in that little town, he'd never have gone on to the next village. Instantly, he saw the little café at Tourbièrecourt where he'd stopped to eat. Where he'd met Marguerite. "Aye of course. Where I found out about Fred. At the CCS there."

"Sad that," Frank said.

"And where I had the first good sleep in a while, thanks to you and your posh nursie friend." Joe looked intently at Frank, hoped he would offer up some information about his hanky-panky with the nurse at the casualty clearing station, but Frank ignored his stare.

"There's a fair at Bercordie starting tomorrow and I thought you, me, and some of the other lads could give it a go. Bit of fun."

"I don't think so. Days off I catch up on sleep." He didn't mention his druthers would have him with Marguerite. Nor did he tell Frank her father had punched him out and scared them apart.

"Hey, friend," Frank said, "We gotta do some living in this miserable life."

Joe stood. "I've got to get back."

"Okay, but I'm not taking no for an answer." He pointed at Joe. "See you there. Saturday."

On his way back to the ADS, Joe saw Adelaide coming toward him and waved at her. "How's the hand?" he said, and pointed to her arm, which was bound up in a sling.

"Doing nicely and all thanks to you I hear. Look." She came so close to him her arm touched his before she took it from the sling and unwrapped the bandaging. "You can touch it. It doesn't even hurt anymore."

Joe's cheeks flushed at the intimacy and he put his hands behind his back. "You should never have put off getting it seen to."

"Lucky for me you have first class sewing skills." She tried to roll the unwound bandage with one hand. "Yes, you're right, Joe. I knew I was in trouble with it, but the work has become very important to me." She gave a little laugh. "I kept hearing my mother's voice."

Joe took the dressing from her. "I'll do that for you. And what did it say? This voice?"

She held out her hand for him. "Oh, all the usual stuff about the silliness of taking on a job, any job, no matter one like this. The very idea of a woman, never mind a married woman, working is not what a person of her generation or ..."

"Social class?"

"It's sounds awful when you say it like that, but that is how my mother thinks."

Joe finished redressing her hand. "There you go. I think your mother would be very proud of you if she could see how good you are. You've a caring heart for others Nurse Adelaide." He hoped she didn't think he was speaking of himself as one of the others. Maybe he overreacted to her touching him. "And if you don't mind me saying, if you were half-ways as good at looking after yourself this never would have happened."

"Are you scolding me, corporal?"

Joe reddened. "It's just lance corporal."

"It's official then?"

"Aye," Joe said, and pointed to the single chevron stripe pinned to his sleeve.

"Let me sew that stripe on your arm. Make it permanent and you can throw away that dirty safety pin. My thanks. You saved my finger. And my ability to work."

"Just helped out."

"That's not what Lieutenant Atholl told me. He spoke highly of you."

"That little twerp? He can't stand me."

Adelaide smiled. "Truly, he did. And I am very grateful. If there's ever anything I can do for you, I'd be happy to. Just let me know." She laid her unbandaged hand on his shoulder. "Anyway I'm off back to Bercordie and duty tomorrow."

"I'll be in Bercordie myself on Saturday. I hear there's a fair."

"Oh, I love fairs. Maybe I'll go. If I do, I'll look out for you. Bye Joe, and again, my thanks."

Saturday, September 9, 1916 Joe was the only one in the *estaminet* in the main street of Bercordie who wasn't drunk, asleep, or close to it. He'd grown restless with only his own company, so he stood and yanked Youngalec by the scruff of the neck. When he let go, Youngalec gave him a glazed look and his head limped back down to the table. No stirring him or any of the others. He dropped a few francs on the table for his share of the wine and walked out to the street.

He heard music—hurdy-gurdy music. It rushed him back home to the annual fair week when the carnival came to Methilane. Loneliness thumped through his chest. He sat down on the edge of the road and surrendered himself to sweet memories of his own childhood and now that of his wee Ellen. He remembered how his dear little daughter clapped her hands and tried to sing as he stood with her in his arms, watching the organ grinder and his little monkey.

He thought of Kate too. She loved the fair. Loved the noises, the crowds, the booths, and rides, and the opportunity to stop every six or seven steps to gab with a neighbour or a friend. She knew everyone, and it struck him for the first time that others enjoyed her company and her chat. Was he just a stupid mooning fool to think he was in love with Marguerite? Should he just give his head a shake and find the good in Kate? Make himself think kindly of her? She was, after all, Ellen's ma.

He saw Kate and Marguerite framed in his mind, side by side. It struck him as funny that the woman he wanted to listen to couldn't speak his language. Yet he had more to say to her than he'd ever wanted to say to his wife. Kate had traded talking to him for using him as a child-minder so she could visit and gossip with her friends. He closed his eyes and could hear her rail at him that he didn't want to listen to her. She was right, he wasn't interested in listening. And absence hadn't made his heart grow fonder. The cacophony of mixed shouts and music from down the street from grew louder. He walked on, his mind peppered with more images of the woman he loved: Marguerite shoving her sunny curls under her bonnet, Marguerite humming and caressing his shoulders that day by the pool. He laid his hands on his chest, wished her sunny laughter had rubbed into him. He tried to force happy images of Kate, but such that came were tinged with annoyance: Kate reaching up to put his wet shirts onto the clothes horse suspended from the kitchen ceiling, moaning about the housework, berating him for coming home late from work, saying how sick she was with only a bairn for company when he had his pals down the pit. He tried to bring his daughter into the picture show that filled his brain, but each time she appeared, Kate was there too: Kate roughly wiping porridge splashes from Ellen's chin, making her bawl, Kate handing off her daughter—his daughter—to his mother so she could selfishly indulge herself down at the snug. Then there was Ma with Ellen on her knee telling a story about her daddy and a magic place called France.

Joe considered going back to the ADS, to the barn and the sumptuous solace of sleeping on a straw mattress. He hadn't forgotten the sodden feet and the itching lice that had plagued him when he had no choice but to sleep outdoors in the fields and trenches. He shuddered when he thought of all the men who had no relief from such savage nights. It would be smart to go back and enjoy a good night's sleep. But he did want to spend some time with Frank, who always cheered him up.

The music enticed his weary body down the street. It didn't look much different from home. The buildings were made of similar grey stone. Shops at street level and housing above where old women sat at open windows. He played a game with himself, matched the words over the shops with the goods displayed in the windows. Sausages and hams–*charcuterie*; long sticks and soft balls of bread–*boulangerie*; jams, sugar, and tins of coffee–*epicerie*; and of course the *tabac*, the tobacconist's, the word in French not so different from home. In the distance, the church tower glowered over the town, a gold figure with outstretched hands on top, as if reassuring them they were taken care of and all would be well.

Joe followed the music into a small park. Pale mauve light lingered in the sky, although it was close to nine o'clock. Still time to look for Frank here at the fairground. He sauntered through the gate, turned his shoulders this way and that to avoid banging into anyone in the crowd. He spent a few moments by a stall where fathers guided their children's hands to hit coconuts with a wad of tightly rolled cloth. Darkness finally overtook the day. Flashing lights lit up the amusement booths and rides. A moment of panic seized him, and for a few seconds, he was flung back to the trenches and the flares and shell bombardments that had tortured his ears and eyes in July. Thank goodness he was alone. No one to see his hands shaking, or the sweat beading on his forehead. No one to see him swallowing against a rise of nausea. No one to lose his rag at as he'd done after that soldier trampled on his boot. He'd heard the doctors talk about the embarrassing reactions soldiers often developed to sudden movements, noises, and flashes of light. Shell shock, they called it. He'd seen men at the ADS driven crazy by the torment. He wasn't like that, of course. Those ones screamed out, shook and jerked, or couldn't move a muscle, their eyes staring and fixed. Shit their pants like bairns. The poor sods he'd seen didn't get much sympathy. Like the rest of the medics, he would turn away and busy himself, unsure of what to say even if it were appropriate to be sympathetic. He hoped the nurses at the casualty clearing stations and the hospitals were less ruffled. Some of the younger ones at least might be more sympathetic to the afflicted. What would Kate do if he came home like that? He realized with some shame that he thought she would ignore him, abandon him to the inside of his own head. But maybe she'd surprise him. And Marguerite? Would she still gaze at him with those fantastic blue eyes?

"Joe!"

Joe looked around and saw three silhouetted shapes heading towards him, one pulling the others along.

"Aye, it is and who might be asking?" he asked, his hand shielding his eyes from the flashes of green, red, and yellow that jabbed at his face.

"It's Adelaide." Joe stopped suddenly, bothered by the flush in his cheeks at the welcome sight of her fresh, rosy face. "Oh, aye. I couldn't see you 'cause of the lights. How are you?"

"Good. Very good." She held up her injured hand. The big bandage on her hand had been replaced by sticking plaster. "Almost all better. These are my colleagues." She indicated the two women with her other hand. "Nurse Wilkinson. Susan." She pointed to the taller blonde woman. "You remember Phillipa from the moribund ward at the ccs?"

Joe wiped a hand on the seat of his trousers, took off his cap, and offered a handshake to Adelaide's friends. "I'm glad you told me about the fair," Adelaide said. "I hoped you'd be here. Are you alone?"

"Aye well, I just heard the music and ... well the lads in an *estaminet* back there are a little the worse for their night off, if you know what I mean. I'm supposed to see Frank." He spoke to Phillipa. "Have you seen him?"

"Seen who?" she said.

"My pal Frank. We was both at your ward back in July."

"July? My God, that was a lifetime ago. Sorry I don't remember him."

"But you and he ... I saw you."

"Dear boy, many men go through my ward." Phillipa laughed. "A girl needs relaxation." She put her arm through his. "Come and join us. We were going to ride on these new dodgem cars. You can be our escort." She ushered them all over to a booth where a young girl, no more than twelve or thirteen, sold tickets. "My treat. *Quatre billets, s'il vous plait,*" she said at the booth and produced some money from her coat pocket.

The four ran over to the cars, which circled a wooden floor raised over the sparse grass. Adelaide's friends pushed their way ahead and climbed into a car painted bright blue with silver stars. Joe took a step back, but Adelaide made a move toward him and steered him by the elbow towards a bright red car. Joe put his cap back on as he leapt into the car, allowing her the driver's seat. A dirty-faced man climbed onto the bumper, wiggled the pole that attached them to the ceiling, and off they went. Joe sat with his hands in his lap. Adelaide gripped the wheel and moved it in a dramatic circle only when it was already too late to avoid a collision.

"I've driven a real car, really I have," she said. "My father bought one just before the war and I used to steer it down our drive."

"Oh, I believe you. I'll not interfere! It's all yours." With each crash, Joe relaxed and smiled at the tense set of her mouth. She kept flicking glances at him. He chuckled. "I'm just along for the ride." He fished in his breast pocket for his cigarettes. Took two from the packet, and asked her if she wanted one.

Adelaide leaned over to take one from him, and the car careened to the left as she let go of the wheel. “Okay Nurse Armitage,” he teased. “Eyes on the road. No cigarettes for us just yet.”

“I thought this would be easy. Sorry.”

“Don’t worry,” he said. “It’s a wee bit different driving down a straight road and doing this. Want me to show you?”

“That would help,” she said.”

“Like this.” He leaned over, placed his hands over hers in a better position. Her fingers shifted and mingled with his. She stared at him and smiled. He untangled his hands and pointed ahead. A rush of awkwardness danced around his ears. “It’s all about anticipation,” he continued. “You have to look around, all around, to see what might come at you.”

“A bit difficult to do,” she said, “when one has to steer at the same time. A bit like patting one’s head and rubbing one’s tummy at the same time.” She laughed and loosened her grip on the wheel.

“It’s likely no harder than your work at the hospital. Doing a ton of things at one time. I know when I’ve been to deliver the wounded, the wards seem like bedlam and you nurses run all over the place, and by my reckoning, you keep it all straight. Look to your left, there’s one coming at us now.” He guided her hands to steer to the right and she made a large circle away from the challenging car. “See, you’ve got it already.” He took his hands away. “Get us out of this safely and your prize is a cigarette.”

“Right,” she said. Then their car shuddered and came to a halt. They looked up to see her friends’ blue car jammed against them.

“Susan, Phillipa! You rotters! I’d just got the hang of this.” And all four laughed.

“I can’t give you first prize for that performance,” Joe said. He took Adelaide’s elbow and helped her step over the rim of the car. Once she was safely on the ground, he lit the two cigarettes and gave her one. Adelaide took a short puff, threw her head back, and coughed as she blew out the smoke. “Second cigarette of my life,” she said. “Do you remember when we worked on the hospital train you gave me one?”

“Glad you’re not making it a habit,” Joe said, and nudged her jokingly. “That’s a good thing for a woman.”

"Things are changing for women, Joe. My mother, as you know, is not pleased. She didn't like me leaving England. And actually doing work. What about your women?"

Joe reddened, thinking of Marguerite. His woman. "My women?"

She gave a little laugh. "You know what I mean. Mother, sister. Can I guess by your colour you have a sweetheart at home? Or a wife? Yes?"

Joe ground his cigarette end into the ground and stomped on it even after the burning ended had died. He looked down and shoved it around with his toe.

"Oh, Joe. Have I put my foot into it? Has something else happened to your family?"

"No, no. Nothing like that. Look, would it be rude to ask you to take a walk with me? These lights are giving me a headache. And I'd like your ear. Again. Like you did for me when Fred died."

She looked over to a stall where Phillipa and Susan threw balls at coconuts. Susan unperched one and the keeper threw the coconut over to her as a prize. "Let's leave them to that nonsense. I didn't mean to pry, but yes I can listen if you have something on your mind. And I can be discreet. Say, why don't I buy you a drink? We women can do that now." She linked her arm through his and leaned into him. His body wanted to relax into the weight of hers, but his mind was embarrassed to be so close to a … lady. He hoped she didn't catch his rigidity.

She was the one who first spotted an open hotel with a restaurant. They both downed two glasses of wine before Joe finished telling Adelaide about his life at home and then Marguerite. He signalled to the waiter to bring them a third drink. He leaned back against the leather banquette. "Well, that's my whole tale of woe."

She leaned forward and stroked her glass. "May I ask a few questions?"

"Aye. Of course."

"What if I were to suggest your attraction to this young lady is merely a reaction to the war. An attempt to have some beauty in your life. An escape from the pain you feel at missing your wife and daughter."

The cords in his neck tightened and he turned sharply toward Adelaide. "This isn't some fancy notion I've took."

She looked down and folded her hands in her lap.

"Some of what you say is right," he said. "I miss Ellen so much at times it makes me crazy."

She was looking at him now.

"But to tell the truth," he went on. "I've never missed my wife. Not even from the first day I was here. I really love Marguerite and I just can't figure what to do. I want to spend my whole life with her. I can't even find a way to see her. I'm not stupid. I know there are problems in the future."

"For example?"

"First she'll have to learn a new language, but that'll come with time, I suppose. And then how do I get her to leave her family and take her back with me?"

"You could stay here in France after the war."

Joe laughed again. "I had fantasies about that. In the summer, when it was hot and sunny."

"What else?" Adelaide said. "What other obstacles do you see?"

"There's the obvious one. Kate."

"You could divorce. If you could convince your wife. On the grounds of your adultery with Marguerite."

"Don't say that."

"Say what?"

"Adultery. What I do with Marguerite's not adultery. She's the woman I should've married in the first place. Besides, people like me, we can't afford divorces like your folk." He took two quick gulps of his wine and sat back with his arms folded. "Seeing it all laid out like that—"

"Joe. I'm not trying to upset you and I'm sorry if I have."

"No it's good. I haven't been thinking straight. Too wrapped up in enjoying her, then trying to get to her." He took another swig of wine. "And I should be thinking as well from her standpoint."

"I'm sure she loves you."

"She does. I'm wondering now if she sees the problems. The language and other stuff about her being French for starters."

"And likely the father sees you as taking advantage of your position as a soldier," Adelaide said. "You must strike her as somewhat exotic. To her father, you are only out to seduce her and dishonour the family."

Joe banged his fist on the table. "That's not true."

"I know that. And there is the question of religion. Are you Catholic?"

"Me? Not on your life."

"Well, there you go then. That in itself is enough to want her father to keep you away from her and to raise worries in her mind."

"Aye, the whole Catholic thing wouldn't go over well in my family. My mother's sister married one. She got no help from the family when her man died young, leaving her with ten bairns under fifteen." He put his head down on the table and covered it with his hands.

Adelaide took out some money from her purse and laid it on the table. "Come, I've depressed you enough. Walk me back to my friends at the fair." She helped him to his feet and gave him a hug.

Joe pulled back.

"I'm sorry", she said. "It was not my intention to upset you."

"It's not that at all. Your smell."

"My smell. Is it offensive?" Adelaide seemed taken aback.

"No, no," Joe said. "Took me by surprise. It's lovely. Too lovely."

"It's very popular with the French women."

"The woman I told you about smelled like that. *Lavandre* she called it."

"My, your French accent is very good, but then you Scots always were better at it than we English."

Joe felt no relief that he'd told Adelaide the whole sorry tale, as he now saw it. But she was good. Like Ma, she didn't tell him what to do but was genuinely interested. He offered her a cigarette but she shook her head. He lit one for himself and wondered about her problems. There was her missing husband of course, but was there other stuff? He'd always assumed the rich folks like her couldn't have much to complain about. Now that he'd spent all this time with her—on the trains, at the casualty clearing station at Bercordie, at the ADS at Lauretteville, and now this evening—he felt ashamed he'd talked all evening about himself.

"'Ello, soldier!" Frank ran across the street and kissed first Adelaide and then his friend on both cheeks. Joe wrestled himself free.

"You're drunk," Joe said, and wiped his face.

"Just a wee bit, *mon cheri*. Me and my mates were 'aving an evening on the town. I saw you at the fair, but as per usual you ran off with a bint. Excuse me, ma'am." Frank said. "Saw you walking out with a lady." He tipped his cap at Adelaide and almost fell over.

She reached out and steadied him. "I shall leave you to help your friend," she said to Joe. "I'll get back to the fairground and find my friends. They'll be wondering where I am. Good night to you both."

Joe walked away. Frank grabbed him by the arm. "You're not much fun these days. We used to 'ave a good laugh together. You 'ad a fight with your new lady friend?"

"What are you on about?"

"The Armitage woman. I'm sure she fancies you." He leaned into Joe and whispered, "Did you forget she is a *madame*."

"It's not like that. We've helped each other. Enjoy each other."

"I'm sure you 'ave," Frank said, and thrust his hips back and forth.

"You're one to speak. What happened to you and Miss Nursie Phillipa?"

"Just some fun and company. She's like us boys here. Tries to 'ave some good times in this fucking miserable situation. Would do you good to get out more often with me. Any road, what about that French tart you 'ad back at the château?"

Joe's fist flew towards Frank's face, and then Frank was lying on the road.

"That really 'urt, Mathieson. Seeing you're such a good friend, I'll give you three seconds to tell me what that was for or you'll be the one down 'ere 'unting for your teeth in the gutter."

Tears lined up at the back of Joe's eyes, waiting, like the men in the front line, for the signal to pour forth, but he pushed them back and helped Frank up and brushed him down.

"That's what you get," Joe said. "I'll thank you not to be using insulting names. She's my girl."

Frank rubbed his jaw. "You can't 'ave a girl. You 'ave a wife. And a kiddie."

"I'm really in love with her. I can't get to see her. I even tried the café here where she worked off and on. They don't know where she is."

"Bloody 'ell, Joe, it's been two months since we were at the château and you met 'er. I thought you'd be over it." Frank wiggled his mouth open and shut. "I thought after we moved away you'd come to your senses and remember you're a married man. What's 'er name again?"

"Marguerite."

"Right. I remember now." Frank dropped his hand from his jaw. "I thought you were just 'aving me on with all your talking about," Frank faked a swoon, had to grab Joe to stop himself from toppling, "falling in love for the first time. Just your guilt."

Joe looped Frank's arm around his neck and laughed, happy to be talking about Marguerite again.

"You're a daft bugger," Frank said. "A seriously in love daft bugger. But you could 'ave a problem."

"Just one?" Joe said.

16

Monday, October 23, 1916 Joe strolled halfway across the arched wooden bridge that linked the banks of the River Ancre. Thanked the heavens for the day Atholl came to him almost three weeks ago and announced that Captain Rogers and his team were to move from the advanced dressing station at Lauretteville to this casualty clearing station at Bercordie.

"Not sure why he's offering you a special position," Atholl had said. "But he is. An assistant in the operating theatre at the CCS." The outline of Atholl's mouth had crooked into a sneer. "But then you went out of your way to make sure you impressed again at the ADS. Sewing up that nurse's finger. Of course I told him I'd taught you."

Joe wondered if he was supposed to scrape the ground at the lieutenant's feet and didn't let on that Rogers wasn't capable of sewing on as much as a button that day.

He relished these moments, alone by the river at the bottom edge of the hospital grounds. He could loosen up here despite the racket of the trains across the river that grunted and puffed as they shipped the most horribly wounded north to the base hospitals at Boulogne or Etaples. He loved it when he was lucky enough to see an ambulance barge gliding upriver. He hoped the lapping water soothed the agony of the wounded, snug inside the gaily-painted boats.

Autumn still hung in the air. Joe was grateful for winter's delay and for the shelter of the casualty clearing station. He'd been lucky last winter as well, on the trains, away from the rain-soaked trenches and the front line. Sometimes he was ashamed he wasn't more grateful, but he was thankful for this sunny day. He raised his chin, trolled for the sun's warmth. It could certainly be a lot worse. He hadn't had a day off since he came here to the Bercordie Casualty Clearing Station close to a month ago, but he had these peaceful few hours and the work challenged and rewarded him. He'd learned a lot more anatomy first-hand, and better understood how muscles wrapped around bones and how glistening ligaments tied them firmly in place like apron strings. His suturing skills would amaze any seamstress. He quickly learned how bones should be set and had become Rogers' favoured orderly for wrapping plaster casts.

He leaned against the bridge rail, closed his eyes, and soaked up the sound of the water skooshing over the mill wheel. He thanked his lucky stars. As Rogers had promised him in July, this hospital was far enough back from the battleground that everyone here enjoyed relative peacefulness and safety. He lowered his shoulders, shook out his neck, and let the tranquillity soak in. A rustle in the bushes towards the hospital startled him and he crouched. He told himself to stop being so bloody stupid. It was probably only a hedgehog or some other small animal rooting around.

"Sorry, Joe. I didn't mean to give you a fright." Adelaide pushed her way through the birch hedge. "Peace offering?" She held out a sandwich wrapped in brown paper. "Late lunch for me. Hungry?"

"Starving. As usual," Joe said.

"Let's sit on the river bank. C'mon. I'll share my sandwich."

She lifted her black woollen skirt past her ankles and walked ahead, taking care on the copper carpet of fallen leaves. Joe collected an armful of twigs and made her wait while he interlaced them to make a mat for her to sit on.

"Mademoiselle Adelaide," he said, as he made a grand gesture, laying the mat on the riverbank. It still felt strange to him to be calling a woman of her station by her first name, but here they were. All in this war together. All mucking in to help the wounded.

Joe held his half sandwich in both hands and dug into it. The ham was tough and salty, but his stomach welcomed it. Adelaide bit into hers, keeping her shortened finger sticking upright. She chewed slowly and dusted the crumbs from her lips with her handkerchief. "I expect it is a comfort to you to be at the ccs?"

"Bercordie?"

She swallowed. "For your brother. You have been to see your brother?" She looked up over to the hospital and pointed to where the cemetery lay a couple of hundred yards the other side of the main building.

"Aye well, I keep meaning to go but something always comes up. You know how it is. Day after day, hardly ever get the time. We've done eight amputations today already and it's not even dark. Then there's cleaning the operating theatre, the instruments. And the—"

"Joe. Stop." Adelaide's hand was on his arm. "It's important, you know."

"Aye. I know. My ma and Fred's wife would like it if I went."

"I'm talking about you, Joe. It's important that you go."

Joe stood, threw away the remains of his sandwich. "You've said that already."

He turned towards the bridge, wanting to get away from the truth of her words. "My break's over."

Adelaide stood also. He heard her sigh and imagined her shaking her head at him as he hurried away.

Captain Roger's team operated on another six men before night fell around six. They removed eighteen shell fragments and a gemstone ring— intended, Joe assumed, for a future fiancée—from the chest of a nineteen-year-old who was remarkably alert afterward. And delighted the ring was intact. Two men in their early twenties had devastating facial wounds that Rogers debrided as best he could before he tagged them for an immediate blighty evacuation. Three amputations completed the pre-supper list—a partial leg from the knee down, another below the groin, and an arm. As Joe stood by the operating table near the pile of bloodied dressings and severed limbs, he thought how he might as well be working in a butcher's shop, so familiar was he now with cutting and sawing flesh and bone. Maybe he'd leave the mine when he got back and try getting work with Hugh Simpson, the butcher on Main Street in Methilane. Then he studied the arm amputation patient, oblivious that he would wake up missing half an arm. *Nah,* he thought. *More likely I'll never enter the door of a butcher's again.*

"Wakey, wakey, Mathieson. I asked for another swab." Rogers put out his hand to Joe, who handed him the swab pinched on the end of a pair of forceps. Rogers peered inside the wound, dabbed at it a few times. "I'm done here. Sew him up, Atholl," he said wearily to the lieutenant. "I'm calling it a night."

Joe knew he meant he'd gone too long without a tot of whisky. "You all do the same when this one's been seen to. Get some sleep. I want you all fresh and eager at six tomorrow morning."

Joe hated watching Rogers pickle himself, but he hadn't the nerve to bring up the subject. But what if the captain made a terrible hash of an operation one day? He'd talk to Adelaide if he got the chance. She could be trusted to keep her mouth shut, and being a nurse, she was almost an officer. Perhaps her father could recommend someone to have a quiet chat with the captain.

Joe woke, suddenly, out of breath. It took him a second or two to realize he wasn't running. The army of legs and arms without bodies, hundreds and hundreds leaping through the air and chasing him with tremendous speed, was a dream. It had seemed so real, the pearly white skin and the red blood as vivid as gash-red lipstick on a clown's face. He got up, pulled on his trousers, and grabbed his torch. He flung his jacket around his shoulders, went outside, and peed. The sky was cloudless, the air chilled. The black starry night held his gaze until the images from his dream faded. A brilliant light exploded and dashed high across the sky. This one silent solitary blast through the sky, different from the flashes of the roaring artillery in the night that inspired only fear. A shooting star. Were the heavens mocking him with the name of this beautiful, magical light? It brightened his heart and reminded him there was a world outside this horror.

His eyes adjusted from the flash and he stared again at the field of stars above. *Twinkle, twinkle little star.* He could hear Ellen's giggles as he bounced her and chanted the rhyme. *How I wonder what you are.* He saw her rosebud mouth trying to imitate his words, her blue eyes staring intently into his as if he could unlock a secret contained in these magical words. Fred too was a father. Joe had never given this much thought before. His two nephews were just always there, getting underfoot and berated for their boisterousness. His eyes teared. He wiped them with the back of his hand. Looked into the sky again. *Twinkle, twinkle little stars,* he thought. *How I wonder who you all are. ... Fathers ... of fatherless children.*

He sprinted the couple of hundred yards to the cemetery, up and down the rows of wooden crosses, fanning his torch over the inscriptions until he found Fred's resting place. He sat cross-legged before the grave and shone his light onto Fred's name, regiment, and number. With a flick of his finger, he killed the light from the torch, and in the dark, traced the cross. *Never gave much thought to you being in danger*, he said to the marker, so fresh the wood still held hints of the forest. *Never gave much thought to anything till Walter ran off. Not my job, or even Kate afore Ellen came along. Certainly not this world out here. Or you. Sorry. I thought you could take care of yourself.* The sadness and melancholy of the last ten minutes swelled, its edges hardening into anger. He pawed at the earth, wanting to uncover the body and touch the hands that had held his, dodging the carts on the High Street his first day of school. Surely he'd find a stranger's form there. Could it really be his strapping angry brother's head below the cross? He touched the crucifix once more. His anger ebbed and a peace came over him. He hoped Fred lay there snug and intact. "I'll let Lizzie and Ma know where you are, big brother," he said. "I don't know how, but I promise I'll bring them to you after this war. For now, I'll tell them you're safe under the stars."

Monday, November 6, 1916 Joe made his way to the main building to post a card to Ellen for her third birthday. Adelaide came scurrying towards him as he reached the entrance, one hand holding up her hood. He held the door open for her.

"It's absolutely bucketing isn't it?" she said, taking off her cape and shaking it.

"Here. I'll do that for you," Joe said. "Where are you off to?"

"I've a meeting with Matron in ten minutes to go over some plan or other, but I'm gasping for a cup of tea."

"At your service, ma'am," Joe said with a bow. "Where to?"

Adelaide looked down the corridor. "There's an office that should be empty. Third door on the left. I'll just go hang this up." She took her cape from Joe.

When Joe got to the office, she was putting the clunky black telephone back into its cradle. She put out her hand to take the tea from Joe. "Well, I must say you're looking a lot happier than when I saw you the other day."

"I'm right sorry 'bout running off like that."

"Not a problem, Joe. We all struggle at times."

"You too?"

"Well, of course," Adelaide said, her voice chilling.

"I don't mind hearing about it."

"No, no. It's quite all right." She took a sip and seemed to relax. "But do tell why you've cheered up."

"I'm getting some leave. Real leave, so's I can go back home for a while. The plan is to be gone Friday. I'll be getting to see my wee lassie. It was her birthday on the second." Joe rubbed his upper lip. "And I did go to the grave. My brother's. Like you said I should." He told her all about that night. He even told her how it had started with the nightmare.

"I'm so glad you went to the cemetery. The modern thinking is to face into our fears. Have you heard of Dr. Rivers' work? In Edinburgh?"

"Edinburgh?"

"Yes. They've started a hospital for men who have been traumatized, you know, become nervous wrecks if you will, from the war. This Dr. Rivers is a specialist and he gets the men to talk about their experiences, even relive them."

Joe shivered. "I would think they'd just want to forget about them."

"Well," Adelaide said. "That's just Rivers' point. We don't forget. We can't. And the memories come to us whether we want them to or not. In nightmares, for example. But as I was saying, Dr. Rivers claims that by talking about awful experiences, and even talking about the dreams, the men he has under his care actually have fewer nightmares than they once had."

Joe was uneasy thinking about the bad dreams he had. But all the lads had them, even Frank. "Do you get nightmares?" he asked, worried he was getting too familiar with her.

"I have had some."

"Do you want to tell me about them? I'm no head doctor but I can listen."

"Good news about the leave," she said. "And will you see your wife?"

The sudden switch in the conversation took Joe aback.

"I don't know." Joe's good mood was beginning to deflate. "You want the truth?"

"Of course."

"The truth is I'm hoping she can't get away from the munitions factory at Gretna. It would just make things simpler."

"Whatever way it turns out, Joe, I do hope you enjoy it and you come back well rested. What about Marguerite? Have you been in contact with her?"

Joe took a step back. "Aye. I still write. Plenty. But never hear a word from her." He took a deep breath. "You're good at asking questions. And I have to say you ask good ones. Makes me think, but ..."

"But what?" Adelaide said clutching at her skirt.

"You're not as good at answering them."

Adelaide looked up at the ceiling, as if deep in thought. The door opened, startling them both.

"Mathieson, tea break's over. Back on your head, you slacker. Oh, sorry ma'am."

"It's perfectly all right," Adelaide said to the orderly who had come for Joe. "I have to go soon myself."

Joe lifted both the cups and went to follow the orderly, but Adelaide stopped him and pulled him back into the office.

"What is it?" Joe said, worried she was about to tell him off for being so bold.

"Oh, I was just thinking." She smiled. "I have an idea." Her eyes had an impish spark he hadn't seen before. "I was thinking back to the evening at the fair," she said. "How thrilling it was driving that dodgem car. And since you did a reasonably good job as a driving instructor, I thought we could—how can I put it?—borrow a motor ambulance."

"Are you serious? What for? This is not like you?"

"Oh, so now you know me?"

"I just mean, I don't see you as the reckless type."

"Relax, Joe. I'm not offended. I'm enjoying your company now we're working together again. And," she stood and put her hands on her hips, "I'm ready for a different adventure."

"Are you mad? And when exactly were you thinking of doing this?"

"Are you free after supper-time?"

"No, I'm working right through till midnight. Both today and the next two days."

"All right. It'll have to be Thursday then. Let's meet in the canteen that evening and have our supper together."

Joe bit at a fingernail. "We could get into big trouble." His mind flashed back to the hard wallop on the cheek he'd suffered at the MPs' hands back in June.

"I'd say it was all my idea. I'll be the one doing the driving," she said. "For me, that's part of the adventure."

"And the other part?'

"I'd like a change of scenery."

"It's too chancy. Not worth the risk."

"Not even if we went to Gaudechat?"

Joe's eyes opened wide. "No kidding?" He was quiet for a moment; then he smiled. "I can't. It would put you in danger. Having you in charge of the driving and all that. No, I can't put you at risk."

"I'm disappointed. I thought you'd be all for it."

"Well, you're wrong." Joe was laughing now. "I'd never let a lady do the driving."

Adelaide clapped her hands, then went forward and hugged him.

"Mathieson!" The orderly was back again. "Shake a leg. Rogers is waiting on you."

"Aye, aye. I'm coming."

Thursday, November 9, 1916 Rogers gave Joe permission to knock off shortly after three in the afternoon. To get ready for his departure on leave tomorrow, he had a good wash all over and shaved. He dragged his kit bag from under his bed, and stuffed it with spare socks, clean underwear, his toilet bag, and two shirts. He pulled the drawstring tight and laid his greatcoat over the top. Joy of joys. Surely now he'd see Marguerite. He still had to solve the problem of how to get past her father and avoid another slugging but he knew, he just knew, it had to work out.

And first thing in the morning, after seeing her, he'd be on his way home via the hospital train as far as Boulogne. A night boat across the channel and a long train ride up north would have him in Methilane and his old bed in his mother's house. The journey would take close to forty hours, but by Saturday night, he'd be bouncing his newly three-year old Ellen on his knee. What a fuss Ma would make of the evening meal, scrounging the best pork chop she could. Likely she'd already baked the sultana cake for Christmas and would be willing to cut it early. Joe combed his hair and made his way over to the canteen.

He poured himself a mug of tea from the soup-pot-sized urn. Although staff came and went in dribs and drabs, grabbing a meal or having a smoke break, he and Adelaide would have some privacy amid the buzzing chatter to fine tune their getaway. He looked around and saw her seated in the middle of the room. She waved him over and patted the empty chair beside her. Joe had barely sat down when an officer he recognized as Captain Comstock from the château at Gaudechat walked past, carrying a chair over his head. He thought of Gaudechat. His thighs tingled. Comstock wove his way to the front and stood on the chair. The crowd became quiet.

"Thank you," the captain said. "A head's up on what we might anticipate next week. Eight regiments are being moved up around Oroville. We are expecting some intensification of engagement."

Joe looked at Adelaide. He knew this was the soft way of informing them another offensive was looming. More fighting, more wounded, more death. He let his mind wander to his reunion with Marguerite to avoid the ugly pictures in Comstock's message. Thank God, he'd be on leave and miss this one.

"We'll be setting up an additional ccs in that area and five advanced dressing stations. Your company commander will be informing you if you are to be sent to another location."

"This *Horrible*," Joe whispered to Adelaide. "Where is it?"

"Horrible? Oh, I see." Adelaide laughed. "*Oroville*. North. About twenty kilometres, I think."

"Well, they'll not be sending me." He sat back, gave Adelaide a soft prod in the ribs, folded his arms, and hummed Scotland the Brave. Joe liked it here at Bercordie, sheltered fifteen kilometres from the fighting, and the same distance from Gaudechat in the opposite direction. And now that he was over his fear of Fred's grave, he went there at least once a day and would hate to leave him here alone. "I'll send the lads a post card from Scotland. You too. A special one with tartan and all."

"Shh! Shut up you two," Phillipa Wilkinson hissed at them from behind. "I've missed what he said."

"All leave is cancelled," said the nurse next to her.

Joe gripped the edges of his chair, willing himself to stay put, fighting the urge to pick up the chair and hurl it. Was there no winning anything? Was a few days' furlough not earned? Even down the coal pit he had a week off every year.

Dusk had already spread over the winding rutted road to Gaudechat when Joe and Adelaide drove the ambulance out from the ccs. Christ, he was pissed over the cancellation of his leave. He sat in the passenger seat with his feet leaning against the windscreen, tapping his hand on his thigh.

"Please stop that, Joe. It's making it harder for me to concentrate in this light," Adelaide said, grabbing his hand. "I know you're upset, not going home, but we're doing this now." She stopped the vehicle at the château. "Let's see who we can find."

"The place is useless. I'm sure it's a bloody wild goose chase," Joe said, as he walked to the entrance to the château. "Spooky here. Where is everyone?"

"Let's not give up so soon," Adelaide said, running after him. "There's bound to be someone in the village who will know. Come on, Joe. Cheer up. Let's have a look around. You said yourself we're taking a great risk. Let's make it worth our while."

Joe waited for her and they walked into the village without talking. They pushed open the door of the *estaminet* where in June, before he met Marguerite, he had drunk many a glass of wine. They nodded to a pair of old men swaddled in big wool coats who sat facing each other over a dirty table. The place once so full of camaraderie between the villagers and their visitors from over the channel shivered in a gloomy sterility. Outside the light was failing. Pinks and greys streaked the sky. Joe and Adelaide peeped around the side of the bar. From the semi-dark, a near-toothless old woman came toward them with a broom in her hand.

"Madame," Adelaide said, extending her gloved hand. Joe listened as Adelaide spoke French. The old woman began ranting, throwing her hands up in the air.

"What the hell is she saying?" He yanked Adelaide's arm.

"Joe, let go. You're hurting me. I am trying. Be patient."

The woman walked past them and into the street. Adelaide and Joe followed. The woman stopped, turned around, and started ranting again. She finally stopped, took a huge breath, dropped to her knees, and sobbed. She beat at the ground with her fists and resumed her ranting.

Joe wished he knew the French for *shut up,* so he could silence the grating shrieks. He'd never had to use those words with Marguerite. "We're getting nowhere with the old crone," he said. "Ask her if there's someone else."

Adelaide stood quietly, her hands clasped at her middle, acknowledging the old woman's tirade with punctuations of *Oui. Oui.*

Joe tugged at Adelaide again.

"Shh," she said. "I have to concentrate to understand her."

"It's useless. Bloody waste of time. I'm going."

Adelaide caught up with Joe at the ambulance and stood in front of the door, stopping him from opening it. She crossed her arms. "What is wrong with you?"

"I told you it's a waste of time."

"Since when is finding your lady love a waste of time? You've been mooning about this ever since you told me about her." She walked away from him, then came back, her fists clenched. "I'm doing this for you, you know ... and a bit of cooperation on your part would go a long way. What exactly is this mood about?"

"There you go asking your big questions again." He pushed past her, but she grabbed him and spun him around to face her. He shook off her arm. "Well try this on for size." He stepped in closer to her face, but she didn't back off. "Number one. My stupid wee brother runs off and I can't find him. Number two, my other brother is killed and is lying in a hole in this bloody fucking foreign country. Three, I can't get home for my bairn's birthday. Maybe I'll never get home again and now the only good thing that's happened to me seems to have vanished into thin air. That's four fucking disasters. Does that answer satisfy you? And by the way," he said walking away again, "don't think I'm going to return the favour and find your lost love."

Adelaide gasped. Immediately, Joe ran back to her and held her shaking shoulders. "Oh, my God. I can't believe ... I can't believe I said that! I'm sorry. Oh, God." He took her in his arms. "I didn't mean that. You're my ... my friend. You have to accept my apology. Please."

"It's this bloody war," she said softly. He could feel her warm breath as she spoke. "Number five," she said, pushing him away and dabbing her eyes. "I didn't go to all the trouble of inventing a story for Rogers. Yes, friend," she said, a smile lifting the edges of her mouth, "I got him to agree I should bring supplies to the hospital at the Gaudechat château and convinced him I could drive this damn thing. I didn't know they had already shut it down. I hope Captain Rogers doesn't keep track."

"You told him we were doing a delivery?"

She started to cry again. "I was determined one of us would not leave this war empty-handed. I caught him at a moment when he, well ... you know how he can be."

"Drunk?'

"I know. I took advantage, but no one is being harmed."

Joe's shoulders relaxed and he grinned. "So now we are liars as well as thieves. Have you any idea what they'll do to us if they find out? Rogers has bailed me out once already. I'm not sure I can push my luck any further."

"I thought you had more staying power, Joe Mathieson. And it's for you and your precious Marguerite that I am trying out my schoolgirl French."

"Yes, mademoiselle," Joe said, lowering his head in mock shame.

"It's Madame," she said, and strode off with Joe trailing after her. They caught up with the old woman, who was now labouring under the weight of a heavy pail.

"I don't understand the problem," Adelaide said. "I know my French is not stunning, but she doesn't seem to understand anything I say. And I certainly can't understand her. It's like she doesn't speak French. How can she live in France and not speak French?"

"It's the dialect," Joe said. "Rogers told me. Like the Scots and the English. Maybe here they talk different from you and the posh folk in Paris. No offence."

"None taken, Joe. I'll have another go. What is Marguerite's family name? Perhaps we could write it down."

"If the old bat can read."

"I hadn't thought of that. You're right Joe. It's highly unlikely that she can read. Probably very few villagers can."

Joe stopped and slapped his hand against his forehead. "You're brilliant."

"I am?"

"Marguerite doesn't read my English well enough. Maybe she doesn't read that well even in her own language."

"Quite possibly not. But why wouldn't she write to you?"

"Pride, I bet. When she couldn't get my questions. So then," Joe said, "the letters I gave her afore, in Gaudechat ... she must have got someone to read them to her. But she wouldn't be able to write to me." He rushed over to Adelaide and kissed her on the cheek. "You've got to talk to the auld biddy again."

"At your service," Adelaide said, putting her hand to her face.

They chased after the squat old woman. Joe took the pail from her and she pointed ahead to the château. He and Adelaide followed her through the gateway.

"Madame," Adelaide said, coming around in front of her. She put her hands together and bowed to the woman. *"La famille."* She turned to Joe. "The name?"

"Oh-sar is how it sounded to me."

"Marguerite Oh-sar. La famille Oh-sar." She swept her arms around the château farmyard and pointed to the ground. *"Ici?"*

The old woman shook her head. Adelaide pointed into the distance then held out her arms. "Where? *Où?*"

The old woman started to cry, hugged herself, and gushed a jumble of French-sounding words.

"Pardon, Madame?" Adelaide said. *"Encore.* Slowly. *Lentement."*

"*Way. Way,*" her words sounded, as she rolled her eyes at Adelaide. She flapped a handkerchief and dabbed her eyes, formed each syllable slowly and carefully. *"Les Ossarts. La famille s'en va."*

"They've gone away?" Adelaide translated the old woman's words. "When, Madame? *Quand?*"

The woman held up all ten fingers, and repeated the motion twice.

"Thirty. *Un mois?*' Adelaide said. The woman nodded and continued speaking. *"Merci, Madame,"* Adelaide said. *"Merci beaucoup."* She listened a little longer to the woman before giving her some coins.

"Well," said Joe. "Is she here?"

"No, I'm afraid not, Joe. The whole family has left."

"How?"

"On foot. Can you believe that? All that way."

"Woman, I don't care if they went in a fancy carriage."

Adelaide took a step back and put up her hands.

"I'm sorry," Joe said. "Shouldn't have snapped at you. I mean, how come? Why?"

"I imagine they left because they were frightened. They went on foot, as I said, a month ago. To Toulouse."

"Toulouse? Do we have time to go there? Is it close?"

"No, Joe." She linked her arm into his and started walking him back to the ambulance. "It's in the south. The far south. Five, maybe five hundred and fifty miles away."

Joe lay awake all night. Smoked cigarette after cigarette. Tried to blow off the frustrations that hammered against his skull, gripped his muscles, and turned his dinner sour in his stomach. He couldn't think of one more thing he could do to be with Marguerite. Writing letters hadn't worked, seeing her at the harvest feast had only got him a split lip, and now she was five hundred miles away. As far as Methilane. She might as well have gone to the moon. Maybe Frank was right. They'd as much chance for a life together as a snowman and snow-lady in hell. Adelaide obviously shared Frank's view, judging from all the questions she'd asked about their differences the night of the fair. The vivid dreams and plans he'd had in his head in the summer paled around the edges.

With the rain battering against the tin roof above his head, it took effort to fend off the seepage of memories. Freezing nights like this at home with a gale blowing in off the North Sea. Kate came into clear view. *Aye,* he thought. *Kate.* The wife. *My wife.* A month with Marguerite had confirmed the hesitation he'd had on his wedding day three and a half years ago. Ma had tried to blow off his reluctance. But they both knew the truth. Ma had worked hard that June day in 1912 to keep him cheery.

Ma had come up behind him as he looked at his dressed-up self in the mirror and she'd straightened the back of his new white shirt. She put her hands over his shoulders and deftly made a knot in his tie. "There. Very handsome. A rare gift for Kate." She pulled at his cheek. "Why the glum look? I want to see my precious laddie happy." She gave him a playful push out of her way and lifted her hat, the peacock feather sweeping over the top like a filigreed cage. Wistfully, Joe watched her in the mirror as she put it on, until she caught him staring and smiled.

"Don't be watching me anymore, Joe. There's got to be only one woman for you after you wed Kate." She offered him her arm and he ushered her out of the house where he'd lived his whole life. Ma locked the door and dropped the key into her special occasions' bag, a black velvet square with a silver chain handle. "Unless the bairn is a wee lassie," she added.

Joe felt the hand of shame stirring at the morning porridge in his stomach but said nothing. He hoped the guests waiting at the kirk wouldn't notice the bulge starting to show in Kate's belly. But he knew the old aunties would be looking for it. Fred, the best man, was still nowhere to be seen, so Joe sat down on the doorstep, pulled out a big white handkerchief, laid it on the stone lintel, and bade Ma join him. He cleared his throat and looked up to the cloudless sky.

"Ma, I don't think I'm going to do a good job of this. Being a husband."

"Of course you will. You're a good man," said Ma. "Kind, responsible. And clever. Aye, very clever. You and Walter. Fred too in his own way." She tugged at his arm to make him look at her. "Do you love her?"

Joe bit the side of his thumbnail. "I'm just trying to do the right thing."

"And that you will. I have no doubt, but that's not my question. Och, I'm sorry, Joe. Mothers shouldn't pry like this. Forget I asked that. I'm embarrassed just to think on it. But I wished I'd pushed you harder when I told you to leave here. Do you remember? The night of your da's funeral?"

Joe looked straight into his mother's face, framed beneath the blue hat. He noticed, with bittersweet amusement, her rouged cheeks and lips. A couple of grey hairs had pierced through her chin, an accompaniment to the puffy lines that gave her smile a drawn and perpetually tired look.

"I don't even like her that much," he said, in answer to her original question. "She's all right, I suppose. Not very swift. I can't think of any other way to make it right by her."

"Well, Joe, there'd be few of us wed if it wasn't for a bairn coming. Life usually makes choices for us, more's the pity." The lines around her mouth set themselves into deeper furrows. "I see Fred." She stood and called him over. "I'm hoping you can still have a good life," she whispered to Joe as Fred closed in on them. "Aye, but you will. I know you will."

Friday, November 10, 1916 It was a relief to put away those dismal memories and roll off his bed at five in the morning. He ran over to the latrines, pulling his head close to his chest against the biting November wind that drove sharp needles of icy rain onto his bare head. At least he wasn't sleeping outside in the trenches like most of the company. By six, he was shaved, dressed, and had his hands wrapped around a warm mug of tea in the canteen.

"Good morning, Joe."

"I'd not exactly say it was a good morning. I'm freezing here." Joe scraped a chair over the stone floor for Adelaide. "Got time to sit?"

"So you're on the move again, I hear," she said as she sat down. "What a well-travelled man you are. Last night Gaudechat and today a new posting to Mortecourt."

"Look, I'm sorry about last night. Especially getting upset with you. You've been a great help."

"It's not a problem, Joe. I told you I was ready for a little excitement. I'm just sorry it ended in disappointment."

"Aye, well ... thanks. How do you know where I'm off to? I haven't been told myself."

"I've already seen Rogers this morning." She gave his shoulder a little shove with hers. "I reported to him that we had safely delivered the supplies to the hospital at the Gaudechat château. He told me his team was moving to an advanced dressing station at Mortecourt."

"Did he say where it is?"

"About a mile this side of Oroville. The word is we're going to retake that village from the enemy and start pushing them back."

"When?"

Adelaide laughed. "I'm happy to be a lot of things, including translator and tour guide, but I'm not a military strategist. I assume as soon as the weather gets better and the worst of this rain stops. Wouldn't be able to see much ahead otherwise."

"I never thought I'd be wanting this rain to keep up."

"It's awful isn't it? I'm surprised it's not snowing."

"What about you? Are you going closer to the front?"

"No word yet but perhaps the ccs at Colinvillers. About eight miles north. As the crow flies roughly six miles west of you and a bit to the south. It's the closest to Oroville. I'll be seeing plenty of your patients, no doubt." She lowered her eyes and stroked her damaged finger.

"Are you sure you're not still wild with me?" Joe said. "About last night."

"No truly. I am not. Why would you say that?"

"You were rubbing your finger. The one we operated on. You do that when you're annoyed. Or worried, maybe. It got a lot of stroking last night."

"I am worried." She leaned in closer to him. "About Captain Rogers. He's a good man. And a very fine surgeon."

"You're right there. In my books, he's a prince. A bit moody but then we all have our off days."

"When we chatted this morning, it was barely six and he was ..."

"I can guess. He'd already had a few."

"Joe, I've seen him drunk, really drunk, on more than one occasion when he shouldn't have had any."

"Like in the operating room? Aye. I've seen him too. I worry about him killing someone. We're lucky there's not been a nasty accident."

"And I'd hate to see him reported. It would be a disastrous end to his career, and I'm sure the punishment would be awful. I've listened outside his dugout a couple of times and heard him say such strange things. Frightening things."

"Like what?"

"Taking part in Satan's work. Awful things like that."

"But he's doing just the opposite. He's saving lives."

"I know," she said. "It's bizarre. I am really worried he is cracking up."

"Maybe the drink stops him from cracking?"

Adelaide frowned. "I don't know. Nor do I know what one can do."

"Nothing a man like me can do for a captain. That I do know."

"Could you try and talk to him? He likes you. He might listen."

"That's more your department," Joe said, blowing on his hot tea.

"When you leave, would you at least keep an eye on him?"

Joe shrugged. "Whatever I can do to look out for him, I'll do it. I owe him a few. Will you do something for me?"

"Of course."

"As long as you're here, can you visit Fred's grave? I hate to leave him." He got up and tucked his chair under the table. "Good luck wherever you end up."

Adelaide grabbed his arm. "Be safe, Joe. Drop me a note. If not here, then Colinvillers. CCS Number 5. I'd hate to lose touch."

He held her arm for a moment. "You're my partner in crime now. We can't say cheerio for good."

Joe knew he was lucky. As part of the medical team, he travelled with ambulances filled with supplies and had the luxury of riding most of the twelve miles in relative comfort, squished, but dry, between cardboard boxes. For the thousands of men tramping their way to the new front line, it was heads down and bear it. All day long the clouds emptied rain on the marching troops. Their boots squelched louder and louder as the leather no longer absorbed the water that mushed the rutted roads.

The early winter gloom oozed menace. For many, the battles since July had shone the cold light of reality over any romantic notions they'd brought over the English Channel. No longer was there the protecting ignorance of the coming waste and wreckage. Joe hated the words the officers used: Encounter, engagement with the enemy (as if they were looking to fucking marry them), skirmish, and meet (How do you do, Fritz? How's your day going?). Joe wasn't fooled into thinking it was anything other than a savage black mark against the human race. He counted thirty-four wagons alone that were transporting ammunition, and shuddered at the damage that amount of firepower would do. He studied some of the young faces he passed. Which of them would he see in the coming days, laid out on an operating table, or worse, lined up on the ground as one of the dead?

They stopped at a village, this one with many more remaining inhabitants than Gaudechat. The sign read Bus-Les-Comté. Joe read it as Busless County and wondered how Marguerite would say it. They dropped off supplies at the advanced dressing station there, ate some rations from their knapsacks, and continued on for another mile or so to Mortecourt. It was almost five in the afternoon when they arrived, although it had been dark for close to two hours. Once the supplies were unloaded, Joe was shown a sleeping spot in a dank dugout in a trench some two hundred yards forward of the ADS.

Gone were the relative luxuries of the casualty clearing station at Bercordie: camp beds, blankets, stoves for boiling water, and a canteen where food and drink were always available for the asking. Gone too were the nurses. It would be men only for company until this was over. The kitchen wagon came around and Joe lined up to get his rations: two fried eggs and a plate of chips.

Saturday, November 11, 1916 It was light when Joe woke. He checked the time. Already after eight. He dressed quickly, protecting whatever heat was in his body, and climbed over the top. He ploughed through the soggy ground, showers of foul water spurting up over his boots, and dodged through streams of haggard and sopping infantrymen. He lowered himself down a ladder into the twelve-foot-deep trench that sheltered the row of six concrete bunkers serving as treatment rooms. He half expected a bollicking for being late, but when he entered the first room it was empty, save for a mountain of boxes, each marked with a red cross and the words *wound supplies.* The second the same. At the third, Youngalec loaded surgical instruments onto shelves nailed into the timbered walls. Joe remembered the young orderly's deafness and tapped him on the shoulder. Waited until he turned around. "How you doing, pal? Where's everybody?"

Youngalec shook Joe's hand. "Mostly still sleeping. While they can." He scratched the scar where his ear had been. "So much to do. I've only just started unpacking and organizing. I could do with a hand."

"My pleasure, Youngalec."

A half-dozen other orderlies came later in the morning. They milled together, chatted about where they were from and where they'd spent the war. The treatment rooms were ready shortly after one. Joe went for a nap and popped back into one a few minutes after four. Youngalec sat cross-legged in a corner reading a book. Joe banged a couple of kidney dishes against each other to get his attention.

"Seen Rogers?"

"Nobody's been by," Youngalec said. "Except Atholl. Had a quick boo just before four and left."

"What's the book? Any good?"

Youngalec pointed to the cover. "Mr. H.G. Wells. *Mr. Britling Sees It Through*. It's what people back home are thinking about the war."

"I don't think that'll make any difference. The big brass have got their minds made up," Joe said, as he made for the doorway. "And you'd better not be telling folk I said that."

The frosty wind numbed the back of his scalp. Joe pulled his coat up around his head and walked the length of a trench to where the officers had their dugouts. The icy rain pummelled his shoulders as he stopped and listened at entranceways, hoping to catch Rogers' voice. Halfway down the line he ran into Atholl coming through a doorway.

"Watch out, soldier. Oh, it's you, Mathieson."

Joe took a step back and saluted him. "Sir, would you know Captain Rogers' dugout?"

"Any business you have with him can go through me."

"It's personal. Sir."

"And just what kind of personal business would you have with a captain?" Joe had to think quickly. "It's not me, sir. I've a personal message from Mrs. Armitage at Bercordie. She said to give it to him directly."

Atholl flicked the rain from his face. "I'm not standing about wasting my time getting drenched." He pointed his thumb toward the doorway and moved off. "He's in there."

Joe knocked.

"Come."

He pushed the door open.

"Yes?" Rogers said, looking up from a newspaper.

Joe was surprised to see him looking fresh and well rested. Maybe a good time to mention something. Perhaps the captain would be less likely to fly off the handle when sober.

Rogers closed the newspaper and laid it on the floor. "Something on your mind? Problem?"

"Problem?" Joe looked into his teacher's kind face.

Rogers picked up his pipe. "Not often we get to put up our feet." He lit the tobacco, sucking on the briar and blowing out puffs of smoke until he was satisfied the pipe was lit. "The calm before the storm I am sure. But feels good." He put the pipe down on a brass saucer at his side. And leaned his elbows on his knees. "What can I do for you, my trusted pupil?"

Joe imagined the man's face darkening if he brought up the drinking. "Oh," he said, trying to work up some saliva. "Nothing. I just ... I just wanted to report everything's ready. Any further orders?"

"For now we're just waiting. I hope you're getting some rest."

"I am, sir. Can you say when the fighting's going to start?"

"Not until this infernal rain stops. Apparently not tomorrow. Maybe Monday." He wrote something on a sheet of paper. "On second thought, do this, will you Mathieson? It's a requisition for two barrels of whale oil and transport. First thing in the morning, take Young with you and go over to the quartermaster. Then get the barrels to the officer in charge of the first aid posts up at the front line. It's not far. About a mile ahead."

"What's it for?"

"Ah, Mathieson. You'll be interested in this, being the foot expert."

They smiled at each other remembering the march to the front in the July heat, when Joe had brazenly offered advice to the captain about the prevention of blisters.

"For once, I am ahead of you in my knowledge of foot care. Rubbing this ghastly stuff into the feet apparently can delay the onset of frostbite. Would you believe me if I told you there were a thousand cases this past week alone?"

"I wonder if it's just their feet that's freezing. It's hell out there."

"Worse, I'd say, Joe. At least hell's warm." He handed Joe the paper he'd written on. "I'll telephone ahead my instructions for its application. Check back with me tomorrow sometime."

"Yes, sir. I'll be happy to. Right away."

Sunday, November 12, 1916 Joe, with Youngalec helping, delivered the barrels and headed back to the stretcher-bearers' post, a converted barn within easy reach of the numerous first aid posts dotted around it. He was slurping on hot tea and giving himself a silent bollicking for chickening out with Rogers when the flimsy door crashed open. "Well, will you look at what the cat dragged in?" he said.

"Bugger me," Frank said. "You're a sight for sore eyes." He grabbed Joe by the shoulders and thumped him on the back.

"What are you doing here?" Joe asked.

"That's a daft question, mate. Same as usual, unless the war's over and nobody told me. And you? Are you back 'ere?"

"At the ADS up the road."

Frank poured himself a cup from the big iron kettle. "Any word on your baby brother?"

"None, but I'm hoping he's among this lot." It didn't seem much of an answer, but what else was there to say? He knew the routine. Keep asking around, keep his eyes open, keep convincing Ma no news was a good thing.

"It's going to be big again, Frank. I've seen thousands of troops." Joe shuddered. "Poor miserable buggers out in this cold."

Frank stepped forward, hugged Joe, and whispered in his ear. "I'll keep a special lookout."

A burley red-haired soldier pulled Frank away. "Break up the loving, you two." He threw a football at Frank. "Your dribbling talents are needed on the pitch, not in your boyfriend's ear."

The men standing around whistled and laughed. "You must be joking," Frank said. "It's pissing rain."

"You got something else to do? Maybe shopping for a fancy cravat for your friend?"

Frank threw the ball back at the man's chest. "C'mon Joe. Let's show these Jessies what kind of men we are."

A half-dozen or so full frontal falls in the mud and Joe realized the idea of a football game on a November afternoon in the drizzling mist of northern France was more exciting than the reality, which had the lads spitting out mouthfuls of gluey clay. But it got the blood flowing through his veins, and it was a welcome change to be in contact with healthy moving bodies and boisterous cheering. About twenty minutes into the match, the thirty or so players—winded, their legs leaden with the effort—called time and headed back.

"A gang of us bearers are going right over to Busless County, a couple of miles back," Frank said, leaning against Joe. "Stand still, will you mate?" He stood on one foot on the rain-slicked duckboards, a hand on Joe's shoulder, as he took off a boot and rinsed its upper in a puddle. "The locals, such as are left, are putting on a concert and a dance." He shook the water from the boot and slipped his foot back into it. "Do-gooding ugly women mostly, but better than twiddling your thumbs and thinking the worst." He rinsed his other boot and put it back on. "Your turn," he said, taking Joe's arm.

"Can't see the point if we're just going to be tramping through more mud to get over to there. I'm not that keen. Should get an early night."

"Oh, c'mon. Live while you can. We can sleep when we're dead. And maybe not all the women'll be ugly. Talking of which, 'ow's that mamzelle of yours?"

"Nothing doing."

"You've likely saved yourself a lot of trouble."

"Aye, maybe," Joe said. "Sorry pal, but I'm not going. I'm bumming out on you, much as I will miss your handsome face." He threw a kiss at Frank. "Boyfriend!"

"If only they knew what you'd got up to in that department."

Frank's banter always cheered him. "I wish there'd been more of it. Anyway you go on. Rogers said if the weather turns better the fighting'll start the morn."

"All the more reason to shake a leg tonight."

"Thanks for the invite." He patted his friend on the shoulder. "I'll see you soon enough, delivering the poor sods over to us."

Joe thought the bit of football would have relaxed him into a good night's sleep in the cocoon of the enclosed dugout, but he couldn't settle. He thought of writing a couple of letters but couldn't put his mind to it, and now there was no point writing to Marguerite. Youngalec and a couple other orderlies sat round an empty wire spool in a corner, half-heartedly playing gin rummy. He could exert himself and join them, but couldn't decide if that was what he wanted to do. Maybe it was the weather. He was fed up with it. Everyone was fed up with it and with the same old food, the tea that tasted like petrol because water was stored in old oil drums, the dirt, the mud, the cold, and the lack of sleep. They'd all had enough of the boredom disturbed with fear and pain. Sometimes he didn't know which was worse. Even the most enthusiastic youngster learned quickly war games didn't make heroes of them. In the end, he folded a grey wool scratchy blanket and laid down on it. He lit up a cigarette, stared at the timbers supporting the walls, and watched a big black fly pop through a crack, disappear, and reappear through another crack four feet down the wall. *Poor sod,* Joe thought. It was probably wondering where all its fly friends were and why it had survived the annual die-off.

From the direction of the officers' dugouts came the faint drone of bagpipes. A rip of loneliness gripped his throat. He could feel tears coming. What is it with all this crying? He rolled onto his side so that the card players couldn't see him. I've wet my cheeks more this past eighteen month than all my years as a wee laddie. He stubbed out his cigarette, closed his eyes, and let the lilt of Mhairie's Wedding seep into him and lull him into a precious sleep.

He tried to open his mouth, but it was clamped shut. He clawed at his lips, tried to pry them apart, but they were sealed together. His nostrils too had closed over. His chest hurt, ached for breath. He knew where he was. In his tomb, in a tight, pitch-black underworld. Who had buried him? How could he let them know he wasn't dead? He tried shouting, but he had no air. He could hear them, the living, walking over him. He put his hands over his ears to drown out their footsteps pulsing over his head. He tried to rip the seam that had stitched his lips together.

His eyes were wide open now, as he sat up rigid as a pole. His hands clawed at the muffler that had wound itself round his neck and face. His mouth sucked in air. He shook his head, forced himself into a vague consciousness. He lay back down and wiped the sweat from his face with his scarf, wrapped it around his neck again, and tucked it inside his shirt, well away from his face. The pounding above him continued. The infantry was moving into position. It's starting. He lay dazed and confused for an hour before looking at his pocket watch. Ten to six. He got up, pulled on his boots and greatcoat, and crept outside. It was still dark. The rain had stopped. The clatter of a huge explosion rushed at him from the east and fired him back against the trench wall. He dropped to the ground and covered his head. Then there was silence; a muteness that wavered in the air and unnerved him. He climbed out of the trench and looked into the distance, to where men would again be going over the top. The line between earth and sky was lit up as if with flame. He sat down and stared at it, refusing to believe that today could possibly bring the same horrors as July.

Eventually a mist floated up toward a brightening sky, a shy sun just visible on the eastern horizon. On any other Monday morning like this, he would have said it was going to be a lovely day.

"What's taking so long?" Rogers barked at Frank. "It's damn well close to two o'clock." Joe helped Frank roll the comatose patient onto the treatment table.

"It's 'eavy going, sir," Frank said. "What with all the bloody rain. The bearers are 'aving an 'ell of a time bringing them in. Takes them more than a minute to trudge a couple of steps."

"I don't care if it's raining butterflies, these boys have to be operated on."

Frank giggled, lifting his thick woollen mitt to cover his mouth. He leaned over and whispered in Joe's ear. "Butterflies? The man's raving. What's got up 'is arse? Surely to Christ 'e knows the roads are all flooded. Fucking swamp it is out there. I think 'is mouth's been wrapped around a bottle all week. Fucking sucking swamp out there."

"What's that?" Rogers said, squeezing past them to get to the other side of the treatment table.

"I was just saying we're doing our best. Sir."

"Well, it wasn't good enough for this one. He's dead. Get him out of here and over to the gravediggers at Bus-Les-Comté. Bring me one I can do something for."

Frank lifted the corpse and plopped it back on the stretcher. Joe helped carry the stretcher through the door where a sapper would collect it for burial. Frank signalled to Joe that he was stopping for a smoke.

"Who the 'ell does 'e think I am?" Frank said. "I'm not 'is own personal delivery service."

Once outside Joe, still in his blood-soaked gown, handed over the Woodbines. "Have a coffin nail and settle down. I'll see to the body."

"Where's this bloody place? What'd 'e call it? Boo-something?"

"It's where you went Sunday night. To the concert."

"Busless County? Well, pardon me for not speaking it like a real Frenchie."

"The captain's okay. You know he treats me well. All of us. He's no different from the rest of us. Wants the job done and be on his way home."

"Tell 'im to stick around a while. There's plenty out there needing bits sewed back on. We're not likely to see the end of this for at least a few days, so you can tell 'im there's lots more where that last one came from. God rest 'is bleeding soul." Frank threw his cigarette end on the ground. It fizzled in the mud. "Back to the cesspool."

"Aye. And keep your head down."

Joe crossed paths with Frank many times during the next few days. As the unceasing deluge of wounded was delivered to the ADS, the numbing cold Joe endured melted into frustration and boiled into anger as he and the other medics fought their own battle, trying to give speedy attention to the wounded men. Mostly Joe was able to swallow down his anguish over the more terrifying wounds, but unbidden, the grotesque images stained his mind when he tried to get some shut-eye. Flesh ripped from faces, chests and bellies bared open from shells and bullets, and the grey-white sheen of shattered bones. The triage system was often abandoned in the chaos. Cleaning, stitching, and amputations were all urgent. Joe noticed how willingly the wounded accepted the numbing ether, how easily they warmed to his reassurances, and how confidently they surrendered themselves to Rogers' skill. This worried Joe more and more as the hours piled up and whiffs of whisky wafted from Rogers' breath.

The officer grew more taciturn while the teams revved up their chitchat to stave off sleepiness during the night. They were the busiest then, as the stretcher-bearers retrieved the wounded in relative safety during the hours of darkness. During the grim light of daytime while the bullets flew, the injured were left to their own devices. Some screamed, some writhed, some slept. Many died.

On the fourth night, around three in the morning, hunched over the operating table, Joe's fellow medics took to throwing around the rumours.

"Apparently we *are* making ground," said an orderly, syringing out a pus-filled gut. "I heard we got right into the enemy trenches this time," another said, pushing coils of bowel aside so Rogers could get a better look at the source of a bleed. "They didn't think we would attack with the weather being so lousy. There they were, still in their dugouts, having their breakfast, and big surprise, our boys plop on top of them. Easy-peasy."

The first orderly chimed in: "I heard the Alleyman's trenches were full of beer and cigars and woman's clothing. Dancing slippers and the like."

"Is this who we're scared of? Guys that dress up in women's clothing? A bunch of poofters?"

"Perhaps they're allowed visitors."

"Hey, Captain, could you arrange that for us? Some of those ooh-la-la French lassies? And tell them to bring their dancing shoes."

"And some for me too." Joe said. "I can't fandango in these boots."

They all laughed.

"That's enough," said Rogers. "A little respect for our boy on the table." He picked a piece of dirty kilt out of the anaesthetized soldier's thigh.

Joe put in his tuppence worth. "The word is the biggest regiment, the Seaforths, have lost almost half their strength. But on the up side, my pal Frank Gellatley, that cheery bearer, says he heard we've taken thousands of prisoners." He tapped Rogers' arm lightly, wanting to include him. "Did you hear that, sir? We've likely taken as many prisoners as men lost."

"Well lance corporal, I'll be sure to let your mother know, if anything happens to you, we can ship her a new son. A German one." He flung off his apron, and pushed past Joe and the others. A sour gust of alcohol swirled in the air.

Joe rushed out after him but already the dark had swallowed him up. He ran back to Atholl's treatment room, next door to where he had been working. "Sir. Captain Rogers has been taken ill. Suddenly. There's a patient on the table."

"Is he under?" Atholl said, without looking up.

"Aye, he is. But his thigh's wide open and he's bleeding bad."

"I'll be right there." Atholl tossed a pair of bloody forceps into a dish. "Young can finish this one." He leaned over Youngalec and shouted in his good ear. "Bandage him."

"Permission to check up on Captain Rogers, sir?" Joe said. "Someone should."

"I expect so. Young, shut this room down when you've finished. I'll work next door. "You," he pointed at Joe, "report to me in fifteen minutes."

Joe listened at the door of Rogers' dugout. He could hear whimpering from inside. He pushed gently against the door. The captain was sitting in the corner, on the dirt floor, one arm around his drawn-up knees, the other clutching an almost empty bottle of Dewars.

"Sir? Are you okay, sir?"

Rogers shook his head slowly. "I'm finished here, Mathieson."

Joe closed the door, made it over to the corner, and unclasped Rogers' hand from the bottle. He laid the whisky out of reach on Roger's desk, next to his pistol and the photograph of his wife and child. He stood with his back to the table by the door, his hands by his side. "We can't do without you," he said. "You're the best." He got on his knees and crawled over to Captain Rogers. He wanted to take the officer's hands in his but instead spoke softly. "Look how many lads you've saved just these past four days."

Rogers kept shaking his head. "I just never imagined ... this." He stared at Joe, then grabbed his rubber apron. "It gets worse and worse." He gave a little snort, tried to get up, waved an unsteady head in the direction of Oroville. "No wonder you lads call that hell up there Orrible." He put his hands over his head, fell on his haunches, and brought his chin to his knees. "And the noise. The infernal noise. All day long. Even now, during the night when they stop a while, I hear it. Can you hear it, Joe? I can." He tapped his head. "In here. And not just the guns. The screams. Mostly the screams. All the time. And the smell." He rolled over into a ball.

Joe knelt over him. He glanced at the door, praying Atholl wouldn't come checking up. He touched the insignia on Roger's cuff, feeling its shiny chill. The captain turned his head toward him. "I tell you. I'm finished, Joe."

"It's bad right now, but it has to ease up. It will. And you need a respite from operating." He wished Adelaide was here. She would know better than him the questions to ask, what to say to shake the captain out of his despair. "Things'll not look quite so bleak after a decent kip. Take the rest of the night to sleep. Atholl can hold down the fort." Joe chuckled. "Listen to me. Giving an officer orders." He hoped changing the mood would snap Rogers out of his dark hole.

The captain struggled to his feet and swayed up close to Joe's face. "You really believe you can laugh your way out of this? You with one brother already dead and another God knows where?"

Joe took a step back. "That's not exactly what I meant, sir."

Rogers rushed past him to the outside and Joe heard him being sick. He waited a few minutes until he was sure the heaving was over, then went outside and saw the surgeon standing spread-eagled over a pool of his vomit.

"Let's go in," Joe said. "Lie on your bunk and sleep it off. Atholl's waiting for me to report. If it's okay with you, sir, I'll tell him you have a fever and I've given you a couple of aspirin. I'll tell him you said you're sure you'll be right as rain the morn, reporting for duty."

Rogers nodded, put a limp arm around Joe's shoulder, and let himself be led to bed.

Joe woke up Saturday morning feeling something was strange. The four hours' sleep was the most he'd had in one go in the week he'd been at Mortecourt. It took some minutes for his brain to kick into alertness and realize the guns had stopped. He shivered under his blankets, feeling even colder than usual. He lit a cigarette and pulled on his boots.

Outside, the ear-splitting booming that had shaken the soggy brown landscape for the last five days was now a peaceful silence. Joe looked to the east, towards Oroville where an even white deposit of snow dressed the countryside. He thought maybe the fighting had stopped, for the time being, because of the weather. Then he saw that the steeple of the church at Oroville was no longer standing and hoped that meant the troops had taken the village and it was over, this battle at least. He'd go see Rogers. Asking for information would give Joe an excuse to see how he was doing.

Rogers seemed remarkably chirpy and was able to tell him quite clearly the fighting was indeed over. Oroville had been recaptured from the enemy. He put Joe in charge of a team of orderlies that were to go out onto the battlefield to scour for the last remaining wounded and organize burial parties.

Joe was at the stretcher-bearers' post by twelve-thirty, in time to share the huge dollops of food the cooks were dishing out as a kind of celebration: fried bacon, eggs, carrots and potatoes, bread, cheese, and jam. He filled his plate, took off his helmet, and sat against the wall beside Frank. Both were too busy shoving hot food into their mouths to get a conversation going. Eventually Frank wiped his mouth, and gave a satisfied burp. "When will you be giving us our orders? Now you're our trusted leader," Frank said. He gave Joe a friendly shove, hard enough to almost tip him over.

"When I'm good and ready, you insubordinate little fart." Joe flicked a forkful of mushed potato at Frank's face.

"I see your words are getting bigger along with your 'ead since you got that stripe on your arm."

Joe put his arm around Frank. "My darling man," he said, getting up and pulling Frank with him, "when I get to be general and you're still picking up carcasses, I'll still love you. And I'll give you a medal." He kissed Frank on the cheek and ran off, waving behind him, watching Frank wipe his face and shake his fist.

The cooks had cleared away all remnants of the meal. Joe sat alone in the stretcher-bearers' barn to study the orders. He read the words over and over in a soft whisper. His mouth was dry. He'd never done anything like this: assembling and talking to a crew of forty or so stretcher-bearers and infantry who'd survived the battle unscathed. He knew that all up and down the line many other squads would be gathering like this, awaiting their orders from a junior NCO. But still he wasn't sure how he would keep their attention while he read out the instructions.

The men came into the barn in twos and threes and stood around in huddles, talking bull and backslapping. How was he going to get them to be quiet? And how could he ask this grisly task of these once fit men, hefting off their greatcoats plastered with mud, their young backs bent with the weight of sodden wool? He saw Frank, caught his eye, and laughed when Frank flashed him the finger. Joe dragged a table up to the front of the room and stood behind it. What if he couldn't get enough spit in his mouth to get the words out? How could he let them know he was ready to start?

Frank came up and thumped on the table. The men all turned and looked. Joe looked out at the haggard faces, the short bristly beards. Frank thumped again. "This 'ere is Lance Corporal Mathieson from the ADS at Mortecourt." Oohs and whistles shook the chilly air. Frank put up his hand. "Surgical assistant to Captain Rogers, Royal Army

Medical Corps." Aahs and foot stomps. Frank whacked the table again. "I guarantee 'e's saved the lives of many of your mates." *If he goes on any longer,* Joe thought, *I'll have a V.C. around my neck.* "Give 'im an 'and and your attention." The men cheered and clapped. Thankfully, Frank held up his hands after a few seconds and the men looked expectantly at Joe. He swirled his tongue around his gums. First he apologized for the weather, the biting wind and the snow underfoot. He ordered the stretcher-bearers and their temporary helpers to take the wounded to the nearest first-aid post or the ADS depending on the severity of the injured man's condition. They were to stock up on morphine before they headed out. He ended by saying, "Get going. The sooner we get out there, the sooner we can get our pals in out of the cold."

Once they had left and the barn was quiet again, he talked to the burial parties. He cleared his throat. He put his papers down, strolled to the front of the table, and stood directly in front of the men.

"I'm not going to lie. You've got a horrible job. Those lads out there that have lost their lives are your friends, maybe even a cousin or a brother." He stopped for a moment and collected himself. "They are gonna be hard to look at. I won't pretend it'll be a pretty sight. Just keep thinking that it's a good thing you are picking them up and taking them to their resting place. There'll be carts coming around and that's where you'll put them. Make sure you collect their red tags and pay books. Keep them safe afore you bring them back here to the clerk. And mind you leave the green one on the body for identification. You'll see the ground's marked off in sections. When you've finished a section, go with the cart and horses to Orrible. The motor ambulances can't get through that ground. Even those new-fangled monster tank things got stuck the first day. There's a big grave been dug near the village or what's left of it."

Joe folded his arms.

"And I have to warn you all on this afore you go out. There's been bodies out there since July. This week's shelling has blown them out from under the ground. And if you mind, it was a hot summer. I'll leave the rest to your imagination. Get your gear and get going then. I'll be behind you in an hour or so. And ... it's not unmanly to shed a few tears."

The men shuffled their way out the door. Joe walked back to the table to catch his breath. He wiped away the sweat that had chilled his forehead.

"Are you really a corporal now or are you kidding again?"

Joe looked up, hearing a familiar accent.

"Remember me, Joe?"

"My god. Wee Tom Patterson." Joe took him by the shoulders then held him at arm's length. "You look like you haven't a scratch on you."

"Aye. I've managed to keep myself out of trouble. Mostly thanks to you, getting me on with the body snatchers, I mean the stretcher boys. You mind that lad I told you about afore? The one that called himself Willie Melville?"

Joe gripped the edge of the table. All the saliva went from his mouth. "The one you thought might be my brother? You've seen him? Where is he?"

"Look I don't want to get you all excited. I'm not sure. But I know his battalion was fighting here. I used to be with them."

Joe bit down on his lip. "Do you know something? Anything at all?"

"I asked a few. For this Willie Melville. And I asked for any Mathiesons. I couldn't remember your brother's first name."

"Walter." He shook Tom's arm. "And? Anything?"

"Aye. One or two had heard the name—not Mathieson but Melville—but couldn't say exactly where I could find him. I tried myself, walking around, you know. But we've been right busy. I'm sorry. But as far as I know none of us have lifted him. That's likely good news."

"You've done good." Joe's chest was bursting with hope. "Given me something to go on. After we get the wounded in and the burials done at Orrible, I'll check myself if he comes in the ADS. Where's the battalion now?"

"Over Busless County way."

"I'll get there the minute I get a break."

The door banged open against the wooden inside wall of the barn. Frank came running over and grabbed Joe's arm. "You'd better come quick. Your man's out there. Gone bonkers, 'e 'as."

"Walter? Oh, my God in heaven!"

"Your brother? No, no. Your captain! Follow me."

Joe grabbed his coat and scarf and pulled them on as he ran and tried to keep up with Frank. He kept his head down against the wet wind that bit at his cheeks. His legs jarred against the frozen rutted ground. The waterlogged shell holes had iced over, and he had to dance around them and the stiffened bodies as he tore after Frank over the battlefield. An icy ripple went through Joe as he remembered the fear when he'd last crossed a No Man's Land in July.

Frank shouted at him and pointed up ahead to what had been the other side of the enemy wire. Rogers was running this way and that. He fired his pistol up in the air, then down at the ground. Up in the air, down at the ground. Up, down. As if he were performing some rhythmical calisthenics. Eventually he stopped and slumped down on the ground. Joe tiptoed over to within six feet of him. Rogers' shaking hands were reloading his Webley.

"Sir?"

Rogers looked over his shoulder. "Who goes there?"

Joe couldn't mesh the twisted demented look on his Captain's face with the kind officer who had always protected him. And he knew six new rounds lay in the officer's revolver.

"Mathieson, sir. Joe. Can I come and sit by you? Captain Rogers?"

"Of course. I want you to come and have a look at this."

Joe trembled at the slurred words.

"You wouldn't have a piece of cheese on you by any chance?" Rogers said and pointed to the ground. "For him."

Joe jumped back, repulsed by a pair of tiny black eyes peering at him from a pink face. He tried to step on the baby rat but it was too fast for him and it disappeared back inside its home. Joe gazed in disgust and quickly turned his head away. His stomach heaved and he gulped in air. The rat's home had once been a soldier's chest. The face flesh was completely stripped. Tufts of dark brown hair still clung to the skull like a scarecrow's wig. Bits of cloth that had been his uniform flapped in the wind.

"Captain, give me your hand. Come with me. Out of the cold."

Rogers looked at his bare hands, reddened from the weather. "Useless," he said. He rolled his gun between his hands. "Do you know what happened to that soldier I left on the table that night?"

Joe sat down on his left, keeping his eyes on the pistol. "No, I don't. Atholl saw to him and even though he's a … he's a bloody capable surgeon—"

"He died," Rogers said. "The boy died."

"A lot do."

"Don't you see? Joe, he died because of me. I killed him."

"No, sir. No. Not true. There's nothing we can do when they're bleeding out that fast."

"We could've given him a transfusion."

"We didn't have any blood." Joe inched closer. He put his hand towards the gun, but Rogers pulled it away.

"I could have given some of mine."

"Well for that matter so could've Atholl. Or one of us."

"I wouldn't ask that of you," Rogers said. "You boys were all dead on your feet as it was, working round the clock. I'm responsible." He aimed the gun at the rat's nest. "I killed him as sure as if I'd done this." He fired the pistol at the long dead soldier's empty chest. Rogers' hand kicked back from the force of the shot. His arm arced and wobbled towards his forehead. A second shot snapped the winter air. Something warm, wet and heavy knocked Joe onto his side. He gasped for breath and tried to kick and shove it off him, but his legs and arms were like quivering jelly. He heard someone shout his name and the weight was lifted.

"God. No! Joe!" Frank said, pulling Joe under the arms, away from Rogers' body. "Can you move your legs?"

"Aye. They're just shaky."

Frank went over to the khaki bundle and lifted Rogers' flaccid corpse by the shoulders to a sitting position, then flung it back on the ground.

"You stupid fucking bastard," he spat at the lifeless captain. He pointed to Joe while he spoke to the mangled head of the officer. "You could've taken my friend with you."

"Shut up Frank. Just shut up." Joe stayed slumped on the ground. He looked up at Frank. "I should have stopped him. I saw the gun."

"Joe. Don't start that. You weren't responsible for 'im." Frank stood towering over Joe, pulled his cigarette packet from his trousers pocket, and lit two. He handed one to Joe. "Look at all this." He gestured over the frozen body-strewn ground. "Don't you think this 'ad something to do with it? Not you, not me, 'ave any blame for this." He went over to Joe and helped him stand. "C'mon. I'm taking you back to the post. I'll find something that'll drown your sorrows."

"I need to see to the burial parties."

"Come back to the barn for a bit. They know what to do. Their instructions were clear. Thanks to you. You did well, mate."

Sunday, November 19, 1916 Joe was on his hands and knees with Youngalec in the treatment room, stuffing scraps of bloodied uniforms and sodden bandages into the jute sacks used primarily as sandbags. He stood and arched his back, stretching it out.

"I'd say we're done here, Youngalec," he said. "Spick and span. Thanks to you, you fussy wee bastard. You'd hardly know we'd been up to our knees in body parts this past week."

"I'm thinking of going over to Busless County. There's a service at the church, being Sunday and all. You could come with me."

"I don't think so. After taking Captain Rogers over there for burial, I'm not in the mood for going back in a hurry."

"Any word on your brother on your way back?"

"Bloody frustrating that was. Tried to get talking to the NCOs but it was madness. The poor buggers not hurt are shoring up the old trenches and digging new ones in the ground we took. All I got was the big shove off and told to get out of the way."

"I'm sorry," Youngalec said, putting more elbow grease into polishing surgical instruments.

"Ta. I had a feeling, though, that this time I was getting close." He tapped the side of his head. "Maybe I'm not the mentalist I thought I was. Thanks for keeping things going while I was away."

"Atholl was a bit grumpy," Alec said, "but I think he was glad you went with the captain to bury him right. He just couldn't say. You know what he's like." Youngalec moved in close to Joe. "What happened exactly? I heard from your pal Frank you were with him. There's talk—"

"Sniper." Joe fiddled with some bandages on the shelves. "One that was left hiding in Fritz's trench."

"You were lucky the bastard didn't get you too."

"Aye. Damn, bloody lucky." Joe pointed to the bags on the floor. "Let's get this stuff burned."

"Did we capture him?" Alec said, flinging a sack over his shoulder.

"Capture? Oh, aye, the sniper. Aye. We did that."

"If it were me," Alec said, holding the door open, "I'd shoot him myself. Right in the goolies. Fine man Captain Rogers was. No more wounded coming in then?"

Joe was relieved Youngalec was the one to change the subject. He wanted to kill the speculation around Rogers' death. "Nope. That's it. The last convoy for the ccs leaves around two this afternoon. The rest are either patched up and sent back to their platoons or ... well, they're at rest."

"I'm not sure which is worse," Youngalec said and left.

Joe stepped outside and lit a Woodbine. He took a long drag, felt the cheap tobacco rasp at his lungs, and blew out the smoke while he looked up at the sky. It had clouded over since yesterday, but the temperature had risen. A great relief on the one hand, but the sudden warmth had brought a rapid thaw and the ground outside was once more a quagmire. An airplane droned overhead. Joe flattened himself against the door of the treatment room while he checked out the markings. He relaxed when he noticed the familiar circle of The Royal Flying Corps. They were seeing more and more of those machines. Funny this new-fangled idea: fighting from the sky.

He remembered one of his last long conversations with Rogers, asking him about the planes that zipped and turned through the sky like four-winged insects. The captain, always eager to teach, told him of the two types. The fast little fighters chased their prey three thousand feet above them at speeds over a hundred and twenty miles an hour. It flabbergasted Joe when he calculated that a plane like that could get him home in five or six hours. Then there were the bombers, slower but still capable of flying close to a hundred miles an hour. It gave him the creeps to think of the pilot and the gunner having a secret bird's-eye view of him down on the ground. It made him want to cover his head, like he might if a seagull flew above him and he felt in danger of being shat upon.

He continued to look up as the airplane dipped for a moment then rose again and flew off to the east, vanishing from his sight. He thought ducking would do him little good if one of those metal birds decided to empty its bowels on him.

His eyes stung from tracking the silver stiff-winged bird. He closed them and remembered Roger's body, wrapped in burlap, disappearing under shovelfuls of dirt. Now all he could see was Rogers' head, dead on the white snow, his blood spilling along with the whitish-grey ooze of his brain. He wasn't sure Atholl had bought the story he and Frank made up about the sniper, but he was sure the young lieutenant wanted to believe it. He tried blinking away the image of Rogers that wouldn't stop haunting him.

He'd go over to Atholl's dugout and tell him the work in the treatment room was done and ask for permission to ride with the last of the injured to the casualty clearing station at Colinvillers. He was keeping his fingers crossed that Adelaide was there. She needed to hear about Rogers from him first hand. Talking about it with her would settle him. She had a talent for saying the right words. He'd have to return to the ADS before bed. Certainly didn't want to piss off Atholl, but he'd work out how to return once he got to the CCS.

In the evening, when the men stood down, he'd be able to put the word out again, asking about Walter to the corporals. In the lull after the day's work, they'd pass it down the line he was looking for a Walter Mathieson or a Willie Melville. This time he was pretty sure he'd find him, because Tom Patterson had found out that the whole 51st Division, all the Highland regiments, was in the area. It struck him he had no plan for what he'd do when he did find Walter. He was of a mind to give him a good thrashing. But he'd cross that bridge when he came to it.

"I'll jump out here," Joe said to the motor ambulance driver, at the sign that announced the village of Colinvillers.

"Sure? The CCS is way the other end."

"Feel like a bit of walk."

He got out, shut the door, gave it a friendly rap, and waved the driver away. He walked the length of the short street, looking for an open café or *estaminet* where he might get a beer, but everything was shuttered. Some of the old half-timbered and plastered buildings Joe thought were used for storage and as barns had dates engraved over the lintels. He played a game with himself trying to find the oldest. He found one, sagging and wedged between two newer solid stone houses: 1692. None of the buildings showed any sign of damage. Hard to believe, he thought, that only a few miles to the east lay such carnage and destruction.

The road took a sharp turn to the left and Joe found himself standing at the top of a hill. He saw the church at the bottom end of the cobbled street, and beyond it a landscape of colourless farmland rolled into the distance. Behind the church, angling to the left, stood some railway carriages. They were being loaded with stretchers, the giveaway that a hospital was nearby. Joe cast his eyes to the right and could make out a collection of large tents, maybe forty or fifty. These always made him think of the big tops of the circus, but what went on inside was far from entertainment.

Inky dark had settled by the time Joe arrived at the CCS compound and asked the way to the canteen. It brought back the familiar warm comfort of Bercordie CCS, with staff coming and going and lots of chatter. He helped himself to tea and a couple of slices of sweet bread with raisins. Shoving the food in his mouth, he looked around but didn't recognize anyone. He went over to two nurses chatting together at a table, with their hands wrapped around mugs trying to keep warm.

He pulled out a chair and sat. "Do you mind?" he said, putting his cup down on their table and wiping his mouth.

"It seems we don't have any choice, does it, Annie?" said the younger of the two, who looked no more than seventeen or eighteen. "Be our guest."

"I've got a message to deliver to a nurse. Adelaide Armitage. Do you know her?"

The older one went pale and put her hand up to her throat. "Oh, God. Is it bad news?"

"It's not her family or anything like that," Joe said. "I need to talk to her directly though."

"She's in charge of resuss," said Annie. "We work under her. I'll go tell her." She got up and gave a cheeky curtsy. "Who shall I say is calling?"

"Tell her it's Joe. Joe Mathieson. And that it's important."

"Look after this young gentleman while I'm gone, will you, Marjory?"

The younger one giggled, then straightened herself. "Sorry," she said.

Joe took another swig of his tea. "I worked with Nurse Armitage," he said to the young nurse. "Different places, off and on. Last time was the CCS at Bercordie. I'm over at the ADS at Mortecourt now. We've been sending lots of lads to you."

"It's just awful," she said. "This is my first posting. I had no idea. I wouldn't have coped without Nurse A. That's what we call her. She's a gem. Funny that, isn't it?"

"What?"

"Nurse A. I didn't know her name was Adelaide. That's pretty. I guess we could call her Nurse double A. Oh, I'm sorry. I do go on. It's all a bit much, you see. I expect I'll get used to it."

"I wouldn't count on it," Joe said.

"I just tell myself that, with all the new ways of doing things, we are saving lives that would have been lost in my father's day. He was a doctor, a major, in the South African war. It's such an irony don't you think?"

Before Joe had a chance to reply, she babbled on.

"Because of war, we practise these wonderful new methods of surgery, anaesthesia, antisepsis, resuscitation ..."

Joe turned his head away, looking to see if the nurse named Annie was on her way back with Adelaide and could save him from the prattle in his ear. He just wanted Adelaide to appear, give her the news about Rogers, and hurry back to the ADS, do his search for Walter: a search he was sure, this time, would uncover him. To shut out the nattering, he let his mind wander to home and wondered how Ma was managing being cooped up with Ellen on a miserable dark winter afternoon like this. His focus drifted in and out of what Marjory was saying. "... neurasthenia ... so young ... cleanliness ... brave Scots ... blood transfusion ... shock ... Melville ... infection—"

"What?" Joe interrupted, his head jolting back toward her.

"I was saying we need to learn how to control the infections. It is estimated that—"

"I don't need to keep hearing about that." He pushed his chair back, stood, and leaned over her. "Will you please shut up?"

"But you asked me what I was talking about." She turned around and looked up at him. "Do you want to listen or not?"

"I'm sorry," Joe said. He sat down again and tried to rein in his irritation. He put on his most winsome smile. "Just tell me about this Melville lad."

"Melville? He's just one of the many horribly hurt patients. I was talking about the infection rate. If we could stem the infections or cure them when they occur, many more lives would be saved."

"I know." He patted her on the hand. "You seem very smart. I can tell you know all kinds of stuff, but I really want you to tell me about Melville."

She smiled at him. "He's a good example to do with blood transfusions. Are you interested in that?"

Joe put his arm around the back of her chair. "Yes, I am. Go on. Tell me about blood transfusions. And this Melville. You say he's one of your patients?"

"Joe. What brings you here?" Adelaide said, coming toward them. "Nurse Gillingham, you can go back to your ward now."

The young woman chucked a weak smile at Joe and scurried away.

"Nurse Foxman said you had a message," Adelaide said.

He couldn't stop the trembling in his arm as he led her away. He was desperate to ask her about this Melville boy. It could be his own brother lying there, bloodied and near death. He took her hand and pulled her closer to him.

"Joe?" Adelaide said. "You're shaking." She put her hands on his sleeve. "What is it? You're alarming me."

He took her elbow and pushed her in front of him. "Let's walk. Outside."

"Joe, it's dark and freezing cold. Let's sit and you can tell me."

He sat down and she slid next to him. He told her about Rogers, both the true story and what he'd told Atholl: the version that would be reported to his senior officer and recorded. "I did try and keep an eye on him, like you asked me afore I left Bercordie." Joe sighed and told her about Rogers' drunken collapse the previous Thursday night. "I'd no idea he was suffering that bad. Enough to ... well, you know."

"To kill himself," Adelaide said softly. "Don't be afraid to say the words. In fact it'll help."

"But I should have ... I don't know what I should have done, but I should have done something."

"Joe. You must not take any of the blame." She laid her hand over his. "Nobody could have known what thoughts he was harbouring. It was his decision not to tell you or anyone what he was planning. If indeed he did plan it. Where is he now?"

"He's buried. At Busless County."

"Busless County?"

"I don't know how you say it right, but I could write it down for you. I made sure he got his own spot. And it's marked."

Adelaide nodded her head slowly. "Graves," she said. "More and more graves. I wish I had one."

"What? Are you saying ...?" Joe still couldn't say the words out loud. "Like the captain?"

"Oh, God. I'm sorry. No. That's not what I meant." She gave a little laugh. "I'd like to think that's not me." She looked down at her hands in her lap and took a deep breath. "My husband Robert doesn't have a grave. He's one of the missing. I know now he will never be found. It would be a comfort to have somewhere to, you know, visit him. Like you did with your brother at Bercordie."

At the mention of Fred, Joe's mind darted back to Walter, but he didn't want to interrupt Adelaide if she felt like talking about her husband. He wanted to offer her some of the comfort she had always been so willing to give him. Her eyes had become wet, so he made to touch her arm but she pulled away, smoothed out her apron, and stood.

"I should like to get back to the ward now, if you don't mind."

"There's something else," Joe said. " I think so. Maybe."

"My goodness. What?"

"That young nurse? Marjory something."

"Gillingham. What about her? Good Lord. She has brothers. Not one of them?"

"No, no. Can you stay a couple more minutes?"

Adelaide checked the watch pinned to her apron bib, then sat down.

"I feel a bit stupid, but I need to ask. That nurse mentioned you have a lad called Melville in your ward."

"We might have Joe. I'm not the one who keeps track."

Joe ran his fingers through his hair. "Remember back in July I heard about a lad named Melville? The one I thought sounded like my brother?"

"Walter? Well, of course I remember."

"Aye well. I know this sounds mad, but I'm wondering if it's the same lad."

"You think this Melville is actually your brother?"

"I could be off my head."

"Only one way to find out. Come," she said, getting up.

Joe's heart thumped in his chest. A terrifying and muddling debate went on inside his head as he followed Adelaide down the resuss ward. The inside of his mouth felt like sandpaper. *It can't be him. I would have seen him come through the ADS.* Unless he came through Thursday, when I was trying to sober up Rogers. *I don't want to see him all beaten up.* Then turn on your heel and get back to the ADS.

Adelaide tapped him on the shoulder. "Here," she said, as they approached the foot of a bed. He shut his eyes. *Please don't make it be him. No, no, no. Make it him. Better here than already rotting under French mud.*

Joe breathed in slowly, forcing his attention on the cold air going up his nose and down into his chest. He opened his eyes and looked at the chalky face of the young man lying on his back. He turned to Adelaide and gripped her arm. She wheeled out a round stool from beneath the bed and lowered him onto it. He covered his face with his arms. Adelaide knelt down beside him.

"Joe?"

"This is not Willie Melville," he said.

Adelaide stood. "Let's move on then," she said.

Joe glared at the floor.

"I want to do this with you," she said. "But we really do have to speed it up."

Joe shifted himself on the stool, spread his legs, and let out a long slow moan.

Adelaide swung around. "What is it? Have you become unwell?"

"This is Walter Mathieson. My wee brother. Age seventeen years and eight months." Adelaide gripped his knee.

Joe stood and stroked his brother's smooth face. "Wee Walter." He turned to Adelaide. "Our gran called him that to her dying day. He should never have been here. Too young for the army."

"Joe. He's in the best hands possible. Sit here and talk to him. I'll get some sweet tea and see if there's a doctor available."

Joe watched her walk up the ward, her heavy shoes squeaking on the wooden floor. He looked back to the bed, knowing he had to force himself to look again at his brother's face. He moved himself onto the stool, closer to the low bed where Walter lay on his back, his head slightly tilted toward Joe as if he knew he had a visitor and at any moment would open his eyes and speak. Joe leaned against the bed, confused for a moment by the heat rising from the bed-cover. Resuss. Warm and water the patient. Get them well enough for life-saving surgery. Joe patted his brother's hair, matted and stiff with dirt, its normally bright sandiness now a dark halo ringing the pallid skin. He licked his finger and cleaned off a smudge of blood on Walter's cheek. He felt his forehead. No fever. He was cool, almost clammy, despite the hot water-filled stone jars in the bed. Joe blew gently on his brother's lips, hoping to prime a rosier glow. Walter's eyelids flickered and his head jerked away. Joe laid his cheek against his brother's, listening to him softly but steadily breathing in and out. He felt the soft teenage down on his chin that no doubt made Walter proud. He thought of how his gran, Annie, planted wet smacking kisses on her youngest grandson and how he would flip his head away and make a face, his budding manhood offended.

Joe reached under the blankets and took his brother's hand. The metallic smell of dried blood and the meaty rancidness of a wound slithered out. With both hands, he lifted the covers higher and saw the blood-soaked dressings that bound his brother's naked body from armpit to groin. He carefully covered him again and checked the paper wound tag tied to his toe. *Melville W. 16-11-16 Multiple shrapnel wnds to chest/abd. Organ involvement unknown.* Joe went back to the bedside and clutched Walter's hand to his own heart.

Anger spurted through him. He tossed off his brother's hand, watched it flop onto the cover. How could Walter have been so wrapped up in his own fancy ideas? Inflict on him the job of writing to their mother with more horrible news? He wanted to grab his brother by the shoulders, shake him, and tell him to get the hell home and stop making their mother crazy with worry and grief. He let Walter's cold hand lie limp on the bedclothes and wrapped his arms around himself. Fiendish voices of anger, anguish, and crushing chaos screamed inside his head. He understood how easy it must have been for Rogers to put a bullet through his brains just to stop the noise.

He looked again at Walter lying there. He seemed even younger and paler than before, as if his skin were painted with a brilliant whitewash. A flashing picture show shot through Joe's mind: the sparkling summer light when he'd been with Marguerite at Gaudechat, the dazzle of her flimsy white dress, her golden curls dancing in the sun as they ran hand in hand to the swimming place, the glitter on the ripples of water as he held her close to him. All his fury left him. His body let go. He leaned forward onto Walter's shoulder, wrapped his arms around his brother's head and cried.

He felt the tap on his back and sat up. Adelaide was standing behind him holding out a cup. "Drink this," she said. "Would you prefer to be alone for a while?"

Joe wiped his nose on his sleeve. "Sorry," he said. "Not very dignified." He took the cup from her. "No, I'd like you here." He took a slurp from the cup and gagged. "Bloody hell. That's like syrup."

"Just the universal remedy. Four teaspoons of sugar. Look, Joe, I've talked to Major Saunders. He's in charge here and he can explain the situation with your brother, but first drink your tea and we'll talk somewhere else out of earshot of the patients."

Joe's heart pounded again. He blew on the tea to cool it and watched Adelaide shake down a thermometer and place in under the motionless Walter's tongue. She checked under the covers while she waited for the temperature to register.

Joe sucked up quick mouthfuls, the sweetness mercifully distracting him.

"His temperature is not elevated," Adelaide said. "That's a good sign. We can assume no infection has set in." She put the thermometer into a breast pocket beneath her apron. "Bring the tea with you. Major Saunders has agreed to meet with you in the canteen. You're in luck on two counts. He went to university with Captain Rogers, and I've told him all about you and how loyal you were to him. And I bribed him with the offer of a chocolate biscuit. Cadbury's no less.

My mother's always sending me these luxuries. Can be valuable currency sometimes."

Joe followed Adelaide to a quiet corner where a small dark-haired man was bent over a textbook.

"Major, this is Lance Corporal Mathieson. I spoke to you about him. He was with Captain Rogers when he was shot."

The man closed his book and Joe saluted, expecting a nod or a grunt as a reply. Instead the officer rose to his feet and shook Joe's hand. "I want to thank you for the great care and compassion you showed Martin. Captain Rogers. I had the utmost admiration for him." His face flickered. "And fondness."

"He was the best surgeon I worked for, sir."

"With," the major said, in the same posh Scottish burr that Rogers had. "With. We're all in this ghastly mess together. Come sit. Now I understand this young Melville in resuss is your brother, and that you've already lost a brother."

"Aye. That's right, sir," Joe said. The major nodded to the chair and Joe sat. "My brother's name is Walter Mathieson. He didn't tell us, any of his family, he was joining up back in '15 and has been using this Willie Melville name so nobody would find out. I've been hunting for him all this time—never neglecting my duties, sir—and thanks to Nurse Armitage, he's found at long last ... and in your good hands."

"I wish I could give you some hopeful news, but the situation is dire. We've put him in resuss to lessen shock by keeping him warm. But without an operation to remove the shrapnel and get him stitched up properly, it's only a matter of time before infection sets in and ... well, I'm sure you've seen enough to predict a not happy outcome. I am so sorry."

"But sir, you can operate here, can't you? We can even do it at the ADS."

The major leaned toward Joe. "You've seen his colour? That young man has lost maybe half his blood volume. And he may be still bleeding internally. As soon as I cut into him, and he starts bleeding again, he'll go further into shock and we'll lose him for sure. Our only hope is that in time he may get stronger, in which case I might consider surgery, but for now I can do nothing except leave him in the resuss nurses' capable hands."

"But we don't have time, do we? You said yourself, sepsis is the enemy. That'll do him in unless you get that stuff out of him, irrigate, and sew him up cleanly. With good nursing ..." He looked over to Adelaide.

"You know your stuff, young man."

"Aye, well. Your friend was the best teacher ever."

"I'm sorry. I won't do it. I know he cannot survive any further blood loss."

"Sir, please. You could transfuse him first."

"The problem there is we get very little usable blood. Much of it clots in the bottle before we can use it. All that we had we've used up."

"I could do it," Joe said. "He can have my blood. Man to man like."

"In theory, that's a good idea. But we have two problems with that, the first being that, although you're a close relation, we cannot assume your blood is the same category as your brother's."

"With respect, sir, I am willing to take responsibility for that risk. If you want me to sign something, I will. Something that would say I'll take the blame. You said yourself he doesn't have a chance otherwise."

Saunders smiled at Joe. "That's all very noble, but that still leaves me with the second problem."

"What would that be?"

"I've never done it before," the major said.

"I watched Captain Rogers do it a few times. What he did was—"

"I do understand the premise. Connecting a donor artery to the recipient's vein. It's the experience I am lacking at this point."

Joe was breathing heavily. He tentatively laid his hand on his superior's forearm. "Well then, here's your chance to practise."

Saunders looked across at Adelaide.

She shrugged and held out her arms to the surgeon. "Captain Rogers always spoke very highly of Joe. I know he'll be a very able assistant, even while he donates his own blood. Besides we're always taking risks with these boys, aren't we? Trying new things. And sometimes it works."

"She's right," Joe said. "And afterwards, I might have a brother. If we do nothing, my mother'll just have … me. One son out of three."

Saunders turned to Joe and grinned. "If you are as competent as you are persuasive, I might just consider it. But this is your brother's life you're messing with."

"Sir," Joe said, "like I said, I'm willing to take the blame if anything goes wrong. You can do what you want to me. Court-martial me if you have to."

"I'm sure that won't be necessary." Saunders rubbed his chin. "All right. Give me a couple of hours to read up, then I want us three to talk this through step by step. Nurse Armitage, can you make the arrangements to do the donation in resuss? That young man's too weak to move."

"I'll get his bed wheeled to the top end, screened, and I'll lay out the equipment. It'll be ready when you are, sir." She looked at Joe. "Let's get you set."

Major Saunders got up, grabbed his textbook from the table, took a few steps away from them, turned, and came back.

"Nurse, this'll cost you a whole shipment of chocolate biscuits."

Two orderlies in Wellington boots steered a bed to the top of the ward and brought it up close to Walter's. Joe watched Nurse Gillingham roll the portable curtained screen round both beds. He lay down and faced his brother. In Ma and Da's house, he and Walter had divvied up the three-quarter bed in the small back bedroom. Always kicking each other and parrying for the lion's share of the lumpy mattress. What each wouldn't have given back then for a bed to themselves. What a funny relief that here, in France, he didn't have to share a bed with Kate. But he wished he'd been lucky enough to sleep with Marguerite. That would have been fine. Just fine. He shook away those thoughts and held his brother's very cold hand. Walter looked chalkier than an hour ago, his breathing slower and shallower.

Joe turned around when Adelaide pushed her way through the screen, carrying an enamel basin covered with a crisp white cloth.

"Ready?" she said.

"Aye." he said. He extended his arm and rubbed the bluish artery at his wrist.

"Major Saunders will be here shortly."

Joe pulled Adelaide toward him and whispered. "I hope he's swotting up the procedure."

"He's good, Joe. No need to worry." She rubbed Joe's wrist with an alcohol-soaked chunk of cotton, and with another swabbed the crook of Walter's elbow.

Saunders squeezed through the screen, his floor-length white robe tied at the waist with string. He tapped the veins in Walter's elbow, raising one enough to insert a hollow needle attached to very narrow rubber tubing. He told Adelaide to hold it in place while he watched Joe's wrist pulse. "This'll sting a bit," he said to Joe. "Here we go."

Joe tensed at the sharp cut and turned his head away. Adelaide came round to his side and raised his arm. "Doing all right?"

"I'm great. I'm just not much in love with the sight of my own blood."

"The tube went into your artery very nicely. I'll hold your arm up until we are finished. It'll slow down the blood flow and help us control the amount that goes into Walter."

"How much?" Joe said.

"About as much as would fill two milk bottles. You'll never miss it." She touched his cheek. The softness of her hand surprised him. "Keep still."

Joe ordered his mind to summon up a soothing Marguerite picture, but his brain would not cooperate; the only show a young boy, lying as still as death. He looked away, worried Saunders would see the panic in his face and think him a coward. He pressed his knees together to keep them still. "How much longer?" His arm ached from holding it in the air.

Adelaide chuckled. "Four days, if you won't stop asking questions." She tapped the rubber tube. "Flowing well. Won't take too long." The tube jerked and sprang from Joe's arm like a cobra, stiff and strong, readying for a strike. Blood spewed over Adelaide's face and chest. She raised her hands like a boxer to fend off the drenching. She spluttered Joe's blood from her mouth and nose as she reached for the tube, now hosing the floor. Joe's pulsing ulnar artery jetted more blood into the puddle slithering across the floor.

"Leave it!" screamed Saunders. "Tourniquet! Tourniquet!" Joe instinctively pressed his fingers into his forearm. He leapt from the bed, grabbed a thin rubber tourniquet and towels from the equipment cart and threw them to Adelaide. "Wipe your face," he whispered to her and nodded to the tourniquet. "Can you see well enough?"

"Yes, yes. I can do it."

"Tie it tight." It was so unlike her to be flustered. "It'll stop quickly."

"That's it," Saunders said, and threw off his gown. "I'm aborting this." Nurse Gillingham picked the robe from the floor. Joe looked at Adelaide and cocked his head.

"Joe, I don't blame him for not taking the risk," she said. Huge bloody splotches clumped her hair and stained her apron.

"Risk? Risk?" Joe held his arm and ran after the major, "Sir, you can't stop now. I'm fine." He tugged at the doctor's sleeve.

Saunders lifted Joe's hand from his arm. "I'm sorry. But I won't risk your life. What if for some reason we couldn't stop you bleeding? Best we leave it." He touched Joe on the shoulder. "Hard as it is to see your brother like this, it is, as I've just said, best left alone. If it's God's will, he'll come around enough for us to operate."

Joe stood in front of the major and blocked his way. "Hear me out. Please. Sir." He took a deep breath. He knew this exhalation and the words it shaped might be the most important in Walter's life. "I've had injuries. Fights. Bloody noses. Split my head open once. Fell off a swing." He pointed to his ankle. "A really bad accident in the mine three years back." He gasped, bent his wrists up and faced his palms towards Saunders. "Never, never had a problem. And look." He held out his arm with the tourniquet. "It's stopped already."

"I wasn't too eager to do this in the first place. I told you I hadn't attempted it before."

"All the more reason, you—we—should try again. Practise. For the future. For others. Sir, please, I'm begging. The only chance Walter has is the operation, and without trying this, he'll stay in shock and not be able to have the operation, and if he doesn't have the op—"

"Shh," Saunders said and waved his index finger at Joe. He crossed his arms, shifted his weight, and pinched his nostrils together.

Joe's heart revved up. Thumped. Thumped. He dug his fingernails into his palms.

Saunders' lips twitched. "Your logic is very compelling, young man. Nurse." He pointed at Gillingham, who cowered by Walter's bed. "Bring me a clean gown." He looked at Joe on the way back to Walter's bedside. "I want you to hear this." Joe nodded. "I cannot promise anything."

"Turn your head," Adelaide whispered in his ear. "Look."

Joe rolled his head to face Walter's bed. His brother's eyes were open, fixed on him, pale and staring. Joe tried to detect if Walter was afraid, but his own dread clogged his ability to think. Walter shuddered, closed his eyes, and let out a huge sigh. He lay still as a dark winter night. Joe froze. Then the lad's cheeks blushed pink with new blood. He trembled and reached for the tube in his arm.

"Lie still, boy," Saunders said. "The last thing we need is you jerking around."

"Hiya, Walter. It's me. It's Joe."

Walter blinked.

"Aye, it's me," Joe said, and turned his body toward his brother's. "Do as the doctor says. Lie still."

"What's going on?" Walter said, his voice soft and raspy. "What are you doing here?"

"Joe," Saunders said, "you too must lie still. For another five minutes at least. Until your tube's out. I want to get as much blood into him as I can."

Joe did as he was told until Saunders spoke again, this time to Walter. "Bend your wrist up as much as possible." He nodded over to Adelaide. She relieved Joe of his tube. Dribbles of blood mizzled onto the floor. "Nurse Gillingham?" she said, pressing on Joe's artery and looking over her shoulder. "Sticking plaster."

"Keep up the pressure," Saunders said. "I'm going to pull the other end from Walter. There'll be some splatter." Saunders slipped the tube from Walter, doubled up his arm, hand to his shoulder, while pressing the inside of his elbow.

Nurse Gillingham bent over Joe and stroked an adhesive bandage onto the cut.

"Perfect." Adelaide nodded to the young nurse. "Take everything away, clean up, and bring four teas." She smiled over at Joe. "Extra sweet and dip into my biscuit supply for us all." She checked his wrist. "Bleeding stopped, but I'll keep the pressure on it until the tea comes." She smiled. Joe felt every muscle in his face relax.

"What's happened to me?" Walter said, throwing a puzzled look at Joe. Adelaide and Major Saunders sipped tea at his bedside. He tried to prop himself up on one arm but winced and froze.

"Lie down," Saunders said. He moved in and pushed gently against Walter's shoulders. "You've taken some shrapnel in the belly, so you should lie still. Don't want it poking your insides. Your brother can help you sip some tea." He flicked his head towards Joe. "Gave you a little present. Fresh blood. Should perk you up quite a bit."

"Am I better now?" He lifted the covers and looked underneath. "What the hell?" He looked to Joe.

"Hush, wee man. Drink your tea." Joe lifted his brother's head just enough so that he could take a sip. Walter winced again and his eyes filled with tears. He held his brother's gaze. "Hurting?"

"Aye, like a bugger. Did I have an operation, Joe? Is that why I'm wrapped up like a bairn?"

Joe turned around when he heard the screen's wheels scrape the floor. "We'll leave you two for the moment," Saunders said, and ushered Adelaide away into the ward. "I'll send someone for your brother, let's say in an hour." He checked his wristwatch. "Yes, around eight. No more tea for him."

"Right," Joe said. "And thanks. To you both." He stood and saluted the major.

"No need to do that. Just doing my job."

Joe pulled out the stool and sat down at his brother's bedside. Walter was shaking.

"You haven't had an operation, Walter. But here's the thing. You need one. That's why the doctor said he'd be back in an hour."

Walter started to cry. He sniffed and wiped his nose on the sheet.

"Go ahead. Cry," Joe said. "I've seen many afore you do it. We all do from time to time."

Walter sniffed again. "I feel like a lassie."

Joe laughed. "Aye well, you look like one and all." He tugged gently at a tuft that had fallen over Walter's forehead. "When did you last have a haircut?"

Walter flinched and laughed.

"Do you remember what happened to you?"

"Not much," Walter said. "I remember we were walking. Slow and steady like we were told. We'd gone over the top, all in a line. An explosion. I remember that. There were others, maybe four or five lying next to me. Maybe they were dead. They were still, bent up and quiet. Then I was at the dressing station. I heard my name. Heard some posh doctor, right grumpy he was, shouting, *Where's Mathieson?* I tried to say, 'I'm him. I'm here.' I don't know how he knew my real name. But I couldn't get the words out. Lucky for me or I would've got in real trouble for lying and calling myself Melville. Then someone said my name again. Mathieson. And something about going to a burial. I thought they were saying I was going die." Walter started crying again. "The next thing I remember is I opened my eyes and saw you here." He clutched Joe's arm. "Am I going to die?"

"You silly wee bugger," Joe said. "Course not." He stroked his brother's hand and laughed. "I've a right mind to bash you up myself for running away on us. I would if you weren't here hurting and waiting on an operation."

Now that the words were out, Joe's sympathy for Walter vanished. He stood and leaned into his brother's face. "What the fuck were you doing running off like that? How could you put Ma through all the worry?" He shook his finger right between Walter's eyes. "You'd better have a good story. A really, really good reason for putting us through this. I could ... I could ... "

Walter started sniffling again, and tried to shift away. He cringed, pulled the bed-cover up to his eyes, and peeped over it. Joe took a deep breath and stepped back from the bed. He picked up his shirt, threw it on, furiously worked the buttons, and leaned over Walter again. "You blithering, drivelling moron." His spit settled on his brother's eyelid. He grabbed his jacket and pushed his way through the screen.

Outside, he lit a cigarette and pulled his collar up. He stomped up and down, took deep drags, and blew out the smoke in huge puffs, like a dragon bent on incinerating the world. Rage about everything pushed to explode from him. With each exhale, he hoped to burn off enough of it that he wouldn't stride back down that ward and shake the bejesus out of his brother. And why not? If Walter hadn't run off like he did, he wouldn't be here, would never have seen all that he couldn't unsee. Like Rogers' brains plastered, sticky and slimy, over his chin and on his lips. Like all the other body blobs he'd seen. Bits that before this he never knew existed, the colours inside a body he'd never given a thought to, the amount of blood that could drain from a man. The muck, the dirt, the shit. The screams and the wails of lads and men that likely hadn't shed a tear since their last scraped knee at five or six.

Stupid, fucking wee Walter. His head riddled with the romance of battle from the books he buried his nose in. Joe could remember the pictures: Admiral Nelson dying a smiling hero in someone's arms, the false glory flouted in the Charge of the Light Brigade. Fucking fables. Fucking lies seducing Walter's brain. Joe would certainly not be painting any victory pictures or writing any noble poems about his last year and a half. He felt the bitter bile of his anger rise again. He started to run.

He ran in a wide circle around the resuss tent. Same with the next tent and the next and didn't stop until he covered the whole casualty clearing station and found himself back outside Walter's tent. Spent, he plunked himself on the cold ground. He saw the flickers of light from inside. Calm now, he'd be able to see his brother off to the operating theatre with concern and kindness and write to his mother while the surgeons did their work. He pushed open the flap and went to his brother's bedside.

Walter gave him a thumb's up. "They're coming for me any minute," he said.

Joe caught the fear behind the gesture of bravado. He laid his hand on Walter's forehead. "You'll be fine. I've seen thousands get the same op done." He didn't add that only a third survived. "I'm sorry I lost my rag."

Walter presented a weak smile. "What'll happen to me? After?"

"That's the good part, wee brother. You'll spend a day, maybe two, here ... then you'll be on a train. Homeward bound."

"To Methilane?" Walter hoisted himself up a little.

Joe rearranged the thin pillow behind his head. "Likely not there. But some swank hospital, somewhere safe in Blighty. You can count on your fighting days being over." He sat on the edge of his brother's bed. "What made you do this?"

"The lads at school. They was on me, always, for reading too much. What's wrong with being interested in why the war was coming? And I liked to tell them the history and ways to settle differences. Diplomacy and stuff like that. Stuff I'd got from the library. More than once I got beat up for my opinions."

"And here was us thinking you were safe in that school with the other bright laddies."

"They shouted I was one of them objectors. Called me a conshie, a sissy, and a coward."

"Well maybe you should have kept your mouth shut. You're the only one in the family that got the chance to stay at school and get on. That was your job, not pretending you was the knight in shining armour." He leaned into his brother's face, almost touched his nose. "I'd have killed for your chance." Joe shivered at the expression, how innocently such expressions fell off the tongue without thought to what they might mean.

"I'm sorry," Walter said. "I'm sorry."

"But why not write? Even to Ma?"

Walter smiled. "Maybe she scared me more."

"You daft wee bugger."

Walter lowered his head and fiddled with his fingers. "I just wanted to be a man like you and Fred."

Ah, shite. Joe hoped Walter wouldn't bring him up. "Well, what's important is to get you seen to."

"Have you heard any news?" Walter asked. "About Fred?"

"Not for a while but he's fine. I can't mind exactly what he's up to or where he is, but I know for sure he's out of harm's way. Don't you worry about him."

"Excuse me, but we need the patient now." Foxman and Gillingham stood at the foot of Walter's bed. Nurse Foxman laid her hand on Walter's forehead. "Good. Good. Maybe a slight fever but certainly nothing to worry about. And you look so much livelier. We've come to wheel you away for the op. Say cheerio to your handsome brother here." She turned to Joe. "Off you go."

Joe took Walter's hands in his. "I'll see you in a couple of hours. Minus that metal in your belly."

He pushed through the screens and left the nurses and the surgeons to do their work.

Dear Ma

First off, Walter is found. He's alive. I hope you get this with the good news afore the telegram about his injury arrives. I hate the way they write them things. 'Regret to inform you' is a stupid way to start. Scares people mad. Sounds like the worst is coming but Walter's going to be fine. For the now, your wee boy is not kicking too hard. I won't kid you. He's hurt pretty bad. Took some shrapnel in the guts and when I first saw him a few hours ago he wasn't very spry but he's had a blood transfusion and has perked up. Amazing what the doctors can do. He was sitting up in bed a few minutes ago and chatting away to me. He's in surgery as I write getting fixed up better. I'll post this letter straight away to set your mind at rest and write later as well to tell you how the op went. And here's even better news for you. He'll be shipped home. I don't know exactly when or where he'll be sent for convalescence. It could be anywhere. Up in Scotland or somewhere in England. I don't know that part of the system but I think you'll have him home for Christmas.

Joe rocked in his chair in the canteen where he'd come to write the letter. He lit up another cigarette and wondered what else to say to his mother. Fred was dead. Walter had come close to death and still might not survive. If all went well, he'd be sent home but once he recovered and turned eighteen, he could be sent back to France. Joe banged his fist on the table. And me? What's the fucking point of me being here now?

He got up and refilled his mug. He looked at his watch. Twenty after ten. They should finish with Walter soon. He paced the canteen, dragged on his cigarette, and took gulps of tea. Every time there were footsteps, he looked up, hoping to see Adelaide. Someone had left a magazine on a table. He picked it up and settled himself at a table, one leg folded over the other knee.

"What is this shite?" he said, flicking through the pages. Elegant English ladies in summer frocks played croquet on pristine green lawns. Men wore expensively tailored jackets and arrogant smirks and splayed their legs astride huge sleek horses. Hounds yapped in packs. Joe stopped at a page with the header: Preserving the Virtues of Rural Life. He groaned, thought of the churned up fields, the trees reduced to charred sticks or blown right away from their roots, and the piles and piles of stone and brick that had once been country cottages and farmhouses.

"Mad, mad," he said. "The whole world's gone fucking mad."

Someone rapped him hard on the shoulder. He put out his hand to field off the blow and turned round.

"Not as mad as I'm going to be if you don't let go my stick and tell me what you're doing here?"

Joe jumped up and saluted. "Lieutenant Atholl. Sir."

"Captain Atholl, Mathieson. Captain now. I'm your commanding officer."

Joe wanted to laugh at the former lieutenant's slicked back hair, fuzz-free skin, and polished buttons. He might have just stepped out of the magazine, escorting an English rose from a croquet game to her cucumber sandwiches.

Atholl tugged at his jacket hem. "Well? I'm waiting."

Joe stubbed out his cigarette in the metal ashtray.

"I was assisting Major Saunders with a procedure. The patient is due to come from surgery and I was told to wait on news of his condition." He kept his eyes fixed on Atholl's. "Sir."

Atholl looked toward the entrance. He stiffened and saluted as Saunders and Adelaide came towards them. Atholl stretched his hand toward Saunders, but Saunders ignored him and put his arm around Joe.

"He's all patched up. A few nicks to his liver. I've taken out the spleen and repaired a tear in the stomach and another in the duodenum. A lot of perforations in the bowel but I stitched up all I could see. He still has a pound or so of metal in his belly, but he, and half the males in Britain, can live another fifty years with that debris in situ. I'm confident there's no internal bleeding and no sign of infection although ..." He turned to Adelaide. "Pyrexia? Increasing or not?"

She pursed her lips. "Slightly up. Almost hundred."

"Not bad given what he's been through. I'd say he's a lucky one. We'll keep an eye on him, but he's young and well equipped to put this all behind him. Both in body and spirit." He nodded his head. "Yes. A complete success, I hope. One we can all be proud of." He turned toward Adelaide "Don't you think?"

Adelaide stepped forward and took Joe's hands in hers. "He's doing really well. Truly. We'll keep him sedated for the next twenty-four hours, then he'll be on the train. For home."

Saunders turned to Atholl. "I'd like Joe to stay here tonight, if you can spare him. It will do his brother the world of good to see him when he wakes up."

"His brother? Another brother?"

"Yes sir," Joe said.

For a moment, Atholl's eyes softened. Joe heard his swallow. "It turns out that will be very convenient. We've closed all the dressing stations and first aid posts up and down the line. All personnel have moved over here." He gave a little cough. "That's what I came to tell Lance Corporal Mathieson. Before I reported to you, sir. I knew he had permission to leave the ADS for a while and was a little concerned when he hadn't returned. It's not that I thought he was AWOL or anything like that."

"Of course he's not absent," Saunders said. He smiled and clapped Joe on the shoulder. "Your man's right here. Been with us for hours. Walk with me, Captain, and I'll bring you up to date." He headed toward the entrance. "We've dealt with about half the patients. I reckon we have close to two hundred more lined up for surgery." Before he left the tent he turned to Joe. "Sister will take you to the recovery tent and you can sit with your brother."

"Sister? I'd prefer Nurse Armitage if you can spare her."

"Sister now. This lady here." He pointed to Adelaide. "We've promoted her."

She folded her hands demurely in front. "Only acting sister," she said.

"And doing a fine job," Saunders said, and disappeared with Atholl into the dark night.

"Congratulations. No one deserves it more," Joe said. He blushed with pleasure. "You're not just good at your job. You have a special good way with folk. All kinds."

"Thank you. And you too are a talented man." She flicked both ends of her veil over her shoulders. "All right, enough mutual adoration. I'll take you to your brother. Is there anything else I can do for you?"

"Could you put in a word with Saunders? I want on the train with Walter. You know I have the experience. I'll come straight back from Boulogne when he's dropped off."

"Joe. Major Saunders respects my *work*. Not me personally. I don't have that kind of influence."

Joe turned away. He didn't want her to see the desperation in his face.

She put her hands on his waist and swung him around. "I'll go with you, but you have to do the persuading." She smiled. "You've already succeeded over the transfusion."

She's brilliant, he thought. He had an impulse to kiss her smiling mouth but instead took her hands from him and kissed them. "Okay. Let's do it. Now."

"Then I really must get back to work." She wiped her brow in mock weariness. "Is there anything else that is your command? I've helped with girlfriend, brother. Been translator, psychoanalyst. What about ... oh, I don't know, tinker, tailor?"

He laughed, landed another kiss on her cheek, put his arm through hers and led her over to the surgeons' quarters. "Aye. One more thing." He pulled her tighter into him. "I'm racking up a lot of favours here. Atholl said everyone from the front's sent here. Can you put the word out that I'd like to see Frank and let him know where I am?"

She unlinked her arm and ran ahead of him, laughing. "I'm on my way!"

"What's up, old mate? 'Ow's the patient?" Frank pulled up a chair and sat at Walter's bed next to Joe.

"Good. Really good. Thanks for the visit."

"I wouldn't miss meeting this young lad for the world." Frank nudged Joe in the ribs. "If it wasn't for 'im I wouldn't 'ave 'ad the pleasure of your miserable face for nigh on two years." He leaned over the bed, smoothed out the swaddling over Walter's abdomen, and took his hand. "First class brother you've got 'ere," he said, and nodded toward Joe. "I 'ope you appreciate that, young nipper. You take care of yourself now and get some rest. Your brother and me's going for a dander and a smoke." He gave Walter two thumbs up.

As they walked outside, he turned to Joe and laughed. "'Ow about you wrap me in bandages and sneak me with you onto the 'ospital train? Then I'll head straight for 'ome."

Joe smiled. "Knowing you, you'd get away with it. How do you do it?"

"What?" Frank said.

"Keep cheery all the time. I've never seen you pissed at any of this. Drunk, yes, but you always come up smiling."

"I try not to look ahead or back. Just what's in front of my nose."

"Not possible when the voices of hell scream night and day," Joe said.

"Sometimes I force myself to see what's going on like a dartboard, a 'uge circle what fills my mind, blotting out everything else."

"Never been able to do that."

"I've 'ad practise," Frank said. "Done it all my life. Worked when my dad 'ad a skinful and battered on my mum. I couldn't do nothing about it except try and cheer 'er up with my jokes."

As Joe listened, Frank's Cockney twang that once grated his ear became the soft sound of friendship. "Are they … still around?"

"Old man buggered off when I was twelve. The cancer got my mum. Summer of '14. In all that 'eat."

"I never knew," Joe said.

"Well I never told." He shrugged and smiled. "The stretcher-bearing is good 'cause my banter seems to cheer the patients up, give them 'ope or whatever to keep them focused on being alive and staying that way. You've 'eard me tell them the wounds will get them back 'ome to regular life." He laughed. "Wife, kids, a bit of shagging. Saturday afternoon at the football match, the evening down the Red Lion with their mates and maybe a girlfriend." He laughed again. "And maybe more nookie."

"You're good at that. The best."

"Shagging? I am that. Little do you know, my friend."

"I'm sure you are, but seriously, I mean there was many a day I couldn't have kept going if it wasn't for you."

Frank fiddled with his cigarette packet and offered one to Joe. "Enough sop. Light up."

Joe lit a match for them both. "Seeing my brother so close to death's made me soft, I know." He faced Frank. "You're a real pal. I'd hate it if something happened and I hadn't told you."

"Nothing going to 'appen to you."

Joe blew smoke into his friend's face and gave him a shove. "I meant you, you muttonhead." His laughter evaporated quickly. "Look what's happened to Walter. My wee brother. Lying still and bound up. Clever. Had a future. What's ahead for him when he recovers? Killing and more killing. Where's it supposed to get us?"

"Maybe the generals 'ave a grand plan but they 'aven't let us in on it," Frank said. "Fuck me if I know. Anyway, your brother'll be 'ome soon. Can 'e pick up where 'e left off? Yeah?"

Joe pinched off his cigarette between his thumb and index finger and put it behind his ear for later. "Maybe." He sighed.

"This miserable weather got us all down," Frank said. "We'll all feel better when the winter's come and been and it warms up." He pushed

Joe's shoulder. "Remember the summer at Gaudechat? Those were the days. Sun, easy work, nights of music and drink. Autumn wasn't all bad either. Me and some other mates duck 'unting and catching eels in those ponds round Frise. Made a nice little profit, I did."

"But don't forget what happened in between. Especially July."

"I 'aven't. I just can't see the point of putting it in the spotlight. I try and think of the good parts. You're the last person to say no good 'as come of this."

"How's that?" Joe said.

"Mamzelle Marguerite and all that."

Joe gave a little laugh and shook his head. "For sure, Frank. Being with her was the best thing what ever happened to me."

"Was?"

"Aye. She's gone. Away with her family. There's only one place I'll ever feel her again." Joe stood and put his hand against his heart. "In here." He sucked in some air. "Got to catch some kip. Thanks for coming by. You are a pal, Frank. Aye, a real pal." He shook Frank's hand with both of his.

Frank pretended to wipe tears from his eyes. He threw himself against Joe. "And I love you too, mate."

Joe laughed and pushed him away. "You fucking goof. Away to your bed."

Joe woke around seven. On a cot in the orderlies' tent, his body had yielded to sleep almost immediately. His night was dreamless and he woke up the most refreshed he'd felt in weeks. He dressed quickly, so as not to let the November damp cold ruffle his good mood. He reminded himself Walter was on his way home. He grabbed a mug of tea and three slices of toast and marmalade from the canteen and hurried over to the four tents huddled into a square that made up the recovery ward.

"Over here." Walter was sitting up, and waved at him.

Joe strolled over to his bed, the third in a row of ten or more. "Well, look at you." He lifted the covers and looked at his dressing. Only a spot of blood on the bandages. Good.

"Anything else you'd like to check out, Doctor Mathieson?"

"I see your little holiday from home hasn't rehabilitated you from your insubordination toward your more senior brother."

"Where'd you learn those big words?"

"Enough cheek." He pulled the bed-covers up to Walter's armpits, and shoved the last of his toast into his mouth. Walter kicked the covers off.

Joe pulled up a chair. "Do you feel as good as you look?"

"Aye. I do. I'm just sore if I move."

"Well don't move then."

"Thanks for the sympathy,"

Joe pulled his chair in closer to the bed. "This is what's going to happen, Walter. And this time, I want you to listen good and for once do as you're told. You'll be put on a stretcher and then on the train heading to the coast. It could take a long time, but I'll be by your side the whole road. I've written to Ma, told her the op went well, and that you're leaving today, so don't muck this up doing it your own way. You'll be well looked after on the journey. You get that? So take the chance to rest and get better. I know what I'm talking about. I worked on the hospital train when I first came to look for you."

"You came to look for me?"

"What do you think, you daftie? I came over here 'cause I wanted a foreign holiday?"

Walter started to sniffle.

"Stop it now."

Walter lifted the edge of the sheet and wiped his nose.

"I would have got sent here anyways. Later. When they started the conscription. But now, you listen. Listen good to everything we tell you to do."

Walter started to whimper again.

"I said no crying. You'll do as you're told. Ma's expecting you for Christmas. You ruin that for her, I'll personally come after you and rip that belly open again. Got that?"

Walter managed a weak smile. "Aye, I got it. Sir."

"And afore you go, I'll write a wee letter to Ellen. And draw a few pictures. She likes cows. Three now she is. Can you believe that? When you get home, I want you to take her on your knee and read it to her. Cuddle her tight for me."

"What about Kate?"

Joe looked away. “I'll write to her too. I will, but I've no time to do it afore you go. I'll send it by the post.” He pulled his chair in tight to the bed, took the porridge bowl from Walter, and laid it on the floor. He folded his arms over the bed and leaned forward. “Walter. There's something else.” He took Walter's hand and rubbed the knuckles. “Fred's killed.”

Walter gasped. “No, no.” The sniffles heightened to a wild weeping.

Joe stood and put his arms around his brother.

“I'm sorry,” Walter said, trying to stem his sobs.

Joe held Walter tighter. “No. Go right ahead. This time you can cry as much as you want.” Joe too cried. And the two brothers buried their heads, each in the other's shoulder.

Wednesday, November 22, 1916 2:00 p.m. At the train siding, Joe and Frank hoisted Walter over the rows of stretchers laid out on the hard cold ground. “Wave bysie-bye to the ccs and the nice nurses. You’ll never see more beautiful girls in all your life,” Frank said.

“Get on the train. Bloody stretcher’s digging into my neck.” Joe blinked sweat from his eyes. “Curl your toes and hold on,” he said to his brother, as they angled the sagging stretcher from the ground up to the train. “We have to tip you a bit.”

“Insides slopping around enough?” Frank asked.

Walter panted in short stiff breaths. “Only a few seconds more,” Joe said, “and the hurt’ll die down.”

Once on the train, the familiar rows of injured men and nurses scurrying up and down the aisle filled him with confidence. Joe was raring to begin Walter’s journey home. The move from the ccs to the train was another hurdle passed. Every mile the train ate up, the closer the finishing post and safety. He stared the length of the coach, relaxed a little in the well-known scene: the low row of footed cots fixed to the floor on either side of the coach, and the hammocks stiffened with wooden rails slung above for the more stable patients.

“Name?”

“Walter Mathieson,” Joe said to an orderly with a clipboard, checking in the patients.

“Wound tag?”

“Aye. And surgical notes.” Joe lifted the cover on the stretcher and showed the orderly Saunders’ scribblings.

“Bed fourteen. Right-hand side. Settle him in and get out the way.”

“I’m going with this one. To Boulogne. Major says so. In the notes.”

“I’ve not time to be reading doctors’ stories.”

This was exactly what Joe had been counting on, but nevertheless could feel the sweat on his neck. When Saunders had told him to take thirty-six hours, he hadn't said he couldn't take a train ride. He took his place with Frank in the line-up of bearers taking wounded to their berths.

Joe spread-eagled his feet for balance in the connecting gangway that allowed staff to trek from coach to coach. He blew smoke from his cigarette out the window. As the train clanked its way through the countryside, he refused to let the shattered landscape or the miserable November afternoon get him down. Walter was taken care of. More or less. A long healing time lay ahead, but he was on the road. Frank was right. His brother was still too young to be conscripted. He could go back to school. He'd damn well buckle down after his little adventure. "Hardly little," Joe said to a burned-out village that flashed by, with its church spire pointing defiantly to the sky. "Still, a grand tale to tell his children and grandchildren."

He threw his fag end out the window, and yanked it closed with the leather strap. He swayed with the train, legs apart, at the entrance to Walter's coach. He held onto the doorframe to steady himself. Nurses and orderlies silently went about their duties. The light of day was fading fast, but the hanging lamps had not yet been lit. The door at the far end stood open, as was the one in the coach beyond that. Joe peered and squinted as far as the dim light would allow. He shivered. A dark tunnel of endless wounded, winding and weaving with no light in the distance.

He let go of the doorframe and moved to Walter's bed, a little more than halfway down the coach, where a nurse sat on her haunches giving him water from a spouted cup. Walter squeezed out a laugh. "Hey, big brother. Tell her enough of the water. I'm famished. I want a fish supper."

Joe introduced himself to the nurse and took the cup from her. "I'll do this, let you get on."

"Oh Lord," the nurse said. "Your brother? I am sorry."

"Aye, you would be if you had this rascal for a brother. No end of trouble he's caused me." He brought Walter's head to the cup. "Water only for a couple of days. Your tum needs a chance to rest. So for once in your life, do what this nurse..."

"Celia."

"Do what Nurse Celia tells you. You do that and I'll make sure your order for fish and chips goes in when we get to the hospital. Drink up. You'll not starve to death if it takes a week to reach the fish suppers."

The soup pot came up the aisle and the able ones were helped to some nourishment. After the slurping, choking, clanging, and banging stopped, Walter's eyes closed. Joe smiled and smoothed his brother's hair. When he was sure Walter had fallen into a deep sleep, he crawled over his feet to the bulkhead side of the cot and sat hunched and cross-legged, halfway up the bed.

The train screeched and jerked him awake. The wheels grated over the rails and shuddered to a stop. Joe rubbed his eyes, goading his brain to remember where he was. Men hobbled up the aisle. Nurses squeezed past to answer calls and moans. Orderlies strode down the aisle, some with armloads of laundry, others with pots of steaming water. He had to twist and contort his upper body to turn around in his cramped space. Once on his knees, he reached up and rubbed away the condensation on the window above his head. It was pitch dark. Flashes pricked the night as matches lit cigarettes. Piss break. Could do with one himself, but he was too stiff and cold to stir. He settled into a ball again and covered his legs with the edge of Walter's blanket. He threw up a prayer to whatever power might be. Please, please, get the train moving. Let Walter and me sleep the whole night through. Until the light of day. Until Boulogne. He needed to feel this train move under him, check off more and more miles from the front. Patience, he ordered himself. Only a handful of hours more.

Walter's right hand twitched, his eyelids fluttered. Joe wondered what dreams darted behind those eyes. Football in the park down by the shore? A supper of black pudding and peas? A daring grope for a lassie's titty? Or was he seeing nightmares of mud, stones, and blood streaking towards him? Maggots the size of grass snakes guzzling the endless supply of human offal? He touched the spaces between Walter's long, slim fingers spread on the thin cover. How like his own. Not a sissy hand. Nor a boy's. A man's. Strong with tiny tufts of ginger hair on the fleshy mounds between the joints. He traced the length of his brother's arm and marvelled at the muscles that shaped his forearm, the outside of his upper arm, and the bulge of his shoulder. Nearly as powerful as his own, over-developed from carrying loaded stretchers. More than a few in the family had remarked on their resemblance, but until now, Joe never paid heed to those matters of kin and kind that seemed to fascinate the women folk.

The train lumbered into a slow roll toward the coast. Joe regretted not taking advantage of the stop. He really needed a piss. And a smoke. It had been hours since he'd had either. He edged himself down to the bottom of Walter's cot and slid into the aisle. Crept among the snores and soft whimpers of the wounded. He slipped into the connecting gangway through the sliding door at the end of the coach, closed it behind him, and looked about. No one up and about. He lowered the window its full extent, stood on his tiptoes, hung his willie out, and emptied his bladder, closing his eyes against a possible back splash. Then he treated himself to a cigarette. He'd just enjoyed his last puff when a couple of orderlies appeared from the coach behind Walter's. Both could have been patients in the past judging by their limps and scarred faces. Joe nodded to them and, with a smile, refused the cigarette the short red-faced one offered him. They exchanged stories for a half-hour or so. Proud, they said, of the village they came from, high on the Yorkshire moors.

"Joined the same Pals regiment. Went arm in arm. February '15."

"We was wounded the same day too," said the other. A scar from the bottom of his nose travelled around his mouth and disappeared down his collar. "Warrant tha' right, Tom? Both in same leg," one said and nudged the other. "Just like 'ome. One always 'as to be same as tuther. Best friends." They both chuckled and spluttered on their cigarettes.

Joe told them about his brother.

"Summat we could do for 'im?"

Joe smiled and shook his head. "Ta. He's in good hands and'll be even better when we get to Boulogne."

Each shook Joe's hand and reminded him what a grand thing was coming. A mother's reunion with her son for Christmas.

"Better yet," Joe said. "Home for Hogmanay."

"Bah goom," said one. "We've 'eard 'bout you Scotch on New Year's Eve."

"There's aye a party at my ma's on Hogmanay. Look me up when this is all over. Standing invitation. You can visit my brother." Joe nodded ahead. "I'm away back." He slid open the door and gave them a wave.

The drained bladder, the surge of tobacco through his veins, and the chat with the friendly Yorkshire men had relaxed him. Enough to get a few more hours kip while Walter slept. Barring any interruption on the line to let troop trains or ammunitions wagons through, they'd arrive at Boulogne around eleven or noon. Another step towards home checked off. Home. What wouldn't he give to see Ma's face! Tears nipped his eyes as he thought of her happiness.

He swayed down the coach, legs apart to keep his balance, to Walter's bed. His brother was awake, panting. Joe knelt down at his side. "Hiya. Okay?"

Walter scrunched his face and shifted. "It hurts."

"Aye. It will. You've just had big cuts made in you. And you know how even a wee cut on your finger stings when it's healing."

Walter moaned.

"Shh. It's okay. I'll see if I can get some tablets." He combed his brother's hair with his fingers.

"Don't. I'm hot," Walter groaned and flicked his head to the side, away from Joe's hand.

Joe bent over his brother's bed and gently laid his hand on Walter's abdomen. A malicious heat stabbed his hand, shooting it off the covers as if he'd been stung. "How long have you been like this?"

"Dunno. I just woke up. Joe, it hurts. Bad."

"Worse than afore?" Joe laid a hand on his brother's forehead. Hotter. Guilt pricked at his skin for whiling away the time, shooting the breeze and smoking out in the gangway instead of being vigilant by his brother's bedside. He pushed the bed-cover down to Walter's knees. Greenish-brown pus seeped through the bandages. Joe dragged his haversack from below the bed, took out his scissors, and cut away the fetid cloth, snagging a few wiry pubic hairs. The swelling, complaining bowel had forced open a line of stitches. They lay on Walter's skin like a defeated army of ants.

Walter opened one eye, a flash of fear on his face. "What are you doing?" he said, his voice barely audible over his rapid panting.

"Nothing for you to worry about," Joe said. "I can take care of it." He pulled up the bed-cover. "I'm off to get you something for the pain. From the nurse down the way. Something to get you back to sleep too." He squeezed Walter's hand. "There, there. No touching your belly now."

He wanted to rush up the aisle, scream for help. Yell for a surgeon to come instantly and cut away the rank flesh of Walter's suppurating bowel. Tidy up all the rotten parts, sew his brother up and say, *Phew, that was close but all is hunky-dory.* Instead he rushed down the swaying aisle, hand over hand on the upper bunks to steady himself. At the far end of the next coach, seated on the floor next to a black stove heating a dozen or so kettles of water, Celia and an older nurse well into her thirties chatted softly and blew on hot soup. Joe tapped Celia on the shoulder. *Stay calm, go slow, speak clearly.* He described the problem. "He was doing fine until a wee while ago."

The older one handed off her soup to Celia and reached over her head into a little wooden chest and collected dressing pads, bandages. "Fetch a jug of hot water, Ceece. You a kettle of cold," she said to Joe. "On the floor, next to the stove."

All three strode with their comforts to Walter's bedside. He stared, glassy-eyed, at Joe.

"Ceece, clean up the wound best you can. We'll redress it." The more senior nurse turned to Joe as she unpacked a dressing and handed it to him. "Estelle. Lawson. Hold this. And cool him down." She nodded over to the black kettle. "Lucky for him it's winter. Water's good and cold. Talk to him."

Joe knelt at the head of the cot and patted Walter's arms and chest with the icy water. His own forehead dripped with sweat and he gave it a quick wipe before laying the chilled cloth over Walter's face.

"Close your eyes, wee man. Picture you and me standing together. See that long rope? Can you see you and me holding one end? Ma's got the other end tied around her waist. See? She's at the frying pan cooking your tea. Look at her. She's happy. She knows you're on your way. What's she making for you?"

Walter grimaced and arched his back, let out a crackly sigh.

"Make him lie still," Estelle snapped.

"Aye, aye. I will." He turned back to his brother. "Here's the thing, Walter. You, you lucky wee bugger, you're gonna get a nice warm bath.

From these bonnie nurses." He leaned over to Walter's ear and whispered. "Down there. Jewels and all."

Tears dribbled from the corners of Walter's eyes.

"We want Ma to see you all spick and span. Right?"

Joe tensed at Walter's fixed stare. *I can't let him see anything in my eyes but a cheery smile.*

"Temperature?" Estelle handed him a thermometer.

Joe stuck it under his brother's tongue, wished he'd never have to take it out and confront a horrible number.

Walter pounded his hands on the thin mattress.

"Sorry. The old bandage got a bit stuck to your skin. Want you to have a nice clean one," she said. "Almost done." Joe saw her look from his brother's spread-open wound to her partner and shrug. He dabbed Walter's face with the cold cloth. His brother breathed faster.

Joe cleared his throat. "You sound like the train, puffing away like that." He hoped he was making a good job of the fake calm. He connected the symptoms. Rising fever, rapid breath. He touched Walter's chest. Increased heart rate. He pulled the pyjama top off his brother's shoulders. Add angry red striations on his upper arms to the list. He bet Walter's thighs were the same. He'd seen this a million times. Septicaemia. He wanted to fling himself against his brother and breathe his own life into him.

"Keep talking to him," Estelle said. "Keep him awake. Got to do what we can to stop him going into shock."

He heard the nurse's voice as if from far away, like an echo. Joe swiped his tongue around his lips to get enough spit to talk. "Aye. Aye. Do you see Ma like I told you? Look. She's in the kitchen. Oh, here's my Ellen. She's running to you. Look at her big smile. My God, she's happy to see her uncle. You're her favourite, you know."

Walter clutched Joe's hand as he eased the thermometer from his mouth.

"Ma?" Walter's voice was thick and gurgly.

"Let go now. I need my hands to help you." The glass thermometer slipped from Joe's sweating hand and landed on the pillow. The mercury a black line. Straight. Tall. Joe counted the marking bars. Ninety-eight, a hundred. A hundred and one. The mercury risen still higher. A real fever. Not a post-op reaction. He mouthed the terrible result to the nurse. *104.* She nodded and pointed to the end of the coach. Joe stuck Walter's hands under the blanket and covered him. "Nature calls," he lied. "Back soon."

In the gangway, the nurses already sat on the floor with their legs outstretched when Joe caught up with them. Joe pulled at his hair, felt his control slipping. *104. He'll fry his brains if it goes any higher.*

"I'm sorry," said Celia. "Didn't realize at first it was so serious. He spiked really fast. Sit." She took off her veil, rearranged stray strands of fair hair with her fingers, drew in her legs and rested her chin on her knees. She looked to Estelle. "What do we do?"

She looks all of fourteen, Joe thought. This country, this war, makes us grow up in a hurry.

"There may be nothing we can do," the older nurse said, her long oval face a canvas of concern.

"Nothing? This is my brother with a fucking high temperature. One hundred and four fucking lethal degrees."

Celia tugged at Joe's leg. "Sit a minute. Smoke if you want. We can at least make him more comfortable."

"May I have one?" Estelle said and pointed to the pack Joe had just taken from his breast pocket. "Helps me think."

He handed her one and offered the lit match before lighting his own. Her pale freckles hopped around her mouth as she savoured the first drag. "I've seen these youngsters rally. Seen many weather a crisis like this. You have too."

"And I've seen hundreds die. You've seen *that* too."

"Let's all keep our heads on." She leaned her back against the wall and looked to the roof. "What we need is a surgeon. And that's what we don't have." She tightened her mouth and turned to Joe. "Time?"

Joe checked his watch. "Twenty past six."

"Five or six hours till we can get him seen to. I hate this about the trains. If some emergency comes up we have to wait and wait, sitting in this bloody barely moving slug feeling useless."

"Then it's up to us," Joe said. "Walter can't wait that long. We need to open him up, cut away the infection, maybe a bit extra for good measure."

"Lance-corporal, without disrespecting you or your poor brother, *I* have no need for cutting into anyone. Or to be court-martialed for exceeding my authority." Estelle turned away and drew on her cigarette. "Besides, I don't have the nerve for assuming that kind of responsibility. Nor do I have the skill."

Joe fixed his eyes on her. "I do. I've stitched everything. Fingers, toes, heads." His hand twitched, remembering Captain Rogers' spilled brains dribbling through his fingers. "Arse wounds too." He cleared his throat. "My last C.O. said…" He pinched his nose. Hard. He wanted pain to stall his urge to fling himself against her bosom and cry. Pinched harder. "He said I could sew like a country lady."

She stood and straightened her skirt. "All we can do is pray he can hang in until we get him to Boulogne. Then he can get fixed." She lowered the window and threw out her cigarette butt. "And he'll have a good shite every day for the rest of his life."

"A sh—"

"What?" She faced Joe. "Shocked to hear a woman talk like this? After all we've seen?" She tapped Celia on the arm. "Come on. We *will* do a check on this young man's brother. Then we have others to see to."

"Take a proper look," Joe said. "Please."

She folded her arms. "A proper look?" she said. "I'm sorry. It's Joe, right?"

He nodded.

"In my opinion, Joe," she said, "there's nothing to be done. I think he's past our help. Like I said, if we had surgeons here …"

"Then I don't need your *help*." He pushed her away and jumped up. "Thanks for nothing." At the doorway he turned back. "Look, I didn't mean that." He moved carefully into her space, put his hand on her arm. "If you think he's going to … go ... then what does it matter? I'll not be telling anyone. Nobody'll know. They'll think it was the operation he had at the ccs. You'll not be in any trouble." He held her gaze, and saw indecision in the slight twitch in her lower lip. "There's no medical officer what would know. Not on the train. No surgeons you said." He waited for his words to settle. "Please. I need your help."

She pushed past him and disappeared into the next carriage. He sank to the floor. He tried to think, keep his mind clear, but the slow throbbing of the train wheels underneath grated on his brain. He lit another cigarette and used each puff to still his frustration.

"Well, are you coming or not? I thought you were in a mad hurry." Estelle stood over him, a scalpel, forceps, and a stitching kit atop a pile of bandages and towels. "Bloody stubborn, you Scots." She turned to Celia. "Follow me with that jug of hot water, then get some more." She pointed a finger at Joe. "I'm doing this to protect the patient. I don't trust you alone with this ... this *operation*."

Joe led Estelle to his brother's bedside. Walter had thrown off the covers, the fever governing his body, his arms and legs jerking in stiff spasms. Joe laid two fingers on Walter's wrist over the radial artery. He didn't need a watch to tell his heart was racing wildly. Dangerously. More rigors. Joe held Walter's legs down. "Walter, Walter. Speak to me." Walter's breathing came in rapid weak bursts. Celia arrived at the bedside with two jugs of steaming water protected by linen scraps. Joe waved away the mask, jury-rigged from a bandage, that Celia handed him. Estelle ripped off the elastic band on the canvas instrument holder and unrolled it. A set of forceps was placed in Joe's hands.

He'd seen other bodies like this, hundreds of lads with spilled guts. Months and months he'd stood beside Captain Rogers at the operating table, unworried, relying on Rogers' skill and training. But this was his wee brother. He remembered him being born, squawking into the night, and keeping him and Fred awake. Plumping into a toddler, stealing his comics or scribbling all over them with his chalks. Walter's new bandages were already soaked and stained brownish-green. As Celia peeled them away, a torrent of pus squirted into her face. Joe wanted to run from the stink. He blew out as much air as he could and looked at the forceps in his hands. He leaned over Walter's belly but the rushing stench pushed him back, sent its tentacles up his nostrils, smearing the back of his tongue with its foul reek and filling his throat. He retched, glad he'd had nothing to eat since breakfast. Celia offered the mask again and this time he let her tie it around his head. Glistening black slime had pushed through the widening rip in Walter's wound, a couple of inches above his left groin. If only Joe could reach inside and grab the mess like a string of sausages, cut off the rotted ones, stuff the whole lot back in again. *Can't this fucking train go any faster?*

"Walter, Walter. Can you hear me?" Estelle steadied Walter's head. "Walter?" She squeezed cold water onto his face. Walter arched his back, his body as stiff as iron, and screamed. His eyes opened wide and rolled.

Joe knelt on the floor by his brother and looked at Estelle and Celia, kneeling beside him. He saw the doubt in their eyes peering over the top of their masks. "Is the scalpel clean? I need to cut through this mess."

She nodded.

"Chloroform?" asked Joe.

She shook her head.

"Morphine?"

"Plenty, but I'm worried it will adversely affect his breathing. He's already having trouble."

"What choice do we have?" Joe said. "If morphine's all we've got to make it easier for him, morphine it is. Inject a double dose for starters. I'll give my hands a good scrub while it's taking hold."

Celia shuffled the last of the blood-and-pus-streaked rags into a dustpan. "Don't get up, Joe, but if you could just move your legs? Sorry."

"No, no. I'm sorry. I need to sit." Walter hadn't moved in the hour since Joe had snipped, scraped, and scooped inside his gut. "My knees are still aching from kneeling by Walter." He shifted his legs and spread them out again on the icy floor without letting go of his brother's hand. Celia scraped the debris into a paper bag and scurried up the coach, giving him a pale smile.

He brushed Walter's cheek with his free hand and then traced a diamond shape into the perspiration puddling on his brother's forehead. "Do you remember," he whispered, "Da sometimes came home from the mine unwashed? Do you mind us drawing pictures in the coal dust on his face? You drew a right good robin one time. Remember? And a rabbit. Wee Ellen likes rabbits. Maybe you could get her one and a hutch when you get home? That's a grand idea, eh?"

A shallow in-breath, the first in what seemed to Joe over a minute, was Walter's reply. Then a gravelly exhale. His chest fell and lay unmoving. Joe took out his watch. Almost ten. Walter breathed again and moaned softly.

"Tea?" Celia was back again, a mug in her hands. Joe shook his head. "It'll pass the time," she said. "More so if you have some porridge. Still a couple of hours to go. And," she pointed to Walter, "he needs you to be strong. Besides the morphine you gave him is doing its work. He's sleeping quietly."

Joe shook his head again. She put her hands on her hips. He couldn't help but smile at this little young thing taking charge. "I'm sitting with him. You're going up the train to get some food. Now go." She dropped her pose and laid her hand on Joe's arm. "I promise I'll come and get you if there is the slightest change. I promise. Really."

Joe heaved himself from the floor and dragged himself to the kitchen three coaches ahead.

The bit of food, the three cups of tea, and two cigarettes had revived him. In the waxy morning light, he saw Celia, up by Walter's bedside, peer at her fob watch. *Ten past noon,* he heard her say. The train stopped with a soft hiss. He tapped her on the shoulder. "I'll take over." And he saw. Without a doubt. Walter had died. Through the window he could see the station, the grey wooden shingle swinging on its chains.

Boulogne.

Saturday, November 25, 1916 At the ccs at Colinvillers, Joe marched up and down between the tents, his hands under his armpits to keep them warm. He tried hard, so hard, to think of something good, or at least better. Nothing came. Walter was gone. Found but dead. Already buried in Boulogne. He willed his mind away from a devil in his brain that sought to touch his grief. A grief already settled so deep inside him he could barely detect it. Something in him wanted to worm his way toward it and touch the solid bundle of pain. Unravel and soothe it. But his body was terrified of its ability to sting.

He looked around this little makeshift hospital town. A part of his brain could not grasp that so much had changed when, all around, the dots of canvas making up the ccs were the same as when he'd first set eyes on them less than a week before. Resuss wards, operating tents, pre-op and post-op tents. Doctors' quarters, nurses' tents, tents for orderlies, and for food. Tents for tetanus, frostbite, scarlet fever, dysentery, peritonitis, meningitis, gangrene, heart mischiefs, and varicose veins. The moribund tent off in the distance. The ugliest detail in this forest of fabric—that Walter had *died*—was a sled on an icy hill, sliding just out of his grip.

He stamped his feet, and urged his blood to warm. Easier to dwell on the misery of the biting cold and the freeze to come when November gave way to December and January. *Think of the good,* he urged himself. The worse the weather gets the longer the guns will be quiet. Perhaps long enough to get a decent amount of leave. If he went home, he'd face a new terror, Ma and her anguish. Two sons dead. How would she and all the other families live on with such heartache? How many were there? Thousands? Hundreds of thousands? He didn't have it in him to write more words of comfort to his mother, when he ached for his own relief. He wanted to seek out Adelaide but worried he'd already asked too much of her. She had her own sorrow. He bit his lip. The freezing air pinched his tongue. So, he mused, Adelaide was the first woman he thought to turn to. Not his wife. Nor … not even … His throat closed over her name. He forced his breath to shape it. *Marguerite.* A new, sweeter wave of sadness blanketed him. He pulled his arms tighter around himself.

His fingers tingled from the frost. Without thinking, he stuck them in his mouth as Gran had done when he was a bairn: put his fingertips under his own tongue and blown her hot breath onto the backs of his mitten-covered hands. He remembered, when he'd tried it himself, how he had gagged on the fluff that itched the sides of his tongue and threatened to dam up his throat.

Warmth and life prickled back into his hands and he remembered how they'd baked under the constant heat of June. His mind leapt back to Marguerite, and a thought that brought energy surging through his torso. *If I get leave, I won't go home. I'll find out where Toulouse is. I'll go to Marguerite.*

He strode through the entrance to the operating room, ground his teeth while he scrubbed his hands with carbolic soap, and pulled on the long white gown over his uniform. Youngalec was counting out surgical instruments and laying them on a white cloth when Joe leaned over him. "Good job. Seen cheery chops Atholl?"

Youngalec laughed. "You're right there about that little lump of misery. Not the chirpiest of men, is he? Not like Captain Rogers." Youngalec crossed himself. "God bless his soul. Yes, I have seen our laugh-lacking leader. You're not in his good books, that's for sure. What's his problem with you?"

Joe shrugged. "Dunno. Maybe didn't like Captain Rogers taking an interest in my learning. Me, one of the common-as-muck soldiers. His whole opinion of himself is in those pips on his shoulders. Now his knickers are in a twist 'cause he thinks I'm pally with Major Saunders."

"A right gentleman him. Pretty decent to you over … you know." Youngalec sobered his voice. "Your brother."

Joe shut his eyes against the battering image of Walter thrashing with fever on the train. He shoved out a couple deep puffs. "Aye," he said, his composure mostly restored. "No pulling rank with him. We'll stay out of Atholl's way as much as possible. Keep our heads down.

The major says we've a backlog of about two thousand, so likely it's another all-nighter for us all." Joe squeezed Youngalec's shoulders. "Then, my friend, I'm hoping we'll all be getting a bit of a holiday. Maybe even until after the New Year. Your ma and da'll like that."

"And my wife." Joe's mouth dropped open.

"And three nippers."

"Never," Joe said.

Youngalec took up a sponge and started swabbing the rubber cover of the operating table. He turned and tapped the side of his face. "It's only one ear that doesn't work."

"I didn't mean—"

"I don't want any idle chitchat." Atholl stood between them and the table, pulled on rubber gloves. "Let's get started. This is not a soiree." He dipped his head at the orderly. "Bring in the first patient."

Youngalec brushed past Joe to the injured man, silently mouthing a pursed-lipped imitation of Atholl. Joe couldn't help laughing. Atholl bounded over to him and stuck his face so close Joe could see the shapes of the spaces between his teeth.

"You'd be doing yourself a favour, Mathieson, if you remember what you are. You're a nobody in my books, so you can drop the high and mighty impression you seem to have of yourself. I don't know how you charmed Sister Armitage. Or Captain Rogers. Now I see you working your game on Major Saunders."

Joe took a step back, but Atholl came towards him again, flecks of saliva escaping from the sides of his mouth. "But I am telling you, it won't work with me. I'm in charge here and I'll suffer no lip. You'll do exactly as I say and I'll be the one making the decisions. Do you understand?"

Joe heard the squeak of a wheel and turned around. Youngalec was bent over, pushing a bed over the uneven floor.

"Give him a hand," barked Atholl.

Joe stared at him.

"Lift my patient onto the table, lance corporal," Atholl said.

Joe kept his eyes firmly on Atholl's. "Yes, sir. Whatever you wish. Sir." He helped Youngalec transfer the unconscious man to the table. He was not much put out by Atholl's words. But his moods interfered with the calm that had descended on the hospital since the guns quit, and invaded the space in Joe's head where he preferred to imagine the longed for leave.

Joe put his feet up on the empty chair next to him in the canteen. He checked his watch. Just after nine. His belly was quiet and sated with chips and some sort of stewed beef. He preferred not to think what animal had donated its flesh for his satisfaction. By some sort of miracle, there'd been custard and tinned pears as a pudding. He fished in his breast pocket for his cigarette packet, lit one, and eased out the smoke. Now that he'd decided he'd use the time to find Marguerite, if he got leave, he allowed himself an oasis of optimism in the desert of hardships he'd endured these past seventeen months. He was sure the re-taking of Oroville had to be a turning point. Soon it would all be over for him, for them all. If he were a general, he'd continue to pursue the enemy back east, now they had them on the run. Never mind the cold. They couldn't suffer much more with the weather than they'd already done. And wouldn't this be a great chance, when the enemy army had to be depleted, dispirited and in disarray? But what did he know? More likely they'd replenish troops and supplies, and the lads, like himself, who had been in the thick of it since July, would get a break. Yes, he could feel some leave coming, taste it as sure as he relished the tobacco surging through his veins. The cells in his body tingled as they remembered the softness of Marguerite's limbs wrapped around him in the juicy summer grass at Gaudechat. Would Walter lying under the cold ground think of this as a betrayal? Deserting their mother? Joe assured himself he'd have years to see to Ma. She'd grieve for Fred and Walter the rest of her life, as hordes of mothers, fathers, brothers, sisters, sons, and daughters would miss *their* Walters. Besides, it had been a bugger of a day. He'd assisted with six surgeries since this afternoon.

He did a quick calculation in his head. Twelve or so operating rooms. At this rate they could get through a couple of thousand in forty hours. Of course, the teams would need to sleep a few times. At the outside, they'd be done in three days. Maybe another three or four days to get the injured shipped out or put into graves. The image of the burial grounds brought a jolting shudder. He took a long, long drag on his cigarette, stubbing out that reality. A week at the most to close down the ccs. He marked off the days on his fingers. December 3rd. Sounded like a good day to start leave. If it were true the guns wouldn't fire up again until the weather got better, they might give leave right through to Christmas or even New Year. He gulped. How could he not go home to Ellen and play Santa Claus? Kate would likely get time off from the munitions factory, if the guns didn't need to be fed. But how would she know he had leave unless he told her? Ma had Lizzie, Kate, and the three grandbairns to get her through Christmas. It was settled then. Keep the surgeries licking along as fast as he could make possible, stay clear of Atholl's childish tyranny, and find out how to get to Toulouse. Adelaide would know that.

He stood, brushed the crumbs from his jacket, and put his white robe back on, tying the cords as he braced himself for the frigid walk back to the operating tent. Outside, he trod carefully to find his path in the dark of night, barely lit by the remaining sliver of an old moon. A plane hummed over him, a sound he was becoming more used to. He liked these machines of the RFC circling the skies, like guardian mothers doing the rounds, checking on their children. This one flew more slowly than usual. The soft hum increased to a nerve-jangling drone, lowering in pitch and rising in volume, finishing with a thud that flung Joe face-down to the ground and smeared a cover of silence around his head.

The shaking ground rocked Joe on his hipbones. He lifted his head, wanting to track and save the pilot who had fallen from the heavens. Sky and tents around him glowed. The hush confused him until he saw soldiers and orderlies shambling from what he remembered was an operating tent with patients, their mouths shaped into silent screams, flung over their shoulders. He raised himself to a sitting position and hit his ears. The left one popped, and from the mouths of the scurrying people came a high-pitched wailing that threatened to shut down his hearing again. Atholl was pushing a nurse from the tent.

"Mathieson! Are you all right? Are you hurt?" the surgeon called through the swirling orange haze.

"Someone get to the pilot. Can't get up," Joe said.

"Taken care of, I'm sure." Atholl ran and squatted beside him.

"I'm fine," Joe said.

Atholl shone a torch into Joe's face and patted his legs and torso. "My responsibility as a medical officer to my men."

"Joe!" A flash of white veil knelt beside him.

Joe shielded his eyes. "Adelaide?"

"Sister, help me. Lift him," Atholl said. Together they staggered and helped Joe to his feet.

"I have to get an evacuation co-coordinated," she said. Her strong voice cut through the stinking air. "Gillingham," she said to the nurse Atholl had saved from the burning tent, "run to the guard post. I need all the orderlies over here to get the patients out. Tell Foxman to get the patients as far away as possible. Each man's to have at least two blankets."

Joe was shaking his head, trying to get both ears working again.

"You sure you're all right?" Adelaide said.

Another thud. Joe dove for the ground, pulling Adelaide with him. Sheltering them both with his gown, he held her head down while he peeked out from the folds. One of the post-op tents was lit up like a Guy Fawkes effigy. Above it, in the blaze of light it threw up, Joe saw the plane—the enemy's black cross outlined in white on its fuselage. Another thump. Joe flattened and covered them again.

The plane's whir faded. When all was quiet, he left Adelaide and crept toward another post-op tent. Behind it, the bomb had blown a massive hole in the ground. Flames licked at the bottom of the tent. Joe ripped at the canvas flap. "Get out! Get out!" He ran the length of the ward. Flung back bed-covers. "Get up! Help someone who can't. Go. Go."

"Wake up!" he screamed into the face of a young lad whose left leg, shot through with metal pins, was hoisted onto a pulley. One arm lay flush with the bedclothes, where his other leg should have been. "Outside," Joe said, unhitching the pulley.

The young lad opened his eyes, smiled, and pushed Joe away. "Let me be," he said. "I lost this boy back in July." He patted the smooth bed-cover. "Last week I took a second hit. I'm not lucky enough to survive a third. Save someone else."

The lights went out. Joe edged his way from bed to bed, grabbed a patient under each arm and dragged them toward the outside. He urged his eyes to adapt to the blackness. Outside, he found Adelaide giving out hand lamps to her nurses.

"Three dead in there I know of," he said. "I'll get more out."

"No. The stretcher-bearers and their muscle are on the way," she said. "You get over to the operating tents." Frank and half-dozen men emerged from the dark into the shadow of the lamps. "And troops are coming from Oroville and from wherever else they can be mustered." Adelaide pushed a lamp into Joe's hands. "Go. I'm in charge of my wards. Until more help arrives, my nurses and I can at least get the living up and under their beds. Safer there if we take another hit. If it makes you feel better, I'll collect the enamel washbasins and we can all wear them as helmets. Now get going over to surgical."

An engine whined overhead again. Joe kept turning and staring above him, trying to locate the plane. Another bomb hit the ground some distance behind him and he took off at a sprint, head down, one arm outstretched to keep the lamp level, the other furiously pumping, urging his legs toward the operating tent. Another crack. That one he heard with both ears. Another burst of light gave him a vivid snapshot of the double dragonfly-like wings of the enemy bomber heading toward his operating tent. It hovered for a moment, then veered to the east as if thumbing its nose.

Youngalec stood outside the operating tent, waving his fist at the sky. "Bloody cowards. Not enough you mush up our lads on the battlefield?" He had one hand on a hip now, the other pointing back to the tent. "Yellow-bellied bastards." He pushed aside the tent flap and went back inside.

Joe followed and laid a hand on his shoulder. "Feel better now?"

Youngalec nodded. "I thought they were going to drop one right on top of us."

"Where's the patient?" Joe said, nodding at the bare operating table. "And Atholl?"

Youngalec pointed under the table. "Patient's lucky. Finishing him up when this all started." He winked at Joe, and pointed again. "We thought it would be safer. Under ... the ... table."

Joe held onto the table with one hand and looked underneath.

Next to the blanketed patient, Atholl was scrunched up, as round as a hedgehog in a ball, his arms drawn together over his head and tucked under his toes. Joe crawled underneath the table and knelt in front of him. He gave Atholl a gentle poke on the shoulder. The young surgeon raised a hand and pushed Joe away. Another bomb exploded, off to their right. Atholl threw himself at Joe and clung to him, his fingers digging in so deeply he hurt Joe's upper arms. He tried to pry him loose, but Atholl's limbs were around him now in an octopus hold. Staccato panting came from the young officer's throat. Joe encircled his shaking body with his arms. He rocked him and shushed him as he might do to wee Ellen after a bad dream. Atholl's breathing slowed down and became more solid. They sat locked together under the shelter of the table for a few moments, until Atholl pulled himself away and started to move out. Joe slithered out the opposite side, jumped up, and when Atholl stood, Joe was waiting for him with a salute.

"What are my orders, sir?" Joe said, careful not to look Atholl in the eye.

"I-I-I'm not sure."

"Should we get the patient outside?" Joe said.

"Yes. That's right. Of course. You and Young. Take him. Somewhere safe. Then find out what the evacuation plan is. I'll ... I'll wait here for word."

Joe and Youngalec crouched and drew out the still woozy patient from under the table, then lifted him outside.

Outside the whole camp was filled with men in khaki, orderlies and stretcher-bearers carrying, lifting, dragging, pushing, and urging patients towards a fleet of motor ambulances. A procession of horse-drawn carts arrived from the village. Joe and Youngalec handed off their patient to a pair of bearers running back from an ambulance with an empty stretcher.

"What do we do now?" Youngalec asked Joe. "How are we supposed to get the answer the captain wants?"

"We're not," Joe said. "We'll just let him be. It's clear we gotta help get everyone out of here and transported."

"Where to?"

"Do I look like I have a turban on? And a crystal ball? Away. It doesn't matter where. Maybe the village. Colinvillers. Likely they'll commandeer some of the bigger houses."

The snarl of engines burst through the sky again, blanking out all sound. Joe saw Frank dash into one of the post-op tents some thirty yards away and he ran toward it. "C'mon. Alec!" he yelled behind him, hoping Youngalec would hear something. "It's your turn to be a hero."

A flash blinded them both and forced them to stop. When the lights behind his eyes stopped dancing, Joe saw that the tent had collapsed. A figure with long dark hair was inching out from under canvas.

"Adelaide!" Joe sprinted to the tent and knelt down beside her. He pushed her hair out of her eyes.

"I'm not hurt," she said. "Grab me under the shoulders and pull me out."

"What about your back? Can you move your legs?"

"Yes, I can move my legs. Will you please just get me out of here?"

Youngalec was beside him now. Adelaide grimaced as the weight of the canvas pressed against her body. Before she was even fully out she was giving them orders. "Get a squad over here and get this tent upright. There are four patients and two stretcher-bearers in there still."

Joe put his hand to his mouth. "Frank?"

"I'm afraid so, but he could be all right. We need air in there."

"I'm going in," Joe said.

Adelaide grabbed him by the elbows. "Don't be an idiot. If you get stuck in there, I can't pull you out. Just make sure air's getting in."

"Okay, but I'm staying here. Close to Frank." Joe turned to Youngalec. "Get help. Run."

Among the scattered debris were iron bed legs that made perfect props, but Joe and Adelaide could barely lift the heavy canvas enough to allow in some air. Joe lay on his stomach and put his nose and mouth through one of the three gaps they'd been able to make.

"Frank? Frank, it's Joe. Can you hear me?"

"'Ello."

Joe didn't like the short reply. Not from Frank, who always had a lot to say, always had a joke.

"Are you hurt?"

"More like. Blood."

"Where?" Joe said. "Can you stop it? Tie it off?"

"Arm's stuck."

"Don't worry," Joe said. "We've got the cavalry coming, so to speak. What about the others?"

"Dunno," Frank's voice was flatter than before.

Joe wriggled back from the gap. "What's keeping them? What time is it anyways?"

"Five after ten."

"Geez. It feels like four in the morning already."

Adelaide gave him her apron. "Hold this and push it in after me. I'll use it as a tourniquet. I can squeeze through."

Joe stared at her.

"Here, take it," Adelaide said. "And get out of my way." She was already on her belly, wiggling her way forward like a fish chasing an ebbing tide.

"Did you hear that, Frank?" Joe shouted through the air hole. "Adelaide, Sister Armitage, is coming in to help you. She'll have you fixed up in a jiffy."

Once she was in, Joe sat up and looked around. Where was Youngalec? When the hell was help coming? The swish and clatter of an aircraft carving through air hit his ears again. He looked to the sky, still lit by the fires set by the bombings. The plane came straight for him, like a moth to a flame.

Joe scrambled on his hands and knees, faster than he knew he could, away from the plane. He dared to pause and grab a look over his shoulder, shooed and waved the plane away. Circles. Circles. Was he really seeing lovely blue, white, and red circles painted on the plane's side? He blinked and looked again, but the plane had already risen steeply and was heading away. He stood and watched it become a streak in the eerie orange light from the fires.

He ran back to the tent. Adelaide's muddied shoes stuck out from the small gap. He tugged one of her black stockinged ankles. "Are you getting anywhere?"

"Few more minutes."

The plane roared back, the sound closer. This time he didn't even bother to look up. His concern now was for Frank, Adelaide, and the others trapped under the tent. The wonderful Royal Flying corps pilot up above was the guard with the shotgun. His stomach relaxed a little. The big bad wolf had been scared off from the coop. But where the hell was Youngalec and help?

The noise overhead grew denser. Ha! We've got reinforcements. "Frank, the cavalry's arrived just like I said." Joe looked to the sky, ready to give the thumbs up and a great cheer. Instead he saw again the fierce white cross of an enemy plane. In pursuit was one of the RFC spewing burps of fire from its maw. The enemy plane responded with flashing farts from its rear. He stood, pulled at his hair, mesmerized by the dreamlike vision of a metal beast pursued by a contraption wielding a sparkling whip.

The planes passed right over him. The faster fighter had caught up to the enemy bomber and thrown a net of gigantic sparks over its backside. The bomber was alight, swirling and twirling towards the ground. Joe braced himself for the impact by hitting the ground, curling up, and covering his head. An excruciating burning pain made him grab his shin and roll back and forth on his bum. He emptied his lungs, trying to breathe the sting from his body. But the pain rose in intensity and he let out a howl. He grabbed his shin and rolled on the ground. Adelaide? Frank? The tent was now completely flattened. The pain in his leg whipped up again, like a spear thrusting from his ankle through to the top of his head.

"Joe. Joe." Youngalec was shaking him. "Thank God! I wasn't sure whether you'd passed out or ... well ... worse."

"Leave me. Get them out." Joe tried to slither toward the tent.

"Stay still," Youngalec said, gripping Joe's arms. "It's all under control. Look."

Two pairs of horses dragged the canvas away. A team of medics walked through bodies laid out on the ground. Joe counted. Six. There are four patients and two stretcher-bearers in there still. Wasn't that what Adelaide said? Joe tried to wriggle from Youngalec's grasp, but the orderly held on tight.

"Have you even checked yourself?"

"No," Joe said. He winced as he tugged at his tattered puttees.

"Lie down. I'm doing this. And that's that. And no discussion, even if you are my fearless leader."

Joe lay down and lifted his injured leg off to the side. "Okay. But tell me what you're doing. And can you see Frank? Adelaide?"

"With respect. Shut the fuck up and let me get on with it." Youngalec cut through Joe's puttees with the scissors from the first aid pack.

"Clean off the guck and tell me what you see. I think I need to lie back for a bit. Got any water?"

"Sure thing," Youngalec said, and took his water canteen from his belt.

Joe tried to keep his mind off the bodies lying a few yards away from him, but he had to see, had to get to Frank and to Adelaide.

"There's a big black hard thing and a white strip of something," Youngalec said.

"Is the white thing hard too?"

"Okay, I'll see. I'll touch it." He stopped. "What if it hurts?"

"Then it hurts," Joe said. A throb pulsed up his leg.

"It's not exactly hard. More like tough elastic."

"It's a tendon. Is it ripped at all?" Another pulsing as Youngalec probed inside his leg.

"A bit shredded."

"Shit." Joe slammed his fist against the ground.

"What about the black thing?"

"Shrapnel," Joe said. "That's got to come out."

Youngalec's breath came in quick gulps.

"It's just like yanking the stone out of a stewed plum. You can do it Youngalec. Breathe steady. Okay?"

"I can do it."

"Four things, Youngalec. Get a swab pack ready, 'cause the bleeding could start up again. Soak a piece of gauze with iodine to clean the area, then snatch the bugger out. Bandage me good and tight and you've got your surgeon's wings." He put out his hand. "And I forgot. Give me one of them morphine pills afore you start." Joe closed his eyes and let the drug embrace his brain.

"Wakey, wakey, pal. Put your arm around me," Youngalec said, and eased Joe upright. "All done and here's your souvenir." He handed Joe a blackened piece of metal, the size of a watch face. "And I'm putting you in the ambulance and that's all there is to it. No pulling rank on me."

"Where's Frank? Adelaide?" Joe looked over to where he'd seen the six bodies. The tents were still smoldering, but the ground was cleared of bodies. "Find out for me. I can't go myself." Joe tried to put weight on his bandaged limb, but it buckled under him.

"For the love of God, sit down." Youngalec went to the front of the ambulance, spoke to the driver, and called over to Joe. "Okay. The driver'll wait, but only for a couple of minutes."

"Tell him to go without me," Joe said.

"Her. It's a her what's driving, but I'm telling you that ambulance is not going anywhere without you in it."

Joe sat down and nursed his shin.

"Do as you're told now. And ... and keep in touch. I'll pray for you." Youngalec walked away and waved to someone. Joe peered through the darkness and recognized Atholl coming toward the ambulance. *The last person I bloody need to see.*

"Don't get up," Atholl said.

I wasn't planning to. "Thank you, sir."

Atholl crouched down beside him. "Lance-corporal Mathieson, Young said you wanted to know about Gellatley. I know you were friends."

Joe looked into Atholl's face, into the soft sadness veiling his eyes. "He's dead?"

"I'm afraid so. Only one survived in that tent. But look, you need to get going, get your wound seen to properly."

Joe tugged at Atholl's sleeve. "What about Sister Armitage?"

Atholl motioned to the ambulance. "It's my understanding she's in there, badly hurt. Don't keep her waiting. Get in." The surgeon helped him to his feet, and together they climbed the couple of steps into the back of the ambulance.

"Mathieson, one more thing," Atholl said, holding open the door.

"Yes sir?"

"I'll be informing Major Saunders at our debriefing of all the efforts you have made during this ... this incident. If there is anything I can do to help your recovery, don't hesitate to contact me."

"Thank you. Sir."

Joe sat on a metal bench that ran the length of one of the inside walls of the vehicle. He heard the doors close and someone, Atholl he presumed, rap on the side panel. The ambulance lurched. Joe held onto the struts framing the wall and quickly scanned the floor for Adelaide among the stretchers lumped together. They all looked the same: bundles of dirt and blood, strips of bandages, and shreds of clothing. His eyes closed again from the dregs of the morphine, but he forced them open, to adjust to the darkness lit only by Youngalec's hand lamp. As the ambulance bounced over rutted ground, he picked out a person here, a person there. He lowered himself to the floor and squeezed himself through the injured.

He barely recognized her with her head swaddled in bandages. She was squished into one corner up by the driver's cab. He wriggled himself over to her side, careful to avoid jostling his leg. He held his breath against the pungent smell of burned flesh. He found her diagnostic bulletin on her wound tag and read *2nd degree burns, back torso/legs, scalp lacerations, ?fract R femur, ribs Rx morphine stationary hospital Amiens*

Her eyes were wide open, staring, as he leaned over her. A brilliant smile washed over her face when she saw him. She reached out and took his hand. "My darling." Her eyes flickered and closed.

Joe put his ear to her chest. Her breathing was slow but reassuringly strong. The weight of his head roused her and she opened her eyes. "Robert?" Her voice rose to a husky scream. "Robert!"

"No. Adelaide. It's Joe. It's okay. It's okay. You're hurt but on your way to the hospital.

"Where's Robert gone? I saw him."

"It's the morphine. Adelaide. There's no Robert. Remember?"

"But I saw him. He was here."

"Oh Adelaide," Joe said. "I'm sorry. Your husband's gone. Killed. Remember."

She tried to sit up. "No. No I saw him." She stared at Joe. "He's dead?"

"Yes."

She grabbed Joe's face and pressed her fingers into his cheeks. "Then he wants me to go to him. That's what he wants. I want to go." She sucked in a huge lungful of air.

Joe lowered her hands and held onto them. She tried to squirm away, but he held her fast. He whispered in her ear. "No, Adelaide, you don't. You told me yourself, when Captain Rogers died, you weren't the type. Remember? You'll get past this. You will. You have to. We all have to." He felt her relax. She started to tremble, then cry softly. She leaned into his chest. "The missing? They are all gone then?" she asked. "All gone?"

"All gone. I'm sorry. All of them. Why don't you try and sleep now. We can talk more after."

"And your brothers too. Joe. Dear Joe. I am so, so sorry." A flood of pain spilled through his shin.

She jerked away from him. "Frank? And the others under the canvas? What's happened?"

"Him too. He didn't make it. Only you came out alive."

She clutched at his breast pocket. "Joe, I tried to stop the bleeding. Truly I did. It was a massive haemorrhage. I did try."

"I know that," he said. "I saw you. Hush now." He held her and stroked her bound head. He waited until the rocking of the vehicle lulled her to sleep before he laid her down.

22

The growls and grunts of the ambulance did little to mask the moans of the injured. Some, like Adelaide, had mercifully fallen asleep. Joe lay down and squirrelled in amongst the stretchers on the floor but couldn't get his leg comfortable. He had expected it to hurt after Youngalec removed the shrapnel, but didn't remember that when the morphine wore off it would still throb like a bugger. He put his hand to his forehead. Sweat oozed through his pores. *Maybe more morphine,* he thought. But if he was showing symptoms of infection, he needed to stay alert and not allow himself the possible relief of drifting off to sleep. Infection. The word, since Walter's death, had become a vile and treacherous fiend. A swell of anger heaved up through Joe's torso and competed with his frustration and distress at the stubborn image of Frank bleeding to death, the weight of singed canvas robbing him of air.

The ambulance stuttered to a halt and threw Joe on top of a middle-aged soldier, who gave him a reactionary kick. His hands shook as he tried to massage away the unceasing pain in his leg.

The back doors opened, letting in a stinging draft of icy air and a blast of light. Joe shielded his eyes and managed to sit up. Men in civilian clothes gathered at the rear and held up lamps, while orderlies unloaded the injured. A pair pushed Joe aside, lifted Adelaide's stretcher up to the exit, and handed her off to another couple. Joe watched with a heavy heart as she was carried beyond the lamps. The night absorbed her into its blackness and she was gone.

"Hey you." Joe called through door, and tried to edge his way through the spaces. "Orderly!" He waved his arms. "Sir? Please."

The orderly stopped writing on the clipboard he held and climbed into the ambulance, as Joe crawled toward the front and lowered his good leg over the lip. "Get back in," the orderly bellowed at Joe, lifting his dangling leg and pushing him along the floor on his bottom.

Joe grabbed the orderly's legs and tried to stand up. "What's going on? Where are they taking her?"

The orderly lowered Joe back to the floor and knelt beside him. "We're at Amiens. The Aussies have commandeered a city hospital. We're dropping off the worst of the wounded here."

"I want off too. I'll get them to check my leg."

"No. Our orders are to take you lot back to the ccs at Bercordie. In fact, most of the personnel from Colinvillers will likely turn up there."

"I'm getting out." Joe leaned over and whispered in the orderly's ear. "There's someone I need to wish luck. Say cheerio to."

"No, you can't." He handed off the clipboard to another soldier directing the unloaded injured. "That's them all. You can tell the driver to get going." He turned back to Joe. "Sweetheart, eh? Write her a letter when you get to the hospital at Bercordie. I'll personally make sure she gets it." He fished into his pack. "Swallow this." He lifted Joe's head, handed him a tablet and put his water canteen to Joe's mouth. "Take a swig and lie down. Do as you're told now, soldier."

Joe opened his eyes and strained to keep them open. An insipid dawn squiggled through his eyelids, and then he whooshed back into a black hole. Gradually the fuzziness drifted off and he could take in his surroundings: the smell of hospital disinfectant and over boiled tea, the chatter and clatter of nurses, the slight dampness of stiff sheets, a pillow under his head. An arced cage lifted the covers from his legs. Panic shot through him, the memory of the hit on the shin slunk into his awareness. His mind slammed into a black wall. Frank. Walter. Fred. He beat his fists against the mattress, gulped down the urge to scream and kick. He gripped his legs. He thought he could feel them, both of them, but he knew of the 'phantom limbs experience' amputees described. He could definitely feel pain in his shin, but those who'd lost their legs talked about that too. He hauled himself to sitting, dragged his legs over the sheets, and slapped his thighs to reassure himself they were real. He started to cough, his lungs dry and inflamed. His mouth was filled with the cloying taste of chloroform as he puffed the noxious gas from his chest. His stomach heaved.

He leaned over the side of the bed and splashed his last meal onto the floor.

Soft hands pushed him back against the pillows.

"It's just the anaesthetic. No need to worry."

Joe opened his eyes and saw a nurse he'd met at Colinvillers. She dabbed his face with a cool cloth.

"Hi Joe. Remember me? Marjory Gillingham." She put the cloth away and held a bowl under his chin. "Are you going to be sick again?"

Joe wiped his mouth. "No. It's over." She called to an orderly for a clean-up.

He pushed away the bed-covers.

"Stop that," the nurse said. She grabbed his hands and tugged at the blankets. "You'll catch your death." She put her hand up to her mouth. "Oh. I am sorry. You know what I mean."

"I have to see what they've done to my leg."

"All fixed up."

"I still have it?" Joe said.

"Of course you do. See for yourself." She drew back to the covers and pointed to his swaddled lower limb before she remade his bed. "Lie down now and get some rest. I know Captain Atholl wants to check on you. I'll tell him you're awake."

"Atholl? Did he operate on me?"

"Yes. Yesterday. First thing in the morning. Before breakfast even. Said he wanted to attend to you personally. Now lie down."

She started to leave, but Joe tugged at her skirt. "One more thing. Have you heard anything about Adelaide? Sister Armitage?"

The young nurse looked close to tears. "No. Nothing. I haven't heard a peep."

Joe tried to sleep but pounding filled his head. He sat up, leaned against the pillows, and laid his hands out in front of him, palms down on the top sheet. They shook from the dread of losing his leg. He watched his fingers relax and become still as he repeated inside his head, *I have two legs. I have two feet. I have two legs. I have two feet.* He stopped himself from muttering aloud, *Fred, Walter, Frank. Fred, Walter, Frank.* But the four-syllable beat wormed into his brain.

Wednesday, November 29, 1916 "Must have dropped off," Joe said, waking up to Atholl prodding him.

The surgeon smiled. "Here, let me help get you comfortable." He laid the tray he carried at the foot of the bed and fixed the pillow behind Joe's back.

"I must be going mad," Joe said. "Never thought I'd ever be waited on by … an officer."

"I was coming to do a round when I ran into the nurse with your lunch." He set a bowl in front of Joe. "A hearty soup of some indeterminate vegetables, but I'm sure nonetheless good for you."

"Would it be pushing my luck to ask you for a urine bottle or a bedpan?"

Atholl backed away quickly.

"Just joking, sir."

Atholl's pursed lips widened into a smile. "Yes, lance corporal. That indeed would be pushing your luck."

"What time is it?" Joe turned and looked out the window at the murky weather and the rain drizzling down the pane.

"One. In the afternoon."

"It feels like the middle of the night."

"Well you've been sleeping a lot. The best cure. But now the nurses want to feed you up before you're shipped out. Good news, lance corporal. You'll be on your way home in a week at the most." Joe slurped on a spoonful, realizing as it went down he was very hungry. He took another spoonful and wiped his mouth, worrying that Atholl would judge him uncouth. "Tell me about my leg."

"May I?" Atholl said, indicating the edge of the bed.

"Be my guest."

Atholl sat down. For a moment, Joe thought the young doctor might take his hand, but he stood again and put both hands in the pockets of his white coat.

"I-I … About the night of the bombing. Well the thing is—"

"Can't remember a thing. My mind's a blank. Totally wiped out." Joe smiled. "Sir, my leg?"

"Yes, yes. Of course. The leg." He sat on the bed again. "That orderly, the deaf one, I forget his name …"

"Youngalec. Alec Young."

"Yes, well, you can thank him for the timely attention he gave you. I noticed some dark purple blisters around the edges, suggesting infection or possibly even gangrene. Anytime you come in contact with soil there's a risk. God knows those bloody germs are having a field day with all the, the …"

"Decaying matter?" Joe said.

"Quite. And your temperature was somewhat elevated. I didn't want to take any risks. There was no gas under the skin, but I took the precaution of cutting away as much tissue as possible, and as close to the bone as I could get. You'll end up with a rather large ugly scar. Between that and the tendon fix I did, you may never walk without a limp. I'm sorry." Atholl gave a little shudder and stood. "Well, there you are. As we, you and I, say in Scotland, France has seen the back of you. You'll be served a medical discharge." He patted the covers as tentatively as if they might jump and bite him. "Our loss."

"Sir, what is your first name?" Joe said.

Atholl's shoulders stiffened and then relaxed. He turned to Joe. "It's Simon."

Joe put out his hand. "Thank you, Captain Simon Atholl, for saving my leg."

"And thank you lance corporal for … for all your exceptional help. Yes, thank you."

"Captain, you said once if there was anything you could do ... well there is something. Nothing medical. A personal thing."

"If I can, of course."

Joe ran his tongue around his dry gums. He knew he was pushing it, but he had to try everything before he left this country, maybe never to come back. "Back in the summer, when we were at Gaudechat, I made a friend in the village. A special friend. If I'm going home and be scarred and limping for the rest of my life…" Joe hoped Atholl wouldn't think he was laying it on a bit thick. "The fact is, sir, I'd like to see my friend one last time."

"That's a tall order." Atholl stroked his chin. "Must indeed be a very special friend."

Joe was a muddle of feelings. Excited. Perhaps he could get to Gaudechat. Depressed. Marguerite likely hadn't come back. Ecstatic. What if she was waiting for him? Elated. Atholl hadn't turned him down—yet. And weaving through it all, the dark threads of his sorrow.

Atholl grinned. "I have a full schedule today and over the weekend. It'll have to wait until next Monday. I can spare a few hours in the afternoon."

Joe thought he would cry with relief.

"Oh, I almost forgot, I also brought a letter for you. From your other friend. Mrs. Armitage. I caught the post boy and wanted to make sure you got it." He pulled the letter from his trouser pocket. "Monday then?"

Joe nodded.

New Zealand Stationary Hospital
Amiens
Monday, November 27, 1916

Dear Joe,

It's hard to believe it was only a week ago that we were going about our business as usual. A normal day for us, if indeed there is such a thing. Your pain over Walter's death was written all over your face, and I could read the sadness you felt, still in France, far from home and your family. However you went about your duties with such commitment and diligence. As usual. I have managed to get news of you through Major Saunders. He says you have 'copped a blighty' as the boys say. I am glad for you and your family that hopefully you may never have to return and face the awfulness that stalks this beautiful part of the world. And I am relieved that your injury, although serious, is one from which you will eventually recover.

What does that mean? Joe thought. Recover? So different from *un*cover, where Fred would rise from his grave, push aside the sod that had covered him for months, stripping his bones and dissolving his flesh. And Walter and Frank? Covered too. He shuddered, remembering the countless nights he'd seen them under the covers asleep. For how long would they look the same?

*Re*cover. Would all the skin that had been burned off, blown off, and shot off slide back intact onto all those damaged bodies? Would all the land that been churned and pitted be filled in again, cover all the corpses, the diseased soil? And with what? He couldn't imagine how it could be recovered. He leaned over to the metal bedside table, found his cigarette packet, and pulled himself from his dark thoughts.

I was bashed about somewhat extensively, but I have very little memory of that night so I am not being haunted by images like so many of our poor boys whose nightmares have driven them mad. I do have rather a few broken bones and some nasty cuts, not one life-threatening. I am so fortunate. It will take a while, I am told, to recover fully but recover (that word again) *fully I will. Did you ever think we would both end up on this side on the fence? I somehow felt immune to it all, that I was here to help, not to be helped. But there you have it. I am very well looked after at the moment and have been told they will keep me here in the city, as it is now a safe distance from the enemy lines.*

Major Saunders informed me yesterday that I am to receive a medal. I feel very embarrassed about it, as I only did my duty in trying to get as many of our patients out safely. A piece of silverware in no way compensates for what so many have lost.

Joe lit his cigarette and coughed. He lay back for a moment to catch his breath. Atholl had told him among the bombing raid death toll were forty-seven patients and one doctor. Two nurses, Annie Foxman and the Phillipa woman Frank had played around with, had been killed too. And Frank. What was the silly expression the generals used to bond the men together? Comrades in arms? *No,* Joe thought, *Frank was my friend, a man I am not ashamed to say is fixed in my heart as surely as if he were my own flesh and blood.* He took another drag on his cigarette and turned back to the letter. He didn't want to think anymore of blood and the gluey ocean of it that had flooded this country.

But no doubt the honour will please my parents no end. For me, I hope it will turn out to be a blessing in disguise and they will give their *blessing to me having work. You know how dead set they were against me nursing. They thought that as soon as I found out what had happened to Robert I would hightail it back to the manor, as it were. As it is they have arranged to send me to a hospital near their home, but that won't happen for at least a couple of weeks. They are probably already plotting to marry me off and carry on as if none of these momentous events in my life had even taken place.*

"Bloody hell," Joe muttered. He shivered, realizing he didn't have a 'manor' of his own any more. After Kate went to the munitions factory and Ma took over Ellen's care, it made no sense to pay rent on an empty house. He shook his head in disbelief. He'd been living mostly underground, in no more comfort than the rats. At best he'd had a bed on a barn floor with a bunch of hay stalks for a mattress. Except for Gaudechat. He stroked his arm. Except for Gaudechat. Then he trembled with anger when he grasped that to get a bed, with a sheet and a real pillow, he had to be shot at, lacerated, and riddled with pain and worry. When he did finally get home, he'd be homeless and wouldn't even have a trough in a field. He lit another cigarette and read on.

But you know me better than that. I am determined more than ever to take further training and make nursing my life's work. I suspect this war will change things for us women and I am sure I will be fortunate to find a fulfilling place in the world. Unlike the future I see for many women. I mean those for whom it will be a tragedy, as they struggle to feed their fatherless children. Life will not be so hard for me. In anticipation of going off to war, Robert made sure I would be well looked after. Especially since we might have had children and I may have had to rear and educate them without him. I hope you can tell that I have come to accept that my husband is gone. You played such an important role in getting me to that acknowledgement, sad as it is.

Joe swung his legs around and sat on the edge on the bed, flicking his cigarette ash furiously into the ashtray on his bedside table. *I'll have no job either,* he thought. *At least not a regular decent-paying one at the pit. Not with my injury.* He ground out his cigarette butt when he thought of the stripe he'd be given to wear on his sleeve, apparently to proudly declare he'd been wounded in the service of this country. There'd be no blissful homecoming for him, having to sort out the house and the job. And Kate. One day she'd be back. This might be the biggest problem of the lot. He'd put off thinking about that until after his Monday afternoon outing with Atholl.

Dear, dear Joe, we may never meet again, but I will not say goodbye in case we do. I will say though that you were an enormous help, inspiration, and source of comfort and friendship to me. Not only in my early first days on the hospital train, when we first met, but throughout all our dealings with each other and particularly when I had my 'little breakdown' in the back of the ambulance.

I hope to return to France and the nursing service when my own wounds have healed. I would like you to write, if you are so inclined. It would do a lot to cheer me in the dark days of the war yet to come.

Fucking, fucking shite. He was assuming it was over. All over. Forever. He looked at his bandaged leg. For everyone. Not just him. He placed his hands over his ribs, felt the crush of this realization. What if it never ended? Fred had said, had *assured* him, that it was unimaginable it *wouldn't* be over 'by Christmas'. That was almost two years ago. How many more thousands—no hundreds of thousands—would continue to slog and suffer? It all felt hopeless, endlessly black. He replaced his hands on the last sheet of Adelaide's letter.

The irony of the casualties and loss I—we've—seen is that I've lost my fear of death. My only fear now is that I waste my life. You and I have learned so much. I do so hope, Joe, that you can put your experiences here to good use as you return home. I wish you the very, very best in life. I know it will come to you.

With the greatest affection,

Adelaide

PS I heard a good friend will also receive a medal but perhaps that's still a secret!

Joe folded the letter into the envelope and put it in his pyjama pocket. He held onto the bedside table and eased his feet onto the floor. He stood, lifted his injured leg, and did a hopping turn toward the window. The afternoon inched toward early winter darkness. He could just make out blinking flickers of light through the sheets of rain.

Monday, December 4, 1916   6:00 a.m. Joe'd been awake for over half an hour. He heard the nurses' natter in the duty office, as the staff handed over the nightly report to the day shift. He twitched with excitement, couldn't believe that in eight hours, maybe four, perhaps even two, he'd be in Gaudechat. Why hadn't he asked Atholl what time they were leaving, so he could relax knowing how long he had to wait?

December fourth. One day after he'd reckoned they'd be finished at Colinvillers and he'd start leave, on his way to Toulouse. *Why was it,* he thought, *that his leave never worked out? Bloody war. That's what happened.* The best laid plans ... but now it was working out. In a way. Today he'd actually be in her village. He'd cross all his fingers and toes, if it would make sure she'd come back. He looked down at his wrapped leg. What would he give up to have her back? *Dear love,* he whispered, *you have to be there.*

Breakfast came. He got out of bed and ate it at the table in the centre of the ward, with the other ambulatory patients. Chatting to them and swapping injury stories passed the time until seven, when the nurses came with shaving and washing water. Shortly after eight, the nurses started their dressing rounds. The sister would check his dressing. Either she'd give the okay to have it re-bandaged or refer him for a further consultation with Atholl or one of the other surgeons. A senior nurse charted all the activity.

Fed, shaved, bathed, and with a fresh dressing, he hopped over to the window. The rain had stopped but a dense hoar frost painted the landscape, hiding all but the closest trees. He held onto the windowsill and moved his injured leg in circles, urged the blood to hurry and repair the tissue. He checked his watch in the drawer by his bed.

Ten past nine. What should he do next? If he got dressed, the nurses would make his bed and not let him sit on it. He'd have to sit on a chair and suffer and couldn't tell anyone, as it would be reported back to Atholl, who then might cancel the trip, deeming him not fit enough for the journey. And then he'd have to give up the slightest of chances to see Marguerite again. He fisted the sides of his head. *Stop it. Stop it. Wait. Wait.*

He sat on the floor and opened the door of his bedside locker, where the nurses would have stored his clothes. As soon as he saw it was empty, he realized he'd lost his uniform, torn to rags in the blasts. If he were on his bed in his pyjamas when Atholl came for him, *whenever that might be but hurry up, please,* he would think he wasn't ready and might withdraw his offer. *Pull yourself together.* His nerves were on edge more than they had ever been on the battlefield, or in the operating rooms among the desperately wounded who relied on him. The only time it had been worse was on that gruesome last train ride with Walter. He pressed his hands against his diaphragm and willed his breathing to steady. He'd sit on his bed, in his pyjamas. And wait.

Joe had eaten only a few forkfuls of the hash served for lunch when he saw Atholl coming toward his bed, a pair of crutches slung over his shoulder.

"Did you forget?" Atholl asked.

"Forget? God no."

Atholl pointed to Joe's pyjamas.

"I have nothing to wear," Joe said. He gulped down another mouthful.

Atholl shouted the length of the ward. "Someone bring this man trousers, a pullover, and a coat. And a pair of shoes!" He looked down at Joe's leg, bound from above the knee to his instep, and reddened. "Sorry. What size?"

"Nine," Joe said.

Atholl barked down the ward again. "Make that one left shoe. Size nine."

At the street end of the château's driveway, Atholl ground the gearstick of the lorry into neutral and pulled on the brake. He got out and came around to Joe's side, and helped him upright with the crutches under his armpits. He checked his watch. "I'd like to head back by two thirty. It'll start to get dark around three with this murky weather, and I want to be able to see my way. Here in an hour and a half?"

Joe nodded and adjusted the crutch on his right side.

"Good then. I'll go into the village and keep myself warm in the *estaminet.*"

Joe watched him climb back into the lorry and move off into the fog. He leaned heavily into the crutches and stared at the stone arch, the entranceway to June and so much happiness. He pulled up the collar on his coat and hobbled through the arch to the apartments where Marguerite and her family lived. No one was around. No pigs snouting for scraps, no dogs guarding the homestead, no cats giving him the evil eye. He started to shiver. *God, it's cold.* The mist wormed its way through his coat and ate up his body's warmth like a moth nibbling on wool. Try as he might, he could not get his skin to recall the summer sun on his bare back. He knocked on doors, urging someone, anyone, to open up so at the very least he could shelter from the bitter cold that was now stiffening his bones.

Door after door remained closed to his knocking. *I'd move away too,* thought Joe. *I'd take my loved ones and run if my home was this close to the front line.* He walked up the driveway until he could see the château, closed two months ago when the enemy front line had advanced too close for its safety.

He sweated with the effort of hauling himself up the roadway, the moisture boosting the chill on his skin. The estate already looked neglected and forlorn. The windows were shuttered, weeds sprouted in cracks in the paths. The leafless trees held out their branches in frozen distorted poses. The flowerbeds had not been cleared; the wilted blooms and blackened leaves leaned over as if pleading for a merciful burial. It was as if all the work they'd done in June to prepare the glorious building, in readiness for July, had never happened. The life that Frank had raved about—the fresh farm food, the bands that played in the evening, the good spirits—had packed up and left. All that remained was an impression of ghosts. *And,* he thought, *somewhere in villages all around here, cemeteries full of young bodies.*

It came rushing at him. He felt it in his gut. Never again would he see her. He knew now she had not come back. No one had. He gasped and dizziness grabbed the back of his head. He eased himself onto the ground, put his head between his knees until the wooziness passed, then lumbered back to the apartments. He sat on the stone steps and lit a cigarette.

What would he have done if she had been there waiting for him and running into his arms? He really hadn't planned for that. Wished for it, fantasized about living in the sun with her, with Ellen and their children to come. But truly, he had not prepared himself for a future with her. Nor had he planned for *this* reality: that she had vanished to Toulouse hundreds of miles away. That fantastic June seemed so unreal now.

He pulled a wilted dahlia head to him with his crutch. He picked it up and whispered to Marguerite, as he ripped each paper-dry petal from the flower head. "Thank you. Thank you for your sunshine, your love. For what was."

In the still of Gaudechat's early winter, two years into the relentless battles, he had to believe the guns would, surely, one day stop for good. They, the generals, the officers, the men, the wives, the mothers, the brothers and sisters, the world, would one day talk about the war in the past tense. They'd say, *'During the war, I remember one time, at Christmas of '14 ... in the summer of '16 ... since the war ... because of the war ...'* They'd tell stories of deprivation and hardship, of terror and bravery. The survivors would laugh at how silly they were to have doubted their continued existence.

Eventually it would be a bored discussion about who did what to whom and why and what for. He flicked his cigarette away, reached forward, and stubbed it out with the tip of his crutch. All of it, ten years from now, would be reduced to facts in history books for Ellen, her children and grandchildren, and their children too (if the world still cared) to memorize and regurgitate at exam time, just as he'd had to do at school. He and his pals had laughed about the relief of Mafeking during the Boer War. They'd tittered, imagining officers and soldiers perched over latrines collectively straining at the stool. As to that war's significance, or even the dates? He hadn't a clue. Dates. Names. Places. Facts.

Facts? Fred Mathieson fooled himself into thinking he could change his world. Now dead and buried in the wet wormed earth of a foreign land. Young Walter got a thick-witted notion into his head he was not tough enough, and thought a war would prove his manliness. His family, along with a hundred thousand others, was broken. Could it be put back into working order? Unknown fact.

And what about these facts? Captain Rogers, wise and kind surgeon and teacher, mender of macerated bodies, had had his spirit broken. Frank Gellatley, stretcher-bearer, cheerer-upper of wounded men in their last moments, eeler and rabbit-catcher, misused son, loyal friend ... the best. No one knew where his bits and pieces were or if they even existed any more.

Joe stood, leaned on the crutches, and rubbed his uninjured leg, trying to beat out the cold. And now he too would soon be done with it all. He shuffled a little way up the driveway again, just far enough that he could see the château in eerie silhouette. His foot hurt. He swung around and took in the whole area: the farm, the path through the woods to the pool, the farm workers' homes. Nothing was as he remembered it. He wished he hadn't come. He wished he could have seen it all one last time as it had been in the summer, not as he saw it now. A lifeless lonely place.

He'd have to learn to love back home as much as he'd loved here. But he knew it wouldn't be easy. A part of him would cling desperately to all that was past and so alive. Could he ever make something out of the toil, the struggle, the losses, and the carnage? Maybe he'd take Walter's place, find a way to push himself into more school learning. Ellen for sure, when she was bigger. *I promise you right here and now, my wee darling. I'll give you a proper education, no matter the cost.* He'd make bloody damn certain some change for the good would come of it all. His brothers and friends fought and died for that.

Fact.

Did he have it in him to dig deep enough to find any part of him that hadn't been stained by what he'd seen? Past the rips in his gut, torn when he held the dying German boy in his arms? When he felt the slime of Captain Rogers' brains? Smelled the burned and utterly mangled landscape?

Scary unknown fact.

There would be other facts to deal with. Joe pursed his lips, partly at the increasing pain in his leg but mostly from thinking about his wife.

"Time to go? Finished your venture here?"

Joe jerked and almost fell over at the voice and the touch on his shoulder.

"Steady on there," Atholl said, and grabbed Joe's elbow. "Didn't mean to startle you. Christ, it's raw here. Just as cold inside the *estaminet.* Only two pathetic old souls, staring at the walls. Not even a fire burning in the grate. This place feels like a wasteland. Ready to go back?"

Aye, Joe thought, *I am now.* "Yes, sir. I'm done here."

"I take it," Atholl said, waving his arm over the empty estate, "that you didn't find your friend."

"That's right. I'm sorry. I've wasted your time."

The mist had condensed into a fine spitter. Atholl pulled up his collar and hunched his shoulders. "Actually not. I'm grateful for the outing. Get away from the hospital and all that." He took off his glasses and wiped the rain from them with a white handkerchief. "Time to go though. Come. Can you make it to the lorry? I left it outside the *estaminet.* Walked around trying to warm up. Perhaps I should have driven it here."

Joe turned and stared at the arch over the driveway. "I can manage."

Atholl opened the side door for him before he started the engine. Joe was hurting too much to be amused by the new Atholl's care and attention. Frank would have had something choice to say about it.

"I'd rather lie in the back, if you don't mind."

"Of course, of course," Atholl said, and ran around to the back and lifted the canvas flap. He helped Joe up the step and settled him on the floor.

"Sir?" Joe said.

"Mmm?"

"I'm really grateful."

"I'm a little embarrassed. I should have known you'd be more comfortable with your leg flat," Atholl said.

"It's good now."

The engine laboured to life and they bumped along the road. Joe stretched out. He had half an hour, maybe a little more because of the dim light, to think.

He hadn't been the best husband. What if he tried to treat Kate better? With the same carefulness he had with Marguerite? Listen to and hold onto her words like he had with Marguerite? What if he stopped tuning her out? Would she respond? Many questions. No facts. No answers. Yet.

When he got back, maybe in as little as a week, Kate would still be away in the munitions factory. That would give him time to settle, time to adjust to his damaged leg. Time for him to get used to the idea of being back in his life again. What had the last eighteen months been? Had the time really been part of his life? The rest of his days, be it fifty years or more, would never feel as long or full as the last eighteen months. He crawled over to the back of the lorry and lifted a corner of the flap. All around was a monotone: the muddy grayish brown of the rutted road, the fallow fields, the sky emptying its light. It was hard to bring this together with the vivid colours and events of his time in this broken land. He felt drained. Hollowed out. He could swear he'd lived a lifetime here. Methilane seemed so long ago. His spirits sank deeper, he was becoming as wretched as the washed-out landscape. The task ahead at home was as fearful now as any day with the guns firing all around. He saw himself in bed with Kate, after one of their bad days, calling out for Marguerite in his sleep. He'd have to lie, say he'd had a dream about Ma—his mother, Maggie. Brush it off as the way the French said her name. Did he want Kate's touch, or to touch her? Or would he feel it was an offence against what was true in his heart?

He dropped the canvas, lay down, and breathed away the gloomy thoughts. He closed his eyes. He saw Ellen climbing onto his knee. Saw himself holding out his glass of whisky at arm's length, so she wouldn't spill it. He'd allow himself one, and only one, around eight every evening: the time he'd reserve for himself and his thoughts. He'd have his tot at home, not go down The Brig and have to pretend he was the same as before.

"Managing the bumps back there?" Atholl's voice pulled the shutters over Joe's thoughts. The lorry's gearbox ground like rocks scraping over glass. The young surgeon's mechanical ability made Joe chuckle. It made him think the vehicle was an animal, moaning to escape the hostile elements and an incompetent master, grunting to the safety of its stall.

Aye," Joe shouted back. "I'm doing fine."

"Five more minutes and we'll be warmed up inside."

Joe closed his eyes again. He saw Ellen standing on his thighs, perfectly balanced and trusting. He gazed at her fresh face and tears filmed his eyes.

She pulled his eyelids shut and kissed them. "No crying Dada. Can we go paddling in the sea?"

"Not today. It's time for bed."

"Tomorrow?"

"Aye, my wee love," he would say. "Tomorrow."

ACKNOWLEDGEMENTS

It took two continents and four countries to raise *The Bearer's Burden.* Without the gracious involvement of many wonderful, generous people, this novel could not have gone out into the world.

In the U.K. for research assistance, I thank the staff at East Neuk, Scotland libraries for information on the mining industry in early 20th century Fife, the Army Medical Services Museum at Keogh Barracks, Aldershot, England, and the staff at the Imperial War Museum, London, England. All these places are candy stores for the history buff. Special hugs to my driver, Cynthia Greenwood, for her patience when I had to check out 'just one more place'.

In France, thanks go to the curators and guides at La Grande Historial de Peronne, the proprietor of The Tommy at Pozières, M. Rene O who told me his family stories and shared my hunt for derelict WWI Casualty Clearing Stations, to M. Thibault from Puchevillers for photos of a Casualty Clearing Station that I reimagined as the CCS at Colinvillers. My appreciation also goes to Avril Williams for allowing me access to her museum, preserved trenches and the dressing station at Auchonvillers ("Ocean Villas"), and to historian Derek Bird for literally walking me through the mud over the site of the November, 1916 Battle of the Somme.

I am thankful to Kerstin Wöstefeld Djelloul for hanging me upside down in the Mobilounge and clearing my head to write some more, to Chris and Maria-Dolores Berte for friendship and fabulous food and to Annie for her amazing French cuisine and recipes. Thanks also to the English conversation group in Amiens: Francoise, Louis, Jess, David, Pascal, Sylvie, Annie, and Veronique, for the relief of "English only" evenings – such a respite when my head was so full of my stumbling French I thought it might explode.

Also in Picardie, I had the amazing good fortune to make the acquaintance of Jacques Fauquembergue. Merci mille fois, mon ami for my writing retreat, chauffeuring, guiding, French lessons, breakfasts, dinners, evenings learning French, encouragement, poetry and laughter.

In Canada I first have to acknowledge and thank the expert teachers who have influenced my writing: Julie Paul, Steven Price and the most generous and gracious teacher of all, Jack Hodgins.

I received helpful comments on the manuscript from Patti-Anne Kay, Angela-Lee McIntyre, Edeana Malcolm and Mary Nelson. I relied on the sharp eye, over military and procedural matters, of Richard Gibbons. Giles Stevenson and Ilse Stevenson were my advisors on medical matters. My thanks to all three for your generosity and your enthusiasm—you did a grand job. However, the responsibility for any errors sits solely on my shoulders.

I offer a huge *thank you* to my caring and competent critiquers and biggest cheerleaders this side of the Atlantic: Leanne Baugh, Sharon Carson-Bell and Kathryn Lemmon who lovingly gave their time and energy to turn an early draft inside out and upside down and steer it in the right direction. Deep gratitude goes to the indefatigable and head cheerleader, Tricia Dower, whose critical talent, wisdom and mentorship kept me focussed throughout the birth pangs of *The Bearer's Burden*. I am truly blessed to have you in my corner.

For steering me to the finish line I am indebted to all the talented folk at FriesenPress, in particular Astra Compton. And last, but not by any means least, my appreciation also goes to my family and to Catherine E for psychic sustenance and casting light into dark days when I doubted this novel would ever be a reality.

For more information on the writing of this book see my website at: www.dianaelizabethjones.ca

ABOUT THE AUTHOR

Diana Elizabeth Jones spent three months in Picardie, France, researching and writing much of *The Bearer's Burden*. While there she retraced the boot steps (often with soaking feet and frost-nipped fingers) of soldiers and medical personnel who endured the trenches and WWI battles.

She has previously published and won awards for short fiction and this is her first novel. She is currently working on a collection of short stories and incubating a second novel.

Born in Dundee, Scotland, Diana is a former linguist and educator who now lives and writes in Victoria, BC. She visits Spain frequently pursuing her second passion, flamenco.

Printed in Canada